"*Yesterday is not ours to recover, but tomorrow is ours to win or to lose.*"

—LYNDON B. JOHNSON
Address to the Nation
November 28, 1963

"*. . .when I returned from my travels in other countries and I settled here to think about them, it seemed to me that I had made one discovery. I had found that clever men greatly resemble the insect that made the earrings in my servant's ear. They will elaborate vast structures of thoughts from their very nature. They cannot stop, even though the thing they are building is senseless. They must go on. And we must live in the nooks and crannies of their aimless building, and sometimes be imprisoned in it, as they work, endlessly, surrounding us, closing our escapes, until we live and die a part of the gigantic folly, as blind and in as deep a darkness as its frantic builders.*"

—THE RAMAYAMA

JERRY PRESCOTT, SECRETARY OF STATE, BROUGHT THE PHONE TO HIS EAR. THE VOICE HE HEARD BELONGED TO FRANK MERRIMAN, DEPUTY SECRETARY OF STATE.

"We just got the craziest message over the wire. It's from Saigon, Jerry. And it . . . let me read it to you. 'Grettings to the government of the United States of America. The People's Republic of Vietnam is holding a total of 2,045 prisoners of the imperialist war that the American government waged against the free peoples of Vietnam. These prisoners will be held for a total of seven days until reparations for the damage they have done to our country have been made. The reparations will total one million U.S. dollars in gold per man. If these reparations have not been made by the above stated date, these prisoners of expansionist war will be tried as criminals and executed."

Prescott sank onto the sofa. "Has the President been notified?"

"Someone's doing it right now. Jerry, are we going to pay it?"

"We can't pay. You know that."

THREE HOURS LATER, NANCY HENDERSON, RECENTLY HAPPILY MARRIED, TURNED ON THE TELEVISION AND WAS CONFRONTED BY A GHOST. THE GAUNT FACE OF HER SUPPOSEDLY DEAD HUSBAND FILLED THE SCREEN, A LIVE TRANSMISSION FROM VIETNAM. THE NEWS TORE HER HEART APART. FUTURE EVENTS WOULD DESTROY HER WORLD AND PROPEL HER AND OTHERS TO THE CUTTING EDGE OF TREASON AND WAR.

THE M.I.A. RANSOM

THE M.I.A. RANSOM

Mike McQuay

BANTAM BOOKS

TORONTO · NEW YORK · LONDON · SYDNEY · AUCKLAND

To Marvin and Norma, with love.

THE M.I.A. RANSOM
A Bantam Book / August 1986

ISBN 0-553-25867-2

Published simultaneously in the United States and Canada

Bantam Books are published by Bantam Books, Inc. Its trade-mark, consisting of the words "Bantam Books" and the por-trayal of a rooster, is Registered in U.S. Patent and Trademark Office and in other countries. Marca Registrada. Bantam Books, Inc., 666 Fifth Avenue, New York, New York 10103.

PRINTED IN THE UNITED STATES OF AMERICA

O   0 9 8 7 6 5 4 3 2 1

MONDAY

In a move meant to underscore problems in Southeast Asia, the Republic of Vietnam recalled its delegates to the United Nations in New York today. Though no official reasons were given for the surprise action, experts speculate that the move is linked directly to the inaction of the world body to condemn Cambodia in its continuing struggles against the ailing Communist regime. . . .

I

Vietnam—Highway 1

April 13—10:15 A.M.

Colonel Jason Ridley watched out of the back of the deuce-and-a-half as it bounced along the pitted roadway on rocking-chair shocks. They were heading south; he knew that much. Moving again.

Another work crew, he figured, another month hurrying to beat the rain. Another month repairing roadways and bridges out in the middle of wet green jungles—eternal, inscrutable jungles. But this was farther south, much farther south than he had ever been before.

Rice paddies extended out from either side of the road. Vietnamese in wide-brimmed hats and pants rolled up to the knees were stooped over, always stooped over, working in the sun-glistening water. They were hurrying to beat the rain, too.

He took a breath, leaning his head back against the bouncing canvas of the cargo hood. It was an American truck, left behind when the troops pulled out in '75. He turned his head and glanced at the others wondering why they all had stayed alive. They were lean and leathery, baked brown by years of hard work in the relentless sun. Their peasant clothes were simple but clean, their Ho Chi Minh sandals workable if not comfortable. But their eyes. Their eyes were dead things, windows to the morgue of their brains. They had no home and no country, no ties except to each other. They couldn't even remember the last time they had slept in the same place two nights in a row in this forest land where every night was the same night.

These had once been proud men. Now they were straggly and bearded, heavily scarred from years of unattended injuries. He wondered if he looked as bad as they did. His memory of himself, the one that he kept with him, was of the last time he had looked in a mirror. It had been January 20, 1968, and he had been flying mostly B-52 support out of Korat, Thailand. He had shaved, then zipped into his flight suit and combat boots. After winking at the fighter jock in his mirror, he had left the hootch and gone over to the gun locker to pick up his sidearm and "blood chit" package of survival and barter gear. Then he had gone out, scaled the ladder into the cockpit of his F-4. He had been nervous and excited, and his belly was loaded with 750-pound bombs. He was going hunting, hunting for SAM sites to the north of the provincial capital of Thanh-hoa.

He never came back.

The land outside the truck was much more cultivated than they were used to. Ridley craned his head out as far as the chains would allow. The jungle had been cut back for civilization. The peasants on the side of the road waved as they transported families on the backs of water buffalo or bicycles. Traffic, cars and trucks, was passing them going in both directions.

He looked across the truck bed at Jenkins, who was scratching through his hair, trying to pick out lice. "Pretty far south, aren't we, Harry?" he asked.

Jenkins looked up slowly, coming out of a distant dream

somewhere. "Yeah," he answered, and held Ridley's eyes with pale, dead blue.

"You know the south," Ridley said. "Where do you think they're taking us?"

"What difference does it make?"

Their eyes stayed locked; Ridley didn't answer. Finally, Jenkins shrugged and shifted around to get a look out the truck back. When he came back in, his face was heavily creased in thought. "Son of a bitch," he said.

Ridley felt himself stiffen, couldn't figure out why. "What is it?"

"This is Highway 1," Jenkins said low. "If we follow this all the way down, it'll take us to fucking Saigon."

"You mean Ho Chi Minh City," someone called from the darkness farther toward the front of the truck.

The rain was still coming down when the pitted road turned to hard gravel, then smooth concrete. They were in the city, and many people were watching them, people whose eyes showed pain at their coming, people who remembered.

They were all watching out the truck back now, dead eyes recording a break in routine. No one spoke, no one moved. The rain was easing up, the traffic getting thick and heavy.

They turned onto Le Loi, filled with street stalls and soldiers, smells and jamming crowds of people. They passed a huge plaza, and Jenkins was pointing.

"The National Assembly," he said of a large brown building supported by Gothic pillars and corbeled arches. He was shaking his head. "The central market's farther down this street."

And their noses guided them in. The market was teeming with crowds. The odors were sickly sweet and the flies thick. Old women with betel-nut juice running down their chins squatted on the concrete streets and sold overripe fruit from old army blankets.

The truck drove through the center of town, then turned onto Tu Do Street, the hotel district, and they were passing the fine white structures that had been put up by the French aristocrats. Wide verandas filled with people in white suits overlooked their route, almost as if they were the carnival coming to town. Ridley was puzzled by what seemed to be an inordinate amount of VPA regulars stationed up and down the length of the street.

Tu Do ended at the old, Gothic basilica of Our Lady of Peace, and they jogged to the north, turning left between two large, well-kept buildings.

"Gentlemen," Jenkins said. "Welcome to the French and American embassies."

They watched out the back, Vietnamese soldiers all over what used to be the American Embassy, while the French remained both intact and in use. They drove for another two hundred yards past the embassies, then stopped. Ridley heard a loud creaking, figured they were opening a gate of some kind. The truck was rolling again, through the gate, past barbed wire fences into a large compound.

"My God," he heard Jenkins say. "This is Camp Friendship. We barracked marine detachments here to defend the embassy compound."

And they stopped again, the rain sputtering an easy drizzle. The driver, who they called Dude, came around with armed guards whom Ridley had never seen before. They were laughing and chattering, but Ridley's poor command of the language kept him from getting anything worthwhile from their words.

Putting down the truck back, the guards wound their chains out of the loops, pulling on them to make them move.

Ridley got up and jumped out of the truck back, Jenkins jumping out on the other side. Thirty others followed behind them. They splashed out into mud, Ridley feeling it ooze up over the tire tread of his sandals.

He looked around, astonished. They were in a camp, all right, wooden barracks set up on stilts all around. The compound was filled with other trucks, and more were pulling in. People were climbing out of all of them. Americans. They were filling the yard.

Jenkins stared at him, the man's lips moving soundlessly. All this time, all these years, they thought they were the only ones. But there were others all around them. Hundreds of others. Thousands. He saw Jenkins begin to cry.

II

Silver Springs, Maryland

April 13—2:58 A.M.

Jerry Prescott heard the phone off in the distance somewhere, off in the dreams somewhere. He came around slowly at first, then when he geared on the fact that it was the phone, he jumped up like a bolt.

The pain in his head was the first thing that grabbed him, the middle-of-the-night hangover that he had been sleeping through. Then he realized that he was in the den, sleeping fully clothed on the couch where he had passed out. And then he reached through blurry eyes for the phone on the coffee table beside him and saw which one it was.

The red one. The open line to the State Department.

The headache was gone immediately. He was fully awake by the time he brought the receiver of the dialless machine to his ear.

"Prescott," he said into the mouthpiece.

"Jerry," a voice returned, and it had a peculiar sound to it. "This is Frank."

"What's wrong?" Prescott asked, and he was already slipping into his shoes. Frank Merriman was deputy secretary of state. He ran the night shift crews at the State Department.

"We just got the craziest message over the wire."

Prescott was up, tucking his shirt back into his pants, balancing the phone on his shoulder. "Unsecured?"

"Yeah."

"Go on."

Lights were going on in other parts of the spacious house. A Secret Serviceman poked his head out of the downstairs bedroom that was connected to the den. Prescott waved him in. He nodded once, then ducked his head back into the room.

"It's from Saigon, Jerry. And it . . . let me read it to you. Are you sitting down?"

7

"Just read the goddamned message."

"Okay. Here goes: 'Greetings to the government of the United States of America. The People's Republic of Vietnam is holding a total of 2,045 prisoners of the imperialist war that the . . .'"

"What?"

Tod Barrows, the Secret Service agent, walked into the room, dressed in slacks without a shirt. Another one, Charlie Johnston, was still making noises in the bedroom. Barrow stood looking quizzically at Prescott.

"There's more," Frank Merriman's voice said over the phone. "Listen. '. . . imperialist war that the American government waged against the free peoples of Vietnam. These prisoners will be held for a total of seven days, until noon, Sunday, April 19. They will be held until reparations for the damage they have done to our country have been made. The reparations will total one million U.S. dollars in gold per man. If these reparations have not been made by the above-stated date and time, these prisoners of expansionist war will be tried as criminals and executed if they are found guilty.'" There was dead air on the line for several seconds, then Merriman rasped, "That's it."

Prescott felt himself sink onto the sofa. He could hear footsteps upstairs. Myrna was up and around. She'd be down in a minute.

"Mr. Secretary . . ." Barrows said quietly.

"Put a shirt on, Tod," he returned.

The man turned and walked away immediately.

Prescott took a breath. "That's over two billion dollars," he said.

"I know."

"Has the President been notified?"

"Someone's doing it right now."

He shook his head slowly. "Christ Almighty," he said, and put a foot up on the edge of the coffee table to tie the lace. Myrna was moving down the long, curving staircase, quilted robe wrapped around her body. Her face was set with the hard lines that always came out in times of stress. She had heard the red phone, too. Prescott covered the mouthpiece with his hand. "Coffee," was all he said to his wife of twenty-six years.

She moved without hesitation to the kitchen. Charlie

Johnston was out there now, slipping on his shoulder holster, tying it to his belt to hold it steady.

Prescott glared at the phone, the possibilities just now taking shape in his mind. "Unsecured wire," he said again.

"Everybody's got it by now," Merriman returned. "The boards here are already lighting up like a Christmas tree. What'll I tell them?"

"Don't tell them anything." He covered the mouthpiece again speaking to Johnston. "Bring the car around."

The man left.

Prescott held the receiver for a minute before speaking. He didn't want any part of this. He wanted to tell Frank to call somebody, anybody else. Instead he said, "Tell them we're checking it out. We are checking it out, aren't we?"

"So far, it's all on the up and up."

"Yeah. Well, tell them that they know as much about it as we do, or something like that. This is going to be all over everything by the morning. Jesus. Get the Joint Chiefs on the horn and get them down to the Pentagon for briefings. And get the secretary of defense over there, too."

"What about Benstock?"

Prescott thought for about a half second about the domestic affairs adviser. "Fuck him," he said. "If the President wants him, he'll have to get him all by himself. I'm on my way to the White House. I want as much readable information as you've got on this by the time I get there."

"Gotcha. Jerry?"

"Yeah."

"Are we going to pay it?"

"We can't pay. You know that."

"How are you going to tell that to the folks?"

That's what presidents are for, he thought, but didn't say it. Instead he said, "See you in about thirty minutes," and hung up.

The tie from the day before was lying across the cut-glass coffee table. He picked it up and wrapped it around his neck, then turned a circle, looking for his sport jacket.

Myrna came up with the coffee, steam rising lethargically from the bone-china cup. "You have to go?" she asked, knowing better than to question him too closely.

He took the cup from her, smiled the way he would smile at a waitress. "I'll call you when I get a chance."

"We're supposed to have dinner with the Durbins tonight."

"Better cancel it," he said, and drank half the tepid cup before setting it down to retrieve his jacket from the chair back.

Barrows, in shirt and tie, had come back into the room. He looked steadily at Myrna until she got the message and left quietly, gliding silently back up the thick carpeted stairs to her bed.

"Charlie's getting the car," Prescott said. "I'll need my briefcase out of the office."

"Trouble?" the man asked.

Prescott got one arm into a jacket sleeve, then stopped, looking at Barrows. The man had been a Green Beret. "Does starting up the Vietnam War again sound like trouble to you, Tod?"

The man's eyes widened. He turned and ran for the briefcase.

III

Washington, D.C.—1600 Pennsylvania Avenue

April 13—3:37 A.M.

Washington, D.C. is the capital of the United States of America. It sits on low, flat ground, the north bank of the Potomac River, on U.S. Highway 1, just as Ho Chi Minh City sits on another Highway 1 in another part of the world.

Simon Herrod sat in the swivel chair at the large oak desk that had once belonged to Franklin Roosevelt. The desk was sturdy and imposing, a symbol of sorts. It was dragged down to the basement every time a Republican administration took office and dutifully brought back up whenever the Democrats were in power. Such was the nature of things.

Herrod was drinking coffee to wake himself up and thinking about history. He often thought about history and the way it had of taking control of people's lives, of making out of them something that they never were. The Civil War did it to Grant. The Great Depression did it to Hoover. The Cuban missile crisis did it to Kennedy. Being there was everything; what you did held very little sway. Longevity determined political success, not the job done.

He had come close to negotiating a viable arms control treaty with the Soviets. It had been his major preoccupation throughout three years of office. He had wanted to shape history. But it didn't work that way. A backwater country was going to do it to him. A backwater country that America had been stupid enough to war with years before. They obviously needed the money. And they were going to affect the course of history to get it.

He stood slowly, unwinding his 6-foot-2-inch frame that hadn't had enough exercise in the last couple of years, and walked to the window. He had never felt comfortable in the White House. How can you when you know your residence is only temporary—other people's furniture, other people's ghosts walking the creaking halls?

There was a knock on the door.

He started to yell for entry, then gave way to protocol instead. Moving across the new carpeting that his predecessor had put in, he opened the door to the secretary of state.

They shook hands, eyes locked.

"You look grim, Jerry," Simon Herrod said.

The man walked past him into the office. "I've looked at this from forty-eight different directions," he said, because he believed in getting the bad news out right away, "and it looks rotten no matter how we carve it up."

Prescott watched Herrod walk slowly back to his desk, noticed for the first time how the years in office had aged him. "And on top of everything else, it had to happen in an election year."

"This wouldn't have set any better in an off year," Herrod returned, and sank with a groan into the chair behind his desk. "Anybody gotten in touch with Benny?" he asked.

Prescott thought about Benstock for another half second. "I didn't," he returned, and dragged a red-leather overstuffed chair up close to the desk so he could lean on its top. "Anything new?"

The President picked up a photograph that was lying before him on the desk. He looked at it, grimaced, and handed it over. "Came off the AP wire," he said, then picked up the receiver of the white phone on his desk.

Prescott took the photo, looked at it. It was a picture of a detention camp, fences full of rolled barbed wire and guard towers. There were barracks evident in the background. The foreground was full of prisoners, American prisoners dressed in Vietnamese clothes. Despite himself, he felt a small catch in his throat when he looked at it, a slight rush of emotion that scared him.

"Lolly," the President said into the phone, "have somebody get hold of Benstock. Tell him what's going on and get him over to the briefing with the Joint Chiefs at . . ."

His eyes drifted up to Prescott's. The secretary held up six fingers.

"At 0600. Got it? Okay."

He hung up. "Doesn't that just make you sick to your stomach?"

Prescott looked up at him. "It's going to make a lot of people sick to their stomachs," he returned.

Herrod sighed deeply, visibly aging with every breath. "What's the time difference between here and there?" he asked.

"Twelve hours later there."

Looking at his watch, the President tightened his lips. He said nothing.

There was an embarrassing silence for several seconds, then Prescott said, "What the hell are we going to do, Simon?"

Herrod folded his hands on the desktop and stared. He looked the part of commander in chief. "We're going to preserve the Union," he said in a clear voice. "We're going to negotiate like crazy and hope to God we can get those boys out of there somehow without getting them all killed."

"The ransom . . ."

The President held up his hands. "We'll never talk about the ransom again, Jerry. It's nonnegotiable. That's the only thing I'm absolutely sure about in all this. If I were to pay that ransom, there wouldn't be an American citizen safe anywhere in this world."

Rooting through his jacket pocket, Prescott came out with a new cigar. He slipped it out of the cellophane package slowly, thoughtfully. It was a way of avoiding eye contact with Herrod. They both knew that a whole lot of people wouldn't understand about the ransom. He wet the cigar with his lips before looking up again.

"Mind?" he asked, holding it up.

A smile played quickly on Herrod's lips as he shook his head.

There was a lighter on the desk inset in a small block of granite carved in the shape of Texas. Prescott slid it across the glass desktop and fingered the flame. "They're going to want war over at the Pentagon," he said, and leaned down to puff the green monster to life.

"They always want war over at the Pentagon," Herrod said. "That's what we pay them for."

He swiveled his chair around away from Prescott, thinking. The secretary simply sat, puffing quietly on the smoke. It was the calm before the storm, both of them knew that. It was a time for thoughtfulness, because in a very few hours they would have to commit absolutely to a course of action, and then there would be no time for thought of any kind.

Strangely, Prescott found himself thinking about the canceled dinner with the Durbins. His son, Randy, fresh out of law school, was just about ready to marry Durbins's daughter, June. Randy was just starting out with Durbins's firm, an old, respected New York liberal go-get-'em Park Avenue kind of firm. Durbins himself didn't practice anymore, devoting all his time and most of his money to a no-frills overseas airline he had started as a sideline several years before when deregulation had opened up new routes. Jerry hadn't practiced law for years either, but the prospect of getting out of government was beginning to sound appealing. Maybe Durbins could find a spot for him.

"War in Vietnam," Herrod said, and swiveled around again. "How's that for pulling scabs off wounds?"

Prescott knocked his cigar into the heavy glass ashtray that sat near him on the desk. "I'm afraid that those wounds aren't as healed as we'd like to think."

"That's just what those fuckers over there in Vietnam are thinking."

Leaving his cigar in the ashtray, Prescott walked over to the window and watched the early morning traffic on Pennsylvania Avenue. Reaching out, he rapped on the thick glass. "What are *they* going to want?" he asked.

Herrod chuckled softly. "Are you asking me what they want now, or what they really want?" He got up and moved over next to Prescott. "You know, folks who live on the banks of rivers that flood every spring really hate those floods; but after those floods go down, they sure like the crops they grow in the silt. If we went down and stopped those cars out there, every one of those people would have an idea on what we should do; but not a one of them has to sit in that chair over there and make the decisions."

Prescott turned around slowly, looking at a man he had known well for over thirty years. And in that instant, he knew that he didn't know him very well at all. "Just what are you saying?"

Herrod slowly walked back to the desk, as if he had to be there to let the office speak for him. "I have the welfare of the country to think about," he said. "Those men over there, they're all soldiers. They were expendable ten years ago and they're just as expendable now. The decision I make, whatever it is, will have to be in the best interests of this country, of the citizens of this country. All other considerations are secondary."

"Even if it means the death of those men?"

"Yeah, Jerry," Herrod returned. "We understand one another."

Prescott began wondering if it could be possible to do everything he needed to do, and still work out dinner with the Durbins.

RUSSIA REAFFIRMS FRIENDSHIP

HO CHI MINH CITY,—In ceremonies here yesterday, the Republic of Vietnam and the Soviet Union reaffirmed their mutual commitment by signing a series of nonaggression and mutual defense pacts. At a state dinner held in honor of two hundred

Soviet mining engineers and surveyors who have recently come to Vietnam, Soviet Ambassador Nikolai Brodski said, "Our two countries, united through Marxism, clasp hands in glorious friendship."

Insiders say that Vietnam is not happy, however, with the level of commitment toward recovery the Soviet Union has exercised in Vietnam since 1975. "It seems they only want to take from us," said an unidentified source in the R.V.N. government, obviously referring to the engineers. "The only aid they give is in the area of mineral development, the results of which they take with them as repayment for their help."

—REUTERS

IV

Camp Friendship

April 13—6:10 P.M.

Ridley watched intently out the window of Charlie Building as what appeared to be the last of the trucks rolled into the compound. The ground had already dried from the rain, and a fine fog of gray white dust hung in the air of the yard.

There were people everywhere, laughing and shouting, lining up for identification or shaving sets or another hot dog. God, he wondered where Charlie got the hot dogs. The word was that they were going home, but somehow, he didn't feel that it would be that simple.

The barracks held perhaps a hundred and fifty men, all white, no minorities. It was lined on both walls with single beds, real beds, with clean sheets and pillows. He hadn't seen a pillow since '68. The floors resounded hollowly, like dull drums as the prisoners ran and jumped, filling the crowded room with a steady pounding. Men were pushing all around him, worked up, too worked up he

thought, buying this vision of freedom because they had
had so many years with no vision. And he realized that
once Charlie had gone beyond torture, real torture, with
them that the control became so subtle and so long term
that none of them had any idea that perhaps they had
been changed totally, that perhaps they weren't the same
people they had been—and would never be again.

There were a lot of television people in the yard and
the various barracks, French television, small hand-held
cameras that they could take anywhere, anytime they
wanted. These small cameras scared him; they had the
ability of intruding into his life. They even had one in the
barracks. It was the most frightening technological advance that he could imagine, and he wondered what other
new atrocities the world had to offer him.

"Look at me, will you?"

He turned from the window to see Harry Jenkins,
clean and shaven, wearing jeans with a wide belt and a
paisley shirt.

"Hey hippie." Ridley smiled. "That's not regulation."

Jenkins grinned wide, showing his missing teeth.
"Get with the program, Jase," he said. "I'm ready for
Haight-Ashbury and you haven't even cleaned up yet."

Ridley moved away from the window and sat on the
edge of the bed, smiling quickly when he felt himself sink
down into it. "I'll get around to it," he returned, and felt
the stubble of his beard with a heavily calloused hand.
"Plenty of time for that."

Jenkins sat on the next bed facing him, their knees
almost touching. "What's your problem?" he asked, and his
features were dark. "We're going home."

Ridley looked at him hard. "Are we?"

"What kind of question is that?"

"I just wonder, that's all. I wonder, why? Why now?"

Jenkins patted his leg, but it was more of a slap.
"Don't worry about it, okay? Don't worry about it."

"They've kept us all this time for a reason," Ridley
said, and, reaching across pulled a pack of Camels out of
Jenkins's breast pocket. Putting one in his mouth, he
tossed the pack back to the man. "I'd like to know what it
is."

"What difference does it make?" Jenkins snapped, and there was fire in his eyes.

"They want to use us, Harry," he returned, and lit the smoke on a matchbook advertising money to be made in the field of electronics. "They might want to use us to make the country look bad."

"Fuck." The man spat the word. "They can fucking use me any damned way they want to. Nobody's cared about us all these years. Why should it make a holy shit to us what the deal is? And while we're on the subject, what other shot have we got? We don't buy this package, we may as well just hang it up, 'cause we'll never get out of here."

Drawing deeply on the cigarette, Ridley let the smoke out slowly, trying to use it to keep himself calm. "If I believed that, I would have committed suicide years ago."

"You're a motherfucker, you know that?" Jenkins said. "All I care about is home, brother. Zone Interior. I'm ready to go."

Ridley stretched out on the bed, feeling himself sinking into it. He had been sleeping on hard ground for so long, he wondered if a good soft bed would give him a backache. "Home to what?" he asked, and stared at the ceiling. "Haight-Ashbury was a long time ago. Things have changed, whether we were there or not. I was married for fifteen years. That's a long time, but I've been here longer. I'm sure that Marsha had me declared dead a good ten years ago. I've got kids who grew all the way to adulthood without knowing anything about me. They've probably been calling somebody else Dad all this time."

"Stop it!" Jenkins said too loud. "Everything will be fine."

"Harry, I . . ."

"Stop it, I said! I don't want to hear it."

Ridley shut up. He wanted to be excited about this, but somehow he wasn't. "Sorry," he said, after a minute.

Jenkins leaned way over and stared into his face. "You've taken care of me for years," he said quietly. "I could never have gone on without you. You were strong for both of us, and I'll never forget it; but I've got to believe in this." His eyes were misting over again. "I've got to. I feel like I've been dead and come back to life."

Some enlisted men several beds down began singing "Stop in the Name of Love" and laughing, and Ridley figured, what the hell. He started to join in with the singing, when they were interrupted by loudspeakers outside.

"ALL OF OUR GUESTS AT CAMP FRIENDSHIP WILL PLEASE TO ASSEMBLE IN THE COURTYARD FOR AN IMPORTANT MESSAGE. A MESSAGE OF GREAT IMPORTANCE WILL BE GIVEN OUTSIDE."

Ridley sat up at once, swinging his legs off the edge of the bed. This was the part he had been waiting for, the part he had been dreading.

He stood up and Jenkins was already gone, anxious to get outside for the news. Men were jammed up in the aisle between the rows of beds, pushing and laughing. Ridley waited until the flow had passed to join it. He noticed that there were a few others hanging back as he had done and he wondered if they had been thinking about things the way he had. Then he wondered if the others were thinking at all.

He got to the door, down the four swaying wooden steps to the ground. The compound was surrounded by several layers of fences, all topped with rolled barbed wire. Vietnamese were jammed four or five deep on the outside of the farthest fence, hanging on the wire, looking in. A large stage was being erected in the yard, workmen still hammering away. That's where everyone was congregating. A microphone was set up on a stand in the middle of the stage, but everytime they turned it on, a shrill feedback scream filled the yard.

He wandered over to the crowd, feeling out of place. Nearly everyone had changed out of peasant clothes and was now wearing more Western gear. He hadn't gotten around to it, yet.

These were all hard-looking men, many of them maimed severely, crippled and twisted; but they were all acting like children, eating too much and throwing up in the yard. Moving into their midst, he was interested in a group of several hundred men who had all stayed together. They seemed in better shape than everyone else, their hair was longer, their clothes fit them better. What interested him most, however, was the fact that not one of them seemed happy. They all stood there, staring, talking quietly to others in the group.

"Jase, over here."

It was Jenkins, motioning for Ridley to come over next to him. His cigarette was getting low. Throwing it on the ground, he walked over to Jenkins.

"God, I'm so worked up I can't believe it," Jenkins said. "Christmas was never like this."

Ridley turned slowly, taking in that strange group again. "Who are those guys?" he asked, and Jenkins turned around to stare at them, too.

"AWOLs," he said. "Decided to stay when everybody else got the fuck out. From what I've heard, they've been living free all these years. This is the first fucking camp they've ever been in."

Ridley felt anger flush through him. "AWOLs," he repeated, and he felt dirty just being around them. "What are they doing here?"

Jenkins shrugged. "Who cares?"

The microphone was turned on again. It squealed at first, but they adjusted the volume down. A military man walked up to it first.

"I am General Hue," he said in barely understandable English, "and this compound is my responsibility. We do not wish any trouble from anyone so close to the time of your freedom. You will treat us with respect, and that respect will be returned to you. We ask you to observe certain rules: You may congregate, but only in groups smaller than ten; no one may speak to or for the group as a whole; you will set up no chain of command; you will follow orders without question; and lights out is at nine P.M." Hue smiled quickly. The medals on his uniform glowed hotly in the dying sun, making it look as if his chest were on fire. "I wish you all good fortune."

He turned and walked away immediately, to be replaced by a man no taller than five feet at most. His face was stoic and intelligent, and his suit fit so well it looked as if it had grown onto his body. He smiled constantly.

"Welcome," he said, opening his arms wide. His English was acceptable. "I bring you greetings from the Republic, greetings to our American friends."

"Son of a bitch," Ridley hissed.

"Shhh," Jenkins returned. "Let's listen."

"I wish to dispel all the rumors that you have been hearing the several last hours. My name is Colonel Bui Tin, and I am the engineer and overseer of this operation. As you probably have heard, we have decided that it is time for our American friends to return to their homeland. For the last several years most of you have been most graciously helping us to rebuild our homeland, first from the devastation caused by your own countrymen and your greedy politicians, then from the destruction caused by the Chinese when we fought them. We are most grateful. We are negotiating the arrangements for your release at this very moment. We do not think it will be too difficult. All we ask is some money to make reparations for the damage you did to us in fourteen years of war. You have worked with us; you know how bad things have been. We are a very poor country, poor mostly because your expansionist politicians chose to defoliate our countryside and poison our water so we cannot grow rice. Amends must be made, as I'm sure you all understand."

"Ransom," Ridley said.

The man on his left poked him in the ribs. "Shut up," he said. "Give the man a chance to talk."

"We will ask you to help us with this," Tin said. "We must ask you to help us make the people of America understand the way you understand. I will ask Mr. Boulle to stand up here and explain our needs to you."

Tin stepped back a pace and began applauding himself, the others on the stand joining in. When they were finished, the Frenchman walked casually up to the mike.

"Hello," he said, his voice low and melodious, the accent thick. "I've heard of captive audiences, but this is . . . ridiculous."

Everyone laughed, and he smiled with them. An incredibly handsome man, Boulle looked totally in charge of everything.

"We will be making films of you to send home," he said. "Your country and your loved ones will be able to see that you are well and ready to return home to their loving arms."

A cheer rifled through part of the crowd, much to

Ridley's surprise. Didn't they realize that they were being held hostage?

"I will be asking for volunteers to come to the stage in a moment. We need you to talk to the people of America, to tell them that you will be coming home just as soon as they help undo some of the wrong that was done to the free people of Vietnam. You will be able to help . . . how do you say . . . right the scales of justice. I, myself, am proud to be a part of this glorious event. We will all make history here together."

There was applause, and Boulle held up his hands for silence. "We will applaud when you get on the plane for San Francisco. And now, I need the volunteers."

A wild crush ensued, as well over half the prisoners rushed to the wobbly stage and had to be held back by the troops.

DATELINE WASHINGTON—Political-well watchers have been buzzing lately about the subtle changes affecting President Herrod's cabinet. Secretary of State Jerry Prescott, career politician and longtime confidant of Simon Herrod's, seems to be taking a backseat lately to Domestic Affairs Adviser Maurice Benstock. Benstock, they say, with his casual charm and quick wit has been edging out Prescott for the President's ear.

Such a reshifting of advisers could mean big changes for the country. Prescott is an old-time Democrat, staunch and straightforward in his thinking and values. "Benny" Benstock, however, is a new brand of politician. Media-oriented and shoot-from-the-hip, he has been advising the President to be more aggressive in his handling of state business, more out front in his appeal and his approach. Should he succeed in supplanting the old-line methods, we will see a new look from the White House, and this reporter, for one, hopes the changes work in positive directions.

—"Inside Report"
Washington Post Syndicate

V

Oklahoma City, Oklahoma

April 13—6:23 A.M.

Nancy Henderson had been cooking breakfast when Timothy, her four-year-old, came charging in, crying.

Leaving the oatmeal to plop-bubble in the pan, she bent down to tousle his sandy hair. "What's the matter, hotshot?" she said. "It can't be all that bad."

"Cartoons," he sobbed, and pointed into the den. "Cartoons."

"This sounds like a major problem," she said. "Let's go check it out."

She started out of the walnut-paneled kitchen, stopping just long enough to grab eight-month-old Jeremy out of the high chair.

Toting Jeremy on her hip, she followed Tim into the comfortable den, picking her way carefully around ET hand puppets and Fisher-Price circuses.

Timothy scrunched up his nose and pointed to the TV screen. "Cartoons," he said.

Sure enough, there were no cartoons. It was some news program. Setting Jeremy in the playpen, she moved to change the channel. More news. She changed it again. The same.

Curious, she knelt in front of the set. These weren't regular news shows. Something was going on. She turned up the sound and listened.

The man on the screen was talking. ". . . I must repeat, the things that we are reporting to you have not, as yet, been verified. We have had no confirmation from the government, or any government agencies. All we have are the reports themselves, issued over the Associated Press wires this morning from Ho Chi Minh City, the capital of Vietnam. Once again, here is the picture that we received this morning at 3:15 Eastern Standard Time."

She watched in horror as a photo, apparently showing American prisoners of war, was placed on the screen.

Tim was in her face. "Where cartoons?" he demanded, hands on hips.

She gently shoved him aside. "Not now, honey."

"Cartoons," he said loudly, stamping his bare feet. "Cartoons!"

"Quiet!"

Tim threw himself on the floor, crying. Jeremy, apparently liking the sound of it, began crying, too.

Nancy glared at them and turned the sound up.

". . . The Vietnamese government is apparently demanding a ransom of one million dollars per man, for a total of 2,045 prisoners of war still in that country."

"Do I smell something burning?" came a voice from out of the room.

"Come here, quick!"

"Just a sec."

"We must say again, that this word is unofficial. There has been no official confirmation on this report."

Sid Henderson appeared in the doorway.

"Come here," Nancy said, her heart pounding. "It's something about the MIAs."

He squatted down beside her. "Take it easy, Nance," he said, and put a hand on her shoulder that she never even felt. "You know all this shit just gets you all worked up."

She looked at him, tried to keep her voice steady. "They're alive, Sid," she said quietly. "They're being held for ransom."

The arm went around her shoulder. "No. No. There's got to be some kind of mistake."

"Shhh. He's talking again."

The man on the screen looked off-camera for a few seconds, his brows knotted in concern. When he turned back, his face was slack, his eyes faraway. "We are apparently receiving live television transmissions via satellite from Vietnam. I must stress again that we have verified nothing. . . . We are showing you these pictures as we get them."

Nancy Henderson gripped her husband's arm. He pulled her closer. Even the children had quieted down.

A picture staticked on the screen. It showed a prison yard, the same one as in the photo. Men were milling around, some dressed as Orientals, others wearing the kind of clothes she had worn in college. They were all lean and gaunt, their hair chopped close. They all had strange, staring eyes that make her skin creep.

A voice thick with accent was speaking perfect English. "Some of these poor boys have been with us almost twenty years. Alone, without a home, without a country. They wait for you, people of the United States of America, to give them a home, to give them a country. They enacted a terrible debt on our land. They destroyed our homes and families. You knew that, people of the United States. You forced your leaders to give up that horrible war with the free people of Asia, your Asian brothers. And still we starve, our country still suffering from the attrition you placed upon us.

"It is time to wipe that slate clean. With the money you pay, you will be doing a twofold service. You will be returning your lost men to the bosom of their families and you will be helping to rebuild the country that your greedy politicians destroyed. Listen. Listen to one of your own countrymen."

A face appeared on the screen, a young face gone old. The face was gristle, skull-like, the short hair completely gray. And the eyes, just like the others, eyes that had lived with death and now could see nothing else. Nancy felt something click inside of her. She was gripping Sid's arm with both hands now, her fingers white with the strain.

The face spoke. "I'm Private First Class Billy Phillips, United States Army..."

Nancy heard herself scream from somewhere far away. It was Billy. It *was* Billy. They'd been married in '65 when they were both in college. He had dropped out to work and had gotten drafted almost immediately. He was lost in Bien-Hoa during the Tet Offensive of '68.

She was crying now, strangled moans. She looked up at Sid. His bearded face was unmoving, his eyes set in horror on the screen.

"We tore this country up pretty good," Phillips was saying. "And me and the others have spent the last years trying to build it back. But we're really homesick. We miss all that crazy stuff—baseball, TV... sitting around a dinner table with the family..." Tears were running out of his eyes, sliding down both cheeks. "And I miss my wife, Nancy. I go to sleep every night thinking about her. I . . . I ain't got anything else. You folks have gotta help us. You just gotta. They really need the money down here—their folks are starving and all. And it's our fault. You gotta help us. You gotta."

Sid reached out and turned off the television.

"What are you doing?" Nancy screamed, and went for the set.

He grabbed her, pulled her away.

The children were crying again. Screaming.

"Don't look anymore," he yelled back. "My God. My God!"

She was banging on him, flailing at him with her fists. Getting hold of her arms, he wrestled her to the floor, straddling her.

"What are you doing?" she screamed.

"Get control of yourself. God please, you'll hurt yourself."

Her teeth were clenched, fire spitting from her eyes. "Let me go, you son of a bitch. That's Billy. That's my husband!"

He just stared back at her, his eyes wide and frightened. Neither of them heard the phone that was insistently ringing in the background.

VI

Glen Burnie, Maryland

April 13—7:15 A.M.

Cassady liked the fact that the neighborhood was hilly. It was a lower-middle-class late-fifties neighborhood, built for people who had a lot of kids during the post-World War II baby boom. The houses were ranch-style, Cape Cod, and split-level, and Cassady walked five miles of those Glen Burnie Park hills every morning.

The kids were gone now, the war vets settling into the advancing stages of age. They tended to work on their lawns a lot; they pruned their hedges; they edged their grass; they washed their cars. Most importantly, they left Cassady alone. That was at all times the important thing.

Cassady walked, thinking about nothing, not noticing that the houses were falling into disrepair because the economy was just bad enough that lower-middle class had somehow become lower class, and that the people inside of the houses had hopes and frustrations and dreams and fears. They were five miles of hill to him and they left him alone. That was important.

It wasn't his real name, Cassady, but it was the one that he used the most, the one he liked the most. It was the first one he used back in '67 when they pulled him out of that jail in Da Nang and put him in the SEAL squad, running point in Operation Phoenix.

The road was pitted blacktop, and the sun was just cherrying up the sky. Cars were beginning to grumble out of driveways to make the fifteen miles to work in Baltimore. Glen Burnie Park was just coming alive. It was time for Cassady to get off the streets.

His Cape Cod with the aluminum siding and the peeling wooden carport sat at the top of a steep incline. It was painted flat white with beige trim. He mowed his lawn once a week, early in the morning so fewer people would see him. He drove a three-year-old Chevy and never, ever had parties, loud or otherwise.

Making the hill, he went up the drive, using his key to let himself in the kitchen door that sat off the carport. Walking into the house, he took off his windbreaker and hung it carefully in the hall closet. He would fix himself a breakfast of wheat germ and carrot juice then exercise in the bedroom that he had converted to a gym. He would exercise strenuously for two hours, or until exhaustion overtook him. In the evening, after dark, he would repeat the process of walking and exercising. He related to the pain of it. He was a piece of tightly coiled rope, and he tightened the sinews every chance he had. It was something like being alive, only different.

This morning, however, the phone interrupted him before he even had the carrots in the food processor. Unplugging the machine, he washed his hands before answering. It would be business, he knew, and they would let it ring until someone answered.

Walking into the sparsely furnished living room, he wiped his wet hands on his jeans and picked up the receiver.

"Davidson," Cassady said into the mouthpiece.

"Control," responded a dull female voice. "Scrambled."

"A minute," he returned, and set the receiver on the empty coffee table. Walking into his bedroom, he opened the walk-in closet door and took the extension that he kept in there off the hook.

Retracing his steps, he hung up the phone in the living room, then went back to the bedroom. He went into the closet and closed the door and bolted it behind him.

The closet was full of clothes he never wore. Shoving aside a number of overcoats, he revealed the long table with the scrambler computer. Sliding the stool out from under the table, he sat in front of the typer and flicked the machine on. Picking up the receiver, he said, "Go ahead," into the mouthpiece, then set it on the cradle on the side of the scrambler.

Muffled, off in the distance, he could hear tiny, rapid, beeping sounds. Within seconds, the sounds gave way to writing on the scrambler's blue-green viewscreen.

A series of access codes came up on the screen first, and Cassady typed in the correct responses. When the machine was satisfied with him, it read:

PRIORITY ONE
EYES ONLY
NO NOTES
ARE YOU ALONE?

He typed in:

ALONE AND SECURED

The scrambler answered:

RECORDS INDICATE THAT EMPLOYEE SS# 442 50 6937 CODE NAME: DAVIDSON, CLEARANCE: TOP SECRET HAS EXTENSIVE WARTIME EXPERIENCE IN ASIAN OPS AND IS CURRENTLY UNASSIGNED. CORRECT?

He stared in disbelief at the screen. Asian ops. There hadn't been his kind of Asian ops. for many years. He drew his fingers across dry lips, his insides tightening up, that coiled rope. A small seed of hope was planted in his psyche. He trampled it before it grew.

The screen, impatient, asked again.

CORRECT?

With shaking fingers, he answered in the affirmative. The questions would begin now, he knew, the questions that gave him the illusion of choice, though for people like him choice was never an issue.

WOULD YOU ACCEPT OVERSEAS ASSIGNMENT?

He typed quickly:

WHICH COUNTRY?

The answer came just as quickly:

VIETNAM
BLUE CHIPPER

The last remark was an agency joke. A blue chipper was a high-risk military operation, entailing visibility and nonregulation behavior. He answered immediately:

I WILL ACCEPT ASSIGNMENT
WILL YOU BRIEF?

The answer was several minutes in coming, and cryptic when it did come:

WE WILL CONSIDER YOUR ACCEPTANCE
WILL CONTACT ABOUT BRIEFING AT 1200 HOURS
END MESSAGE

There was nothing more. The screen sizzled to static and a muffled dial tone hummed from the receiver. Cassady sat

there feeling Nam welling up inside of him like a rice
balloon.

Then, all at once, right there in the closet, he tilted his
stool back on two legs, threw his head back and roared with
laughter.

It was the happiest moment of his entire life.

VII

Washington, D.C.
—The Pentagon

April 13—7:45 A.M.

Prescott watched General Layton glare at him across the
table, the man's smooth, unlined face tightly controlled, his
voice emotional, but restrained. "I just don't understand you,
Mr. Secretary," he said.

Gazing across the pool of fuzzy light, Prescott answered.
"What don't you understand, General?"

The large room was dark and empty, like a forgotten
basement. The table held twelve men, most of them in
uniform. Phones with push buttons and small monitor screens
were set at each place. The table was not round; it had a very
definite oblong shape, with Simon Herrod occupying the
head. The tiny screens were all showing the same picture—
American soldiers consorting with a foreign power.

Layton's eyes smoldered darkly. He was sixty-two
years old and had served his country in three different
wars for forty-five of those years. He pointed a long finger
at Prescott. "I don't understand why this doesn't set you on
fire inside, Mr. Secretary." He directed that same finger
toward the small screen. "I don't understand why this
doesn't start a patriotic firestorm inside of you that would
drive you to action."

Prescott took a breath. "My personal feelings are not at

issue here, are they? What we're searching for is a solution for the current problem."

Layton leaned way across the wide table, as if he might like to crawl across it and go for Prescott's face. "I've been giving you the solution all morning," he said in clipped tones. "We've got to come down on these bastards, and we've got to do it right now. Don't you see? They've got our boys on goddamned television f'chrissake. The whole world is watching them make fools of us." His chair scraped out behind him, and he was up on his feet. He leaned heavily against the back of the chair. "We've got to stop this. It's a direct challenge. Don't you understand that?"

"Sit down, General," the President said quietly. "In about an hour, I've got to go on national television and make some sort of statement about this, and it's going to have to be rational and thought out."

Layton sat, giving cursory glances up and down the length of the table. "I apologize, Mr. President," and then more grudgingly, ". . . Mr. Secretary. I did four duty tours in Nam. I have very strong feelings about it."

"I understand that," Herrod responded. "I really do. I dare say that most of us have those same feelings. But dammit, George. I need you clear-headed. This is the biggest thing we've ever faced together. When I do make the decision, I want to be sure it's the best one for the country."

Admiral Hansen spoke up from farther down the table, his white uniform nearly glowing in the indirect light. "George's problem is the same as mine," he said. "We don't see that there could be any other possible solution except military retaliation. It seems obvious to me, too."

Herrod's eyes just touched Prescott's, who nodded imperceptibly. They had arranged in advance that he would be the peace dove, thrusting and parrying the hard lines of the hunters. They had to see it fly.

He spoke up. "The problem here, gentlemen, is that at the conclusion of the war in Vietnam, fully 80 percent of the population of this country was dead set against our involvement over there. How do we justify to them a military action?"

"What in the hell is that supposed to mean?" Layton asked. "We're here to protect the people, not to ask them if they want to be protected. The people don't know what they think from moment to moment."

"At least until someone tells them," said the voice on Herrod's right. It was Maurice Benstock, leaning down into the light, smiling his you-all-know-me smile. Benny was a slick, fatherly figure, who had been close to Herrod ever since he had retired from TV journalism several years before. Prescott didn't trust him. He was from outside the fraternity. People from the outside usually ran on a different energy that he didn't understand.

Herbert Vallens, secretary of defense, sat between Layton and Admiral Hansen. Formerly a banker, he dressed like a mortician, all in black. He was bald on top, the side tufts trimmed to military precision. He was soft-spoken, and hard-nosed. He had removed his black-framed glasses and was holding them in the air.

"Go ahead, Herb," Herrod said.

The man licked his lips before talking, looking at the tabletop the whole time, at his reflection the whole time. Prescott's feelings about Vallens were mixed. He didn't care much for the man personally, but listened to him when he talked.

"Just for a second, let's extend General Layton's philosophy to its logical limits. I assume, General, that you would have us declare war on the Vietnamese?"

Layton turned to him, nodded once. "The sooner the better, Mr. Secretary."

"Suppose we do that," the man continued. "Suppose that we go to the Congress this very day and ask for a declaration of war. Now, assuming we get Congress to go along, which is very doubtful at this point, what would you have us do, then?"

Layton smiled wide, his still-handsome, lean face red from shaving. Prescott knew without looking that he had shined his shoes, too. "I'm glad you asked that question," he replied. "What we do, is send the Seventh Fleet down there to put the fear of God into them, and if that isn't enough we send in the B-52's . . . hell, blacken the skies with B-52's. We level Saigon . . . pardon me, Ho Chi fucking Minh City, and Haiphong, and Hanoi. Then we establish beachheads, and move the marines in and take the country. We've been slapped in the face, gentlemen. The bottom line. We've got to slap back or they'll continue to take free shots. It's the nature of things."

"What about the prisoners, General?" Vallens asked.

"We all die, Mr. Secretary. About the best any of us can do is try and control the circumstances. They took an oath, same as I did. They should all be willing to lay down their lives if necessary."

"If you recall, General Layton, we spent nearly fifteen years trying to do what you just suggested and we got our asses kicked. What would make this time any different, any less costly?"

Hansen spoke up. "We never tried to win the last time; you know that as well as I do. We were supporting them in their civil war."

"This time it'd be us against them," Layton said. "By God, we'd plant the flag within a month. It'd be the biggest shot in the arm to this country since World War II."

"We've got two basic problems with your idea, George," Herrod said. "First off, it assumes as a given that the hostages will be lost. I'm not ready to accept that yet. It cuts off all other options, leaves us no room to negotiate."

"You can't negotiate with these people," Layton returned. "They look at it as a sign of weakness."

"Bullshit," said Dean Gibbons, Herrod's chosen from the Security Council. He was seated on Herrod's left, between him and Prescott. His gray pinstripes looked natural on him, a second skin. Prescott could always tell inherited money. "They're highly skilled negotiators, patient negotiators. My feeling is that they have every intention of negotiating a settlement here. It's just a question of finding out what they really want."

"The other problem," the President interrupted, "is, what the hell would we do with Vietnam if we take it? We'd be just another invading enemy to them. We'd have to settle into trying to hold the damned place against world opinion."

"To say nothing of the money we'd have to pump into it to rebuild it, so that they could ultimately take it back away from us," Prescott said, then poured himself a drink of water.

Layton slammed a fist down hard on the table. "Mr. President, what we're talking about here is firmly establishing American integrity abroad. We can't let these little dink-ass countries push us around. They get away with it there, they get away with it everywhere."

Hansen spoke up again. "What about a limited strike, a retaliatory response if they don't free the hostages?"

"Have you thought it out?" Prescott asked him.

"Not entirely."

"Try this," Prescott returned. "They've given us an ultimatum. Suppose we turn right around and give them an ultimatum?"

"Such as?" Herrod asked.

"We use their own deadline. Tell them that they have that long to free the hostages or we retaliate."

"With what?" Layton asked.

"That's the beauty of it," Prescott returned. "We don't have to say. If they, in fact, don't return the hostages, we can then go to an angry Congress and get authorization for almost anything. Then, the onus will be on them. They will be the ones pushing for trouble. That also allows for the possibility of getting the hostages back. They've given us until noon Sunday, that's midnight here. I think we should use every minute of that time."

Benstock spoke up. He was called Herrod's domestic adviser, but his duties were more along the lines of confidant. He was the most affable man Prescott ever knew, but he feared there was nothing beneath that affability.

"Don't you think that the Vietnamese have already thought of all that?" he asked.

Herrod looked at him. Prescott watched the President; he didn't like the hold that Benstock had on the man.

"Keep going," Herrod said.

"First of all," he said, "I think I know what's on their mind." He pointed to his own monitor. "The ransom demand isn't being made on us, but on the people of this country. They knew we'd never pay. They're hoping that the citizens still feel the way they did and will raise the money themselves."

"We can't allow that," Herrod replied.

"How are you going to stop it?"

The President shook his head. "God, I hope you're wrong." He ran a hand through his hair. "Would the networks voluntarily stop running the transmissions?"

"Who's a network?" Benstock countered. "In this day and age, a network is anybody with a satellite dish and transmission equipment. You might coerce the big three, but what about all the independents? And if you force them, say through the Sedition Act, to stop, how will they respond? They'd attack you viciously, any way and every way they could. They'd blitz you from all sides, until you wouldn't even know your own name, or care."

"Make your point," Herrod said.

Benstock nodded. "General Layton's right in one sense," he said. "We are at war with the Vietnamese right now. It's a media war. We need to fight them on a media front. Let's take Jerry's advice. Return their ultimatum in kind, then spend the rest of the week negotiating in private and countering their media in public. We'll PR them to death."

"We need an alternate plan," Vallens said. "Another front to open up while we do the other things."

One man had leaned his chair back into the darkness of the room. He had been silent for the entire proceeding. He shoved his chair up to the table with an audible scrape. It was Miller Angostis, head of the CIA. He was a grim, humorless man, thin and serious. "We do have an alternative," he said, almost in a whisper.

Every eye turned to him. He didn't speak again until he had served his dramatic purpose. "We have a force in Vietnam."

"What are you talking about?" Prescott asked.

"Are you forgetting," the man replied, "that we have over two thousand American troops in Ho Chi Minh City right now?"

"The prisoners," Herrod said softly.

Angostis tried to smile; it came out as a grimace. "We still have weapons stockpiled in that region. Some of them may have been found, but not all."

"What good is that going to do us?" Layton asked.

Angostis held up a finger. "All we need is one man. One who knows about the weapons. A man, intimately familiar with the region, who can slip into the compound, help the prisoners organize an escape. My intelligence tells me that the hostages are being held in Camp Friendship, a former marine compound. It's not designed as a prison; it can be easily cracked. Those people are all together for the first time. The security is not going to be sufficient to prevent a mass break."

"Sounds complicated to me," Prescott answered.

"Our computers give it about a one in four chance of success if all the elements are right," the man said. "If you can find better odds than that, I'll support your idea."

Benstock cleared his throat. "What happens when they get out of the place?" he asked.

"It's a port city. There will be boats in the harbor. We do as General Layton suggested earlier. We send down the Seventh Fleet. But instead of attacking, we plant them firmly on the twelve-mile limit. Then, when the time comes, they'll be able to support the escape."

There was a murmuring around the table. Prescott and Herrod looked at one another. Prescott could see the question in the President's eyes. He took a deliberate breath and shrugged.

Herrod frowned and turned to Angostis. "I suppose you have someone in mind?"

This time the director did smile. "I have several qualified men," he returned. "I've put them all on alert. It's simply a question of choice."

"If we can get a man in," the admiral said, "why not a small force?"

"These are highly qualified agents," Angostis said. "Technically skilled and knowledgeable about that part of the world. Getting one in will be difficult enough, a force would have to fight its way in, then fight its way back out again. Our computers leveled the odds on that one at a thousand to one against."

"What do you think, gentlemen?" the President asked.

"All this covert stuff ever gets us is a bunch of trouble," Layton said. "I still say we go in with the marines."

Prescott watched a one-armed man on the TV screen. "Will these men even be able to pull off a prison break?" he asked, then said what he didn't want to say. "Will they even want to?"

There was dead air around the table, embarrassed silence. Benstock raised his hand.

"I think that Mr. Angostis's plan could be our ace in the hole. Plus the idea of the fleet down there could work well if we give the media free rein to cover it."

Prescott wrote down the recommendations one by one. None of them was perfect, few of them were any good. What it would come down to was what Simon Herrod believed to be the best possible course of action for the country. He was drawing breath for over two hundred million people, and only he would be answerable for that. Everyone at the table, despite their recommendations, knew that. And not one of them, Layton included, would have switched places with him.

The President's phone on the table was buzzing. He answered it, slowly, tentatively.

"Herrod," he said into the receiver. "Yes...yes...I understand. Thank you."

He hung up the phone. "Gentlemen," he said, "the Soviet Union has just announced that its Navy will be holding practice maneuvers this entire week in the South China Sea, just off the coast of Vietnam."

"...from the reports we've been getting this morning, the government is simply stunned, Howard. No one has any comment, nor should they have. With the Vietnamese ignoring all diplomatic channels, President Herrod is having to rely on *us* for his news.

"The situation is grave here. Limousines have been moving in and out of the White House all morning. The President has canceled all his appointments until something can be resolved in this international crisis."

"Maury, what sort of effect do you think this is going to have on the current summit conferences with the Kremlin regarding disarmament?"

"Howard...I put that same question myself to one of the President's aides this morning. His answer was: 'what summit?'"

VIII

Camp Friendship

April 13—8:37 P.M.

It was steak, real steak. The only meat that Ridley had eaten since his capture was an occasional piece of water buffalo. But this was beef, real beef, fried fast in peanut oil, still juicing blood. He stared at the plate in disbelief, unable to either eat or leave it alone. He could only look and wonder what it all meant.

They were all taking mess together, two thousand refugees from limbo who were sponging up experience faster than their brains could comprehend. Perhaps this was the point, the deal. Perhaps confusion was the answer here.

The mess tent was huge, circus-sized, with triple layers of mosquito netting cocooned around the outside. No one was left in their peasant clothes now, not even Ridley. They all laughed and screamed and ran around the long crowded tables squealing like pigs.

A Vietnamese rock and roll band was blaring away at the head of the tent, phonetically mimicking the words of Hank Williams and Creedence Clearwater Revival. Asian rock bands all had the same style of playing. They'd all do medleys of three songs connecting them with drum solos. Then they'd stop for a moment and do three more songs, Oriental palates wrapping unsuccessfully around hillbilly slang. And the GI's loved it, dancing on the tables, doing mock stripteases—whistles and catcalls—the guts of soldier-boy reality.

An enlisted man named Tom who was sitting next to Ridley talked incessantly about what he was going to do when he got home. At first, Ridley tried to sound interested. Then he realized that Tom needed nothing from him other than for him to be sitting there while he talked.

Jenkins was right across from him, shoveling the steak in. He began jabbing toward Ridley with his fork.

"You gonna eat that shit or name it?" he yelled, to get above the clamor that filled the tent.

Ridley tightened his lips, then sighed loudly. "Aw, hell," he said, and cut into the meat, steam rising from the slice. Spearing it, he brought it to his lips. It practically disintegrated inside his mouth. It was the best piece of meat he'd ever eaten. He rolled his eyes.

Jenkins started laughing. "Goddamn, I knew you'd go for it. I knew you'd love it!"

Ridley could feel himself smiling, could feel his lips stretching across his teeth. "I feel so damned guilty eating this!" he yelled back.

"Would you just stop that," Jenkins called back. "This is the first day of a new world. From now on, it's steak every day."

"I've got a new GTO," Tom said. "I know my folks have kept it in good shape for me. When we get back, I'm gonna take my back pay and put that sucker out on an Arizona highway where they ain't got no speed limit and try to knock that fucking needle off the speedometer."

"We're not home yet," Ridley called to Jenkins.

A bowl of mashed potatoes, melting butter, got passed down the table. Jenkins grabbed it and started scooping a mound of them onto his plate. "What's gonna stop us now? A few days to get the money together, and it's back to the motherland."

"Who's going to pay that money?" Ridley asked.

Tom kept holding the same forkful of meat in front of his mouth. "I'm going to the coast," he said. "First the Pacific, then the Atlantic. I'm gonna see America. I'm gonna cruise America in my GTO and fuck hippie girls, then use the G.I. Bill to get me some college and get a job with General Motors or somebody. Get me a secretary."

"The government'll pay," Jenkins said.

"They can't pay extortion money."

Jenkins's eyes narrowed, and he talked around a mouthful of potatoes. "This is different."

"No it's not."

"It's different, I said!" he screamed, his ragged emotions fraying, then tearing. "They'll pay! They'll pay!"

Two NVA's with rifles pushed through the crowd to stand by their table. They stood, silently watching. Jenkins looked up at them, lips quivering. "It's okay, fellas. Really. Just a little discussion. See?" He began shoveling food in his mouth, trying to show them how interested he was in the meal.

Lieutenant Harry Jenkins had been with Special Forces. He was captured in late '69 in Cambodia while laying charges along a rail line. He had been brought to the Hanoi Hilton, although that was unusual as it was a prison used almost exclusively for fliers. He and Ridley had spent two years together in a French-built cell in a section of the Hilton the prisoners had called Las Vegas. For those two years Jenkins and Ridley supported one another. Through torture and deprivation, through humiliation and interrogation and "confessions," they had kept one another strong and idealistic and clinging to their own humanity. And then they had been put on the work crews.

"And I'm going to have Jack Daniels to drink any time I want," Tom said, his forkful still wavering in front of his mouth. He was in his late thirties, a prisoner since age nineteen. "With lots of ice and Coke and lime."

The soldiers stood for a moment, just to be sure that Jenkins had calmed down. Then they left quietly, disappearing into the crowd like specters.

The band was playing, "Your Cheating Heart," loud sobs from the prisoners filling the tent.

Ridley took another piece of the meat. It tasted as good as the last piece.

When they had gone out on the work crews, Jenkins began to change. They had been treated reasonably well on the crews, despite the fact that they had to adjust to living in chains. Without the torture to relate to, without the pain, his attitude had begun to change. His reasons for staying alive were more and more difficult to remember. This had just made Ridley stronger; he simply looked upon it as another, more subtle form of torture. He took responsibility for his own life and for Jenkins's. It had given him a reason to go on.

After the announcement that the war was over, which was one of the few bits of news they had ever gotten on the work crews, Jenkins had simply given up. He became an emotional derelict, his only connection to humanity coming through Ridley's determination to keep him going. They suffered together, and Ridley had kept him alive.

Only after the guards left was Jenkins able to look across the table at Ridley. "Stop wrecking things," he hissed. "Stop trying to ruin it all. I can't stand you to do that. I can't. I can't hardly stand it."

"The GTO's metallic blue," Tom said, "with moon hubcaps and flames painted on the side. She'll do zero to sixty in four seconds flat."

Then it started, from the end of the room near where the AWOLs were huddled together. Food far too rich for stomachs used to blander fare began coming up. Men started vomiting violently, their sounds mixing with the out-of-tune Asian guitars. And everyone started vomiting, doubled over, a chorus of voices gagging to Hank Williams.

SENATOR CALLS FOR ACTION

PHILADELPHIA, (AP)—Speaking at the national VFW convention here today, North Carolina Senator Ned Bundy called for immediate action on the issue of the MIA hostage situation.

"We've got to go down there and kick some backside," Bundy told a packed house of appreciative veterans. "We must reestablish American pride overseas if we are to survive in the jungle environment of this planet. If these countries think they can push us around, they need to be taught about the spirit that made this country great. War, gentlemen, is the only answer. And the sooner, the better."

Insiders say that the conservative Democrat's speech is the first step toward an announcement that he will be seeking the office of President during the next term.

IX

Washington, D.C.— 1600 Pennsylvania Avenue

April 13—11:17 A.M.

Prescott had to keep moving, to keep walking. If he so much as slowed down, he found himself quagmired in a mud bog of questions and information. The White House was alive, throbbing with aides and minor officials who filled the halls with monkey-house chatter, trailing tails of printout paper.

Outside, across the wide expanse of front lawn that boasted at least one of every species of tree on the continent, citizens huddled three rows deep on the other side of the big iron gate. They stood uneasily, some with placards. Their tone was neutral, expectant. They mostly waited, eye to eye with the marines who stood at parade rest on the other side of the fence.

Inside, the switchboards had been shut down and most communication to the outside severed. Even the grumbling press corps was confined with the demonstrators on the other side of the fence. Herrod had determined that there would be no rumors, or rumors of rumors, leaked to the press, and the only way he could accomplish that was to, in effect, seal off the entire building.

Prescott was pushing his way through the crowds of people who jammed the upstairs hallway. He was trying to get to the elevator.

There were television sets hurriedly hooked to the hallway walls. They were all filled with American newsmen trying to banter while waiting for the President's address. There were no more transmissions coming in from the prisoners. It was after eleven at night in Vietnam and everyone was asleep.

The computers were churning out data, all confirming what they already knew, that this was no joke or trick. The wires were pulling in tentative statements from foreign powers, but it was all rhetoric that said a great deal without saying anything. Everyone was waiting for the Presidential address before choosing up sides.

Frank Merriman caught up to Prescott at the elevator.

"Something in from NATO," Frank Merriman said, speaking loudly to get above the noise.

Prescott pointed his finger toward the floor. "Ride down with me."

The man nodded and they climbed into the elevator. Merriman looked dead tired. His shift should have been over hours ago.

"What have you got?"

The man shuffled through papers. "NATO confirms that the Russians are moving elements of their fleet toward Saigon," he said, and looked up. "What does that mean?"

"It means that those fuckers are going to try and keep us honest. What else?"

"We've confirmed identity on fifteen of the prisoners, the ones who went on the tube. And there have been phone calls from everywhere confirming others in the background. These guys are the real McCoy."

Prescott was beginning to feel dirty and grimy in his clothes from the day before. He was hoping that he'd be able to get to his office at the State Department for a shower and change. "Any angle on public reaction?" he asked, but didn't really want to know.

Merriman faced somewhat away from him, his eyes unfocused. "It's hard to tell so far," he said. "I know that a lot of people are going to be surprised when we don't pay the money." He gave Prescott a sidelong look. "They're not going to understand. I'm not sure that I'm going to understand."

"Yeah," Prescott said as the elevator groaned to a stop.

He climbed out, turned and looked at Merriman on the inside. "Get some sleep," he said, as the door slid closed on the man. He looked at the blank door. "You'll need it," he said quietly.

Turning, he looked at the basement, the past and the future merged as one. It was an old, dusty room, crammed high with wooden crates; legacies from the past—all the famous names, the world-churning decisions, reduced to plywood cartons stamped with the word Fragile. Fully a third of the basement was swept clean, crammed with fiery light, aluminum poles squirting hard brightness, running wires that fed into cables that were banded together and taped to the floor. There were three large cameras aiming into the egg of light, aiming at an exact duplicate of the Oval Office, a fake White House made for the cameras and their artificial fire.

The President was off to the side of the light, sitting in front of a large, self-lit mirror. Benstock was leaning down next to him, helping him get into his makeup. He was whiting out the circles under Herrod's eyes.

"It makes you look more sincere," he was saying. "When people watch television, they expect the people they see to be perfect. You know: no constipation, no tiredness, no bad moods. They don't trust people who act the way they themselves do."

"Don't the words they say mean anything?" Prescott asked.

Herrod turned to him, smiling. "Ah, the voice of reason has arrived."

Benstock simply looked annoyed. "The words really

don't mean anything," he said. "It's the person who says them that the people either believe or disbelieve. I made my living for many years by being the person everyone expected . . . no, demanded that I be."

"Ten minutes!" the director yelled from the Oval Office set. "Where's that damned script?"

"Coming!" called a voice from the edge of the line of darkness. The scriptwriter was typing directly onto the tele-prompter machine, trying to hammer out Herrod's address.

"What's it look like upstairs?" The President asked.

Prescott shook his head. "The Soviets are at sea right now," he replied. "We've got positive IDs on many of the men. Trading on the stock exchange was so irrational and heavy that they've shut it down for the day. The phone calls . . ."

"Never mind," Herrod said. "You're just making me nervous. I have got a question for you, though. How come all the prisoners are white men?"

Prescott shrugged. "Don't really know. One of the reasons may be that blacks and Puerto Ricans remind the Vietnamese of Cambodians, who've been their enemies for thousands of years. They've never really held onto dark-skinned prisoners."

"There's another reason," Benstock said, as he picked up a comb and started running it through Herrod's hair. "I told you this is a media war. The Vietnamese have gone for the straight, average middle-class television watcher by giving them the images that they're most comfortable, most familiar with. Name me a family in Alabama, or South Boston for that matter, who is going to want to put themselves out on a financial limb for a black man? It's almost as if they did a ratings poll and found the mainstream of American thought, then tried to appeal to that thought."

"I think you're giving them too much credit," Prescott said.

Benstock leaned over a touch, staring intently at the job he had done on the President. He nodded reflectively, then turned his eyes to the secretary's. "Humor me," he said without humor.

Steve Tackett, Herrod's speechwriter, walked up and laid a small stack of papers on the makeup table. Tackett was gray all over, his face, his skin, his eyes. He was an old newspaperman, just as most speechwriters were old newspapermen. It had something to do with self-abuse.

"Wear it in good health," he said.

Herrod picked it up, glanced casually at it, then handed it to Benstock. "Is it all there?" Benstock asked.

Tackett nodded wearily, as if nodding was a harder job than speechwriting. "Everything you asked for."

"Has it got a kick?" Benstock asked as he read quickly through the speech.

"Like a bionic mule," the man answered. "If this doesn't leave them crying in the aisles, I'll go back to writing obituaries."

Herrod nodded. "You did good, Steve. Go get yourself some coffee."

The man rubbed his eyes with open hands. "What makes you think I want to stay awake," he said, and wandered off.

"Okay, right here," Benstock said, pointing. Herrod turned in his chair to look at the script. "When it comes to the part about emotional blackmail, I'm going to have them bring the camera in tight. When we do that, lock eyes with that camera, talk to it as if it's your lover, control it. And for God's sake, don't blink. We'll have it on you for about thirty seconds. They say there's a relationship between eye blinks and lying. Burn that lens with your eyes. You can do it."

"We need you on the set, Mr. President," the director called, and Herrod stood up immediately.

The nervousness was evident on the President's face, but Prescott knew it would disappear as soon as he got rolling.

The man stuck out his hand. "Wish me luck," he said to Prescott.

"You don't need it, Simon," he returned, shaking his hand. "Just tell them the truth. We can't go wrong."

Herrod then turned and shook Benstock's hand. "Just remember," the man said. "You control the camera, not the other way around."

The President nodded and started toward the set. On impulse, Prescott hurried and caught up to him. "Is there some kind of open line down here?" he asked quietly. "I'd like to call my wife."

Herrod stopped walking, then pulled Prescott away. "There's a pile of crates marked Harding over by the elevator," he said. "Look behind them. I just called Elaine a little bit ago myself."

"Thanks, Simon," Prescott said, and walked off to the phone.

Myrna answered after five rings. Her voice was detached enough for Prescott to know that she had gotten her Valium prescription refilled.

"It's me," he said.

"Well, it's me," she returned.

"Have you canceled dinner tonight yet?" he asked without preamble.

"I was going to do it after lunch."

"Good. Don't bother. I think I can make it."

"Really?" The surprise in her voice was genuine. "But, I thought . . ."

"I can't really talk about it right now."

"I understand. But, this isn't like you."

"No," he said, "It's not."

"Are you all right?"

"Sure. Plan it for seven; I'll see you when I can." He hung up immediately, then caught himself staring at the phone.

"Two minutes," he heard off in the distance.

It snapped him back to the present and sent him back to the set.

Herrod was sitting at his "desk" while they adjusted the boom mike that hung just above his head.

Benstock watched everything with a practiced eye. Prescott moved to stand by him. He watched Herrod, feeling like he was watching an actor playing the President.

"You're not too hot on me, are you?" Benstock asked, not even looking at him.

Prescott took a breath. "It's not you so much as what you represent."

"What do you mean?"

"You're all this," he said, gesturing around the set. "You're electronic things that poke and prod. You make reality what you want it to be."

"It's a new world, Jerry. Brand new. It's a survivor's world."

"What do you mean?"

Benstock looked at him then. "It's not you so much," he said, "as what you represent."

"I understand," Prescott said.

"Ten seconds!" the director called. "Look serious."

"This is Joel Carson in Dallas, reporting from the grassy knoll, the spot where President Kennedy was assassinated nearly three decades ago. We came to see Jory Dade, local oilman, who called a press conference to make a statement about the hostage situation. Those of us in local media know Jory to be a bit eccentric, but today he's been showing off several gold bars and promising fireworks. He delivered. Listen."

"When Jack Kennedy said, 'Ask not what yer country can do fer you, but what you can do fer yer country,' well, I kinda took it to heart. America's been real good to me, and all our boys fightin' overseas have helped keep it real good. So I thought, what the hell, Jory, all this money ain't doin' you a lick a good less you can use it to do some good fer them that's done good fer you.

"What this here is, is a ten-pound bar of gold, worth about sixty-four thousand dollars. And there's plenty more where this'n come from. What I figgered I'd do would be to spend a little of this stuff. There's gotta be some Texas boys in them hostages. I figger I'd like to buy back about five of them, provided they's Democrats, of course... and born again."

X

Oklahoma City, Oklahoma

April 13—10:35 A.M.

Nancy Henderson paced nervously in front of the television, her insides churning up the half-bottle of Maalox that hadn't done a bit of good. Through the outside window she could see Sid out on the lawn.

The telephone had mercifully stopped ringing moments

before, everyone clearing the lines to listen to the President's address. She had spent the entire morning on the phone with people from her old group, the National Association of MIA Wives. She had been active in NAMWives since its inception in the late sixties, had been spokesperson for it at one time. From the moment of the first satellite broadcast, the group had put its old phone tree into operation and was already lobbying the State Department to get the money together.

Billy's mother had called her, too. They had cried together on the phone. That's when Sid had gone out to "pull weeds."

Nancy paced past the window, noticed that Sid was walking toward the house. Then she looked down and saw the presidential seal filling the TV screen. Leaning down, she turned up the sound and walked back a few paces.

Sid came in without a word and sat on his recliner. "Nance," he said, and she turned with a jerk.

He was motioning her sideways with his hand, and she realized that she was blocking the screen. She stepped aside a bit.

"Why don't you sit down?" he said.

"Can't," she answered.

The calls had been a blessing, actually. The calls had enabled them to avoid discussing what was going on. Both of their minds were full of feelings and devoid of thoughts. Both of them recognized that a major change was taking place in their lives, though neither of them was sure what it was. They needed the luxury of some distance.

The seal was replaced by the President's face. He looked grim, but not distraught, an honest man caught in the throes of a moral dilemma.

He stared directly at the camera as he spoke. "My fellow Americans, I come to you today in sorrow and in anger. This is my most difficult day as your president, my most trying day as a man, as a citizen of this great country.

"Early this morning we received a transmission from the Communist government of Vietnam. The message they sent was a message of infamy, of barbarism."

Nancy watched as Herrod waved a piece of paper in

front of the camera. She didn't like the tone that he was taking.

"The message concedes that over two thousand of our soldiers have been held illegally in Vietnam since the cessation of hostilities in that country well over a decade ago. The note is a cheap extortion attempt, a ransom demand for men whose freedom was purchased at the Paris peace-table and paid for with the blood of America.

"Let me make the position of this government perfectly clear from the start. These demands are just so many buckets of ashes to us." He wadded up the paper and threw it down. "America never has and never will bend in the winds of terrorism. We are a firm and mighty tree, our roots deep and secure. We will never pay this ransom, not one dollar, not one penny."

Nancy heard herself moaning from far away, heard Sid shushing her. Things never changed, never changed.

Herrod's face was set hard, his look unfaltering. "The so-called government of Vietnam knows this, knows we will never bow to their demands. That's why that message is the only one we've officially received from them, and since this message, they have adamantly refused to make contact with us through the regular diplomatic channels. Instead, they've entered into a campaign of emotional terrorism, of bloodletting of the spirit."

The camera began pulling tight on his face, and his eyes loomed very large.

"They are attacking us at the source, at our good hearts. They are trying to stir us up, all the old feelings, all the old pains. They've gone to you, my friends, in a cheap attempt to play upon your nature. It's a game of emotional blackmail where everybody loses. They want you to feel guilty. They want you to feel responsible for a situation that they, themselves, perpetrated. Their methods are sick and inhuman, and we will not kneel to such inhumanity."

The tears were coming again and Nancy couldn't stop them. The cause she had given so much of herself to for so many years was being buried at the edge of success by a man who hadn't even been around when it all happened. She felt cheated.

The camera pulled back showing the President's hands balled into fists on the desktop. "Here is our response to the ransom demands. First, there will be no money, none. Second, you have given us seven days to comply with your lawlessness; we in turn give you the same seven days to free your illegally held prisoners, or we will take immediate action to force you to free them. These points are not negotiable on any level. Those men were officially freed on January 26, 1973 in Paris, France. There can be no other discussion about their release, except for the times that we can pick them up. As a proof of my sincerity, I am now officially ordering the U.S. Seventh Fleet to the South China Sea. The fleet can either be the receptacle for the safe return of the hostages, or the instrument of our wrath should the Vietnamese government fail to take our position seriously.

"To the people of the United States of America, I say this: Pay no attention to the parade of faces that marches across your television screens. Stand unified with me. Raise no money, nor attempt to raise any. It will only weaken our position when we all need to stand together in strength. I challenge the television networks of this country to ignore the transmissions of hatred that come unbidden through our own satellites. Don't show them; let them hang up there in the ether, invisible and harmless."

The camera came in tight again. "I want nothing more in my life than to bring those boys home safe and sound, but the integrity of this country and the safety of its citizens everywhere in the world demands that our prisoners be brought back properly and on our terms. We will be strong, and with God's help, we will prevail."

The camera held there then, held tight on the face of Simon Herrod before fading slowly to black.

Nancy Henderson fell to her knees in front of the screen. She was shaking, vibrating violently. Twenty years of pent-up hostility was leaking its way out like radioactive steam through a cracked reactor.

"You motherfucker," she rasped. "You lousy motherfucker!"

She brought her knees up to her chest, hugging them tightly. Resting her head on her knees, she quaked, shaking wildly from the inside, none of it getting outside. Sid was at her shoulders, holding them as if that could stop the shaking.

She twisted around to him, falling into his arms, crying in earnest, sobbing into his shoulder. "Oh, Sid. Billy never did anything to anybody. Why do they have to punish him this way?"

Sid felt himself stiffen involuntarily at the mention of Billy's name. He couldn't help it. "Nobody wants to punish anybody, Nancy," he said, but the mood was wrong now, his tension evident. "Take it easy. Please."

She turned her face to him, suddenly calm. She forced a cracked laugh. "Take it easy, you say? Take it easy? That son of a bitch has just condemned those men to death, and you say to take it easy." Her eyes were desperate, pleading. "Don't you understand that I can't take it easy?"

Sid stood up, his own face red, his own emotions tied into knots. "What the hell did you expect him to say?" he spat out. "He can't pay that money."

She scooted around on the carpet to face him, her cheeks trailing tear-smudged mascara. "Why not, goddamnit?"

"It's not in the best interests of the country," he said.

She was breathing quickly, shallowly, her usually pretty face twisted ugly by anger. She spoke low, forcibly low to keep from screaming. "Those men are the country," she said. "They've been through things for this country that you can't even imagine. The money's nothing compared to what they've been through." She pointed to the TV screen. "And I don't care what that motherfucker says, I'm going to do everything in my power to raise that money and bring Billy home."

"You're wrong, Nancy," he returned. "You're blinding your eyes to this."

She glared at him. "And you're not? You're so afraid that something's going to upset your little world that you'll just bury your head in the sand to everything. I love you, Sid, but this is something I'm going to do whether you like it or not."

The phone started ringing again, and Sid Henderson knew that it was NAMWives and that they felt just the same as his wife. Nancy stood quickly.

"Don't answer it," he said.

She looked hard at him. "Fuck you," she said, and ran to the kitchen to get the phone.

ISRAEL SUPPORTS THE U.S.

TEL AVIV, (AP)—In an interview outside the

Knesset today, Prime Minister Peres said the United States has every right to use whatever means it takes to free its captive hostages. "The Vietnamese have committed nothing less than piracy and barbarism," Peres told a news conference. "This situation must be dealt with harshly and quickly, or a rash of imitation hostage crises will spring up all over the world."

Citing the problems Israel has had with kidnappings in the past, Peres said there is no need to debate such issues. "It is, unfortunately, a very hard world," he said. "To survive in it, one must also be hard."

Israel has offered to the United States whatever assistance it can render in dealing with the current crisis.

XI

Glen Burnie—Highway 301

April 13—11:58 A.M.

Cassady smiled all the way through the President's address, shutting off the car radio as soon as it was done. He'd never really thought about it, but it was the first time he had ever listened to the radio in the car. The car still had many firsts to be accomplished: a first passenger, a first use of the ashtray. Though the company had given it to him over three years ago, it still had less than five hundred miles on it. It was a go-to-the-store-or-the-airport car that still smelled like it had in the showroom. Even so, Cassady was meticulous about cleaning it. Once a week he washed and waxed it and vacuumed the inside. Cassady liked things tidy. Tidy and clean.

He was making the five-mile trip from the Park to the city of Glen Burnie, a bedroom suburb that only had come alive once in its entire existence. Back in the late seventies, a Russian spy had been found asphyxiated on this very highway, a garden hose running from his exhaust pipe into the passenger compartment of his car. It had been ruled a suicide, and Cassady smiled to think of that, too.

He passed Old Stage Road and the fork where 301 and Ritchie Highway came together and he was just a matter of blocks from the city proper. He thought about going back to Nam, a thought he had lived with since he had been forced to leave when Saigon fell. He remembered the date; it was burned like acid on his brain—April 29, 1975—the date he had stopped thinking of himself as a member of the human race, the date he had stopped thinking about almost everything.

And his eyes were pale brown. He wore a dark blue suit with small pinstripes. He carried no gun, but a box knife was stuck down into the top of his oxblood zip-up boots.

Cassady turned onto Delaware, off the main drag, and the traffic died away to nothing. Pulling up to the trash-cluttered curb, he climbed out, looking up and down the street. A block away, a blue Toyota sat parked, a man behind the wheel reading the newspaper.

Locking his car, he walked across the street to an old movie theater that was bleeding rock and roll music onto the dead street. The theater was a video game arcade now, called The Black Hole, and when Cassady had moved to the Park, it had been an army surplus store. In these days of rapidly rising and falling crazes, the arcades were also dying.

He opened the old double-glass doors and went in. There were about ten people inside, most of indeterminate age, somewhere between high school and adulthood. They were transfixed by their machines, jerking on control sticks, moving in time to the pounding music. In the middle of the room was a small gazebo, complete with its own little roof.

Walking up to it, he laid a five dollar bill on the counter, and a pimply faced teenaged boy with black, stringy hair replaced the green with a handful of brass-colored tokens.

"It's eight-for-a-dollar day," he said, and Cassady nodded, scooping the tokens into the pocket of his suit jacket.

Moving to his left from the door, Cassady slowly walked past the machines, stopping at the eighth one in line. He stared at the graphic display; it showed a little man with a shovel tunneling his way underground, while trying to inflate and pop assorted bad types that chased him through his tunnels.

He reached into his pocket and took out some of the tokens. Shoving one into the slot, he lined several others up on a ledge on the machine to insure that no one would take it away from him.

He pushed the button and started the game, moving the little man with his control stick, but not really paying any attention to where he was going or why. Narrowing his eyes, he concentrated on the outside glass of the machine, watching the bare reflections of the rest of the room and the shadowy shapes that moved through it.

The game ended quickly, and Cassady put another coin into the slot. He played five games this way before someone finally came over to stand at the game next to his.

"Your trouble is, you don't care about the contest enough," came a voice, but when he jerked to it, the voice said, "Don't turn around. Just play."

He shoved another token into the slot, listening to the strange computer music that signaled the start of things.

"You have to take it seriously, but not too seriously," the voice said. "These things are really a lot like life, you know?"

"We have company," Cassady said.

"His name's Morton," the man said. "But his real name's Dobryn. He's been following me for years. Apparently that's his whole job, following me around." The man's machine started playing the computer's idea of what circus music would sound like. "We go ahead and let him, because when he's following me, we know where he is."

"Will he make me?"

"Probably. But I don't think it means anything."

Cassady took a breath, watched his little man get eaten by a dragon. "I don't like it," he said.

"He's just a working stiff like the rest of us," the man answered, and out of the corner of his eye Cassady could see him moving with the machine, working with it. "He's just putting in his time until he can get his pension."

"So, when do I leave?" Cassady asked.

"Just hold your horses," the man said, and plunked another slug into his machine. "I'll tell you when you can leave. We haven't settled on anybody yet."

Cassady started to tell him how bad he wanted this one, then thought better of it. "What are you going to want done?" he said instead.

"Guess you know what's going on?"

"Just what I've seen on the tube."

"That's all we know, too."

Cassady lost his last digger and slugged another token.

"You'd be operating totally on your own," the man said. "No backup or support at all. We have to be very specific on this point, because if you're caught, we don't want to lose our negotiating potential in other areas. Do you understand that?"

"I understand."

"I'm told that you know the location of weapons stores over there."

"Yes."

"Do you think that any of these weapons could be retrieved?"

"Yes. Definitely."

"Are there enough weapons to support a prison break?"

Cassady smiled. That meant he'd be going all the way into Ho Chi Minh City. "More than enough," he answered quickly.

"You sure are anxious for this one."

"Yeah," Cassady answered. "I'm a real company man. Could our friend outside bring some heat down on me?"

"Conceivably. But I think that our Russian friends are too anxious to see us screw up on our own to interfere."

"Would I be restricted in any way?"

The man slapped his machine, put in more money. "I told you that you'd be totally on your own with this. The only restriction would be your imagination. And if you can pull it off, I am prepared to offer you the standard bonus, plus a month's vacation, expenses paid."

"I'm ready to go any time."

"Go home and wait. You'll be contacted."

"When?"

"What 'sa matter, got a date?"

Cassady left the machine in midgame. Walking to the door, he pushed it open and went out. His contact, John Steakly, turned and watched him go, puzzled at Cassady's eagerness for this assignment. It didn't sit right with him, and he determined to check out Mr. Cassady in some detail.

Out on the street, Cassady turned to the right, away from his car, and walked to the end of the block. Rounding the corner, he hurried down a trash-strewn alley into the heavily littered and cracked-boxed canyon of parking areas.

Then he doubled back, coming out behind the blue Toyota, with Mr. Morton/Dobryn still reading his newspaper inside.

Slipping the box knife out of his boot, he knocked its back against his leg, exposing the razor blade. Crouching low, he scurried the distance to the Toyota, coming up by its license plate.

Cassady took a breath, jumped to his feet. Grabbing Dobryn's arm, he jerked it through the window, reaching his other hand around until the blade it held was resting against the agent's throat.

"Don't move," he hissed.

Dobryn's eyes were hard slits as he froze, half in and half out of his car window. A thin line of blood trailed down from the corner of the blade to wet the collar of his white shirt.

"Where's the gun, comrade?"

"I don't know what you're . . ."

Cassady drew the blade a touch, opening a small gash. Dobryn pointed frantically to the right pocket of his tan sport jacket.

"Pull it out," Cassady said without emotion. "Slowly, by the barrel."

Reaching into the pocket, Dobryn fished out a .9-millimeter semiautomatic, swinging it slowly to the window space. Letting go of his arm, Cassady retrieved the gun. He released the man and climbed into the back seat, burying the muzzle into the flesh of Dobryn's neck.

"Start the car," he said.

The man silently did as he was told.

"Good," Cassady said. "Now back up and turn into that alley."

Dobryn backed up, doing it by looking in the rearview mirror instead of turning around. "What are you going to do?" he asked.

"Don't worry, we won't blow your gas allotment. Okay. Go on up the alley."

Dobryn turned into the alley, coming out in that deserted back parking section.

"Don't embarrass me too much," Dobryn said. "My

section chief has it in for me as it is. Any kind of incident, and I'll end up in East Berlin."

"Park it over by that dumpster," Cassady told him, indicating a large trash bin near a stand of dogwood trees that was just beginning to bloom.

Dobryn parked, and Cassady got him out of the car. "Open the trunk," he said, grabbing a quick look around.

"Give me a break," the man said in perfect English. "Do you know how small that trunk is?"

Cassady shrugged. "What do you want from me? I didn't make you get the car."

"It's issue," he returned. "I couldn't afford to turn down a company car."

The trunk came open. It was, indeed, small.

"Get in," Cassady said, motioning with the gun, his eyes darting.

The man frowned deeply, started to say something, stopped. With a sigh, he climbed into the trunk, folding himself into a fetal position to fit.

Cassady smiled amiably. "Good," he said. Reaching out as if to pat the man's cheek, he quickly used the box knife he had palmed to gouge deeply into Dobryn's jugular.

The man's eyes went wide with surprise, and Cassady quickly slammed the trunk lid shut. Wiping off the gun, he tossed it into the dumpster, then waited a few minutes for the pounding on the trunk to subside before walking back to his Chevy and driving home.

NEW YORK (AP)—In an historic communiqué today, all the major television networks issued a joint statement renouncing President Herrod's request that the networks refrain from showing the transmissions they are receiving from Vietnam.

In a not-unexpected move, they cited the First Amendment right to freedom of the press and condemned the President's assertion of national security as an issue, calling it "frivolous drum-beating."

"If the government can use national security as an umbrella once," the communiqué read, "it will then have the precedence to devour us completely."

XII

MOSCOW

April 13—Around Midnight

The word Kremlin means citadel. It was constructed first as a wooden stockade in the twelfth century, but in the early sixteenth century swampland surrounding the stockade was drained using then-modern engineering techniques and a formidable fortress was built, including a mile and a half of surrounding wall fifty feet high, fortified by nineteen ornately structured towers. It sits on a triangle of land bordered on two sides by the Moskva and Neglinnaya rivers and on the third by a deep, artificial moat. The bodies of forty-seven czars are buried within the Kremlin walls.

General Secretary Alexander Doksoi sat in a swivel chair that had once belonged to Leonid Brezhnev and stared out a Kremlin window toward Lenin's tomb. The chair had better fit the former president, its springs sagging wide for Doksoi's large frame. That largeness, Doksoi had decided, had been the Soviet Union's problem for many years—that burning need to be conspicuously large, even if it killed the economy the way draining blood kills the body. He had wanted something smaller, less conspicuous. He had wanted to remain free and protected without being encumbered by that protection.

And now the Navy was on its way to confront the Americans in Vietnam—a totally useless gesture designed as a play of strength in a part of the world that nobody cared about.

Dolgoruki, chairman of the Council of Ministers, had insisted upon this show of force. And there were still enough old-liners left in the politburo that he could make it stick. So Doksoi had given in because he had no choice.

The secretary stood up slowly, rubbing his eyes with the heels of his hands. It was late, too late. Taking off his suit jacket, he dropped it on Brezhnev's chair and moved over to the worn couch that sat beneath the drafty window. Loosening his tie, he lay down.

Both he and Dolgoruki knew that this display of force had nothing to do with the Vietnam issue. The chairman had simply used it as a wedge to drive between Soviet and American accord, a wedge to drive an absolutely necessary arms reduction treaty farther apart. Old ways are hard to change, old minds nearly impossible.

Totally exhausted, Doksoi stared at the ceiling, wishing desperately for the sweet oblivion of sleep that was to elude him for several more hours.

XIII

Silver Springs, Maryland

April 13—7:15 p.m.

Jerry Prescott sat on the edge of the king-sized bed and groaned out of his shoes. As he pulled off the socks, he watched the small black and white TV atop his dresser. Some crazy Texan was on there offering to buy back five of the hostages if they fit his specific requirements.

Shaking his head, Prescott stood and unbuttoned his shirt. The circus had begun. When the Vietnamese decided to fight this battle on television, they opened the door to a whole new way of life.

On the TV screen he watched the news items troop past like the exhibits in a freak show—a Southern Baptist preacher was demanding that television itself be made illegal; in Eugene, Oregon the patients on total disability in a VA hospital, all Vietnam vets kept alive by modern medicine, rioted, a nineteen-year-old security guard shooting two of them before being subdued; in Hollywood, a famous radical movie actress announced that she was volunteering her services to personally mediate the hostage release, citing the contacts she had made there during a goodwill visit to North Vietnam in 1967. There seemed no end to it.

The connecting door to the bathroom opened and Myrna came in, followed by a dissipating fog of steam. Naked and dripping, she was drying herself on a huge maroon bath towel.

She jumped, startled, when she saw him. "You're home," she said.

"Told you I would be," he responded, and pulled the shirt off. He never did have the chance to get to his office to change, so it was the first time in two days that he had been out of his clothes. "When will the Durbins be here?"

"Any time," she answered, and brought the towel up to her hair.

He watched her moving around the Early American elegance of the room. For a woman of fifty, she looked remarkably good. A bit overweight, most of it had gone to her breasts, which suited her well. Her face was rich-girl smooth, her legs strong and tennis muscular.

As he slid out of his pants, he realized that she was looking good to him, and that was an odd feeling, one he hadn't experienced for a long time. Something strange was going on inside of him. After years of pushing away, he was feeling the need for emotional closeness to fill the deep, empty place his insides had become.

It brought a sad smile to him to think of how long it had been since he'd thought of her sexually. He couldn't remember the last time they had made love. It had probably been years—he honestly didn't know.

Dropping the towel to the floor, Myrna began going through the drawers of her polished walnut dresser. "You really surprise me," she said, not turning to him.

Picking up his clothes, he walked to the wicker hamper in the corner. "How so?" he asked, and dropped the sweaty bundle into the basket.

"This Vietnamese thing," she answered. "How come you're not living in your office going crazy with it? You've done it plenty of other times."

He walked up behind her, folding his arms around her middle and resting his chin on her shoulder. "I don't know. It feels . . . different this time."

He felt himself grow hard against her, his erection pushing against the back of her legs. Moving his hands up, he gently cupped her breasts, thumbs and index fingers rolling her nipples.

"Stop!" she said, jerking away from him. She had come out of the drawer with a bra and began putting it on. Looking in puzzlement at his penis, she moved her eyes up to his face. "Didn't get enough at the office?" she asked sharply.

He backed away then, embarrassed at his clumsy attempt at an advance. After so many years of cold, emotional separation, he'd have been appalled if she had shown any interest. He let the matter drop.

"So, how is it different?" she asked, back in the drawers again.

"I don't know exactly," he said, realizing how complicated his own feelings had become. "It's all changing around me, getting different." He shook his head. "Maybe it's age, I don't know. Maybe they finally wore me out . . . desensitized me."

Myrna sat on the bed to shinny into pantyhose. "People desensitize themselves," she said.

It hit him wrong, twitched the wrong nerve. "Why do I feel that I'm defending myself here?" he asked.

She stopped dressing to stare at him. "What do you want from me?"

"A little understanding for starters."

She narrowed her eyes and froze in place, hose pulled up just over her knees. "Okay," she said. "How's this?" She stared vacantly, theatrically. "Is this understanding enough for you?"

He searched her eyes for compassion, then held his wristwatched arm up to look at it. He had already taken off the watch. "We don't have time now," he replied.

Shrugging, she finished getting into her hose. "The kids will be coming with Fran and David," she said.

"Good," he answered, moving toward the bathroom door.

She stood, slipping into a dressing gown. "Can I ask you to try and keep your goon squad out of sight tonight? I don't want to scare the poor people to death."

"I'll have a talk with them," he said, and moved into the john, closing and locking the door behind him.

It was odd, he thought, that in the middle of a truly major crisis, he was mostly thinking about himself, and Myrna. Their marriage hadn't been anything to speak of for a long time, both of them staying in it because it was easier than anything else they could think of. So, why, all of a sudden, did he want to reach out to her? Probably selfishness, that's what Myrna would say. The little boy found life on the playground too hard and wanted Mommy to make it all better.

He smiled at the analogy, perceptive enough to realize that it wasn't far from the truth. He was tired of government, beaten down by it. Some sort of internal drive to succeed had pushed him to the top, but now that he was there, he saw no use in it. He had made a great many high-level decisions and had participated in many others. But none of it made any difference. The country, in essence, ran itself. The only real decisions to be made were the ones that could never be won, the ones that compromised themselves to death. He had always known that. But before, for whatever reason, the process itself had been exciting. Now it was just tiring.

And he wanted to run home to Mommy, only Mommy wasn't buying. Mommy had probably given up on it somewhere about ten years ago, somewhere around the forty-fifth or fiftieth secretary with whom he had shared his office couch instead of the dinner he had planned with her. And even as he was thinking it, he knew that he was still kidding himself. The work had been a harsh mistress, far more demanding on his emotions than any human female. If anyone had come between he and Myrna, it had been Uncle Sam.

The guests were already there when he went downstairs. They were making themselves drinks in the den.

"You're supposed to let the bartender do that," he said, moving into the large room.

David Durbins turned to him, smiling wide. They shook hands. "Bet ah know who the bartender is," he said.

Prescott got behind the bar and took over the line of highball glasses that sat in front of him. "Somebody's gotta water them down," he returned.

David and Fran were Mississippi Jews, he with blond hair, blue eyes, and an expansive, genuine face, she with a full shock of chestnut hair.

Fran was perched on one of the barstools, dressed like a mandarin princess in shiny blue Chinese silk, undoubtedly a remnant of their recent trip to that country. She fixed Prescott with a naive, implacable look. "Why don't we just pay the money?" she asked without preamble.

"Now Fran," David drawled. "We don't want to inundate the po' man right now."

"Really, Mother," June said from the couch, where she and Randy Prescott sat shoulder-to-shoulder. "Leave it alone."

Prescott smiled, shaking his head. "It's okay," he said, and it really was. After fifteen hours of reasoning and counter-reasoning, the concept of simple solutions was a breath of fresh air to him.

"The President's afraid that paying this off would give every terrorist in the world a reason to kidnap Americans and hold them for ransom. He's afraid of extending this any farther."

"But you don't know that would happen," Fran persisted.

Prescott dropped ice into the lined-up glasses. "It's all conjecture," he admitted. "How many scotch drinkers in the house?"

David Durbins and Randy Prescott dutifully raised their hands.

"Glad somebody around here's got taste," Prescott said, and began pouring scotch into three of the glasses, one for himself, also.

"Can you make a tequila sunrise?" June called.

"Sorry," Prescott replied. "You ran me out of grenadine last time you were here."

She sighed. "I'll have scotch, too, then."

June was blond like her father, and just as down-to-earth. She had met Randy while he was interning during his senior year at her father's law office. Prescott had never much cared for his son's taste in women, but he liked June very much.

"Ah, another real man in the group," Prescott said, and poured a fourth scotch.

"An old-fashioned for me," Fran said. "It suits my values."

Myrna moved behind the bar with Jerry. She moved up closely, touching him with her body. "I'll have a screwdriver," she said.

It was Prescott's turn to stare at her. Her closeness was still affecting him physically, but her eyes were unreadable.

Turning to get the orange juice from the small fridge behind the bar, he brushed up full against her, her eyes nearly laughing.

"One screwdriver," he said, and got out the vodka while getting the juice.

"How can we just leave those boys over there?" Fran persisted. "I mean, I understand everything you said . . . the reasoning, I mean, but dammit, we owe them something, don't we? Don't we owe them the chance? Can't we, just once, forget about the rest of the world and just get them back?"

"That's what we're trying to do," Prescott answered, sliding David's drink across the bar to him. He looked across the room at the couch. "We don't deliver," he called.

June and Randy stood up as a unit, holding hands all the way across the room. He supposed that he had been that way once, but couldn't remember when. They reached the bar and took their drinks, smiling at one another before taking a sip.

"And a screwdriver," he said, handing Myrna her drink.

"Thanks, darling," she said, and leaned up close to peck him on the cheek. She looked beautiful in a clinging wide-knit dress.

He smiled uneasily and went to work on the old-fashioned.

"Let's be honest," Fran said.

"Fran . . ." David said.

She shut him up with a look.

"You know as well as I do that if you don't pay the money, you're not going to get those boys home alive."

He stopped and looked at her and he realized why he felt so dirty inside. "You might be right," he said softly.

"It's not up to Jerry," David said. "His job is to give advice, isn't that right?"

Prescott gulped nervously and nodded.

"Well, what advice did you give?" Fran asked.

"Isn't that a state secret or something?" Randy said, coming to his father's aid.

Prescott smiled uneasily. "Something like that."

"Just between family," Fran said. "What was your advice?"

He looked her hard in the eyes and saw no compromise, realized that there shouldn't be any. "Pay the money," he answered, and it wasn't exactly a lie.

Fran smiled in her childlike way and leaned across the bar, kissing him on the cheek, putting her bright ruby lipstick next to Myrna's pale pink.

"This is my lucky night," he said, and set Fran's drink in front of her. "Getting kissed by two lovely women."

"I'll be darned if I'm going to be left out," June said, and she leaned across the bar and kissed him on the other cheek.

"Hey, you're marrying me, remember?" Randy said.

Randy smiled at Prescott, and Jerry thought he had never really seen his son so happy. It made him feel good, like maybe there really was something worthwhile in life. He glanced quickly at Myrna, but she was still unreadable.

He drank half of his scotch, then forced himself to put it down, determined to stay sober for a change. Drinking was a government recreation. Tonight he was going to be a real person.

"Ah've got a little something for you," David said, reaching into the inside pocket of his sport jacket. "That is, if you promise not to get me arrested for sympathizing with the enemy or something."

Prescott put up his hands. "No promises," he said.

"Guess ah'll just have to bribe you then," Durbins returned.

"Bribe away."

The man came out of his pocket with two long, green cigars, handing one of them to Jerry.

Prescott's eyes got wide. "Havana," he whispered, almost reverently.

"The real things."

He took the cigar and smelled it. "This looks like evidence to me," he said, biting off the end and spitting it into a beanbag ashtray. "But it could be counterfeit. I'll have to smoke it to be sure."

"Well, you're the G-man."

"You're not lighting up those smokestacks around me," Fran said. "That's all my allergies need."

"Really," June added. "Can't you do that somewhere else?"

The two men looked at one another, eyes amused. "I was thinking about an evening constitutional anyway," Prescott said. "Care to join me?"

"It'd be a pleasure," Durbins returned.

Picking up his drink, Prescott moved around the bar toward the door.

"Don't be long," Myrna called after him. "Dinner will be up soon."

They went out, walking into the wide expanse of yard. The house was large and white, with plantation pillars lining the front. The lawn stretched out a long way to the metal spiked fence, the street invisible because of the thick stands of trees and shrubs that filled the yard and the fence area. The sky was bright pink, vibrant pink, as the sun set, courtesy of volcanic residue hanging in the air.

"You know, Jerry," Durbins said as they puffed away and watched the sunset, "ah can't think of anything better than this."

Prescott smiled at him. "Neither can I."

"Guess ah'm not very subtle or sophisticated," Durbins said. "Ah never got the dirt out of mah blood. But ah just want you to know that ah think you're a fine man, and ah'm happy that this marriage is going to make us family."

Prescott turned to stare at him. "You really mean that, don't you?"

Durbins stoked his cigar. "Mean everything ah say."

"I wonder if Fran agrees with you?"

The man smiled wide, watched the sky. "Fran's just a little precocious, that's all. Hope she didn't put you on the spot back there."

Prescott sipped his drink lightly. "Not at all. This is her country as much as anybody's."

A siren sounded way off in the distance, got closer. Then it faded away slowly, as if its source turned another direction.

"You plannin' on staying in politics?" Durbins asked out of nowhere.

"Not forever."

"Ah understand you were a pretty fair corporate lawyer once upon a time."

"That was a long time ago."

"So was your first piece of ass." Durbins winked. "But ah'll bet you didn't forget how to do it."

There was a brief silence, neither man looking directly at the other, both of them soaking up the evening. Finally Durbins spoke. "You know, where ah come from, we believe in family . . . family takin' care of family. Ah don't know what your plans are for the future, but Oscar, mah partner, is going to be retiring here in a few months, and ah sure could use a good corporate lawyer in the firm. All Oscar did was act as counsel for World Airways, mah little playtoy. It'd be easy work, but stimulating. And you're a natural, having been around gov'ment regulations all these years."

Prescott stared down at his drink, shaking the glass to

make the ice cubes circle. "Funny you should bring that up . . ." he started to say, when the front door banged open. Myrna was standing there, frowning.

"Your phone," she said. "The red one."

Without thought, he ran back inside. The phone in the den was still ringing when he got to it. Everyone else had moved to the far side of the room, to give him as much privacy as possible.

He picked it up. "Prescott."

"I tried to get you over the open lines, I . . ."

"Frank? That you? I shut off the outside lines, what—"

"I can't do it, Jerry."

"Can't do what?"

"This. Any of this. I can't accept the decisions coming down on this Vietnam thing."

"What are you saying?"

"I want out of it, out of the job. I thought I should tell you first."

Prescott drained his glass, picked up the phone and moved to the bar to fix another. "You can't leave me in the middle of all this. Be reasonable, Frank."

"I . . . I'm sorry," he said, and his voice was quaking. "I think it's wrong, morally wrong to not pay that money and get them back. I can't associate myself with this."

Prescott filled the glass with scotch without bothering about the ice. "What if we simply move you to a less-vital area?"

"I don't want to have anything to do with any of this."

Prescott drank. From the man's tone, he knew he was serious. "I can't afford to lose you, Frank."

"You can't afford to keep me, Jerry."

"This could kill you in politics."

"I know."

He suddenly heard Fran scream from the other side of the room. "Oh God, guns!"

He turned and saw that Barrows had entered the room, his shoulder holster hanging down under his unjacketed arm. He had forgotten to talk to them about staying out of sight.

While Myrna calmed her down, he turned back to the phone. "I'm going to miss you," was all he could think to say.

"Don't hate me," Merriman said softly.

Barrow was at his arm. "Turn on your TV. Quick."

He covered the mouthpiece. "Television," he called to Myrna. "Hurry!"

"I respect your feelings," he said into the mouthpiece. "Good-bye, Jerry."

"Yeah," Prescott said. "Good-bye."

He hung up and moved toward the others at the TV. Charlie Johnston was now in the room, too. At least he had had the foresight to take off his gun.

Getting up to the screen, he looked at it in horror. The picture showed children, thousands of children, mostly teenaged. They were in a gymnasium of some sort, just standing in there, packing the place—a sea of faces. They looked poor and hungry, their clothes in tatters. It was morning in Vietnam, the early broadcasts beginning.

A French-accented voice was speaking. "These are the children of America. The product of years of your soldiers taking advantage of the women of Vietnam. When you went away and left our homeland, you left behind your legacy: Thousands of mouths to feed, in a country no longer able to grow food because of Agent Orange. We have been raising your children, citizens of America. Isn't it time that you shouldered your own responsibility?

"If you respond to our plea to take your soldiers back, we will give you your children, free of charge. They are the seeds of America and need to be there. Their fate if left behind is one of hunger, ostracism, and abuse. Many of them will die if you do not answer their plea. Their lives are in your hands, their futures yours to decide."

Fran was crying softly.

Draining his drink with one swallow, Prescott hurried back to the bar for another. It was going to be a long night.

TUESDAY

"...it's real simple, Don. We just go into Nam, with B-52's and blast them right back to the Stone Age."

"Is it really that simple?"

"Listen. I spent thirty years in the military, served all over the world. The only thing these people understand is a kick in the pants. Believe me. They're not civilized like us."

"What about the prisoners? What happens to them in all this?"

"With God's help, they'll survive."

"What about the Russians?"

" (Bleep) the Russians."

Newstalk
with Don Reynolds
WLS Radio
Portland, Oregon

XIV

Washington, D.C.—Shoreham Hotel

April 14—12:15 A.M.

Maurice Benstock watched a silent video-tape replay of his most recent speech. His eye was practiced and critical as he scanned the face that was one of the most recognizable in America, looking for weaknesses.

"You can't blame us for trying, Wes," he said into the telephone cradled on his shoulder. "They've got us all by the short hairs on this thing and are totally ignoring the regular diplomatic channels. They're using you guys to fight their battles for them."

Wes Roberts's voice was tight on the other end, the network news chief reacting to what sounded like government interference in his business. "It's just TV for chris'sake, Benny. You know how it works. We get the pictures and put them on. People can still make up their own minds. What if we did stop transmitting, then what would happen? First off, the public would start screaming that we're censoring the news, then somebody else who couldn't resist all the numbers this thing would bring in would start broadcasting anyway."

Benstock grunted, using his hand control to freeze-frame a close-up of his face on the screen. The droop was showing around his eyes and mouth—he was looking old. Christ, he *was* old. When he had gotten the face-lift and acid-peel he somehow assumed it would fix him for the rest of his life.

Roberts was still talking. "You know, we've got to be able to stay in business after this has blown over. There's no reason for us to leave it alone. It's just news, right?"

"It's propaganda and you know it."

"What isn't, Benny? What isn't? Hell, we show a man-bites-dog story and the ASPCA is all over our ass. When the liberals are in power, television news is the nasty muckraker for reporting anything bad in the administration. When the Repubs are in power, we're the candyass liberal press establishment. Don't talk to me about propaganda."

"How about equal time?" Benstock replied.

"Equal how?"

"Come on, Wes. We worked together for too many years for you to try and lead me by the nose. They're getting all the air time they can handle. How much do we get?"

"What are you going to do with it?" The voice was tentative, unsure.

"The same thing they're doing."

"Propaganda?"

"Presenting our side," Benstock said, frowning at the television.

"How much time do you want?" Roberts asked cautiously.

Benstock smiled. Talking editorial direction to newspeople was like talking war to Alfred Nobel. It came with the territory, down to the simplest decision on what or what not to run. No newsman would ever admit editorial bias, while knowing that bias was unavoidable.

"Look," he said, "I think the President is going to make me his media liaison and have me handle all press dealings. I'd just like to know that we'll have the same right to disseminate information as the Viets do, that's all."

"You won't abuse it, will you?"

"What kind of question is that?" Benstock asked, trying to keep the anger out of his voice. "They can come on and say anything they want, and you want us to clear every word with you before we say it. It makes me wonder whose side you're on here."

"Don't get tacky, Benny," Roberts replied. "We're doing our best to keep everybody honest. I'm just telling you that the free access you want has its limitations."

"Does that mean we're going to get it?"

Roberts sighed loudly. "What have you got in mind?"

Benstock smiled. Things were falling into place. "I want to use the press room in the White House," he said. "When we've got something to say, I'll come down and announce it, and you guys put it on right away. To serve fairness, I'll make the same deal with the other networks."

"What about press conferences, instead?"

"When you go to Vietnam and have press conferences with the Commies," Benstock said. "I'll be honest with you, Wes. This is a clear case of us against them. You're an American citizen. The President could ask you to go fight and die for this country. All I'm asking is that in a time of grave crisis you treat us as fairly as you treat our enemy. I don't see anything out of line in that."

There was a long pause on the other end and when Roberts answered, his voice was colder. "I'll have to clear it through division head, but I think we can cut a deal. I hope you know what you're doing."

"I'm serving the republic, Wes. And so are you."

Roberts sighed again. "I'll try to have it set up by morning," he said tiredly.

"Good."

"I just want you to know that this wipes the slate clean with us. We're all even on favors."

"Lighten up. You've got no reason to feel guilty for doing the right thing."

"Tell that to my ulcers, Benny. Look, I gotta go. Give my love to Arlene."

"Sure."

Benstock hung up the phone and leaned his head back in the chair, rubbing his eyes. He had been a newsman for forty-five years. He had covered two wars from the trenches and one from the newsroom. During his time in the saddle, he had watched the restructuring of the planet along Communist party lines. And always the world seemed to get a little bit worse, a little bit more insane. Sometimes he had the feeling he was presiding over Armageddon.

He sat up straight, watching himself on the television. Tired, that's what it was. He looked tired—all worn out. Was it age, or was it simply that he had spent too many years reporting too much horror, always talking, never able to do anything about it?

The funny thing about Roberts's attitude was that Benstock would have shared it two years ago. He knew that journalists have all been so overconditioned by accusations of unfairness that they can't even recognize the real thing when they see it anymore. Benstock thought how they try so hard to be fair to viewpoints other than those they represent that they end up representing unfairly. Like giving all the legal rights to the criminals and leaving nothing for the victims of those criminals.

He turned off the TV and the VCR, then moved through the darkened rooms to check on Arlene. She lay sleeping in the big master bedroom, the night-table light on, a book opened across her chest. He gently slipped the book out of her fingers and marked the place, setting it aside. He smiled down at the face he had seen nearly every night for the last forty years.

Arlene looked her age, much more so than he, but there was still an elegant beauty to her that was ageless. Marrying that awkward little Nebraska farmgirl so many years ago had been the smartest thing he had ever done, and he prided himself on his decisions. Lover and friend, she kept him balanced. She kept him whole.

He leaned down and kissed her lightly on the cheek and she stirred, smiling. "How did it go?" she asked sleepily.

"I got Wes," he said. "Why don't you go back to sleep?"

She shook her head, sitting up bleary-eyed. "No," she said. "Tell me what happened."

Benstock shrugged and began getting out of his clothes. "We talked," he said, "and he bought it . . . though he didn't want to. He sends his regards, by the way."

"What you're doing is right, honey. He'll understand when he sees it."

"I think so, too," Benstock replied as he put on his nightshirt. "With Wes falling in line, the others will go along because they don't want to risk me giving an exclusive to somebody else."

He buttoned the cotton nightshirt and sat beside her on the bed. "This is really exciting, Arlene," he said, taking her hands. "After all these years, I might be able to really make a contribution to the country."

"You can't go wrong," she said. "You speak for the people . . . always have. That's why Simon Herrod put you in politics. You're the conscience of America."

"Ahhh." He stood, patting her on the leg. "I'm just an aging journalist trying to go out with a flourish."

Her face tightened. "No you're not," she said sternly. "You're special. You've got charisma. People remember you more than they remember any politician. It's time for people like you to have a say in how things are run."

He moved around to his side of the bed, climbing under the covers. "Well, I don't know about other things, but this television diplomacy is right up my alley." He reached an arm out and she slid up against him, his arms folding her in a protective blanket. "I'll tell you, old girl. Ever since the Iranian hostage crisis under President Carter, television has played a whole different role in world politics. It's become the eyes and ears of the terrorists and the radicals."

"Because they're newsmakers."

"It's so insidious," he said, holding her closer. "By its intrusion into the homes of the world, TV has been able to give credence and respectability to every Third World political maniac who could blow up a building or butcher innocent hostages. I don't care what it takes, I'm going to put a stop to this freak show."

"How?"

"By beating them at their own game," he said. "If they can make propaganda about us, by God, we can do the same thing about them. We'll nullify them on their own turf, take the element of fear right out of their grimy hands. If I know anything in this world, I know how to handle this situation."

Arlene snuggled close, her voice beginning to fade again. "You're a great man, Benny. I know you'll do the job on this."

"My only problem's Prescott."

"Jerry? What do you mean?"

"If anyone is closer than me to Simon Herrod, it's Prescott. That scares me a little. He's too old-line, too... populist to go along with the kind of changes I have in mind. He's a good man, just a trifle stodgy."

Arlene laughed a small, tired laugh and rolled over to her side of the bed, turning off the light.

"What's funny?" he said into the darkness.

He could hear her readjusting the sheets. "I was just thinking of Herb and Dana Skillman," she said. "You know how Dana's always trying to get her nose into Herb's business affairs and tell him what to do?"

"Yeah. So?"

"So every time he has a big deal cooking, he surprises her with a present—an airline ticket. He sends her away on some luxurious weekend, or whatever. And by the time she gets back, he's finished his deal and has everything wrapped up."

"A trip, huh?"

"Works every time. Good-night, my love."

He leaned over in the dark and kissed her on the neck. "'Night," he said, patting her bottom.

He rolled over and lay on his back in the dark. Yeah, maybe a trip was just what Jerry Prescott, and the country, needed.

MOSCOW—In a strongly worded message, the Soviet Union today denounced the United States for what it called "imperialistic saber-rattling" in the American response to the announcement of American servicemen being held for trial for "crimes against the people of Vietnam."

TASS, the official Soviet news agency said that, "threats against the free people of Vietnam by the US are pure barbarism," further stating that the Republic of Vietnam has the "moral right and obligation" to try the POWs and also to demand reparation from the American government.

No mention was made of a hostage-type situation, the word "ransom" never appearing in the news release.

—REUTERS

XV

Camp Friendship

April 14—12:30 P.M.

Ridley and Jenkins sat watching the baseball game. Aging, crippled men laughed and shouted like children as they limped around the campyard, chasing the softball that Charlie had provided.

The noon sky was hot and clear, the overhead sun reflecting bright white off the dust cloud raised by the activity. Ridley was dry and nearly felt guilty because he could now satisfy his thirst whenever he wanted.

The French TV crews were busily running around the yard with their damned portable equipment, filming the game for the folks back home. Outside the fences, the curious still passed by, the younger ones staring in wide-eyed curiosi-

ty, some of the older ones shouting angrily at them, words
Ridley neither understood nor wanted to understand.

He felt like a traitor and hadn't even done anything.
Somehow this all smelled like complicity to him, collabora-
tion, and he couldn't shake the feeling. The moment Charlie's
hand had become gentle instead of rough, the guilt began
and wouldn't leave. He'd almost have rather stayed on the
work crews.

A chicken slaughterhouse ran right up to the fence facing
them. Women in dull, printed skirts and dirty-white blouses
squatted on the hard ground, long, tapered knives in their
hands. Children ran around the yard playing. They would
take the squawking, blustery chicken from a tall woven
basketful of chickens and quickly slit its throat, dumping it
into another lidded basket. The fowl would thrash around
wildly for several minutes, joining others already in the
basket in their death agonies. When they finally lay still, the
children would remove them for plucking.

"My old lady's gonna shit when she sees me," Jenkins
said, and Ridley turned to stare at him, knowing better than
to say anything about it.

The man had caught a rice beetle the size of a turtle and
had tied a piece of string to its leg so he could "walk" it. The
large black bug scurried at the end of its tether on the hard
ground, little legs scrabbling madly.

Jenkins took his eyes from the bug and stared at Ridley,
smiling with black teeth. "Last time I saw her she was
wearing one of them miniskirts and it looked like her legs
could go on till next Sunday." He frowned suddenly, rubbing
a hand across his face. "'Course I'm not the man I used to
be. First time I looked in the mirror in the hootch I thought
it was somebody else. You don't think..."

"You look fine, Harry," Ridley said to the man who
probably looked twenty-five years older than his age of
forty-two. "Don't worry about it."

"I can't help but worry about it."

The beetle had gotten its legs tangled up in the string
and had fallen on its back. Jenkins bent to extricate it. "You're
the stupidest pet I've ever had," he said. "I ought to eat you
like the slopes do."

He righted the creature and sent it back to walk. "I want

to be able to pick myself up when I leave here. I want to go back to my life like it was."

"Nothing can be . . ."

"Don't say it, Jase," Jenkins warned, his face dark.

Ridley nodded, turning his attention back to the game.

"It's only right," Jenkins said. "After what we've been through. It's only right that things go good. That's justice, ain't it?"

"Yeah," Ridley said. "Justice."

One of the prisoners lofted a fly ball deep, toward where Ridley was sitting. The Vietnamese umpire was jumping up and down, screaming happily as the cameramen, unused to the American sport, panned around frantically, trying to figure out what to shoot.

"I got it!" Jenkins yelled, jumping to his feet and throwing his arms in the air. He let the string go, the beetle hurrying off to get tangled up in the first bush he came to.

Jenkins misjudged the ball, moving too far on it. The thing bounced beyond him, rolling to Ridley's feet. Jenkins ran back, the other players screaming for the ball.

Ridley made to toss it back in play, but Jenkins grabbed it from him. "Me, let me!"

He snatched it away, taking two steps and throwing hard. The ball went wild, missing the game completely and sailing over the fences to land in the midst of the children playing in the chickenyard. The children squealed happily, running off with the ball, while Jenkins was roundly booed by the teams.

When he turned back to Ridley, there were tears in his eyes. "What . . . happened to me?"

"You got carried away, that's all," Ridley said, soothing.

Jenkins was shaking his head. "I was all-state in baseball my senior year," he said. "I had wanted to play in the pros."

"Out of practice, that's all."

Jenkins sat back on the stairs, staring myopically at the yard. Ridley started to say something to him when a shadow fell across the both of them.

A man stood silhouetted against the bright sunlight. Ridley raised his hand to shield his eyes, but still couldn't see the towering figure. He stood, dusting himself off as he did.

"Am I addressing Lieutenant Colonel Jason Ridley?" the man asked. He was tall and slightly stooped, his new civilian clothes precise and tidy. His face and head were shaved smooth. He must have used broken glass or tin to do it over the years, his skin pocked full of tiny shaving scars. His head was nicked up and creviced like an exposed brain. His eyes were narrow and hard, his lips a thin slash. He had no teeth.

"I'm Ridley," he said, and stuck his hand out in greeting.

The man snapped to attention, bringing his hand up for a military salute. "Captain James Ferguson, United States Air Force," he said. "At your service."

Ridley looked around before returning the salute. He gave it weakly, as the man snapped off the return. He was still standing at attention.

"At ease," Ridley heard himself say, and it had been more years than he could count since he had said those words. The man slouched to parade rest.

"What can I do for you?" Ridley asked.

"I've been taking a survey of the camp, sir," Ferguson said, he and Ridley sitting. "And I find that you are senior officer in attendance."

"What the hell happened to your head?" Jenkins asked.

The man glared at him. "May I make an inquiry as to your name and rank?"

"Certainly," Jenkins said, and jumped to his feet, approximating a salute. "Brigadier General Westmoreland, Supreme Commander of the Allied Forces, at your service."

The man faced him, gnarled hands balled into fists. "Ease up, soldier," he said low, menacing.

"Sit down, Captain," Ridley told him.

"Sir." He sat.

Ridley turned to Jenkins. "Take a load off, Harry."

Jenkins saluted. "Yes, sir!" he said loudly.

"This is Jenkins," Ridley told Ferguson. "He's with me."

Ferguson nodded curtly, then leaned close to Ridley and whispered. "Can we speak freely in front of him?"

Ridley jerked back, startled. "Of course," he said. "Why not?"

"Hey, if I'm not wanted..." Jenkins said, and made to stand, Ridley stopping him with a hand on his leg.

"What is it you need?" Ridley asked Ferguson.

The man licked dry lips, then spoke, his eyes darting between the other two. "I just wanted you to know that when you assume command, I will do my best to help you in whatever capacity you require."

"Assume command?"

"Yes, sir. Of the force here, sir." He made a sweeping gesture across the yard.

"We are prisoners of war, Captain. There is nothing for us to assume command of."

"We are soldiers, Colonel, subject to the same military regulations as any army. I've counted, sir. There are two thousand and forty-five of us here." Using a finger, he wrote the number out in the dirt in front of him and underlined it. "That constitutes a force of battalion-strength."

"What are you suggesting, Captain?" Ridley said, and his throat was dry.

Ferguson's eyes narrowed even farther, squeezing to slits. "I'm suggesting we do our duty as soldiers as specified by the Geneva Convention."

"You're out of your fucking mind!" Jenkins said loudly.

"Harry," Ridley said. "Keep it down."

"But this motherfucker's crazy," Jenkins said, incredulous. "After twenty years we get a shot at headin' back to the ZI, and this asshole's talking crazy shit."

"Keep him quiet," Ferguson said, craning his head around. "They've forbidden a chain of command."

"You dumb sons of bitches!" Jenkins said, still too loud. They were attracting attention.

"Would you shut up!" Ridley whispered harshly. "You'll get us all thrown in irons."

Jenkins blanched then, drawing up his knees and leaning his head on them.

"Are there...others who think as you do, Captain?" Ridley asked, a strange feeling forming in the pit of his stomach.

"Yes, sir," Ferguson said. "Not many, but we've got a core. Do you have any orders?"

Jenkins groaned, his voice muffled.

"Let me think about this," Ridley said. "We're not allowed to congregate, either. First thing, we'd probably better not let anyone see any saluting. No use arousing suspicions needlessly."

"Yes, sir."

Ridley looked at Jenkins, wondering how many were as bad off emotionally as he. "I know our time is limited," he said. "But I've got to think about this."

Ferguson stood. "I'll get back to you later this evening," he said. Then, he rubbed out the number in the dirt with his brand-new penny loafers and walked off. Someone had come up with another ball and the game had started again, Ferguson walking right through the middle of it. Ridley couldn't help but notice that the NVAs standing around watching them were sloppy and disheveled, the first sign of lax discipline.

"Don't you fuck this up," Jenkins said low.

Ridley started to talk with him about it, but inexplicably backed off. "Don't worry about it, Harry. You'll get your trip back home."

Jenkins pulled his head up and stared with wild eyes. "I mean it, Jase. Don't fuck with any of this."

All at once, there was a great commotion at the gates, prisoners running in that direction, yelling and cheering.

"What the hell? . . ."

"They're bringing trucks in," Ridley said, and stood to get a better look.

Jenkins was up beside him. "Bunch of trucks," he said. "What are they . . . it looks like they're . . . filled with women!"

"Oh my God," Ridley whispered. He hadn't had a woman in twenty years.

"Jesus, oh Jesus!" Jenkins yelled and started running toward the trucks that were unloading the women right into the yard with the prisoners. "Come on, Jase!" he yelled back to Ridley.

But Ridley didn't go. It was all part of the trick, all part of the mental battle to wear them down completely. Looking down, he saw the place where Ferguson had written the number. A force of battalion-strength, the man had said. He thought about duty, about his duty as ranking officer.

And the cameras rolled.

XVI

Washington, D.C.—CIA Headquarters

April 14—5:12 A.M.

The main thrust of the CIA was, and is, research. And on this night the bright, sterile lighting that was so important to Miller Angostis was burning continuously throughout the bureau, hundreds of employees working around the clock to sift through news, technical, and political reports, looking, most often, not for what was there, but for what was not.

Angostis heard the sound of footsteps and turned to see Russel Buchner hurrying to catch up.

"We're getting pretransmission from Steakly," Buchner said, his young face looking bright, his clothes, as usual, impeccable.

"Once he's cleared, Russ, why don't you patch it down to the office."

"Got it. Anything new?"

"Just got off with our man in the Bangkok station," he said. "It appears the television is coming to us through the good graces of some French Socialists."

"Boulle?"

Angostis smiled. "You've done your own homework. Boulle and others. They go all the way back to the war and the "people's revolution" when the North got all the good publicity. Somebody's been pulling in some chits."

"Can we get the French government to put pressure on them?"

"Not this French government, but I passed the information along anyway."

They stopped before the solid-steel door marked Director, Angostis speaking his name into the small grillwork beside, to voiceprint it open.

"You need a note-taker?" Buchner asked.

The door buzzed, then clicked open. "Sure," Angostis

answered, pushing into the office. "And call the files up for me."

"On my way. Need anything else—coffee?"

The director looked at his watch. He hadn't slept for thirty-six hours. "Get me Grinchy's bag, would you?"

Buchner gave him thumbs-up and moved off down the hall, Angostis closing the door and walking to his desk.

He sat heavily in the chair behind, swiveling to face the large viewscreen that filled one entire wall of the large, sumptuous room. The carpets were gold, the paneling white, antiqued oak. It was the office of someone who could afford any kind of office at all, and Angostis was that kind of person. Bright, harsh lighting dominated everything.

Miller Angostis controlled every aspect of his life and his work. Involved with the company since the Bay of Pigs, he had maintained close ties throughout the years by his electronics firm's development and manufacture of clandestine devices for the American security network, finally lobbying for and getting the director's job when Herrod took office.

It was a job he knew his highly organized mind could handle, despite the vagaries of the political winds. Passionless and calculating, he could accept a given conclusion without reaching moral epiphany along the way—a realist in a confused world.

He was a quiet, closedmouth man, and that approach worked well when it came to company publicity. What the public and the politicians didn't know wouldn't hurt them, and when it came to company matters under Miller Angostis, they knew precious little. The words of a German proverb hung, framed, on his office wall: The silent dog is the first to bite.

Buchner knocked his secret knock, and the director reached under the desk to buzz him in. He carried a small, black bag that he set on Angostis's desk.

"The White House has already called several times," Buchner said, pulling a chair up to face the screen that was still filled with static.

"Did you put them off?" Angostis asked as he rummaged around in the bag, finally coming out with a syringe and a small vial of liquid B_{12}.

Buchner nodded. "You'll have to speak with them soon. The Joint Chiefs called, too."

The director stood to remove his gray, pinstriped suit coat. He sat again, rolling up the left sleeve of his white shirt. "Send them through the maze," he said.

"They're riding the merry-go-round now." Buchner smiled, referring to the daisy chain of middle management people that Angostis used to tie up unwanted callers so he could keep his hands free to do what he needed to do. Being a political civilian agency, the CIA was not answerable to the uniformed military. The National Security Council and the commander in chief himself were Angostis's only superiors.

The director filled the syringe, then injected himself right below the elbow. He waited until he got his sleeve rolled down again and his jacket on before juicing the wall screen.

He found himself staring at the round, pleasant face of John Steakly, longtime company desk jockey and coordinator of an inactive register called Asian Ops. Angostis keyed his own camera and watched Steakly react.

"Mr. Director," he said. "I didn't realize you..."

"Have you got a choice for Project Sidewinder, John?" Angostis interrupted.

"Yes, sir," Steakly said, his voice tired sounding. "I think we need to send Albert Sorrel, code name: Cowboy. He's the best we can come up with down here."

Angostis turned to stare at the terminal on his own desk. "Our computer indicates David Bryan, aka Cassady, code name: Stinger, has more working knowledge of the area and also knows where a number of weapons stores are buried."

"Yes, sir," Steakly said, his eyes drifting from the screen to off-camera notes. "I met with that gentleman yesterday and found his behavior to be somewhat... erratic."

"Go on," Angostis said, feeling the B_{12} perking his system, waking him up.

"I decided to go back into his files and sort through it all," Steakly said. "As you know, we've always tolerated Cassady's peculiarities because of his excellence in the field. But something about this Vietnam thing had him hyped up, overanxious. I went all the way back and found this."

He nodded to someone offscreen and his picture was replaced by a scene of confusion, as helicopters were taking off in crowds of people, many hysterical.

"Option four," came Steakly's voice. "April 29, 1975. The evacuation of Saigon. This is a shot of the roof of the American Embassy as the last Americans and Vietnamese sympathizers are being vacked out." Many people were trying to get on board the last helicopters by shoving large amounts of money and gold at the marines guarding the loading bays. They were being shoved back, some forcibly, with rifle butts. In the background, plumes of smoke could be seen, drift-off from mortar rounds even then being lobbed into the city by advancing Viet Cong.

"As you know," Steakly continued, "Cassady was with the SEAL counterinsurgency squads, using VC methods of terrorism in the villages. He worked for us up until the end and was slated to go out with the last copters."

"There he is," Buchner said, pointing to the screen.

Angostis saw him arguing with uniformed troops and several civilians. They wanted him to board the copter, but he wouldn't go, continually moving away, only to be brought back again. The director watched the history unfold without feeling. It was old time, time gone. Buchner watched with detached fascination, being too young to remember the hostilities.

"He was waiting for someone," Steakly said. "Someone who was supposed to go with him, someone who never showed up."

One by one, copters lifted off, some with Vietnamese clinging to the skids, Vietnamese who were so solidly linked with the American forces that they had nothing but painful death to look forward to under the new rule. Only Cassady's copter remained. He was struggling with several uniformed soldiers, trying to break away from them as the ranks of civilians pushed ever in. Finally, a ranking officer drew his service revolver and brought the butt of it down on Cassady's head and his sagging body was lifted onto the chopper.

"A woman?" Angostis asked.

The videotape was replaced by a still picture of a beautiful Oriental woman with long, sleek black hair and a strangely western face. Haunting eyes seemed to be beckoning from the old photo almost hypnotically.

"Her name's Kim Mang," Steakly said. "Her mother was a French clerical worker, her father a Vietnamese government official. Both were killed when she was very young. She worked as a prostitute, mostly getting passed around the high command because of her beauty and breeding. This photo comes from our file on her. She was always under suspicion as a sympathizer. More than likely she simply blew with the prevailing wind. Cassady became involved with her while on leave in Saigon in September of '69. Our sources indicate he continually reupped and worked with SEAL to be near her."

"And you think he wants to get back to her now?" Angostis asked.

"That's my considered opinion. He's had nothing to do with women since his return to the states. Given his obsessional tendencies, I think we have real reason to worry about Mr. Cassady."

"You may be right," Angostis said.

"There's something else, too," Steakly said. "It may be nothing, but I'm worried. When we met, Cassady expressed concern about my Soviet tag, Dobryn. After that, the man was nowhere to be seen. He's left me alone for periods of time before, but I would think given the gravity of the present situation..."

"Say no more," Angostis said. "We'll scratch Cassady from the mission and put Sorrel in his place. Does this man know about the weapons?"

Steakly's face replaced the woman's on the screen. He shook his head. "We'll have to get that info from Cassady."

"Okay," Angostis said. "You've done well. Go home and get some sleep. We'll take it from here."

Steakly looked relieved. This had probably been the biggest job of his life. "Good luck," he said, and blanked from the screen.

Angostis swiveled to face Russ Buchner. "Get Sorrel in here as quickly as you can," he said. "He'll need to be on the move by tonight. Check with Logistics and see what kind of transport we can arrange that's safe and secure as possible. And get me an ETA."

Buchner stood, finishing up writing in a notebook. "About Dobryn . . ."

The director rubbed his face with his palms. "Check on him . . . discreetly, of course." He closed up the black bag and stuck it in his bottom desk drawer. "It may be time to think about putting Mr. Cassady on permanent inactive."

"Yes, sir," Buchner said, and moved out the door and into the rush of activity.

.

SEATTLE, Wash. (AP)—A group of fifteen women entered Seattle's famous underground today, vowing to go on a public hunger strike until the United States government pays the money to release the hostages held in Ho Chi Minh City.

Marcie Andrews, spokeswoman for the group of middle-aged women, said, "We all lost sons during the war. We are appalled that the killing cannot be stopped." Declaring they would rather die than watch more senseless murder, the group sang hymns and carried lit candles into the subterranean city, created a hundred years ago when Seattle raised its streets twenty feet to accommodate underground plumbing.

XVII

Camp David, Maryland

April 14—11:15 A.M.

The Camp David golf course was designed by Ben Hogan, under the direct supervision of President Eisenhower, who loved his golf. Though not a high-risk player like Jerry Ford, Ike was an eight handicapper and shot a very competitive game—especially if there was money involved. They used to tell the story of how during World War II the invasion was delayed because Ike adamantly refused to destroy key enemy gun emplacements on the outskirts of Munich because they were set on the eighteenth fairway of the Munich Golf and Country Club, calling it a "national treasure."

The fourth hole of the Camp David course is a tricky par five, double dogleg to the right.

Three men approached the tee. Their caddies drove steel-plated golf carts, equipped with shotguns, sophisticated radio gear, and a red telephone connected to several of the forty-four thousand Pentagon phones. The caddies wore gray suits and sunglasses and didn't know the difference between a good lie and a good lay. Off in the distance tiny figures carrying rifles could be seen dotting the landscape.

The President of the United States placed his ball on an extra-high tee because of his tendency to pull up when he drove. Benstock had won the last hole, had won all the previous holes, but it was a house rule at Camp David that the President always got the honors.

"I'm going to show you gentlemen the power of clean living," Herrod said, arching his eyebrow as he straightened, prepared to address the ball.

"If that's what we've been seeing this morning," Jerry Prescott called back, "you've convinced me to stay a wastrel."

"Remember to keep your head down," Benstock said seriously, as he always took his own advice seriously. "I'll watch the ball."

Herrod smiled at him. "Benny," he returned, "I've spent my entire golfing career trying to do just that. I can't help it. I've got . . . what do you call it?"

"Target fixation," Jerry helped.

"Right," Herrod said. "Target fixation. I always have to see if those shots are as bad as they sound."

"They always are, Simon," Benstock said. "And it's precisely because you watch them."

Prescott watched the President carefully, looking for the depth of the strain, looking for the reason Herrod had dragged him out here in the middle of an important workday. He disliked golf, but he couldn't begrudge the exercise or the beautiful, crisp morning.

Herrod aimed for the middle of the fairway, but pulled his head up and hooked far right into the trees. It would be a tough out, providing he could even find his ball.

Benstock looked at Prescott, who smiled and pointed to

the tee. The man, looking like he could do this for a living, gave a small salute and swaggered past a frowning Herrod.

The President joined Prescott. "When you used to come out here more to play," he said, "I could at least look good by comparison."

"We're about as far as we can get from the clubhouse," Prescott returned. "You must have something really bad to tell me. I can't even run back from here."

A Secret Serviceman walked up and took Herrod's club. "Three iron, Marty," the President said, and looked deep into Prescott's eyes. "Am I that transparent?"

"I'm just a better politician that I am a golfer, that's all."

Benstock, using a high tee himself, hit a towering shot that cleared the trees by a good thirty yards and left him a nine iron from the green.

"You act like you were born on this course," Prescott called to him.

The man smiled his television smile. "Maybe I belong here," he replied, and ambled over to the cart to replace his club.

Prescott teed up, deciding to try the short cut the way Benstock had done.

"Get under it and air it out," Benstock called to him.

He concentrated to relax, eased into a perfect shot, his body fluidly whipping through the ball. Unfortunately, the shot hung low, like a bullet, scooting quickly into the trees. When it hit a branch, the resultant crack was so loud it sounded like a gunshot, startling many of the Secret Service.

Benstock was careful not to say, "I told you so," but his condescending grin told volumes.

Herrod patted the seat beside him in the back of the cart. "Care to join me in the trees?" he asked.

Prescott hoisted himself into the cart with effort. The driver started them off with a jerk then moved toward the treeline.

"I'm getting flak over my decision to send the Seventh Fleet down to the South China Sea," Herrod said. "Do you think it was a mistake?"

"A little late to worry over that now," Prescott replied, knowing that this old news was not the reason he was brought to Camp David. "I don't know what other real choice you had."

"I could have just ignored the whole thing, I suppose."

Prescott shook his head. "Not possible. Not with television cramming it down our throats all the time. Once the Russians went down, I don't see that you had a choice."

Herrod looked at the head of his three iron, scraping some dried mud off it with his thumbnail. "What do *they* want out of all this."

"Ahh," Prescott said. "They were as caught off-guard by this as we were." They were bouncing closer to the treeline. "Their diplomats have been scrambling ever since it first happened. They don't want to lose face in this, but neither do I think they'd interfere with us unless we confronted them directly. Doksoi is as hot for the arms talks as we are. I'm sure this is some last-ditch statement by the old, hardliners. In fact, that's probably why the Vietnamese picked this week to pull the stunt. They figure we'll pay just to avoid an incident that could screw up the negotiations."

The driver skidded them to a halt in front of the trees.

"Meet us on the other side," Herrod said, climbing out, his three iron held tightly in his gloved hand. Prescott grabbed a club from his bag, and the car drove off.

"This is all media hype," the President said as they walked into the thick trees. "We've got to put on a solid front for the world."

"You sound like Benstock," Prescott replied. "What do you want me to say?"

"It's a new world, Jerry. It needs to be dealt with in a new way." Herrod walked a distance away, futilely searching the craggy ground.

"It may be a new world," Prescott called to him, and he couldn't care less whether he found his ball or not, "but it's still the same old values, the same old ethics. Truth doesn't change."

The President was pushing through stacks of needles with his club. "I'm talking about PR, Jerry, not immorality."

"You didn't bring me out here to debate this, Simon,"

Prescott said, reaching into his pocket for another ball. "Let's get it out in the open."

The President walked back to join him, the two of them somehow conspirators there in the tiny island of solitude amidst the maelstrom. He pulled a ball out of his own pocket.

"I want you to go to Chicago, Jerry," Herrod said.

"What's in Chicago?" Prescott replied, feeling the tension and knowing he wouldn't like the answer.

Herrod looked at him, then at the ball in his hand. "I won't tell if you won't," he said.

Prescott laughed. "I never have," he said. "Be my guest."

"Fore!" the President yelled, and threw his ball up over the trees to land on proper fairway in better position than Benstock.

"Great shot!" Benstock's unseen voice drifted back from the fairway.

"What's in Chicago?" Prescott asked again, and he threw his ball out of the woods.

"The NAMWives are meeting there—"

"No, Simon!" Prescott said.

"Let me finish, dammit. We're getting some opposition to this from them and...others. Benny's af—we're afraid that they are going to use a media blitz to try and raise that money to spite us. We can't have that division now. We need the country behind us one hundred percent."

"Why me?" Prescott asked. "That was the job Nixon gave me back in 1970, and I couldn't handle it then. They all hate me and the lies I told them to shut them up. I'd be the worst person for this you could ever pick. That's all besides the fact that I wouldn't take that job in a million years."

"They're meeting tonight," Herrod said. "You know them, know their leaders. We couldn't train anyone quick enough to even partway know how to handle them."

"'Handling' them is precisely the problem," Prescott said. "They're hardened by years of lies and bullshit. They won't allow themselves to be 'handled' anymore. And you can take that to the bank."

They began walking through the cool, green shade toward the fairway. "Then talk to them," Herrod said gently. "Explain to them..."

"Why we're going to let their husbands die in Vietnam when we have the means to save them?" Prescott said.

"Whose side are you on, Jerry?" Herrod said, anger evident in his voice. "We're taking the only course possible."

"I'm sorry, Mr. President," Prescott said. "This is an emotional issue for all of us. You don't know how I hated myself for the way I dealt with the wives' groups last time."

Herrod stopped walking, putting a hand on Prescott's arm to stop him, too. "I need you, Jerry," he said. "I know how you feel about this. I just have nowhere else to turn. Between you and Benny, I..."

"What about Benny?" Prescott asked, eyes narrowing.

"I'm putting him in charge of media relations on this thing." The President was searching Prescott's eyes. "He's going to make the public relations decisions. With him on PR and you handling the wives, we might just have a chance to pull in the support we need."

"Don't you think that maybe public honesty might be more beneficial in this than public relations?"

"The direction of this rests with me," Herrod said, and his voice was firm, his mind made up. "Please don't question me on decisions I've already made. I need you badly. Will you help me?"

Prescott let his eyes drift to the ground, surprised to see his original ball lying there, nestled in a bed of needles. He bent to pick it up, his mind drifting images from the past: the faces of women searching his words for hope as he told them negotiations were proceeding when none were, when he promised to account for their loved ones when the government had no such plan or intention.

When he stood he had made up his mind. He watched the expectation on Herrod's still-boyish face. "You know I'd never do this for anyone else but you, Simon..."

"You will then?"

"If you promise I won't have to shill for you," Prescott said, and dropped the ball into his jean's pocket. "I'll go to Chicago and honestly present the administration's views, but I won't lie for you."

Herrod stuck out a sportgloved hand. "I won't ask you

to," he said. "We both want the same thing out of this, Jerry. It's going to be all right."

They shook hands and walked out of the woods, Benstock waving and pointing to their good lies. Prescott watched the man, wondering, above all, what it was he really wanted.

"You may as well face it," Benstock said, his voice barely slurring with his second vodka tonic. "The face of diplomacy has changed for good."

Prescott sipped his own scotch and leaned back in the plush swivel chair. The heavily paneled Camp David clubhouse was loud with military, all talking excitedly about the possibility of intervention. Enough brass, Prescott thought, to cast several good spittoons.

"Why is that point so important to you?" he asked the man. "If I didn't know any better, I'd swear you were celebrating."

"Hell, I *am* celebrating," Benstock replied. "The country's finally going to join the twentieth century."

"I don't know as I understand completely," Prescott said.

Benstock spoke low. "Listen," he said, "television is the ultimate form of mass communication—"

"Or mass manipulation," Prescott interrupted.

"You still haven't figured it out. Everything is manipulation . . . politics is manipulation. Let me ask you a question: Why are you a Democrat?"

Prescott shrugged. He'd play. Why not? "I'm a Democrat, basically, because I believe in demand-side economics. I think big business should exist for the good of the people, not the other way around."

Benstock smiled, getting excited. "You believe that's the best way to live?"

"Yes."

"Okay. How far can you go to promote that line of thought?"

"What do you mean?"

The man finished his drink and set it on the edge of the table, raising a hand to get the bartender's notice. "I mean, do you feel it would be right to show people the possible consequences of supply-side economics?"

"There's historical precedent."

"What about the other side? Are they allowed to show the horrors of Communism, the ultimate workers' state, and say that's what you want?"

Prescott began to see the turn things were taking. "I guess in the broadest sense..."

Benstock began to speak, stopped himself while the bartender took his empty glass. Prescott waved off another. When the man left, Benstock said, "It's all bullshit, don't you see? We create our own realities for what we believe to be the common good. None of us are right or wrong, but in the final analysis, wouldn't you rather the world live by your philosophy rather than some archconservative senator's from North Carolina?"

Prescott smiled. "Well, that goes without saying."

"That's all I'm going to do with my media relations job." Benstock beamed. "I'm going to present our position in the best possible light. I'm simply going to use television for the tool that it is. I'm going to present the truth, our truth, to the American public in the way it will be most palatable to them. Diplomacy is getting set to become an aggressive arm of government, a way of molding public opinion scientifically and accurately. The point here is, we've got the tools. We must use them better and more positively than those who would do our country harm."

Prescott stared at him, feeling like an outsider in a system for which he had worked his entire life.

"And how about you, Benny? What do you have to gain in all this?"

"So, what are you asking? Aren't we all looking to advance ourselves in one way or another?" He took a long drink. "We make our own breaks, don't we?"

Prescott had had enough. "I told you yesterday that I simply didn't like what you stood for," he said. "I've changed my mind about that. I don't much like *you* either."

"Is it real dislike, or do you just feel threatened?" Benstock replied, smiling. "You know, there's room for all of us in this thing."

Prescott turned from the man, making his way to call Myrna on the unsecured pay phone next to the rest rooms.

Sharon, the twice-a-week maid with security clearance, answered and got Myrna on the line.

"What's wrong?" she said curtly. At least she didn't sound like she was on Valium.

"Nothing much," he said. "I was just . . . wondering how you were doing?"

She didn't answer for quite a while. "What do you want from me, Jerry?" she asked finally, her voice strained.

"I've got to go to Chicago," he said, "to meet with NAMWives tonight. I—I was hoping I could talk you into going with me."

"Nothing like dragging me along on a business trip."

His mouth had gone dry. He felt like a schoolboy asking for his first date. "I just want to be with you," he said softly.

"I can't hear you."

"I want to be with you," he repeated louder, and could see out of the corner of his eye that the bartender was straining to listen to his conversation. "I want us to be together."

"Or do you want a woman's viewpoint to help you sell your load of manure to those people?"

"That's not fair, I . . ."

"Forget it, Jerry," she said, and she sounded a million miles away. "You're going to have to do your own slave-trading. Enjoy your trip."

She hung up then, the receiver a cold, dead thing in his hand. He started to slam it back on the cradle, but replaced it gently at the last second. He turned to look at Benstock. A group of officers had crowded around him and they were all laughing and talking together.

BAKE SALE FOR VETS

The Four Seasons nursing home has scheduled a bake sale today to benefit POWs in Vietnam. Calling it, "a little sugar for our boys in uniform," Mrs. Judith Palmer Ackerman, sponsor of the event, asks that instead of cash, customers bring a gold item to pay for their sweets. All donations will be gratefully accepted.

—*The Lexington,
Kentucky Star*

LOCAL MAN TAKES OWN LIFE

The Cuyahoga County coroner today ruled suicide in the death of Cleveland resident John Milner. Well-known locally, Milner had been a POW in Vietnam and author of a book, *Seven Years in Hell*, a record of his experiences in Vietnamese prison camps.

He was found dead in his study yesterday by his second wife, Patricia, who called the police. "John had been very upset about the MIA thing," his wife said. "but I didn't understand the severity of it. He was so quiet, you know."

A suicide note was found on the desk in the study. It read: "I should have been with them." Milner is survived by his wife and two children, John, Jr. and Irene, from a previous marriage. He died from a single gunshot wound to the head.

—*Cleveland Plain Dealer*

XVIII

Oklahoma City, Oklahoma

April 14—10:31 A.M.

Sid Henderson watched his wife talk on the bedroom phone and tried to figure out how she could have changed so much in the space of a day. She was suddenly so aggressive, so hard. When the State Department had called just to confirm her first husband's existence, she nearly refused to talk with them. And when she finally did talk, she was curt, almost nasty.

On the dresser the television played silently, scenes of American prisoners of war playing softball in the dusty afternoon. He hated the intrusion of these phantoms into his home, phantoms who were changing his wife just by being alive.

He walked to the set and switched it off.

"Sid," Nancy said, covering the receiver with her hand. "Something may come on . . . an announcement or something."

He stared at her. Her features softened for a second, her eyes quietly pleading. His jaw muscles tightened, but he turned the set back on. She mouthed a silent "thank you," then immediately turned her attention back to the conversation.

"Yes, Marsha," she said. "I'm packing now. My flight leaves in a couple of hours. I know. I feel the same way."

Sid pushed her suitcase aside and stretched out on the bed, kicking his loafers off. This was his second day of work missed because of this thing, and with Nancy going to Chicago, he'd either have to find a babysitter quick or take a leave of absence.

"I've heard the rumor, too," Nancy said. "If they do put that son of a bitch Prescott on this, I'll personally kick his butt all the way to Washington. . . . I don't care, Marsha! We're not going to be screwed like we were last time."

Sid, a geologist, had married Nancy in '82, several years after Billy had been declared legally dead. They had bought the house from a retired colonel a couple of years later when everyone was getting rich in Oklahoma's oil boom. The boom ended as quickly as it had begun, but Sid had managed to pay off the house anyway. It was theirs, free and clear, and he was proud of that.

Nancy had her hand over the receiver again and whispered harshly to Sid, "They want me to be their spokesperson!"

"Wonderful," he said, and couldn't keep the sarcasm out of his voice. He regretted his tone immediately and sat up to apologize. But Nancy stopped him with a withering look, immediately turning her attention back to the call.

"I don't care what they say, we're going to raise that money!"

By the time Sid had met Nancy, NAMWives had already

begun to wind down as an organization, keeping their contact to occasional newsletters and committees. But once the phone team had swung into action yesterday, they had reconstructed the old framework with a vengeance.

"Are we contacting other organizations that might be sympathetic?" Nancy asked. "With the right help, we can get momentum rolling pretty quickly."

Nancy was his wife now, not Billy's. There was some sense in that—maybe, for Sid, the ultimate sense. Why did she have to go against the government and all that was good and holy to save a man she had lived with for a couple of weeks back in the midsixties? What was it about Billy Phillips that made her risk so much? Could she still love him despite Sid and the children? He had convinced himself from the very first that he'd never have to deal with what was now happening. Now his feelings were totally ambivalent. He knew one thing: When he had seen Private First Class Billy Phillips on the television screen, he had hated the man immediately. And that hatred now formed the core of his emotions.

"I think we should schedule a press conference for the morning," Nancy was saying.

"What if we don't have anything to tell anyone in the morning?" Marsha Ridley asked on the other end.

"We've got to," Nancy replied. "We don't have time to waste on this. If we're going to organize, we've got to do it immediately."

"I'll use some of the Illinois wives to start pitching the media," Marsha said. "We'll get the coverage. I just hope we're up to the fight."

"I am," Nancy said simply.

"Nancy . . ." Marsha began, then hesitated for a moment. "I . . . know this is none of my business, but I want you to try and be careful of your husband's feelings in all this. I don't think you should let any of this come between you and Sid."

Nancy looked over at Sid sulking on the bed. "It already has," she replied.

"Nancy . . ."

"Nothing I can't handle," Nancy said to cut off the conversation. "Look, I'd better get off now and get out of here or I'll miss my own press conference."

"Okay, love. I'll see you tonight."

"'Bye, Marsha," Nancy said, and hung up, turning immediately to Sid.

"Don't tell me," he said. "I should be more supportive."

"*Any* support would be more than I'm getting," she said, and moved back to the suitcase. She put her hands on her hips, then slowly looked around the room, mentally running through her packing list to see what she'd forgotten. Her eyes came to rest on the jewelry case on the chest of drawers.

He sat up, swinging his legs off the bed. "My wife is running off to her husband and leaving the children behind with me, and I'm supposed to be excited about it."

"*You're* my husband," she said softly. "You and the children are my whole life. Don't you know that?"

He stood and moved to her, taking her in his arms. "Oh, Nance," he choked, and the fragrance of her hair was all over him like a sweet dream. "I know this is important to you, but I can't say that I like it. I worry for you, for what this is doing to you."

She pulled away from him slightly. "What's that supposed to mean?"

He felt her tighten up and moved away. "This is changing you," he said.

She walked to the chest and took down the box. "No it's not," she said. "I don't know what you mean?"

"You're into different modes of behavior," he said, watching her root through the cedar box. "Old behavior, from before. And this business about going against the government—"

"It's our government, Sid," she said, and found what she was looking for at the bottom of the case. "They work for us, remember? I can meet with my friends if I want to."

"You're oversimplifying and you know it."

She pulled a gold chain out of the box. It had a wedding ring attached, Billy's wedding ring.

"I didn't know you still had that," he said, practically a whisper.

Her stare was quizzical. "I've got to do this," she said. "Why is that so difficult to understand? I've dealt with this for twenty years and I'm going to see it through to the end." She slipped the chain over her wrist and replaced the box. "Billy has spent more of his life in Vietnam than he spent in the States, and now you and Herrod and all those other assholes are simply ready to sit back and let him die. Well, I'm not. And I can't believe your childish jealousy is making you so callous."

"Is it?" he said. "Is my jealousy childish? You're so hot to get him free that you're willing to undermine national security and your marriage to do it."

She laughed dryly. "Since when has national security been your big priority?"

He moved to her again, his eyes locked on the chain on her wrist. "The government is handling this, Nance. They know better than we do. We shouldn't meddle. They probably have access to a lot of information that we don't."

"I don't want to hear about it."

He grabbed her hand, too tightly. She jerked it away. "Well, you're going to hear about it!"

When the anger came this time, it didn't leave. "Okay," she said, lips drawn tight. "You listen to me for one minute. When Billy got drafted we all thought that it was okay, that the government understood something we didn't. When he disappeared, we believed everything that could be done was being done. When the stupid war ended, we listened to their runaround for years, thinking they really were doing something." She stared fiercely at him. "You know what they were doing, Sid? Nothing. They didn't know anything and didn't want to know anything. They wanted us to go away and leave them alone."

"Nance . . ."

"No. You started this. Let's talk about it. You know why they're holding those men? Because Nixon promised the Vietnamese money to rebuild their country and never delivered. Now they're asking for it, bartering with us from the only position of strength they've got. Herrod doesn't want to pay the money because his macho pride would be hurt, because it would hurt our 'image' with the rest of the world. Well, I'm not buying it. They're not going to shut me up this time."

"There's something you haven't thought about," Sid said.

She moved to the blue soft-shell bag and began zipping it up. "You're getting ready to tell me they could call Billy a traitor for making that speech on television."

"They could make a good case for it."

She pulled the case from the bed and stood it on the floor, then sat on the bed herself. "You sound like you've got an opinion on it," she said, leaning back on her elbows, her manner hard.

He felt he was standing there with a stranger. "I'm an Oklahoma boy," he said at last. "I was raised to believe in the flag."

Her eyes narrowed. "And where were you when they were passing out the guns back then?"

He took a step toward her, his fists clenched involuntarily. "You can believe in the flag without going to war."

She sat bolt upright. "Billy believed in the flag, too, Sid. He believed in it the way only someone young and idealistic can." She lowered her eyes, the toughness gone, the softness back. "So did I."

He reached out a tentative hand, placing it gently on her leg. "I—I'm sorry," he said. "This has got me confused. I know what you feel you must do, but it's a hornet's nest we're shaking here. I'm afraid we're going to get stung bad—me, you . . . the kids. I'm scared, Nancy."

When she looked up at him again, her eyes were moist. She put her hand on top of his. "Make love with me," she said. "It may be awhile after today."

"The kids . . . " he started.

"Jeremy's down for a nap," she said huskily. "Tim is wrapped up in the television. He'll be okay for awhile. Lock the door."

Sid moved to the door, pushed it closed, and thumbed the lock. The emotions were tumbling through him, more confused now with a frightening edge of sexuality.

When he turned around, Nancy already had her printed blouse off, long brown hair tumbling over her breasts, and he wanted her more than he ever had in his life. She was breathing heavily, her face slightly flushed.

He moved to the bed and pushed her roughly back, clinging to her in panting desperation. He kissed her roughly, a free hand pawing the length of her body as her hips jerked of their own will.

She was moaning, trying to slide her jeans off. He lent his hand to hers and as soon as her legs kicked free of the garment, moved his fingers to the dampness of her sex. She immediately began working on his pants, their lips still locked together.

She got them down his hips and he was fire in her hands.

"Hurry," she moaned. "Please hurry."

"Oh, Nance. Oh God."

He was in her, pounding like a teenager as she urged him on with gutteral sounds and grasping legs—and it was over in seconds. Even as he shuddered through orgasm, he realized that the excitement of the act was the excitement of something illicit. He felt as if he were screwing somebody else's wife. He looked at her face, at the slackness still there, and saw his own guilt mirrored in her eyes.

He rolled off her in disgust, his pants still hung up around his knees. Then he saw that she still tightly clutched the gold chain in her hand and became genuinely frightened.

"I don't want you to go," he said.

She sat up, avoiding eye contact with him. She looked embarrassed as she searched through the bedspread for her clothes. "I've got to go," she replied, and turned to look at the clock on the nightstand. "And soon. I'll miss my flight."

He stood, pulling up his pants and hooking the belt. "I'm asking you not to go," he said.

She was buttoning into her blouse. "I thought we were beyond that stage," she said coldly, pulling her hair out from where it had gotten caught under her shirt.

He twisted her to him, forcing eye contact. "I'm telling you not to go," he said. "I want you here where you belong."

She returned the diamond hardness of his eyes, then unclasped the chain, fixing it around her neck.

He moved away then, crossing the length of the room. "If you get on that plane, I can't guarantee that the children and I will be here when you get back."

She had become totally impassive. Bending slightly, she picked up the suitcase. "I can't deal with that right now," she said softly, and walked out of the room.

He followed her to the door, watching her moving down the long hallway. "You still love him, don't you?" he screamed. "You still want that bastard!"

Her shoulders noticeably tightened, but she continued walking away without turning around.

XIX

Glen Burnie, Maryland

April 14—NOON

Cassady squatted in the darkness of his living room, the shades pulled tight, and tried to sink back into the jungle. Face blackened, he wore his tiger-striped fatigue pants and black pajama top of the Vietnamese. Each piece of clothing had the number 47 inked on it, his identity. He wore a clutch belt with a K-bar knife stuck in it. He was barefoot.

The trick was to become part of it, part of the life of the jungle. If you could become a part of it, part of a bush, part of a tree, you could exist safely within its protective bosom. Despite what went on around you, you could be invisible. You could be whatever you wanted to be.

The CIA had bailed him out of a jail in Bien-hoa around Christmas of '67. He had wasted several civilians during a bar fight. When they took him out he thought they were arresting him for fragging some candy-assed second lieutenant the week before. Instead, they told him they were aware of the incident but had heard he was a good point man and they had a job for him if he wanted it. Cassady, knowing they knew about the fragging, had no choice.

Within days he was in a provincial reconnaissance unit working directly with the Navy SEAL squads, the Black Berets as they were called when President Kennedy had formed them, and the Green Berets in the early sixties.

Called Project Phoenix, and under the direct supervision of the CIA, its main purpose was to weaken the infrastructure of the North Vietnamese through terrorism. Basically they used the cover of night to sneak into heavily guarded VC strongholds, places where Americans had never been, and to assassinate tax collectors or other public figures, usually dismembering the bodies somehow to let the people know who was responsible.

Cassady got them in and out, and he smiled there in the dark to think of it. The jungle was his companion, dense and inscrutable, it mirrored the impenetrability of his own mind. He blended with it, merged with it, learned to walk like a Vietnamese, learned to make a Vietnamese shadow. In the jungle he had identity. Where strength and cunning were the measure of worth, he had been the most worthwhile member of society.

They had traveled with the SEAL squads and representatives of the Rand Corporation, who were doing what they called "perturbation research," measuring the value of the terrorism tactics on the VC chain of command. The studies had meant nothing though, since the VC worked with an informal, local-leader concept which was totally autonomous. There had been, in other words, no infrastructure to disrupt. But Cassady didn't mind. The longer the operation went on, the longer he got to stay in the jungle, the longer he got to be near Kim.

Kim. He wouldn't leave Nam without Kim this time. Whatever it took, she would be at his side.

After the war, when they had forced him from Saigon without her, they had sent him to the farm in Pennsylvania for regular CIA training. They had liked his instincts. His instincts were just what they needed. Ever since, he had done covert work with various stations in various South and Central American countries—a few coups, a few killings. Nothing very exciting. Nothing like Nam. It was nothing like the old days, when he ruled in the kingdom of the blind.

And now he was going back.

The phone rang. It rang again. He unfolded slowly, standing casually. This was the call that would change his life. It bothered him that they had taken so long getting everything together, but it didn't surprise him, given the nature of bureaucracy.

He picked up the kitchen wallphone, bringing the receiver to his ear without answering.

"Cassady?" came a familiar voice on the other end of the line.

"Who's this?" he asked.

"It's me—Cowboy."

Cassady felt the suspicions climbing his back. The creeps, he used to call it when he was younger. "Should we scramble?"

"Naw. Not this time. I'm going to need to get with you."

"What about?"

"Burial sites, if you know what I mean."

The guns! Why did Sorrel need to know about where the guns were buried? "I must be missing something here," Cassady said. "Nobody's contacted me about you. I need to hear about the operation. When do we get briefed?"

There was a short pause on the other end. "I don't think you're getting briefed, partner. This is a one-man job."

Cassady used his entire concentration to keep his voice casual. "They chose you?" he asked, and it came out just right.

"And I need to know something that only you know. Can I come by and pick up a list?"

Cassady's mind raced. Unsecured phone. Contact at his residence. No one had ever come to his residence. Something big was up. His senses tingled. "Sure," he said. "You can come by."

"How about forty-five minutes?" Cowboy said.

"No," Cassady answered. "I don't keep the list here. I'll have to go get it. It will take some time. How much do we have?"

"I've got a plane out at eight tonight. I'll need this stuff soon as possible."

"It's a distance from here," Cassady said. "Best I can do is about seven. That's it."

There was silence on the line, and he could almost feel Cowboy's thought processes in motion. "Maybe I can leave from your place," he said at last.

"Good. I'll have the list here at seven sharp. Sorry if it's inconvenient."

"Can't be helped," Cowboy said. "We'll have a farewell drink."

"Sure," Cassady said. "See you."

He hung up the phone. Sorrel didn't have nearly his experience in the field in Nam. He had to have been picked because Cassady had been dropped for some reason. No matter.

The never-used yellow pages sat in a kitchen drawer near the phone. He opened to the R section and found the pages headed, Rental. The address closest to him was in Glen Burnie. He picked up the phone and dialed the number.

"Kirkland Rental," a female voice answered on the other end.

"Yes," Cassady said. "I was wondering if you could rent me an acetylene torch."

"Just a second," she said. Cassady waited patiently, his breathing even, controlled. After a minute the woman came back on. "We've got one torch left. That will be twenty dollars an hour, or a hundred dollars for the whole day."

"I'll take it for the day," Cassady said.

"Payment method, Mr. . . . ?"

"Johnson," Cassady said. "Larry Johnson. I'll pay in cash, including the deposit. Can I come in right now?"

"Certainly, sir. We'll reserve it and look for you soon."

"Thanks," Cassady said, and hung up. He glanced at his watch. It was a little past twelve. He had to hurry. There was a lot to be done today.

CONGRESS DEBATES MIA ISSUE

WASHINGTON, (AP)—Both houses of Congress today began debate over the MIA hostage issue in hopes of passing resolutions and recommendations to President Herrod. Emotions were running high in all directions with most of the President's support breaking down along party lines.

Insiders say that Republicans stand to gain the most political ground from the issue because of their involubility as far as the decision-making process goes. "In an election year, this is the worst possible thing that could happen to Simon Herrod," said Rep. Floyd Jackson (D-Fla). "This thing could be the political football of all time."

Asked if the shortness of time involved would make it difficult for Congress to draft anything useful, Speaker of the House Sam Fulton said, "Congress can't turn around and spit in seven days."

XX

Camp Friendship

April 14—5:00 P.M.

Dr. Duong Quynh Hoa bent to look at the indentation in the man's naked shoulder, probing it first with a straight pin, then tenderly, with her fingers. "Any sensation, Colonel Ridley?"

"All very dull," he answered, his steel-gray eyes hard.

She moved away to wash her hands in the basin on the instrument table. "You can put your shirt on," she said, drying her hands.

Ridley climbed off the old wooden table and retrieved his shirt from the back of a chair.

"You're luckier than many of the others," Dr. Hoa told him as he slipped into the shirt. "The broken clavicle and a touch of anemia seen to be your only problems. No malaria, anyway."

A chic woman in her midfifties, Dr. Hoa had been raised in an affluent family of *collaborateurs*, the Vietnamese who embraced French colonial rule in exchange for favors. She had joined the French Communist party while studying medicine in Paris, returning to Saigon in 1954 to join the resistance against President Diem and his U.S. supporters where she had worked as a covert agent while practicing medicine. Ultimately she had risen to the appointment of deputy minister of health in the provisional revolutionary government. A Communist all her life, she was now bitter, decrying the northern rule that was ruining her Saigon hospital through mismanagement, corruption, privilege, and repression.

"It happened about four years ago," Ridley said, as he buttoned the shirt and tucked it into khaki pants. "A rifle butt for helping some Montagnard Cambodians escape from the work crew. The professional torturers we had at the Hanoi Hilton wouldn't have broken any bones."

She smiled at his candor. "I don't think I should do anything with the collarbone," she said. "Your own doctors can take care of it . . . when you return to your country."

It was Ridley's turn to smile. "You almost said, 'if,' Doctor. Don't you think we'll be returning home?"

She moved to a beautiful wooden cabinet and removed one of the hundreds of brown glass bottles that sat within. "Captivity doesn't seem to have broken your spirit."

"Quite the contrary," he returned. "In a strange sort of way, it's given me a sense of peace. I think—no, I'm certain, there's nothing anyone could do to me I'm not prepared for. I've seen it all, been through it all. Are you going to answer my question?"

She clucked her tongue. "Colonel Ridley," she said, smiling. "All right, I'll answer. I don't see your government paying the money. Why should they? It's all a lot of foolishness."

Dr. Hoa dumped several of the pills from the bottle into her hand.

"What will happen to us, then?" he asked.

"You need to watch yourself," she said. "It's not unknown that you're the ranking officer."

Their eyes met, proud people on common ground. "You speak honestly," he said.

She shrugged. "I enjoy a certain amount of, how do you say it, notoriety. I have many friends. But you, Colonel, you're dangerous."

"I'm just a civilian, once removed," he said.

She held out the pills. "Take these for anything you might have caught from the women this afternoon."

"I won't be needing them."

She snapped her hand closed. "See what I mean? Dangerous."

There was a sharp knock on the door. Dr. Hoa let her eyes linger on Ridley's for several seconds. "There's a Caribbean song they sing here that's very popular," she said, then softly sang:

> *"I see a boat on a river, it's sailing away,*
> *Down to the ocean, where to I can't say."*

The knock came again. The doctor put her hand on Ridley's arm. "Good luck to you, Colonel," she said, then turned to the door. "Come!"

A soldier opened the door and spoke to the doctor in Vietnamese.

"He wants you to go with him," she said. "Colonel Tin would like to speak with you."

Ridley nodded curtly. "Good-bye, Doctor," he said, and walked out with the soldier clutching his arm. They passed a line of squatting Americans waiting to see Dr. Hoa. For the first time Ridley noticed just exactly how strategically the guards were placed. They gave the illusion of not being there at all, but they were simply blending, working into the environment. There were also a great many of what Ridley could only assume were small TV cameras set here and there. They were being carefully watched at all times.

They moved steadily through the large administration building, dust dancing in the late-afternoon light that poured steadily through the open windows in the narrow halls. Ridley stopped walking just to see the guard's reaction. His jailer stopped with him, staring at him with unreadable eyes. The man's hand never left his arm, but neither did he apply pressure. After several seconds the guard motioned with his head that they should continue on, his free hand gripping his rifle strap. Ridley walked, satisfied with the experiment.

They moved into the yard. Many of the prisoners had just finished eating, rice with pork this time, and were filtering outside, talking. The AWOLs still kept to their own small group, and he absently wondered if they could be approached.

He slowed way down in the yard, making it look like the forward-moving guard was hustling him along. They passed Ferguson who was talking with a group of six men. Everything stopped as Ridley passed, all eyes following him.

The small cinder-block house at the far side of the compound was a featureless box with tiny windows set by the flat roof and an armed guard on either side of the metal front door. As Ridley neared it he could hear the hum of an air conditioner.

As they neared the door it suddenly burst open from the inside. Jenkins came hurrying out in the grasp of a soldier. They passed one another silently, but the anger in Jenkins's eyes spoke volumes.

The cool air hit him before they even got in the door. He smiled to feel it, cooler than he had known for many years. Inside, the blockhouse was a dark cocoon, wrapping him in cold, sterile air. They moved down a short hallway, past a room full of small television screens inset in the wall, and came to a stop before an unmarked door.

The guard knocked lightly. Ridley recognized the Vietnamese word for enter, and his man opened the door, ushering him into an empty office.

Ridley stood uneasily in the middle of the room, the guard bowing slightly and hurrying out, pulling the door closed behind him. It was a delicate room, smelling slightly of jasmine. Fragile Chinese and Vietnamese porcelain figurines stood in frozen postures of dance and meditation on shelves and polished tables with spindly legs. There were pictures over all the walls, photos of a small, wiry man in officer's uniform. One showed Ho Chi Minh and the officer shaking hands, another an obviously triumphant entry into Saigon, another showed the man looking serious with a group of officials at a long table. Ridley approached the pictures to get a closer look.

"That's a copy of the *Quan Doi Nhan Dan* in my hands," a voice said from behind him.

Ridley turned to see an older version of the man in the picture. Now, though, he was dressed in a western business suit.

"I know," Ridley said. "I've seen many copies of your army newspaper over the years, Colonel Tin."

"You know of me," he said, moving to the desk and taking a seat.

"You accepted the surrender of Saigon," Ridley said. "They showed me your picture in prison."

The man smiled, enjoying his fame. "Sit down, Colonel," he said. "I thought it was time for you and I to have a little chat, as you Westerners say."

Tin's English was good, if slightly thick. Ridley bet he spoke better French.

Ridley sat in a wooden armchair near the door. "What could you and I have to talk about?"

"Your friend Jenkins has told me you are organizing the camp, is that so?" Tin smiled.

Ridley tightened inside, but it didn't show. He refused to believe it. "By the terms of the Geneva Convention, I'm only required to give you my name, rank and serial number. Lieutenant Colonel Jason Ridley, United States Air . . ."

Tin held up a hand, laughing. "That's fine, Colonel," he

said. "But you can relax. There's nothing I could really want from you after all these years. You see? No guards are present, no stenographers. I was just corroborating what your friend has told me."

"You couldn't be," Ridley returned, speaking again after he saw the man's eyes narrow. "If Jenkins wouldn't give you people real information after years of real torture, why should he make up information after no torture?"

"That could be a point of debate," Tin said. "But perhaps another time." He shrugged. "You can't blame me for trying."

The man picked up a pen and began to write on a pad before him. He didn't speak again until he was finished. "This is my operation from top to bottom," he said, fixing Ridley with strong brown eyes. "I have conceived it as a way of getting you and your people back where they belong and getting my country some needed capital. I'm very proud of this operation. It's modern and up-to-date, and it's working smoothly. If all goes well, it should make a great many people happy when it's finished, and no one unhappy except a few petty Washington bureaucrats."

"You hold us against our will," Ridley said. "I fail to see the happiness."

"Yesterday is gone, Colonel Ridley," Tin said. "To dwell upon it is madness. Look ahead. Look at what you have left, not at what you have left behind. All is happiness."

"What if you don't get the money?"

Tin laughed again. "Your countrymen hated the imperialist war," he said. "Of course they'll pay. America is a very rich country. Surely they can spare a little for those they very nearly destroyed. It's the Christian thing to do, Colonel Ridley."

"This isn't why you brought me in here," Ridley stated.

"You're quite right," Tin answered. He opened his top desk drawer and pulled out two small cigars, Ridley shaking off the one he offered across the desk.

The man slid a glass ashtray near him, then lit the cigar with a silver Zippo lighter. He puffed delicately, savoring lightly the taste as if it were fine wine.

"This operation is my crowning achievement," Tin said quietly, "my magnum opus. I, of course, want it to run smoothly. Our American . . . guests are part of the operation, and you are their leader."

"You requested that we not organize," Ridley said.

"Yes, Colonel. That is exactly what we said." Tin puffed thoughtfully on the cigar for a moment. "And I meant just that. I want your assurance that you will not organize a chain of command."

"I will do what you require of me," Ridley said.

"My dear fellow," Tin replied, "can we not pull down the walls between us. As one man to another, will you not promise me that you won't organize?"

"Will you promise me that we will be set free, even if the money is not paid?" Ridley said.

Tin looked slightly annoyed, but it faded quickly. He shoved the piece of paper he had been writing on across the desk. "This is an agreement that you will not use your rank to organize your men. You will sign it please."

Ridley never even glanced at the paper. "I haven't signed anything since the day I was shot down nearly twenty years ago. I don't intend to start now."

"This is nothing, Colonel. A formality. Please sign it."

Ridley stood. "May I go, Colonel Tin, or am I being held here?"

Tin slid the paper back and placed it in the desk drawer. "You know, Colonel Ridley, we could just as easily send one man fewer back to the United States of America."

"That would leave someone else as ranking officer, wouldn't it?" Ridley put his hand on the knob. "May I go now?"

Tin's face was blank. "We'll speak again tomorrow," he said.

Ridley left without a word.

The heat blasted him as he stepped from the air-conditioned building. He'd have to have a talk with Jenkins. Thirty paces away, Ferguson and his cadre were watching him carefully. Ridley angled his walk slightly to move near them.

"Tonight," he said quietly as he passed and, without breaking stride, walked quickly away.

WASHINGTON, (AP)—In response to the current crisis in Vietnam, President Herrod announced today that Domestic Affairs Adviser Maurice Benstock would be assuming the position of Media Liaison to help speed the dissemination of information to the

American public. Benstock, a familiar figure in national television for many years, hopes to "close the information gap" between the administration and the public.

"We have a lot of faith in Maurice Benstock," the President said in making the announcement. "He is an expert in the field of communication and has a deep commitment to the people of the United States."

XXI

Glen Burnie, Maryland

April 14—6:58 P.M.

Cassady sat in front of the computer, picking out the last passport from the stack sitting beside him on the desk. He opened it using his .45 to hold the page while he typed in the name next to his picture.

PERKINS, RICHARD.

SMOKING OR NON, came the response.

SMOKING, Cassady typed, remembering that Richard Perkins smoked a pipe.

CLASS?

He had made the last reservation coach, so he decided to mix it up on this one. FIRST, he typed.

VALID PASSPORT?

YES.

It had been easy enough to break into the TWA reservation computers. He had used his company codes to access the DOD computers. There he was able to simply punch into the alphabetical listings of passwords the government kept on the computers of airlines that had overseas service. The purpose of the list was to give DOD unlimited access when checking into the background of possible Soviet bloc agents coming into the country. Cassady was using it to book himself some free rides.

PYMT METHOD.

DINERS CLUB, he typed, then made up a number for the machine.

There were several seconds of nonaction, then this appeared on the screen: THAT FLIGHT IS AVAILABLE ON A STANDBY BASIS ONLY.

Cassady stared for a minute, then smiled and typed. CONFIRMED STATE DEPARTMENT PRIORITY AJ-15. They'd track him down eventually this way, but by then it would be far too late.

RESERVATION CONFIRMED—FLIGHT 467—SYDN, AUS TO BANGK,THAI.

He picked up the notebook near the phone and scribbled down the data on the flight beneath the serpentine line of flight information. Then he wrote Richard Perkins next to the information, so he wouldn't forget who he was supposed to be.

The doorbell rang.

Cassady jerked to the sound. Albert had arrived. He quickly extricated himself from the program and unhooked the telephone modem.

The doorbell rang again. He stood in the narrow closet picking up his notebook and the three passports he'd be using. These were his personal identities; the company knew nothing about them. The pistol he stuck in the back of his pants.

The computer/scrambler stood humming on the low desk. He shut it off, smiled once over at the surprise he had made for Albert, set the passports and notebook on the empty dresser top, and answered the door.

"Beginning to think you'd slipped out for a cold one," Albert Sorrel said when Cassady opened the door.

Cassady smiled amiably and stepped aside for Albert to enter. "How you doing, Cowboy?"

The man strode in. Tall and lean, he wore a western-print shirt tucked into tight jeans.

They shook hands. "Been a long time," Albert said, fixing him with cold eyes. "Rico in '81, wasn't it?" The man looked around at the newly welded bars on the windows. "You expectin' some kind of trouble?"

Cassady shook it off. "Security," he said, turning to lead him into the house. "How about that drink?"

The man moved into the living room, sprawling his large

frame out on the sofa. "Just a short one, pard," he said. "I got a plane to catch."

Cassady nodded and went into the kitchen, made them each a bourbon and water. When he came back he placed Albert's drink on the table, then took a chair across from the sofa, realizing he'd never sat in it before.

"I was kinda surprised when they picked you instead of me for this one," he said, sipping the whiskey.

Albert's face betrayed no emotion as he pulled his legs off the table and sat up straight. He shrugged, then said, "Don't know nothing about any of that," and drank half the glass in one swallow.

Cassady leaned forward watching the man closely. "But you called me on the unsecured line."

"They told me it was okay," Albert said, cocking his head slightly.

"Wonder why they'd say that?"

Albert looked at his watch. "I'm going to be needing that list, ole buddy."

"You were only in on the tail end of Nam," Cassady said, putting his drink on the floor. "You probably don't even know the Bangkok contacts. I assume you'll be jumping off in Thailand."

Albert smiled wide, a gangly hand scratching his leg, moving slowly down toward his boots. "Now you don't want to know that." He chuckled. "Don't worry about it, Cass."

The .45 was in Cassady's hand. "I have to worry about it, *partner*," he said, snapping the barrel back quickly to cock it. "And let's get your hands out where I can see them."

Albert's expression never changed. He brought his hands out from his body, holding them there. "Never figured you to turn—"

"Shut up," Cassady said. "We don't have much time, remember?"

"Are you going to kill me?" Albert asked casually.

"Are you going to make me?" Cassady returned.

Albert took a deep breath and stared at the gun. "This ain't that big of a deal to me," he said at last. "Is it to you?"

Cassady nodded slightly.

"Son of a bitch," Albert said. "You didn't turn at all. It's that woman, ain't it? It's that damned Frenchy whore."

"She's not a whore," Cassady said low.

Albert threw back his head and laughed. "Call her what you want," he said. "You're still the dumbest fuck I've ever seen."

"That's enough," Cassady said. "Okay?"

Sorrel tightened his lips and nodded. "Look," he said seriously. "Have you thought this all the way out—"

"Where are your orders and the chit?" Cassady asked.

"In the car," Albert said, his face now blank, his eyes staring, shifting continuously. There was a tension about him.

"What's in the boot?" Cassady said.

"A little .25 automatic," Albert said. "Lady's gun. Nothing special."

"What else?"

"That's all."

Cassady held the gun out level in front of him. "I want you to take your clothes off," he said. "Fish out the .25 first."

Albert did as he was told, dropping the tiny, black automatic on the table.

"There's no way you're going to make it," he said when he was naked. "The whole damned company's in on this one."

"Yeah," Cassady said. "Walk away from the clothes."

Albert moved off several feet as Cassady went through the clothing. He found a knife in the other boot, then fished the man's car keys out of his pocket.

"I assume you're supposed to check in when you have the data," Cassady said. "Secured or no?"

The man licked his lips, eyes blinking.

"Don't think, Albert," Cassady said quickly. "Just answer. It would be a lot easier to kill you than keep you alive."

Albert nodded, his face relaxing somewhat. "Unsecured," he said. "They want everything to seem casual."

"What else do you know?"

Albert shook his head. "Nothing, Cass. I swear it. But I figure same as you. Unsecured wire, sudden change of plans . . . it sounds like permanent inactive. Probably because of the woman."

"Call them," Cassady said, using the gun to point toward the kitchen wallphone. "Remember. I know all the same words you know."

Albert nodded, dialing his section number. The connection was opened without a verbal response. "This is Cowboy," he said immediately. "The horses are in the corral. I'm heading out."

He hung up, turned to Cassady. "Not too late to change your mind. Promise I won't say anything."

"Save it," Cassady said. "Come with me."

He led the naked man through the house, to the master bedroom. He took him through the closet door and into the room with the terminal. There, at the back end of the room, stood a cage. It was lopsided and rusty, welded from junk metal. There were a few center bars missing. Just enough room for a thin man to squeeze in.

"Just like the Dinks used," Albert said.

"Get in," Cassady said, and watched Albert struggle his way through the small space. On the cage floor sat a canteen and a large bowl of rice. There was also an empty bucket.

"Even a pot to piss in," the man said, looking at the bucket.

The cage was not tall enough to allow Albert to stand erect. He was forced to adopt the Asian squat, his knees cracking loudly as he got down.

"Turn facing away," Cassady said, and when the man moved to face the back wall, he set the gun down and fired up the torch. He donned heavy gloves and goggles and welded the remaining bars in place, closing Albert Sorrel in completely.

When Cassady was finished, Albert, crablike, turned back around to face him. "This is really embarrassing, you know?" he said.

Cassady ignored him. He turned the still-lit torch toward the computer, melting and fusing the keyboard, then burning right through the CRT to destroy the guts within. "When they find you," he said, "tell them I'll do their job for them, but that I won't be coming back."

Cassady hurried around the large closet dragging everything away from Albert's reach through the bars. When he was through, he went into the bedroom and picked up his small suitcase, sticking the passports into his inside jacket pocket.

When he was ready he poked his head back into the closet for one last look. "Sorry it had to be you," he said to the squatting man.

Albert shrugged, flashing his toothy grin. "Hey," he said, "thanks for not killing me."

"What are friends for?" Cassady said, and walked out of the closet, then out of the house without another thought.

He got in his car and drove it a block away, parking in front of a vacant house. Then he walked back and climbed into Albert's old Karmann Ghia, driving it to Friendship Airport.

XXII

Chicago, Illinois —Sheraton Hotel

April 14—8:10 P.M.

Nancy Henderson stared across the small, round table at Marsha Ridley. Even in the subdued lighting of the lobby's open-air bar, Marsha was showing her age. What had once been highly toned, smooth-as-milk skin was now dry looking. The latest crisis had etched dark circles under her eyes, and it was in the eyes most of the age seemed to stay. They seemed dull and hopeless, the eyes of an old woman waiting for death.

"So Jason's been confirmed?" Nancy asked, staring down into her glass of white wine to avoid watching Marsha's face.

"He hasn't shown up on any of the films," Marsha answered, looking over at a commotion by the registration desk. Two women stood holding one another, crying loudly, as a TV crew ran around furiously, trying to capture the moment. "But they read his name off a list a few hours ago."

"I wonder what that means?"

Marsha shook her head. "Maybe he's hurt...I don't know." Her face flushed for a second and she clamped her eyes tightly shut, taking a deep breath. When she opened her eyes again, they were glassy. "Maybe he just refuses to go on television." She laughed dryly. "Jason always was a hard-headed son of a . . ."

Her shoulders shook and she began to cry, quietly, with dignity. Nancy reached out and took the woman's hands, letting her come along at her own pace. Sometimes she felt guilty for remarrying when women like Marsha gave up all claims to life when their husbands disappeared.

"I'm sorry," Marsha was saying, and she daubed at her eyes with a cocktail napkin, smearing mascara. "I was stronger than this until I got here. I suppose it's seeing everyone, how they've changed. God, so much time has gone by."

"Some things haven't changed," Nancy replied, a purposeful edge to her voice.

Marsha stiffened physically. "How right you are," she said sternly. "Have you heard anything more about Jerry Prescott coming here?"

Nancy nodded. 'I confirmed it myself with the State Department," she said, and took a sip of wine. "He's going to try to talk us out of any action, you know."

"Well, it won't work this time." Marsha absently fingered the ring on the chain around her neck. "I don't know how we're going to do it, but we've got to raise the money."

"And find a way to negotiate with it and transport it. And all in a few days' time."

"That's going to take some organization," Marsha said, "and strong leadership. Have you thought anymore about what I suggested on the phone?"

There was more noise from around the lobby. It was starting to fill up now; the carnival was in town. Besides the NAMWives, the TV and newspaper correspondents, other groups were intruding on the media time. Small camps of antiransom groups were counterdemonstrating in the ultramodern lobby. A Texas millionaire and his entourage were present, plus parents of MIA groups who as yet hadn't committed to a plan of action. Local labor unions were there to tender their support, plus feminist groups and other organizations with strange, eclectic-sounding names.

The noise level had risen so high it completely drowned out the woman in formal dress who played the harp in the lobby.

"I'll do whatever the organization needs me to do,"

Nancy said. "If my duty falls in a leadership position, I won't deny it."

"Good," Marsha said, and drank from her scotch and water. " I think whatever we do, is going to have to happen fast."

Nancy agreed. "We've got to show some kind of solid front by tomorrow. How long until our first meeting?"

Marsha held up a wristwatched arm. "Fifteen minutes," she said.

"We'll get our leadership first, then settle the moral issues, then figure out how to raise the money." Nancy picked up her purse, fishing through it for money for the drinks. "Nobody talks to the press officially until we've done those three things," she said. "We must act as a unified group. It's the only way to make this work."

A sudden hush had fallen over the lobby. Both women turned to stare back toward the big glass entrydoors. A contingent of marines in full uniform, rifles on their shoulders, marched in, in perfect step and began taking up positions around the lobby.

"You don't think they'd arrest us?" Marsha said anxiously.

Nancy stood, dropping a five-dollar bill on the table. "They'd better not," she said. "We haven't done anything to get arrested for."

"Do you think that matters to them?" Marsha asked, standing, clutching her handbag tightly in both hands.

"I don't know," Nancy said.

They walked toward the elevators. NAMWives had a suite on the twentieth floor where all their regional leaders would be meeting for preliminary recommendations. Larger meetings with the membership present, would be held later to vote on proposed ideas. It would be a process that would probably go on all night.

They made their way through the thick lobby crowds, waving to friends or yelling encouragement. Nancy was amazed at the turnout. It seemed there were a thousand women in the lobby, all wearing wedding rings around their necks. She was having the beginnings of an idea.

"I hope Mary Ann thought to have a lot of coffee sent up," Marsha said. "It's going to be a long night."

"And painful," Nancy replied, but her thoughts were elsewhere.

"Come on," Marsha said, waving above the crowd. "Sandy Miller's holding the elevator for us."

Nancy squeezed her arm. "You go on. I want to check the desk for messages."

Marsha stared, her eyes reading more than Nancy would have liked. The woman started to speak, then thought better of it. She smiled instead. "See you in a minute," she called, and hurried off to the waiting elevator.

Nancy moved between the lines of people at the registration desk, catching one of the red-jacketed staff between customers. "Messages for four twenty-one," she said.

The woman smiled automatically and moved to the honeycomb behind the counter, coming out with a small handful of messages.

Nancy took them, reading as she walked to the elevator. Most were from media people wanting interviews or statements. When the group had been active, Nancy, through a combination of circumstances, had become their spokesperson. She *was* the organization in the minds of many because of it. Perhaps it was only natural that she be the one they thought of now. Several of the messages were from old friends making contact, and several more were from well-wishers. Two or three were hate messages.

There were two messages of particular interest, though. One was from a Mr. Nhu who requested an urgent conference at her convenience, giving his room number and begging that she stop in when she had a free moment. This message went into the pocket of her suit jacket.

The other message was from Sid. Though it was simple and straightforward, she read it several times: Come home now. If not, children and I will be gone when you return.

Nancy had cried out her tears on the flight to Chicago. She simply crumpled the message and dropped it in an ashtray near the elevators.

Jerry Prescott sat like a condemned man in the back of the limo. He could see people streaming in and out of the front entrance of the hotel. But he sat in the shadows of the car watching them watching him. They would stop, pointing out the limo to their friends and talking behind their hands.

This was a mistake. They should have sent anybody else but him. The maddest part was that this whole venture was probably organized by Benstock to get him away from the President. If only Myrna had come with him. If only.

Charlie Johnston and Tod Barrows came out of the hotel, walking down the small flight of stone steps beside the drive. Charlie stayed there on the sidewalk looking around while Tod crossed the drive to the limo.

He opened the door and leaned in his somber face. "You're checked in," he said. "Got you a suite on the twentieth floor with room for Charlie and me to sleep."

"You look unhappy, Tod," Prescott said. "What's wrong?"

The man took a breath and looked around. His tie dangled lazily in the cool spring breeze off Lake Michigan. "Security's going to be a bitch," he said, still looking around. "Every crazy in this part of the world is here right now. We got a squad of marines in the lobby which might discourage something big, but that leaves only the two of us on you."

"What about local help?" Prescott asked.

Barrows shook his head and straightened. "Got no use for 'em," he said, and moved away from the door. "Wouldn't be good to sit out here too long."

Prescott climbed out, into the cool night, and walked to the hotel flanked by his Secret Servicemen. It doesn't project a good image, Jerry thought, to come to something like this with your bodyguards visible. But the alternative scared him to death.

They walked into the lobby. All eyes were on them. They wore no uniforms, commanded no fanfare, drew no special attention to themselves—yet there was not an eye or a camera that wasn't turned in their direction.

A marine had cleared and held an elevator for them. Jerry entered it gratefully, surprised at his own relief when the doors slid shut and they started up. He knew then that this was going to be the most difficult time of his entire life.

Nancy Henderson stared at the lake down below. The wind was up, whitecaps just barely visible frothing the dark waters, banging the sailboats gently in their slips. She had come here once with Sid, her first time away after Timmy's birth. They had had a wonderful time, one they both fondly remembered. The memory could never be the same now.

"What about the money?" asked Ginger Mowery, the

western regional director. "I assume we'll ask for donations, but how will we process it?"

"That's the part that has given me the most problem," Marsha said. "Once we raise the money, we'll have to purchase gold or something. Could we just run it all through some international broker or something?"

Nancy turned away from the window. The suite was large and elegant, with French provincial furnishings that made it look like a small house. The ten women meeting there fit comfortably into the place, and it could accommodate more if necessary.

She went over to the big silver coffee service the hotel had provided and poured herself a cup, while listening to all the money ideas the others had. She had her own feelings about it, but wanted to hear what everyone else had to say first.

A TV played soundlessly. It was morning of the third day in Vietnam and the latest string of testimonials from the prisoners was running. She wondered how they determined who spoke and when.

"This all seems so large," Jane Pickens said. The woman wore jeans and a tie-dyed T-shirt, almost as if she had stopped time back in '69 when her husband had disappeared. "Could it all be too big for us? I mean, the whole tone of the organization from the first was support for wives, then passive coercion of government agencies. This is so . . . active for most of us."

Nancy flared. "We lost before. Last time—and you used the right word—we stood passively by while they condemned our husbands to living death. I could never do that again. I don't care if none of you go along with me. I'm not going to sit by again, and so help me, I'm going to convince as much of the membership as I can that I'm right. We're so overburdened by our conditioning to be weak that we accept it ourselves. No more."

She sipped her coffee then carried the cup to an end table. "I've got an idea about raising the money, too." She looked at Marsha, the woman nodding encouragement in return. It helped. "I did some calculating awhile ago. Gold is sitting at about four hundred dollars an ounce right now. That means we have to come up with about two hundred tons of the stuff to make a deal."

She walked to the wet bar and picked up an empty plastic ice bucket. She returned to the group and held out the bucket. "I know it's not much," she said, "but here's a start."

She pulled hard against the chain around her neck and the ring came off in her hand. She let it slide into the bucket. "A few grams," she said, "but what if every woman in the country, every mother, every wife, were to contribute her wedding ring? It would add up in a hurry."

Marsha stood up almost immediately and walked to the bucket. Her eyes closed, she pulled the ring from around her neck and dropped it in with Nancy's. The others stood silently and moved to the bucket, each one pulling off her ring.

"This is *our* fund-raiser and *our* sign of solidarity," Nancy said, as she watched the rings plunk into the container. "By this action we will show just how serious our intentions are, while at the same time coalescing the rest of America."

"It will also embarrass the government," Marsha said. "So many 'poor women' giving up such important possessions to free those men."

"Yeah!" Mary Ann said, dropping her ring in with the others. "I hope you choke on this, Herrod."

The women laughed and applauded so loudly they almost didn't hear the telephone ringing in the separate bedroom. Marsha ran to get it, coming back solemnly a moment later.

"Jerry Prescott's here," she said. "In a suite just down the hall."

"Good," Nancy said, moving toward the door. "Let's get the ball rolling right now."

Jerry Prescott sat nursing a scotch and a headache in the barely lit living room of his suite. Johnston and Barrows, sometimes knowing him better than he knew himself, moved quietly around in the other rooms, checking security precautions and leaving him be. Somewhere in a back bedroom, a telephone man was installing his open line to the White House.

He closed his eyes and leaned his head back on the couch. He felt like a child throwing a temper tantrum. He had always done what was expected of him, always the "right thing" by someone else's definition. And now he was balking.

At his age, he suddenly was questioning what he had always *known* to be right. It was stupid.

Didn't the government need him to do what was best for all? And his childish reaching out to Myrna after all these years, what was that supposed to accomplish? He had gone to her like a kid to its mother when things got tough. No wonder she resented it. Even so, he wished desperately that she was there. His life, his values, were in a turmoil he had never known before. He didn't know if he could handle it alone.

He heard the sound of angry voices in the hall and sat up straight. There was a knock on the door, Tod Barrows hurrying silently across the room to get it. He opened the door a crack, and Prescott could see the black marine on duty outside. Barrows and the man talked in low voices for a minute.

"What is it?" Prescott called into the darkness.

Barrows turned apologetically. "Some women out here," he said. "Say they represent NAMWives and want to talk to you. I told them you'd meet with them tomorrow."

He recognized a voice outside, vigorously protesting— Nancy Henderson. They had gone at it more than once in the Nixon days.

"Let them in," Prescott said, and straightened his tie. His shoes lay near him on the floor. He almost left them off, but changed his mind at the last second.

"But, Mr. Secretary..." Barrows began.

"Let them in, Tod," Prescott said wearily. "May as well get it over with."

He was still bent over tying his shoes when Nancy Henderson walked in with five others. He remembered most of them from the old days, but couldn't bring up their names. Tod turned the lights up.

"Hello, Jerry," Nancy said, and Prescott knew the familiarity had a purpose.

"Hello, Nancy," he replied, smiling wanly at the others. "Never thought our paths would ever cross again. Sorry the circumstances are—"

"We protest your presence at our meeting," she interrupted.

"Sit down, would you all?" Prescott said. "Can I get you anything...coffee...?"

"You can get us a couple of billion dollars," one of the other women said. She was totally gray-headed, much older than last time he had seen her, but it seemed her name was . . . Ridley.

Most of the women sat, though Nancy Henderson kept her feet, staring.

"Do you . . . represent the group as a whole?" he asked.

"We will," Nancy said. "We'll have our list of demands by tomorrow. But I refuse to negotiate with you."

He looked at them, at the determination in their faces. "Afraid I'm it," he said. "The President's not real excited you people are even meeting."

"Is that what you came to tell us?" Henderson asked.

"In a sense," Prescott replied. "I want to tell you several things, and . . . ask you several things."

"Here we go," Nancy said with contempt.

Prescott looked at his drink on the table, figuring it would be bad form for him to take it now. "I want you to know," he began, "that I'm totally sympathetic with your problem, I . . ."

"You're a hit man!" Henderson said. "You've been sent down here to shoot us down, to make us promises that will shut us up. You've had experience fucking people, Jerry. Of course they sent you."

"Now, wait a minute . . ." Barrows said, moving to the group.

Prescott put up a hand. "Go back to what you were doing, Tod," he said quietly.

"Yes, sir," Barrows said, moving reluctantly away.

"I'm here only to present the President's views on this subject," Prescott said. "Nothing more."

Nancy walked up to where he sat, her face vicious, animal-like. "I hate you," she whispered. "I watched you day after day for years tell us with such sincerity that Nixon and his people were doing all that was possible to bring our husbands home when you weren't doing anything. I sat by while hundreds of grieving women clung to your words of hope like life rafts to keep themselves from drowning. Did you feel proud of what you did? Did it make you feel like a big man to dig our graves a little deeper each day?"

Prescott brought a hand to his face. It was shaking. All of it came back, all the lies, all the deceptions. It was as if the clock had been turned back. "It wasn't like that," he said. "I didn't really..."

"You and your friends," she said, "selling out those who had shed their lifeblood for you at the Paris talks just to buy a quicker pullout so your boy could get reelected. You're slime, Jerry, and we don't want to be around you. You're worse than the worst criminal who ever lived. How can you stand to live with yourself after what you've done? How can you come up here and try to do it again?"

"That's about enough!" came a voice from the doorway.

They all turned to see Myrna Prescott standing there, a light coat and overnight bag in her hands. Her eyes were hard as she threw her things to the floor and strode up to the group.

"How can you possibly know the hell my husband went through back in those days?" she demanded. "Were you around when he woke up screaming in the middle of the night? Were you there when he drank himself into stupors and contemplated suicide for what they made him do?"

"Nobody makes anybody do anything," Nancy said, but her voice had lost some of its edge.

"He didn't know anymore than you did," Myrna said. "They kept him in the dark, too. When he found out, he wanted to die. I've never seen a human being so torn up."

Jerry sat, incredulous. He thought he had hidden all his feelings from Myrna to spare her.

"Jerry Prescott is the kindest, most compassionate man I know," Myrna said, and her eyes drifted to his for just a second. "He'd never intentionally hurt anyone... he couldn't. All he's ever tried to do is the right thing. Sometimes in politics it's difficult to figure out what the right thing is. He's not perfect."

She walked up nose to nose with Nancy, and said, "Are you?"

Nancy retreated a couple of steps, then motioned for her people to get up. "We'll have our demands in the morning," she said. "We'll listen to yours, then. But be absolutely certain—you're not going to bullshit us this time."

"I don't intend to," Prescott said, and looked at Myrna, who smiled tentatively at him.

The women left, Barrows going discreetly into the bedroom, leaving them alone.

He stood, moving to his wife. "Hi," he said.

"Room for one more?" she asked.

"You were pretty good."

"Somebody's got to look after you."

"Myrna, I . . ."

"Look," she interrupted. "I'm here. I don't know what it means, okay? Just one step at a time."

"Sure," he said, and they embraced there in the Sheraton as if they'd never embraced before.

CHINA CONDEMNS VIETNAM

PEKING, (AP)—In an official communiqué, the People's Republic of China today condemned Vietnam's holding of American servicemen, calling the action "reprehensible."

The communiqué, issued at a diplomatic function honoring trade agreements between the U.S. and mainland China, also said, "These are the actions of an irresponsible and dangerous regime. The whole world should stand together in protest."

China and the Republic of Vietnam have been unofficially at war since the midseventies over border misunderstandings.

XXIII

Camp Friendship

April 14—11:32 P.M.

Lieutenant Colonel Jason Ridley, stripped to his underwear, lay on top of the covers in the darkened hootch. Overhead fans cranked noisily, their circulating air keeping the cherry end of his cigarette glowing bright in the blackness. Double-thick mosquito netting was drawn on the windows,

light from the yard filtering through the cracks. The smell of
DDT hung heavily in the air, an odor he hadn't been around
for years, but one that was instantly recognizable. Outside,
he knew four guards were posted at the building, just like at
every building. He also knew that at least some of them were
probably asleep. The barracks camera pointed down the line
of bunks, its red eye gleaming. He wondered how effective it
was in the dark.

Ridley waited, tensed. Earlier in the day Jenkins had
patted him on the back, then walked off. It was their old
POW-camp code. The man wanted to talk, but wasn't going
to do it unless it was absolutely safe. Around the hootch he
could hear other voices whispering to one another, telling
stories of what they'd do when they were released; but
even those voices were dying down now. Camp Friendship
was finally going to sleep. Jason Ridley's night was just
beginning.

Harry appeared to be asleep in the bunk beside him, but
he knew better. The man was waiting, waiting as he had done
so many times over the last decade. He knew Harry, knew
him better than he had known his own wife. He knew Harry
was lying there, feigning sleep, while his brain was racing
furiously. What frightened him was the thought of what was
going through that brain.

There was the sound of movement from down the end of
the long room. Ridley rose slightly on his elbows, looking
down the rows of shadows to see Ferguson sitting up in the
last bunk. With a quick motion, he waved him back to
reclining.

It had been easy enough to get his key personnel
into his hootch. Charlie wasn't used to them yet, so
they simply substituted people and names with others
sympathetic to them. There was a chance involved, the
biggest Ridley wanted to take for awhile, but he felt it
necessary.

When Ferguson lay down, Ridley turned back in his own
bunk to find Jenkins staring across the darkness at him. "I
could kill you," the man whispered.

"Cigarette?" Ridley asked, holding the pack across the
space separating them. Jenkins just stared at the pack until
Ridley pulled it back.

"What are you trying to do to us?" Jenkins said, his voice

too loud. He looked around quickly, then lowered his tone. "You're trying to ruin everything."

"What are you talking about, Harry?" Ridley asked, and it hurt him to lie to the man.

"Don't bullshit me," Jenkins said. "Something's going on. The air reeks of it. And I notice your bald-headed friend from the yard is bunked in here now. He wasn't yesterday."

"What's the point, Harry?"

"That's what I'm askin' you. What are you trying to do to us?"

Ridley pulled another cigarette from his pack, lighting it on the stub of the one he was finishing. Then he leaned over the edge of his bunk and crushed the old one out on the wood floor. "I don't know what to say to you," he whispered around a lungful of smoke. He almost told the man he was taking over as CO, then backed off, lying instead. "I'm not doing anything."

"Then why did they interrogate me today?"

Ridley lay on his back and stared toward the sound of the fan blades. "They interrogated us for the same reason," he said. "They know I'm senior officer and they don't want any trouble starting, that's all."

"I covered your ass today," Jenkins said. "I didn't tell them about your meeting with old skinhead out in the yard."

"Well, I appreciate it," Ridley replied, taken aback. "Though I wouldn't think that..."

"I did it for old time's sake," Jenkins said harshly, and there was real agitation in his voice. "I won't do it again."

Ridley sat up abruptly, swinging his legs over the edge of the bunk and staring. He and Jenkins had lived with abuse for years, had stayed alive by their ability to take punishment for one another without losing their inner strength. "What are *you* saying?"

"I'm saying that I'm not going to let you fuck this up," Jenkins hissed. "I'm saying if I catch you trying anything that could mess up our release, I'll turn you in myself."

"Harry..."

"I mean it, Jase."

They looked at one another, the friendship and support of many years dissolving in seconds. Even in the darkness

Ridley could see how small and frightened the man had become.

"I don't have any more fight left in me," Jenkins said softly, sobbing. "I just can't hold it together anymore, not now. I've got to protect myself from now on."

"I understand," Ridley said, but he really didn't. No matter what else, they were both still representatives of the United States government. Jenkins's words were treasonous and dangerous. The man was willing to sell out his own kind, and despite all that existed between them, Ridley knew that much of their bond had been based on principles that he still felt were operative.

There were no more words between them, nothing more to say. They rolled away from one another, facing opposite directions.

Ridley lay that way for another two hours, making sure Jenkins was asleep. Passivity he didn't mind. What scared him was the thought that Jenkins could take an active part in trying to catch him at something, all under the guise of "protecting himself."

Finally, when the guards had made their 2:00 A.M. check and there was no noise save the fans, Jason Ridley rolled quietly out of his bunk and crawled like a baby to the back of the hootch.

"I was beginning to think that something had happened." Ferguson said as he joined Ridley on the floor between the last bunk and the wall. Several others huddled around, Ridley shaking hands with each in turn.

He told them about Jenkins and about his fears concerning the man.

"We may have to take care of him," Ferguson said. "We can't let him jeopardize the entire operation."

"I've been with this man for over fifteen years," Ridley said. "It isn't that simple."

"Besides," one of the others, a one-armed man, said, "how could we do it without raising suspicion."

"Let's just table this, okay?" Ridley said. "If problems with Harry ever get out of hand, *I'll* take care of it."

"This is bigger than you," someone said. Ridley stared at him. He had long hair and a beard. His was not the look of someone who had spent half his life in a prison camp.

"You're out of line, soldier," Ridley said, surprised at how quickly the trappings of command came back. "Who are you?"

"Larry Frank," the man said, giving no rank.

"Where did they keep you?"

"Nowhere," the man answered defiantly.

"He's one of the AWOLs," Ferguson said.

"What?" Ridley was amazed. "What's he doing here?"

"We all need each other," the one-armed man said.

Ridley looked at them. Besides Ferguson, Frank, and the one-armed man, whose name was Shinsky, there were two others Ridley remembered from the old days at the Hanoi Hilton. Both fliers, captains, and good men.

"I ain't never been in prison before," Larry Frank said. "I hate it. But the shit of it is, if I go back like this, they'll slap me in prison for the rest of my life. If we can fight our way out, maybe me and the others will get a break back in the states."

Ridley looked through the darkness, appalled at the man, at everything he stood for. "So, while you've been collaborating with the enemy, living off the fat of the land all these years, the rest of us were suffering and dying for our country."

"Who was the 'enemy' in Vietnam, Colonel?" Frank said. "*We* were the only intruders I ever saw."

"I don't like it any better than you do," Talbott, one of the captains, said. "But what he said about needing to make this work makes sense. Besides, his people are in better shape than ours, they're stronger, healthier."

"Let's stop kidding ourselves," Ferguson said. "There's no love lost between us and them, but we can't get by without them. Many of them are local and really know the area. If we do get out of here, we'll have to have someplace to go. They can fix us up."

Ridley stared over at the man. This was a night of change, of shifting values. They called it situation ethics. "If we're to work together, you and your men must be willing to take orders from me. The chain of command must be observed."

Frank nodded. "We've already discussed this and are willing to go along."

"I'll have to be honest and tell you I'm not completely

happy with this, but," he stuck his hand out again, "if you are in my command, you will be treated with the same dignity and respect as my other men."

Frank took his hand, responding warmly. "I do believe you mean that."

"Now what?" Shinsky asked.

"Now we begin," Ridley said. "First we've got to understand this situation for exactly what it is. American soldiers are being held in an enemy prison camp for ransom. Ransom implies the threat of death should the ransom demand not be met. Therefore, the government of Vietnam is acting illegally in holding us this way. According to the terms of the Geneva Convention, it is our duty as soldiers to try and effect a prison break at the first available opportunity.

"You must never acknowledge me in public," Ridley said. "They're going to be watching me closely." He nodded to Ferguson. "Jim will be my liaison. Orders from him will be like orders from me. He is the only one I'll maintain any contact with. Now, we've got to know what we're dealing with." He pointed to Frank. "Can you get me a map of the area?"

The man nodded. "We'll have to make one, but it should be no problem. We should probably head west and get across the Cambodian border, then make our way to Thailand. We should try to get transport."

"We may have enough trucks here at the compound," Slater, the other captain, said. He had a small, regulation moustache. "I'll check it out and see if I can come up with somebody to pick the motor-pool locks and hot-wire the machines."

"Fine," Ridley said. "We'll need to know the number, disbursement, and disposition of all VC military in the compound. I want to know where all those blasted cameras are, too. Also, we'll have to know about the numbers and locations of weapons."

"I'll delegate it," Ferguson said. "It shouldn't take too long to come up with all that."

Ridley nodded. "Good. We'll meet here again tomorrow night and see what we have to work with. Whatever we do, it will have to be put together in a hurry. By tomorrow night I want each of you to have a tentative escape plan. We'll think on it all day, then put our heads together."

"Colonel," Shinsky said, resting his chin on a crooked knee. "What about . . . what about the ones who won't want to go? There might be a lot of those."

"I know," Ridley said, thinking of Jenkins. "We'll have to think about that."

He scooted out of the group, not wanting to tempt the fates at this time with a long meeting. "Tomorrow night," he whispered before crawling back to his bunk. "And nobody but you gentlemen are to know I'm in charge."

"Yes, sir." Their whispers followed him down the rows of sleeping men.

He took one look at Jenkins. The man was faced away from him, his breath rising and falling in a steady pattern. He climbed into his bunk, trying to force sleep through his excitement. It wasn't going to be easy.

In the bunk beside, Harry Jenkins pretended to sleep through barely controlled anger. Ridley was trying to ruin everything. And they were so close to going home. Why couldn't the man just leave well enough alone? They had done their duty, done it over and above the call. It was time to rest now, to let others work out the details.

What to do? To turn him in now might get Ridley but leave his plans intact. He'd wait for awhile. He'd watch for awhile. He'd keep his eyes and his ears open, then make his move when the time was right.

STUDENTS DEMONSTRATE

WASHINGTON (AP)—For the first time since the late 1960s, college students are protesting again in large numbers—only this time the stand is a lot more hawkish. "We're watching our country go down the drain," said David Eddings, protest leader on the USC campus in Los Angeles. "For years weak, liberal politicians have slowly been selling out a great nation. It's time we took a stand and showed the world we can't be pushed around anymore. This hostage thing is just the tip of a very large iceberg."

Spontaneous demonstrations have broken out on campuses all across the nation this week, all demanding solid, military action against the govern-

ment of Vietnam. The demonstrators have spurned
what they term the "Great liberal conspiracy"
that is trying to raise money to buy back the MIAs,
missing since the end of the war.

"What we're seeing is an inevitable backlash,"
said Harvard sociologist Dr. Morris Goodman. "This
is all part of the backwater that comes from times of
extreme politics. Besides, these kids are the children of the Vietnam War protestors. What kid ever
embraces his parents' ideals?"

XXIV

Chicago, Illinois—Sheraton Hotel

April 14—Around Midnight

Nancy Henderson stood hesitantly in the hallway checking the number on the door against the one on the paper she
held in her hands.

Hearing people coming down the hall, she raised her
hand to knock, feeling uneasy. She saw no reason why she
should be going to a strange man's hotel room in the middle
of the night, especially *this* night, when so much was happening. But there was something about the note, its simplicity,
that drew a response from her. And the name—Mr. Nhu.
Vietnamese?

She knocked lightly hoping no one would answer and
she could walk away clean and go back to the meetings she
had excused herself from.

But it wasn't to be. Seconds after her knock the door
opened a crack, and she was looking at a pair of liquid-brown
eyes.

"I'm Nancy Henderson," she said.

"Are you alone?" a voice said in perfect English.

The words caught her off-guard, frightened her into taking a
step back. She suddenly felt very tiny and very vulnerable.

The door opened, even without her response. An Oriental
man dressed in jeans and a Grateful Dead T-shirt walked

into the hall with her, looking up and down. He motioned with his arm.

"Welcome," he said amiably. "Come in."

She took a step, hesitated, then walked in, feeling foolish. If the man had wanted to rape or mug her, having her come to the hotel room in which he was registered seemed a poor way to do it.

The room was the same as hers, except for the color scheme. The hotel was new and looked it.

The man directed her past the bed toward the open curtains that gave the same view of Lake Michigan she had from her suite. This part of the place was like a sitting room, with sofa, chair, and a round walnut coffee table.

Nancy sat down on the edge of a chair, just in case.

"Can I get you something?" the man asked. "A drink? A coffee?"

"No, thank you," she replied. "You speak English very well," she said, waiting for Mr. Nhu to make the first move.

"I ought to." He smiled. "I was born in L.A. and have spent most of my life here in the States." He stuck out his hand. "Joey Nhu, at your service."

She took his hand, flustered. "I'm sorry, Mr. Nhu. I just thought . . . I . . ."

"Don't worry about it," he said, smiling to show even rows of perfect teeth. "It's an understandable error. My father had run the University in Saigon in the early fifties. He came over here when the French pulled out and Eisenhower began U.S. involvement. Back in those days they were very afraid of the Communists, so my dad acted as kind of adviser and interpreter to the Joint Chiefs for a time. I was born here and my folks just never thought to leave again."

He laughed, pulling a cigarette out of a pack on the table. He held the pack before Nancy, but she shook it off. He lit the cigarette, taking a drag before continuing. "But I'm sure you're not interested in all that, Mrs. Henderson . . . can I call you Nancy?"

"Sure."

He bobbed his head up and down. "Good, good. You can call me Joey. Anyway, you're probably wondering just why you're up here."

"I *am* quite busy," Nancy replied. "And if you want some kind of interview. . . ."

He waved the hand holding the cigarette, the smoke jagging crazily. "No, no interviews. I'm here about the prisoners, Nancy."

"I don't have any information you haven't already heard," she said, sitting back and crossing her arms.

"But I have information for you," Joey Nhu said quietly. "Information of an important nature."

Nancy straightened, leaning forward. "What information?"

Joey sat back and put his feet up on the table. His face was smooth, his hair sleek and black. He could have been any age between twenty and seventy, but Nancy figured him to be in his mid to late thirties.

"We'll have to get some things straight first," he replied. "First, no one will know of our . . . acquaintance. Secondly, I will remain in the background at all times. My role loses all effectiveness if I'm discovered."

"What role is that, Mr. . . . er, Joey?"

"I'm here to negotiate with you, to help secure the release of your husband and the other prisoners."

Nancy looked hard at him, a young, slick Asian American whose eyes were hard, almost cruel looking. Despite his outward friendliness, she found him extremely difficult to trust. "I thought Jerry Prescott was here to . . ."

"You misunderstand," he said. "I represent the government of the Republic of Vietnam."

She felt the wind go out of her. Speechless, she slumped for just a second, recovering quickly. "You are the ones holding my husband?"

"My government . . . yes."

"I thought you were an American."

"You're going to have to accept my conditions."

She shook her head. This was all happening too fast. "Why do you come to me with this?"

"Come on, Nancy," he said, cocking a finger in her direction. "I've studied your group. You are the logical choice for leader. Is there someone more in authority?"

He was so aggressive, so sure of himself. He was looking at her impatiently. "Probably not," she answered.

"There," he said with finality. "Now stop hedging and tell me you appreciate my position in all of this."

"I won't say anything about you," she said, seeing no harm in it.

"Excellent." He pulled his feet off the table and sat up straight, resting his hands on his legs, the cigarette dangling from his right hand. "Am I right in assuming that your group will be trying to raise the reparation money to our government?"

Reparation money, she thought. So that's what they call it. "Am I . . . allowed to negotiate with . . . a foreign power?" she asked.

His eyes narrowed and hardened even more, impatience evident in his voice. "Legally, you cannot," he replied. "Though if you try to raise the money, you'll also be violating your government's wishes. If you raise the money, how else did you assume to handle its disposition?"

"I'm sorry," she said tightly, reacting to the harshness of his tone. "I haven't had time to work it all out."

"Well, I *have* had time," Joey said. "I've had years to think about it. I was drafted into the Marines back in '69 and sent to Nam to fight. When I got there, all I could see was the misery we had caused my people. I went over to the other side to see if I could help. Then, when Carter declared a general amnesty, they just fixed me up some papers and I came back through Switzerland. I've been preparing for this for years."

"You're a secret agent?" she asked.

He leaned close to stare deeply at her. "I'm the hinge of this operation, Nancy. Without my end, it couldn't exist." He sat back looking self-important. "Besides, if you get the gold, you must have someone to take care of it for you, am I right?"

She shrugged, insides tight from his condescension.

"Your government won't do it for you. They're going to want you locked away somewhere. I'm here to take care of things for you, such as planes for transport, and a factory where the gold can be smelted down to size."

She thought about that. This, in fact, was the treason Sid had talked about. But Nhu was right. To defy the government in raising the money meant to defy them in all things. The actual fact of what she was doing had never been this clear before, and it was something she had to face up to.

"You offered me a drink before," she said. "I believe I'll take it now."

"I have bourbon and Coke. Is that all right?"

She nodded absently. "You say you have smelting facilities?" she asked as she watched him cross the room to the bottles sitting on the desk.

"All owned by my own people," he said. "We also have a warehouse. It's all located in Baltimore, near the harbor. Air France will fly the gold to Vietnam."

"I think secrecy would be the keyword here," she said, surprised at the amount of information he was already divulging.

"Absolutely. I don't trust Herrod or his gang of pigs to leave it alone."

She flinched at the word pigs, though she had used it herself a thousand times in reference to the administration. Somehow, coming from Nhu, it aroused a patriotic anger in her. Everything could be so confusing. She didn't want to betray her government. All she ever wanted was the return of those men. She had to start thinking about this in logical terms. Now she was beginning to see Joey's insistence on absolute anonymity. Should her relationship with him get out, all would be lost.

The man came back and handed her the drink. "Do we have a deal?" he asked sternly, standing over her, crowding her space.

She held the drink up, staring at it. "How do I know you're who you say you are?"

Anger darkened his face, and she could see his jaw muscles clenching. "You little bitch," he said.

She started. "I beg your pardon?"

He moved to the desk, banging his drink down to slosh on its top. "You need me for this," he said without looking at her. "And the sooner you start appreciating that, the better off you'll be."

He turned and pointed at her. "You want proof? Okay." He reached into the chair-well under the desk and dragged out a satchel-type briefcase. He bent and strained picking up the thing. It looked heavy.

He held it in both arms and carried it to the coffee table where she sat. "Go ahead," he said. "Open it."

She leaned over, pushing the metal flange that held the closing strap in place. It reminded her of a bag a schoolboy would carry. She set the drink on the table and used two hands to pull open the top of the valise.

She felt the breath go out of her when she looked inside. The bag was full of dog tags.

"I ask you again, Nancy Henderson," the man said, "do we have a deal?"

He held his glass up. Dazed, she picked hers up and matched the salute.

"To success," he said.

"Success," she echoed, and tilted the glass to her lips, not stopping until she had drained it.

Myrna Prescott sat on the edge of the king-sized bed and watched Jerry struggling through a round of sit-ups.

"I've never known you to exercise before," she said.

He was naked, his face red with exertion, his body glistening with sweat. "I...can't keep the weight off," he said through clenched teeth. "Been doing this for almost six months."

"God," she said, and reached for the glass of water sitting on the nightstand. "How long since we've known each other?"

"Years," he replied, and let himself slump to the floor. "Too many years."

"I want to say up front that I'm not going to make love with you," she said.

He was wiping his face on a towel. His only reaction was the cessation of the movement for just a second. "I understand," he said, and tossed the towel back on the bed.

"I don't know that you do," she said, and stared at his eyes just long enough to see the little-boy hurt edge into them. "So many nights over the years I lay in bed alone late at night, knowing you were out with one of your women. I wanted sex, too. I wanted it so bad that I began to hate you for every desire that ran through me. When I hurt, I wanted you to hurt."

He sat beside her on the bed. "I'm sorry," he said. "You really don't have to..."

"Yes I do," she said. She leaned against him, resting her head on his shoulder. "God, I've loved you and hated you so. You've made me happier and more miserable than any other human being could ever do. When you started acting like you wanted me to be your wife again, I honestly hoped you meant it so I could make you hurt like you made me hurt all these years."

"Why did you come here, then?" he asked, and slipped an arm around her shoulder, pulling her close.

She laughed, a dry, cynical laugh. "I think I wanted to watch you in pain," she said. "Isn't that a laugh? The things human beings are capable of. Anyway, I walked up to the door and listened to the things that woman was saying to you." She shook her head. "I remembered those days and how they nearly destroyed you. Then it occurred to me that maybe you've been living in pain all this time, too, and that maybe we're both scarred-up pretty badly and need to help each other."

She turned her face to his, and her eyes were wet, glistening. "Do you really need me?" she asked in a small voice. "'Cause I need you so damned much."

"Oh, Jesus," he said, and took her in his arms, hugging her fiercely. "I was always such a big shot that I knew I needed nothing. And that's just what I got . . . nothing. And here I am, getting old and lonely, and giving my soul to people who use it for target practice.

"I know I've screwed things up pretty badly, and you've every right to hate me. But please . . . give me the chance to make it up to you, I'll do—"

"No!" She put a hand to his lips, silencing him. "You don't need to make any promises. You don't need to *do* anything, except be my husband. Share with me, Jerry. Let me share with you. We live our lives in moments. Let's make the moments loving."

He stood up, walking to the suitcase that lay open on the low dresser. He took out a pair of pajama bottoms and put them on to cover his growing erection. He turned to her and smiled, a big, toothy grin. "I feel great," he said. "Like a kid again with things to look forward to."

"Like kids," Myrna said. "That's why I want to wait on the lovemaking. Let's get to know each other again. Covering things over with sex is too easy and we both know it."

He drew her to her feet and held her again. "You've got a deal," he said. "But I warn you I can be very persistent."

She pulled away from him, a look of shock on her face. "You'd better be," she said. "I'm a damned desirable woman."

"And a tease."

She wiggled her eyebrows. "Sometimes," she said, smiling and meaning it for the first time in years.

Outside, in the halls, they could barely hear a group of women chanting slogans about him. Moments later, several marines came through with hotel staff and cleared them out.

WEDNESDAY

WEDNESDAY

VATICAN CITY,—Pope John Paul today called for an end to what he termed "cycles of repression" in international politics. Speaking before a crowd of one hundred thousand in St. Peter's Square, he called the actions of the Vietnamese "desperate but not justifiable," and the reactions of the United States and the Soviet Union, "conditioned responses."

The Pope went on to suggest that the time limit be dropped, and that all involved parties should "sit down and strive toward a peaceful solution." The Pope offered to mediate personally but that, first, the "hostages must be freed." The American government had no comment on the Pope's offer of mediation.

—REUTERS

XXV

Arlington, Virginia

April 15—4:02 A.M.

Miller Angostis opened his eyes at the first ring of the phone, immediately awake and alert. It was a trained discipline. The water in the bathtub he was sitting in had turned cool.

He took several deep breaths while drying his wet hands, then reached for the phone on the third ring.

Emotional pressure was a totally internal phenomenon to

147

the director, something to be buried deeply within him and never allowed external release. He could control his waking that way, but not his sleep. Unreleased tension translated as insomnia. The only way he could ever sleep was in a tub full of hot water, water he would reheat several times during the night.

He brought the phone to his mouth. "Angostis," he said in a low voice. The meticulously clean bathroom was lit to gray by the small night-light plugged into the wall socket.

"Mr. Angostis? It's me, Russ Buchner. I'm sorry to bother you; I know you needed some sleep—"

"What is it, Russ?" Angostis asked, impatiently.

"Something's wrong with Project Sidewinder, sir."

Angostis stood, climbing out of the tub. "Is this line secure?" he asked, slipping on a terry-cloth robe.

"Yes, sir."

He moved to turn on the light, brightening the huge, white-tiled room to a brilliant glare.

"What happened?" he asked.

"Cowboy never got on the plane, sir." Buchner's voice was controlled, but obviously strung tight.

"Did someone else?" Angostis asked.

"No, sir. The ticket was never used."

"Tell me what steps you've taken."

"Norwood was on duty at the time. Cowboy was supposed to fly MAC to Oakland where he would be met by a contact there. We never knew he wasn't on the plane until the contact informed Norwood through channels when his boy didn't get off the aircraft."

"Several hours already lost," Angostis said.

"Norwood tried to reach him through all his channels, then called the place of his last contact."

"Which was?"

"Code name, Stinger."

"Cassady. What happened?"

"Nothing, sir. No answer."

"Did you send anyone by there?"

Buchner cleared his throat. "Norwood did," he said. "They sent one of Steakly's people over. The house was dark, no cars in the drive, no answer on a knock."

"More time lost." Angostis was already frustrated with the delays, all of it through bureaucratic handling of procedures according to SOP. "Did they attempt entrance to the house?"

"No, sir. That wasn't called for by Steakly."

Angostis held the phone on his shoulder while he slipped his robe off and folded it neatly, leaving it by the tub. His suit from the night before hung neatly on a rack by the bathroom door. He moved over to it and slipped into the pants, balancing on one leg, then the other. "Then what?"

"Then they called me in," Buchner said, voice tight. "I knew you needed sleep, so I figured to handle it myself. With Cassady also unavailable, I had to assume that he had something to do with the disappearance. I had our computer people check to see if he had flown anywhere, military or commercial. But I came up blank. I also moved through the net to see if either man had made any moves that involved our contacts. I've come up blank all the way around. That's when I called you. I'm sorry, I..."

"Never mind," Angostis said, his thoughts turning to their next moves. There would be ample time afterward to punish incompetence. "The first thing we've got to do is get over to Cassady's house and get inside. I don't care what it takes."

"Yes, sir."

"Then get back in the computers and look for anyone who's routed a flight from Friendship Baltimore to Bangkok leaving around the same time as Cowboy's flight."

"You think Cassady was involved, then?"

"He's the only link we've got," Angostis said. "Until proven otherwise, we'll have to look at him as our logical suspect."

"Suspect?"

"What would you call it, Russ? I'm on my way in."

He hung up immediately, his mind locked on the image of Cassady fighting with the marines atop the embassy in Saigon. "The son of a bitch is going back," he said, then laughed loudly. "That son of a bitch is fucking with the whole world so he can get back to some withered bar girl."

Cassady was on his way to Bangkok. He was sure of that. Tracking him down would just be a matter of time. No matter how determined or clever the man was, Angostis knew he could be stopped. For contests of mind and will were the

director's stock-in-trade, and Miller Angostis never entered a
contest he could possibly lose.

XXVI

Camp Friendship

April 15—10:42 A.M.

Ridley stood in the midst of the small crowd that had
gathered to watch the filming. The sun had already burned
off whatever coolness had come with the night and it glared
brightly in the dusty yard. Far to the east, however, the
sound of small rumbles would occasionally drift over to them,
a portent of monsoon rain that would come later that afternoon.

"No! No!" the director called, running into the cordoned-
off area. They were filming a small group of Americans with a
somewhat larger group of Vietnamese children. All were
supposed to be happy, smiling. The trouble was a dog.

One of the children, a six- or seven-year-old in shorts
and dirty-white shirt open down the front, insisted on holding his dog in the shot. Unfortunately, the dog didn't want to
be held and squirmed around crazily, yelping and crying the
whole time. It was driving the film crew crazy. Ridley thought
it was great.

Everytime they'd turn on the cameras, the dog would go
into its routine, thereby breaking everyone up. Since it was
supposed to be a serious shot, with the Americans telling the
folks back home about the sanctity of life in Vietnam, it
ruined the filming every time.

Boulle, the director, was furious but he couldn't do
anything about it. Since this kid and all the others were the
children of camp personnel, he couldn't exclude any of them
from the shots, or all the others might walk off in a show of
solidarity. Apparently the people's revolution had never heard
of the autonomy of a film director.

The longer it went on, the more impatient the children became until it was nearly impossible to keep them from wandering away while the cameras were rolling. The more it happened, the louder the spectators roared.

Ridley laughed right along with them, but his intention was more serious. He was watching the jailers, studying their level of commitment to all this. He found it interesting that none of the professional terrorists he had run into during his years of captivity were here at the camp. There was a lightness of spirit to these captors. Though businesslike most of the time, they weren't cruel or even hateful. They were there simply to do a job, and Ridley couldn't help but reach the conclusion that Colonel Tin had done it that way on purpose to put everyone at ease—a great concept as long as there was no trouble. If there was a weakness in Tin's scheme, it was here with his personnel.

"Okay," Boulle called through his thick accent. "Action!"

This time the dog broke away, jumping from the boy's arms and charging around the group, yelping. The children all began chasing it as the crowd roared again.

It was then that Ridley saw Jenkins on the other side of the cordon. His friend was watching him intently, trying to be subtle but not succeeding.

Today wasn't the first time he had caught Jenkins watching him. He had known the man too long not to know what was going on. All morning long Jenkins had avoided direct contact with him, but everywhere he went, the man was always there, always watching while pretending not to.

The man who had been closer to Jason Ridley than any other human being was contemplating turning him in to the authorities. He and Jenkins were on opposite sides of the fence, and at that moment, it made his best friend the most dangerous man alive.

He decided to test it one more time to be sure. He moved very obviously out of the crowd and across the yard toward the barracks. Several vendors had been allowed inside the gates, selling wares to the G.I.'s just as they had done so many years ago. Only this time it was the enemy that supplied the money for the incidentals—cigarettes, keep-sakes, T-shirts with strange names, like Adidas, written on them. Ridley stopped at a bomity-bom stand and bought an iced beer in an unmarked brown bottle, then wandered away in the direction of the hootch.

Something must be done about Jenkins, but Ridley found it impossible to dwell on it. The idea of causing harm of any kind to a patriot like Jenkins, while working with traitors like the AWOLs was too much for his unsettled state. He had survived all these years by doggedly accepting a rigid code of values and sticking to it. Now, everything was turned around.

Colonel Tin, dressed in a white silk suit, was out wandering the yard. He spotted Ridley and motioned him over.

"My friend," he said loudly at Ridley's approach. "How nice to see you."

He stuck out his hand, but Ridley ignored it, choosing to bow slightly instead. "Good morning, Colonel Tin," he said, staring down at the man. " A little hot to be out of your air-conditioned office."

Tin smiled without humor, his dark eyes unreadable. "Do not fear, Colonel Ridley, such conveniences are meant merely to maintain the delicate balance of my equipment. The revolutionary ardor burns hot in me at all times."

Ridley drank deeply from the beer, spitting some of it on the ground near Tin's feet. He wanted to push the colonel a bit to see what he was made of. "Hope I didn't get any on your shoes," he said with contempt.

Tin's expression never changed. "You are an unrepentant sinner," he said. "Perhaps I should simply have you locked away elsewhere."

"Your prerogative," Ridley said. "But I must once again remind you that the Geneva Convention..."

"I know what the Geneva Convention says," Tin interrupted without a sign of hostility. "Please, listen to me. Already, forces in your country are working hard toward obtaining your release. I'm asking you as senior officer to let this matter take its course. I want to harm no one. Believe that. In a few days, I guarantee this will all be resolved peacefully."

"Just let us go," Ridley said. "You can resolve it peacefully right now."

"Can I not appeal to your humanitarian nature?" Tin asked. "Our Russian 'allies' send us only enough economic aid to get our natural resources from the ground. In return, we must send those resources to them for world sale. We have no capital to rebuild our country. We need this money badly. Can we not work together?"

"Go to hell, you fucking slant," Ridley said.

The man's fists clenched for just a second, then loosened. "Why not face the facts, Colonel Ridley? Your thoughts of escape are pure fantasy. Even if you got out of the gates, where would you go? What would you do?"

The song kept going through Ridley's head. *I see a boat on the river, it's sailing away* . . . .

"You would all die, and for what? Your government forgot about you years ago. What a waste!"

Down to the ocean, where to I can't say. Ridley finished the beer, dropping the bottle on the ground. "You're the one who's fantasizing," he said. "There are no escape plans. We could never get out of here."

"Then you'll sign my paper?" Tin said, reaching into the inside pocket of his suit coat.

"I don't know how to write," Ridley replied, and turned away from the man, walking off.

"Don't be foolish," Tin called to him. "Temper yourself with good judgment. Please!"

Ridley didn't turn back. Hands in the pockets of his tan slacks, he looked at the dust-colored shoes which had been black when he put them on. Tin was polite now, but he didn't think it would stay that way. It was essential to formulate plans that could be carried forward even if key personnel were taken away.

He got into the hootch, glad to be out of the relentless sun. He felt a pristine sense of awareness as he walked down the rows of beds, a sense of everything around him that develops in warriors if they are to survive. Nothing escaped him. Two men he didn't know were playing gin on a forward bunk. Ferguson sat in the back of the room, waiting for him. He walked back slowly, casually, for the camera.

When he got back to Ferguson, he silently jerked his thumb in the direction of the cardplayers.

"Ours," Ferguson said, "watching anyone coming for the door."

"I'm hot as a pistol," Ridley said, sitting at the foot of Ferguson's bunk. "If something happens to me, I want you in charge. We've got to establish a solid chain of command here, so that plans can continue."

"What's happened?" Ferguson asked, his dull eyes filled with worry.

Ridley stood, moving to one of the windows and siding the mosquito netting. Ferguson joined him, both of them looking through a small crack. Jenkins stood, a discreet distance away, watching the hootch.

"He's been following me all morning."

Ferguson wiped sweat from his pitted skull. "You think he's working with Charlie?"

"Not yet," Ridley replied. "I think he's waiting to see what's going to happen first. If Tin were using him, it wouldn't be so obvious."

"They said Tin stopped you in the yard."

Ridley nodded, dropping the netting back into place. "He's waiting, too. I believe he's simply letting us get organized so he can break it up at the top levels and cause so much confusion that we won't be able to reorganize in time. That's why it's essential that we be able to work without our top people."

"What are we going to do?"

Ridley walked back to the bunk and sat. "We're going to fuck him, that's what. We're going to walk out of this crackerbox clean. How're things going?"

Ferguson returned to the bed, sitting stiffly on the edge, back straight, disciplined. Discipline was his god, the action that kept him going. "They're working on the maps now. Should have a good one by tomorrow."

"Have them include the harbor area."

"Why?"

"A feeling . . . I don't know. Just do it. How's morale?"

Ferguson's lips tightened to a hard slash, his frown etching his face. "It looks bad," he said. "I don't even think we can count on thirty percent. The highest numbers are with the fucking AWOLs. They've got the most to gain by an escape."

"They're also our best shot," Ridley said reluctantly. "Vietnamese could never understand our ability to work with someone who has betrayed us. It's not in their makeup. I'll bet our Colonel Tin has a blind spot where the AWOLs are concerned. I hate to say it, but we may need to transfer a great deal of this onto their shoulders."

"That makes me sick," Ferguson said, "but I've come to

the same conclusion. By the way, I think we've got enough trucks in the compound to pull it off if we need to."

"Good."

"If we can only get our people ready to go."

"I'm working on that," Ridley said. "What we need to do is wake everybody up, remind them of what's really going on here."

"What are you thinking of?" Ferguson asked, an edge of suspicious worry in his tone. He was too protective, and Ridley knew it. "Don't do anything crazy."

Ridley ignored him, changing the subject. "I want everybody back in their own hootches tonight," he said. "We can't risk being all together again."

"Right."

He looked in the man's eyes, using the contact as a lever. "And I want you to do something for me," he said, "something that won't be easy for you."

Ferguson licked his bloodless lips, his expression stern. For a second, Ridley wondered if the man ever smiled.

"I'll do anything you say," Ferguson replied.

Ridley nodded. "I want you to sell us all out," he said.

In a move sure to agitate already angry NAM-Wives, newly appointed media liaison, Maurice Benstock announced that the administration was sending Secretary of State Jerry Prescott to Chicago to personally negotiate the President's position with NAMWives spokesperson, Nancy Henderson. Prescott, you may remember, held roughly the same position under President Nixon and was accused at the time of "inhumanly conspiring against truth" by the very same Nancy Henderson.

Benny Benstock's an old friend, and when we got him on the phone to congratulate him on his new position, we asked him about the wisdom of sending someone to Chicago whose credibility is already in question.

"Jerry's a good man," Benstock said. "He already knows these people, knows the issues, what they want and we want. They'll all forget about the past soon enough and get down to business."

We couldn't resist getting in touch with NAM-
Wives to see if they could really forget the past. An
unidentified spokeswoman told us, "Sending Jerry
Prescott to negotiate a NAMWives issue would be a
lot like sending Adolf Hitler to chair a B'nai B'rith
meeting."

So much for niceties.

—"As I See It"
Max Robbins
Chicago Sun-Times Syndicate

XXVII

Chicago, Illinois— Sheraton Hotel

April 15—8:37 A.M.

"Oh, Jesus, no," Jerry Prescott said, and reached out to
change the station on the hotel TV. This one had the same
thing. It was an old file film from some obscure local station
of a woman named Jeannie Daggot being dragged into a
police van after being arrested for selling cocaine to under-
cover policemen. She was yelling, rattling off a string of
obscenities that were bleeped off the screen.

"Did you get through yet?" he called back to the bedroom. "We've got to do something about this shit."

Tod Barrows, in shirt and tie, got partway into the
bedroom doorframe, as far as the cord of the red telephone
he held would allow. "We're working through channels now,"
he said.

"Jesus Christ," Prescott said again, settling back into the
love seat in front of the set. Myrna sat beside him, face
drawn, her arms crossed.

On TV Jeannie Daggot made an articulate gesture with
her hand before the doors were shut on her and the van

began to pull away. At the time the woman had been heavily involved in NAMWives.

"How old is this footage?" Myrna asked, irritation lacing her voice.

Jerry reached over to the table and picked up his coffee, leaving the saucer. "It's got to be fifteen years old if it's a day," he said angrily. "Fucking Nixon was president when it happened."

"Where did they get this?"

"This is White House footage," he replied, and drank. The coffee was cold. He finished it anyway. "Benstock must have dug it up someplace."

"But why?"

Thunder rolled outside. The curtains to the suite-length window were open, ominous gray and black clouds seemingly boiling right up to them. It was bleak and nasty, rain coming down in sheets.

"That's what I'm trying to find out." He set the cup back on the table. "I think the woman may have ultimately been cleared. I don't quite remember. But what that has to do with this, I don't understand."

The picture on the screen switched to a shot of ambulance personnel carrying a wheeled-stretcher out of a house in a middle-class residential neighborhood. More file footage. A body was on the stretcher, covered with a sheet. An announcer was speaking.

". . . was married a month after her husband, MIA Derek Mazgate, had been declared legally dead. Nearly a year later, she, herself, lies dead after drinking a bottle of liquid drain-cleaner."

The picture changed to show an obviously distraught man talking to the camera. "She never could get used to it," he was saying, tears rolling down his face. 'I tried to help her, but she felt such a sense of . . . loyalty to the man that she could never get over the guilt feelings . . .'"

"This is awful!" Myrna said. "How old is this one?"

Jerry reached over and put a hand on her shoulder. She was still dressed in her robe, her own eyes glistening. "I don't even remember this one," he said, shaking his head.

"Got it!" Tod called from the bedroom.

Jerry was up, slipping on his suit coat. A marine stood at parade rest in front of the door to the outside, looking out of place in the delicate elegance of the room. Jerry moved through the length of the suite, passing Charlie Johnston with orange juice and toast at the bar.

Barrows stood in the bedroom, holding out the receiver in one hand and the body of the phone in the other. His brows were narrowed in concern.

"The President?" Prescott mouthed silently.

Barrows shook his head.

Jerry took the phone, the Secret Serviceman vacating the bedroom immediately, closing the door behind him. "This is Prescott," he said into the receiver.

His blood went cold when he heard Benstock's voice on the other end. "Good morning, Jerry," he said cheerily. "I hear it's raining in Chicago."

"The rain is nothing compared to the snow job you've been dishing out on the television."

"I don't know that I'm exactly pleased with the tone of your voice," Benstock said. "Maybe we'd better go back to the beginning and—"

"Don't patronize me, Benny," Prescott said, and heard a light tapping on the door. Myrna had stuck her head through the crack, and he motioned her in. "You're digging for every cheap, lousy story you can find on these women and running them like they all happened yesterday. What are you trying to pull?"

"Hey," Benstock said. "These are all legit newsclips. If they're not all flattering, that's life. NAMWives has declared war on us from where I'm sitting. Their statements haven't exactly been complimentary, you know."

Myrna was sitting on the bed, watching him quizzically. He shrugged at her. "This isn't a game," he said. "These women are fighting for the lives of their husbands here."

"You're wrong about that, Jerry," Benstock said smoothly. "It is a game. And you'd be wise to remember whose side you're playing on."

Prescott stood there, feeling gutted. "I finally get it," he said. "You're trying to run them into the ground so nobody will help them and you don't care how you do it."

"They're going against their own government," Benstock returned, "siding with Communists."

"You wouldn't know a Communist if you fell over one," Jerry said, burning with an anger he didn't know was still in him. "This is just your chance to see what you can do with your toys. And while you're at it, you're sending me down to their meeting to defend this shit."

"Don't get paranoid on me. You're making a big deal out of nothing."

"Easy for you to say," Prescott replied. "Where's Simon? I want to talk to him."

"He's in a meeting with the NSC and can't be disturbed. Sorry."

"Tell him I need to talk to him."

"He's pretty busy, but I'll pass it along."

"How did I end up getting hold of you, anyway?"

There was a pause on the line, then, "Luck of the draw, I guess."

"You set this up, you son of a bitch."

"Watch your mouth, Jerry."

"And you watch your ass, 'cause I'm not going to go down that easily. You just get Herrod."

He slammed down the receiver, then slammed the whole phone down on the dresser. He looked at Myrna. "I can't believe it," he said.

She stood, her face lost in confusion. "A hatchet job?"

"On a grand scale. he's trying to get rid of me and NAMWives at the same time. I've been led down the garden path."

Myrna embraced him. "I'm so sorry."

"Yeah," he said, smoothing her long hair. "I'm sorry, too—for those poor women."

"Are you going down to the press conference?" she asked pulling away from him.

He nodded grimly. "I've got to."

Her face hardened. "I'm going with you," she said and took off her robe. She wore a slip underneath. "I've just got to put on a dress."

"It won't be a pretty sight."

"We've been through worse," she said, and moved to the closet, shoving dresses on hangers aside one by one.

"Oh yeah?" he responded. "When?"

She came out with a simple black dress and held it up to her body. "What do you think?"

He sighed. "Very appropriate."

There was a knock on the door, then Barrows's voice. "Mr. Secretary, they've called the press conference."

"Be there in a minute."

"Yes, sir."

He sat on the bed and watched her dress, grateful beyond words that she would be at his side through the ordeal to come. He had no idea what to do or say at this point. His own loyalties were shaken. He blamed Benstock, but wasn't the President responsible for those who worked for him. He had been a close friend of Simon Herrod since the Camelot days of Jack Kennedy's administration, but time changes things. To get elected president a man had to sell many small parts of his soul to many people, at the risk of becoming the unknowing instrument of a cadre of strangers, at the risk of becoming a stranger himself.

"I'm ready," Myrna said as she slipped into matching shoes.

He stood. "You look good, hon. I mean it."

She brightened, giving him a tight-lipped smile. "What are we going to do down there?" she asked nervously.

"Play it by ear," he said and moved to the door, opening it. "And be as honest as we know how."

They swept through the room, Charlie Johnston draining his juice and hurrying to wipe his mouth on a linen hotel napkin. Jerry stopped at the bar, picking up an unused ice bucket.

"What's that for?" Myrna asked.

"For my head," Jerry said seriously, "after they cut it off."

The hallway that led to the ballroom was a twisting jungle of flesh, all reaching hands and yelling voices. Nancy Henderson, face severe, pushed through the noise and the waving arms, surrounded by a phalanx of her people. Bright lights from TV cameras flooded the pathway, while popping flashbulbs held above the heads of the crowd flared like lightning.

Nothing in Nancy Henderson's previous life had prepared her for this moment. In one sleepless night she had been swept into a position of international prominence, consorted with a foreign power, and, most probably, lost her husband—at least one of her husbands, she reminded herself bitterly. As newsmen called for comments and hands reached out to grab her, she no longer felt a human being, but rather a repository for the feelings of others. She had resigned from the human race and become a symbol.

It was a frightening feeling, a totally empty feeling.

The questions, always the same questions, never ended. Marsha Ridley, who held Nancy's right arm, her face set hard, always had the same answer. "We will make a brief statement, then answer questions."

Nobody listened. They kept pushing in, shoving and grabbing, as if through sheer brute power they could force the answers they wanted.

After the initial broadcasts from the government that morning, the entire atmosphere of the hotel had become supercharged. Already-high-pitched emotions grew even more in intensity.

Nancy's entourage burst into the large ballroom, crystal chandeliers reflecting television lights in brilliant sabers. There were chairs, but no one sat. Banners, for and against, adorned the walls. Others were being carried on poles. A group of young men stood somewhere in the back, chanting "Traitors, traitors..." over and over.

It brought Nancy's anger back, the only emotion she had left. *They* were the ones who had been betrayed, over and over. The arrival of Prescott proved it. The televised hate campaign proved it. She thought of poor Jeannie Daggot, wrongly arrested so long ago, living the tortures of hell before being quietly let go months later. It was all hatred and repression and she was angry enough to know her judgment wasn't as sure as it should be and not care.

A small man with wild eyes pushed through her people, grabbing her by the lapels of her suit jacket. "Commie bitch!" he yelled in her face, his breath thick with alcohol. "You're nothing but a bigamist, a harlot!"

There were other words, but she tuned them out, barely feeling his hands on her. He was dragged away seconds later and she moved on, feeling disembodied.

A portable stage was set up at the far end of the room. A long table was set on the stage, a podium and mike in the center of it. Hotel security guarded the steps, keeping all but necessary personnel away.

Marsha got her past the guards and up the stairs, guiding her by the arm.

"I can't believe all this," she said, looking out over the crowds. "Everybody in the world must be here."

"No," Nancy replied. "Just the nuts."

Marsha moved her to the mike, hitting it with her finger to see if it was working. There was too much noise to tell.

"Are you okay?" she asked.

"Fine," Nancy said mechanically, wanting to scream. This was too big. How was she supposed to handle something like this?

Marsha patted her arm. "Good luck," she said, and was gone.

The others trooped up and seated themselves behind the stage. Her executive committee, going up to the guillotine with her.

And then, as she stood there—alone, anchored only by her anger, she watched an extraordinary thing happen. The crowd took notice of her. By her presence at the podium, she commanded their attention. They hushed by degrees, and in a matter of seconds, had quieted completely.

They watched her, all desperate to hear what she had to say, and in that moment she understood the nature of power. It was a liberating feeling. The moment was hers to control and it gave her confidence.

Just as she made to speak, there was a commotion at the door. Jerry Prescott, surrounded by marines with rifles, entered the ballroom.

"That's right, Mr. Secretary," she said into the microphone, amplified voice booming. "Come right in. I especially want to talk to you."

A wave of laughter rippled the room, nervous laughter. A loud whistle came through the sound system, persisting until a man in a hotel blazer ran up near the stage and adjusted the mike level.

She put her hands in the air, the silence returning immediately. Far in the back of the room she could see Joey Nhu standing with his hands in his pockets, big sunglasses hiding his eyes. He was smiling.

She had a written statement in her jacket pocket, but decided to go without it. "Ladies and gentlemen," she said, "my name is Nancy Henderson, and I have been chosen as the representative of the National Association of MIA Wives; in so saying, I embody the thoughts and emotions of all of us in the organization.

"Two days ago the President of the United States said officially that the government would not pay the ransom demands for the return of our husbands. He also asked that no one else try to raise that money, regardless of our personal involvement and feelings."

She could hear the cameras clicking all around her. "We find that position reprehensible and dangerous. Reprehensible in that it takes into account neither the lives nor the feelings of the people involved, dangerous in that such action can take our country to the brink of war."

Out of the corner of her eye she could see the container holding the rings being passed down the line. A large bucket sat beside the podium on the table.

"I am here to officially announce that NAMWives rejects the President's foolish demands and is going ahead with plans to raise the money to return those unfortunate men to us!"

There was some applause to the last remark, and some angry shouts, including the continuation of the chanting in the back of the room. It was several minutes before quiet returned.

She reached into her pocket and pulled out the wad of telegrams, holding them in the air. "Support for our movement comes from everywhere, the ACLU, labor unions, support organizations and veterans groups. As our symbol we choose the wedding band." She pulled a ring out of the container and held it up. "Gold and perfectly round, symbolizing the everlasting nature of our union. The most treasured possession many of us own, we donate to the cause."

She dropped the ring in the bucket and picked up the container. "Others have already joined me," she said, dumping the rings into the bucket, "but we need two hundred tons of this stuff. We need the help of the people of this great country . . . mothers . . . wives. Many of us have lived in the hell of not knowing for nearly two decades. You must excuse us if we seem anxious now. We want our husbands back!"

Shouts of support from the audience.

"And we mean to have them back, no matter what Mr. President Simon Herrod says!" She pointed across the room. "No matter what Judas Jerry Prescott says!"

There was no quieting the crowd now. She looked over at Marsha, sitting between Terry Jacobs and Adele Rogers. They were all nodding at her, faces set in determination.

"There's not much time either," she called. "We have barely five days left on the deadline. Five days to try and bring our men back before our government embarks on some insane nuclear confrontation in the South China Sea.

"I'll tell you something else, too," she said loudly, to get over the noise. "We've been in contact with our lawyers this morning, and they say we can sue for the slander that has been filling the television screens of America and the world this morning. Mr. President may be protected from prosecution, but the government isn't. You've all seen it: lies, distortions, half-truths. The amount of our lawsuit has been easy enough to reach—two-and-a-half-billion dollars! Payable in gold!"

Cameras and reporters swarmed the stage, pushing one another, yelling for attention. "One at a time!" Nancy said, pointing to a man in a blue network blazer. "You!"

"Mrs. Henderson," the man yelled up. "What response do you have for those who would accuse you of treason for going against the stated policy of the government and negotiating with a foreign power?"

"We are a free people, sir," she responded. "Free to talk with whom we choose. I do not conspire against my country. I'm simply paying my husband's room and board for the last twenty years."

"It's a very simple situation, gentlemen," Prescott was saying from his small brightly lit corner of the ballroom. "The United States government feels that terrorists cannot be negotiated with, nor unlawful ransom demands paid. It has been the official position of the government for many years—it wasn't invented for this crisis.

"We are working through every possible diplomatic channel and feel that we will be successful. Negotiations by any individual or group of individuals are not in the best interests of the United States and could very possibly damage our own process of negotiation. It must stop."

He felt Myrna beside him, taking some of the sting out. Nancy had been good, inspiring. She'd gotten better since the seventies. After answering questions for twenty minutes, she hadn't faltered once, even when they asked her which husband she'd live with. Now she was trying to make her way off the stage.

A woman journalist was looking at him sternly, her mike pushing insistently toward him, like a weapon. "Mr. Secretary," she said. "Why did Ms. Henderson refer to you as a 'Judas'?"

"You'll have to ask her that," Jerry replied.

A man with a minicam on his shoulder, his right eye glued to the viewfinder, said, "What about the charges of slander in connection with the government's release of footage about NAMWives?"

"That's Mr. Benstock's department," Jerry answered, glad to air that one out. "Talk to him. You all know him. He's one of yours."

There was some cautious laughter attached to that remark, its slashing nature left unsaid.

"Jerry Prescott!" a voice yelled through the now-mulling crowd, pressing against the wall of marines that separated the newsmen and the secretary from the rest of the room.

"It's her," Myrna said, taking his hand and squeezing. "She's coming over here."

Barrows stood near at hand, his face twisting in worry. He moved toward the disturbance.

"Tod," Jerry said. "Let her pass."

"Mr. Secretary . . ."

"Tod."

The man nodded, moving through the crowd of reporters and speaking to the marines.

"Will there be any legal action taken against NAMWives?" someone was asking him.

"Only if they do something illegal," Jerry responded. "We will be watching the situation very closely."

"And we'll be watching you closely," Nancy Henderson said. She stood several feet from him, the reporters moving aside to give them a clear shot at one another.

Their eyes met, hers cold as marble. "I want you to know," he said, "that I am genuinely sorry for our differences of opinion."

"And I want you to know that I'm going to get my husband back no matter what."

"We both want the same thing. Perhaps we can talk."

"All liars like to talk," she said, breathing hard. "Liars can talk you to death."

He looked at the floor, teeth clenched. He deserved that. He didn't even blame her.

Taking a deep breath, he said, "I am empowered to meet with you and see if this situation can be resolved to everyone's benefit."

"I want someone else," she said coldly. "I could never believe a word you'd say."

It hurt—every word—like a punch. "Your objection to me is noted. If negotiators cannot be changed, will you consider meeting with me?"

She didn't even blink. "I'd meet with the devil himself if he could get my husband free."

The television ground relentlessly in the background as Sid Henderson helped little Timmy on with his sweater. Jeremy lay in his carrier, bundled against the Oklahoma April winds, idly toying with his bottle of apple juice.

"Go Gramma's," Timmy said, his little face round and innocent. "Go now."

"That's right, champ," Sid replied. "We're going over to Gramma's. Then maybe we'll go on a trip somewhere."

"Go bye?" Timmy said, eyes bright.

"That's right."

"Mommy go bye?"

"Not this time," he said, standing and picking up his own jacket. "Not this time."

He looked to the television, at the woman he no longer recognized, talking to reporters. Telling them how she was going against the government.

He picked up the carrier, Jeremy crying for the bottle he had dropped. He bent again, retrieving the bottle. He didn't know much, but he knew that she was willing to throw over all they had had for a man she hadn't seen for years. Well, that was all well and good. If she didn't want him, fine. But he'd be damned if some stranger was going to waltz in and try to raise his kids. His kids.

"C'mon," he said, holding out a hand to Timmy. The boy toddled over, taking hold of one of his fingers. They moved from the den to the front of the house.

Sid had already put the suitcases in the car. he had done it the night before in angry anticipation, secretly hoping he'd have to sheepishly take them out again when she returned. But it wasn't to be.

He turned, took one last look at the house, and opened the front door. "Oh, my God."

The front lawn was a madhouse of pointing neighbors and television cameras. One of the TV trucks had pulled up on the lawn and ground through the garden that he and Nancy had just planted.

Timmy, frightened, began crying, hugging himself against Sid's leg. Sid took a tentative step forward, and they descended upon him. They surrounded him like hungry wolves, nipping.

"Would you get back?" he asked. "You're scaring the children."

"Are you going to Chicago to join your wife?" someone asked him, jamming a microphone in his face.

He pushed the mike away, trying to make his way to the car. "No," he said. "I'm not. Now if you'll . . ."

"Do you approve of your wife's actions?" a woman reporter asked.

"No comment. Now, please . . ."

"Has the discovery of Billy Phillips had any adverse effect on your marriage?"

He stopped walking and picked up Timmy, holding him close, the boy hanging on in fright. "What kind of stupid question is that?" He blamed Nancy for every bit of this. Why was she putting them through this hell?

"Are you and Nancy legally married?"

"Yes!" he screamed. "Are you calling my children bastards?"

"Is there a chance she'll now live with her first husband?"

Sid Henderson tightened in rage. He shoved his way through the crowd, ignoring the questions that still bombarded him and settled the children safely inside the vehicle.

"You want a statement?" he asked. "All right, try this: I'm an American and a patriot. I married that woman after her husband had been declared legally dead. I don't know why she's doing this; I don't know where it's going to lead. All I know is that she's there instead of here with me and our children where she belongs. If she's committing any treasonous acts against this country, that's her lookout, not mine."

One of the reporters laughed. "At least if she's in jail you won't have any trouble retaining custody of the children."

He went for the man then, punching him as hard as he'd ever hit anyone in his life, flashbulbs and TV cameras recording the event dutifully for a world that was suddenly very interested in Sid Henderson and what he thought.

BANGKOK—Elements of the Russian Navy under the command of Admiral André Nabov dropped anchor today just off the mouth of the Saigon River, Vietnam, in the South China Sea. The flotilla contained nearly one hundred warships, the largest Soviet show of strength in recent history.

Soviet governmental sources actively denied reports that the Navy was sent down as a message to the Americans to stay out of Vietnam, saying this was simply a training exercise scheduled for nearly a year.

The Soviet contingent boasted the latest in firepower, including an aircraft carrier, submarines, and cruisers, all with nuclear capabilities.

—REUTERS

XXVIII

Glen Burnie, Maryland

April 15—9:13 A.M.

Jesse Harris stood patiently at the carport door while his partner, Thurman Washington, looked through the small leatherette case, trying to choose just the right pick for the job. Both were black men, fresh off the "farm," recruited for counterinsurgency in Nicaragua. This was some of their domestic practice, though Harris wasn't exactly happy with the Baltimore Gas and Electric uniform he was having to wear for the job. He had joined the company to get away from this sort of thing, but it was almost as if a blue collar were destined to follow him around anyway.

"Would you come on," he said. "Let's get this over with and get out of here."

"Keep your pants on, gasman," Washington said calmly, and selected a stainless steel instrument with a long slender wire on the end, a universal key. "You got a date or something?"

He slipped the wire in the lock and began maneuvering it around while Harris watched out both sides of the carport for nosy neighbors or real gasmen. He hated this work. He hadn't signed on to be a cat burglar.

"There," Washington said, backing away slightly and removing the tool. He tried the knob. It freewheeled in his hand. "Now for the deadbolt."

"This isn't for shit," Harris said. "I could have stayed in my old neighborhood and did this."

"Got to take the good with the bad. Every job carries its own value," Washington said, and stuck the chisel in the door crack by the key slot. "Practice on this easy stuff'll pay off for us later on."

He bent the chisel in the door, pushing back the bolt, the door opening partway.

Harris watched Washington reach for the handle, but something was wrong. There was a tiny sizzling noise, like frying bacon.

"No!" he screamed at the last second, and grabbed the man, throwing him away from the door just as the explosion went off.

The concussion threw them to the ground, the door blowing outward in orange fire and wood shrapnel. As gray smoke and sawdust drifted through the carport, the two men picked themselves up, unhurt, and stared at the damage.

"It never did *that* in my old neighborhood," Harris said.

"The motherfucker booby-trapped it," Washington said calmly, apparently unmoved by the turn of events.

They walked over to the place. "So much for secrecy," Harris said, looking at the neighbors who were now coming out onto the surrounding lawns to see what was happening. "There'll be cops here and we're without ID."

"That's not our only problem," Washington replied, pointing to the door space.

The door was gone, completely blown away, but in

its place iron bars had been welded into the frame
from the inside.

"I think we've come across something," Harris said,
wiping dust off himself as the last remnants of smoke dissipat-
ed from the carport.

"What have you told the police?" Angostis asked, the
phone to his ear, his eyes riveted to the screen of the portable
television on his desk. A picture of a towyard operator was on
the screen, talking to reporters. In the background he could
see an area cordoned off by yellow police ribbon, white-
suited ambulance attendants hoisting a body from the trunk
of a car onto a stretcher.

"They know we're government," Steakly replied, his
voice hollow sounding on the carphone, "but not which
branch."

"Can you keep it that way?"

"For now. They'll start wondering about the mumbo
jumbo I gave them when they fill out their reports."

"Maybe we'll be gone by then," Angostis said, turning
up the volume on the television. 'Have you gotten in yet?"

"Working on it now."

". . . dead man was carrying a Russian diplomatic passport," the TV announcer was saying. "His name is being
withheld pending notification of the proper authorities."

"I think we found your tagalong, John," Angostis said.

"Where?"

Angostis watched the body laid out on the stretcher,
incredible amounts of blood soaking the front of the man's
suit. He was being covered with a sheet. "In the trunk of his
car with his throat slashed."

"Cassady," Steakly said.

"I'm on my way over there." Angostis got to his feet. His
black three-piece suit hung perfectly on his lean frame. "For
God's sake, see if you can get rid of the police. Chase the
neighbors off, too. Hold it together as much as you can."

"Do we search when we get in?"

Angostis had his briefcase out, looking through its contents. "Yes," he answered. "But please be careful. There was
one bomb, there may be more."

"If I were Cassady, I'd figure you to figure that way and

just plant one bomb in order to hold us up while we searched."

"I know," Angostis said. "But if you were me, you'd still be obliged to do what I'm doing. Unless, of course, you're willing to accept the complications of killing off your agents in a suburban Baltimore residential neighborhood."

"Think I'll stick to my own job," Steakly said.

"Yeah. I'll be there in forty-five minutes."

"Is Cowboy in there?"

"Something must be."

Angostis rang off, then pushed the switchhook several times until the receptionist came on. "I need a car and driver," he said without preliminaries. "And get Buchner up here."

"Yes, sir."

He hung up and waited for Buchner. Cassady was no dummy. He was using every device he could imagine to hold them up as long as possible, knowing every second was precious. The man had kept them effectively at bay for thirteen hours now, time enough for him to be nearing his destination if, indeed, he had a destination. The killing of the Russian showed just how finally Mr. Cassady treated this business. He was burning bridges for good and letting them know it. Not a good sign.

Buchner gave the proper knock and was allowed immediate passage to the inner sanctum.

"We've found Cowboy's car," he said.

Angostis picked up the briefcase, taking Buchner by the arm. "Tell me as we walk," he said.

"Where to?"

"Cassady's house." They got out the door and moved along the halls, busy people in glassed-in rooms working on either side. "Where was the car?"

"In a ditch near the airport," Buchner said, hurrying to keep up with Angostis's long strides. "Within walking distance."

"Any sign of violence in the car?"

"None," he said.

They passed the television room, banks of screens receiving signals from all over the world, with technicians before them, all gleaning data from news and eyewitness reports.

"Any luck with the computers?" Angostis asked, his attention diverted to the screens they were passing.

"Maybe," Buchner replied uneasily. "We've found several men who are traveling alone to Bangkok from various places in the states. We've already contacted the Bangkok station and they will be detained."

"If Cassady used just one name to get there, you may have him."

"He didn't register any of his company names or passports."

They arrived at the bank of elevators that would take them to the garage below. "I have the feeling this has been planned for quite some time, Russ," Angostis said as he pushed the down button. "We'll need to dig deeper. There's not much time if we're to get him before he's out there on his own."

"He's fucking us, isn't he?" Russ asked.

A muffled bell sounded, announcing the elevator. The doors slid open. "Not yet he's not," Angostis said. "He's merely announcing his intentions."

Angostis's limo slid up to the curb in front of Cassady's house exactly forty-three minutes later. He and Buchner got out quickly, sending the car away.

"Sloppy," the director said, as he slipped his sunglasses on. There were cars parked everywhere, and neighbors still standing on the periphery of the lawn. A uniformed police sergeant stood in the carport, arguing with Steakly.

They moved up the drive toward the conversation. Steakly saw them coming, his face falling. "Get into the house," Angostis told Buchner, "and have those cars driven away from here. Make sure the neighbors hear that everyone is leaving."

"Yes, sir," Buchner said.

They came up to Steakly and the policeman, Buchner walking past the group to the blown-out door. Several iron bars had been burned through to allow passage. He started into the house.

"Now, just a minute there," the cop said. "Where do you think you're going?"

"He's going in on my orders," Angostis said sternly, then nodded Buchner through the doorway.

The policeman was probably in his fifties, gray and

severe, used to giving orders, not taking them. "And who might you be?" he asked the director.

Angostis pulled out the wallet with the fake FBI identification and showed it to the man. "My name's Johnson," he said. "I'm Baltimore bureau chief. You are hindering our investigation, Sergeant."

"Why didn't your man say he was with the bureau?" the cop answered, examining the ID closely. The name Meyers was written on his name tag. "We've always cooperated with you boys in the past."

"This is a problem with domestic espionage, Sergeant Meyers," Angostis said. "National security is involved. My men are not allowed to divulge such information."

"Spies?" Meyers said, eyes widening before resettling to their practiced all-knowing look.

"It's essential that we're free to conduct this investigation in private. I promise that we will share the findings with you as they become available and are declassified." He pointed to the card. "Our Washington number is written here. When you return to the station house give them a call and they'll explain everything."

"Well...I..."

Buchner came back out the door with several agents in tow. They trooped past Meyers and headed to the cars, chatting loudly.

"What is the level of your security clearance, Sergeant?" Angostis asked.

The man looked bewildered. "Well...during the Korean War, I..."

"Anything more recent?" Angostis said impatiently.

The man just stared at him. Angostis took the card away and pocketed it. "You're not cleared for any of this. Please, call the Washington bureau and tell them about all this. They will explain. Now, you must clear the area immediately. You are presently in violation of the National Security Act of 1963." He looked at Steakly. "Come on. We don't have much time."

The two men walked into the house. Meyers watched them for a second, then turned to find all the cars pulling away, leaving him out there alone. Buchner came back and walked to the door. Meyers stared after him, but was turned back.

"This is a security area," Buchner said and disappeared into the house.

Meyers stood for a moment, realizing he had forgotten to write down that phone number. Then he wandered back to his black-and-white, shooing away nosy neighbors as he did.

Inside, Angostis and Steakly stood in a narrow hall of the lower-middle-class house. The director hadn't been inside anything like this for years. Several agents were still left, using electronic gear to slowly move through the place, looking for concealed bombs.

"We've got to be out of here in thirty minutes at the outside," Angostis said. "Meyers will start thinking soon, and we don't need any of this spread around."

Steakly nodded. "We've found no other devices," he said. "I don't think Cassady was trying to hurt us."

"What does it matter what he was trying to do?" the director replied, watching Buchner walk up.

"Every entry in the house is barred," the man said with grudging respect.

"Russ," Angostis said. "I noticed a trash can in the kitchen. Why don't you go dump it and see what's in there."

An agent hurried down the hall to them. "We've got something," he said. "In the bedroom."

They followed him. The sweep had concentrated here, the last unchecked room. The mattress had been dumped off the bed, and all the drawers had been pulled out, their contents scattered across the carpet. Three men stood before a closed closet door, a muffled sound barely coming through to them.

"Is it clear?" Angostis asked.

One of the men, in beard and jeans, nodded.

The director grunted, reaching for the handle. "Grab anything that looks helpful," he said, nodding toward the junk all over the floor. "Put it in pillow cases or whatever's handy. Just do it quickly."

They scattered.

He opened the door and stepped in the soundproofed room. Albert "Cowboy" Sorrel stood naked behind bars, his face red from yelling and embarrassment.

Angostis's gaze took in the small room, stopping on the destroyed computer. "Get him out of there," he said, Steakly hurrying to fire up the torch which had been left behind.

"He was waiting for me," Sorrel said. "Had me set up from the word go."

"What does he have in mind?" Angostis asked as he watched Steakly light up the torch and start on the bars.

Sparks began squirting from the process, forcing Sorrel to back up in his cell. "He intends to go back to Nam," he said calmly, "free the prisoners, and find his girl friend."

"Is he crazy?" Steakly asked, looking up from his labors and bending out a bar he had cut through.

"He's always been crazy," Sorrel said. "You've just controlled its direction before."

"How is he getting there?" Angostis asked.

Sorrel shook his head. "He didn't say, but the last thing he did before he left was to destroy the computer."

Buchner moved into the closet, startled by Sorrel. "I found these at the bottom of the trash," he said, handing Angostis a stack of passports.

The man glanced at them quickly. None were company-issue. He could have used any number of identifications to book flights.

"There," Steakly said. He had cut through several bars at the bottom. Sorrel pushed against them, making a large enough space to climb through.

"Has anybody seen my clothes?" he asked.

"Cassady left some behind," the director said. "Put his on."

"But he's so much smaller than me..."

"You can leave here naked if you want," Angostis said, then turned to Buchner. "What would have been the easiest way for him to book reservations with identities and a computer?"

"Simple," Buchner replied. "He's accessed to our computers, which are authorized, by law, passage into overseas airlines."

"Can we trace that?"

"Maybe," Buchner said. "Last-minute bookings on overseas flights are usually tough to get. If he had trouble, he would have used State Department authorization and forced booking."

Angostis moved out of the closet, watching the other agents hurry around the room. "Use the unsecured line and check it out," he told Buchner, "then go get one of the cars. We need to get out of here."

"Yes, sir."

Angostis stared around the room. There may have been a hundred security leaks in there, and they didn't have time to cover them all.

Albert Sorrel came out of the closet, wearing a sport shirt and a pair of sharkskin trousers that ended at midcalf. Angostis stared hard at him.

"You look like the fool that you are," he said.

The man stared at the floor. "I'm sorry," he said quietly.

"Do you know who I am?"

"I saw your picture once."

"Well, I'm not very impressed with you, Cowboy," Angostis said. "You've just screwed up the biggest mission of your life and been made to play the fool."

"Yes, sir."

"You've got one chance to redeem yourself. Are you man enough to take it?"

Sorrel straightened, the knit shirt riding up on his stomach. "Yes, sir."

"Take the trip as scheduled," Angostis said. "We've arranged somewhat speedier, more obvious, transportation. When you get there, find Cassady and kill him, for your own honor if nothing else. Then complete your mission as planned."

"Yes, sir," Sorrel said sharply.

"If you can't do it," the director warned, "don't bother coming back. Got it?"

"Yes, sir."

"I hope so." He turned from the man, addressing the others. "Gather your findings together and get out."

They hurried around the room, Sorrel helping them. Steakly stood nearby, watching. Angostis motioned him out into the hall.

They moved into the confining space. "I thought I told you to get rid of the police," Angostis said.

"I did. That one came back and wouldn't leave."

The director just stared at him, eyes burning right through. He didn't say a word.

"I—I'm sorry about all this," Steakly said finally. "Those men were my responsibility, I . . ."

"I want you to do something for me," Angostis replied. "I want you to stay after the rest of us have gone."

Steakly's eyes narrowed. "Why?"

"We've got to get rid of this place, understand? This house could possibly be linked to the company."

"Get . . . rid of it?"

"Burn it, Jerry. We don't have time to declassify it because your people brought the whole world down on us."

"I'm just a pencil pusher," Steakly said. "I've never . . ."

Miller Angostis put up a hand to silence the man, then moved to the bedroom door and poked his head in. "Let's go now!" he said, and the men hurried out, led by Albert Sorrel.

"Outside," the director called, hurrying them along. Then he followed them out without a backward glance, leaving Jerry Steakly behind to face the consequences of responsibility.

MAN FOUND IN TRUNK OF CAR

Police are investigating the slashing death today of a man found by a tow truck operator in the trunk of an abandoned car. "The man, one Jacob Morton, died of blood loss after having his throat cut," said Maryland State Police spokesman Tom Petroglio. From his papers it was learned that the man was a Russian citizen who had been living in this country for several years. "We've checked with the FBI and the State Department," said Petroglio, "but we haven't heard back from them yet. Robbery wasn't the motive. His wallet was still in his pocket."

At the present time, state police are working under the assumption the man was murdered because of his citizenship. "I wouldn't want to be a Russian living in the United States this week," Petroglio said. There are so far no suspects in the fatal slashing.

—*Baltimore Sun*

*   *   *

XXIX

MOSCOW

Alexander Doksoi sat in the state box at the Bolshoi Ballet and watched the new season's presentation of *The Flames of Paris*. The first secretary loved the spectacle and the dance above all, and his attendance at the ballet was a passion in life second only to his duty to the party. Andrew Voznesensky once said that the Russian poet took the place of the philosopher, the political commentator, and religion in people's lives. If that were true, Doksoi reflected, ballet was the most beautiful poetry of all.

Chairman Dolgoruki sat beside him, idly tapping his program on his leg in time with the music, and Doksoi knew the man's thoughts were not on Nina Pavlova's beautifully executed grand jetés as the orchestra reached its crescendo, but rather drifted somewhere in the waters of confrontation.

Illa Dolgoruki was one of the surviving politburo members who had participated in the October Revolution, helping the Red Guard drive the provisional government from Petrograd in 1917. He and other survivors formed a cadre of hard-liners who still tried to keep the spirit of the Revolution alive in all phases of life. He hated Doksoi because of the younger man's "one world" economic policies, and live-and-let-live attitude toward America.

When the Vietnamese made their surprise announcement, Dolgoruki rallied his old guard to a show of force against Doksoi's hand's-off approach. He had even coerced President Youskevitch, the weakest member of the triumvirate, into backing him. So the Navy was sent to Ho Chi Minh City above the first secretary's vehement protest. The resultant loss of face when Doksoi was unable to garner enough strength to beat him could be nearly enough to topple his regime. Whatever the outcome, a power struggle was sure to ensue, on that would, no doubt, destroy the spirit of détente that Doksoi and President Herrod had worked so hard to build.

Dolgoruki leaned across the seats. "I like this one," the old man said when the music had lowered to a mourning wail. "Very strong. Very military."

"It's a love story, Illa," Doksoi said.

Dolgoruki laughed, cuffing him on the shoulder. "Just for the women, my friend. In men, the dance is meant to stir the blood."

The music came up again. Doksoi stared down at the stage in sadness. He would fight Dolgoruki for the new world, but he feared he would lose against this last gasp of old-man conservatism. Their military spending was eating them alive. Should it increase, he feared that most worthwhile programs wouldn't survive, beginning with the traditional state support for the ballet.

He looked over at his associate. The man's gray face was pulled tight, like a bag with a drawstring. So much trouble from someone who was simply too old to recognize change as a necessary component of life. He hoped that when he reached Dolgoruki's age, he would be capable of passion beyond simple bloodlust.

If he ever reached Dolgoruki's age. Failure in Mother Russia tended to have a note of finality to it.

Capitol Office Complex—Washington, D.C.
April 15—Midafternoon

Representative Hugh Martindale lay on the couch in his office and watched University of Southern California students protesting the lack of military response to the Vietnamese situation. Earlier it had been groups of older people and handicapped veterans who still had bad memories of the war and wanted the money paid. Before that, American POWs were on with Viet Cong begging for money. And before that, thinly veiled attacks on the MIA-wives organizations. That one had hurt.

When he had left his Georgetown condo that morning, Janie had been crying. She, herself, had belonged to NAMWives when he had been a "guest" of the Hanoi Hilton so many years before.

His bad leg began to hurt, and he put it up on the couch

back to help the blood flow. It had been a long time ago, memories buried deeply to make it seem longer. But as soon as the TV had delivered the first ransom demand, it all flooded back as if it were yesterday—the beatings, the starvation, the message-tapping system, the "confessions," the humiliations, the courage and patriotism.

Hugh was, by nature, a patriotic man. Raised in the Ohio heartland, he had believed in the flag as a matter of course. He had gone to Kent State on an ROTC scholarship, then entered the Air Force as a second lieutenant. When he had been shot down near Haiphong, it was his intrinsic sense of patriotism that had seen him through captivity. And when he had run for office, it was patriotism he had called upon again to help him get elected.

But for some reason, he couldn't fire up patriotism over this. For some reason, doubt clouded every thought that entered his mind on this issue. He didn't know what was the right thing to do here. Did simple patriotism have its limits? Was there room, somewhere, for compassion? Perhaps he was simply too close to the problem. Perhaps . . .

The phone rang. Della, his secretary, had gone to lunch. He'd have to answer himself. He swung his legs off the couch and stood, running a hand through his shock of bright, white hair.

"Martindale," he said, when he picked up the phone.

"Hugh," came the voice of George Keller, minority whip. "How are you?"

"Hi, George," Hugh said, sounding tired even to himself. "My damn leg's been giving me fits."

"The old injury?"

"Yeah. What's up."

"It's this Vietnam thing," the man said. "You know we want to introduce some kind of resolution tomorrow, condemning the ransom and somesuch . . ."

"Uh-huh."

"Well, the party's been trying to figure on directions for this, you know, the best kind of handle to stick on the thing. And this is what we came up with."

There was a slight pause while Keller, who had notorious hayfever, blew his nose. The minority leader had never called him before. Martindale wished the man had left that record intact.

"We've decided to take a tough public stance on this," Keller said. "You know, in the long run, this thing can't help but be positive for us."

"How so?"

"Okay, lookit. If we get in there and really talk up the traditional values and call for the immediate bombing of Saigon, we can turn tomorrow's debate into a fund-raiser and plank for November's platform. The House is up for reelection, and we could sure stand to add a few seats."

"Bombing Saigon would kill the prisoners," Martindale said simply.

"Well, Herrod's not going to do it," Keller said. "That's the beauty. We'll call for it. If Herrod wins, we're no worse off than before. In fact we can say we've lost face abroad because of our weak stance. If this thing blows up in his face, though, we got a shit pile of I-told-you-so's to throw at him."

Martindale looked at his dark walnut desk, at the dogtag that was set in a block of Lucite on top. "Should we even think in terms of winning and losing here?" he asked.

"Hey, I know how you feel," Keller said, "but the party has got to make a commitment, and we want you to be a part of that commitment."

The pain in his leg was excruciating. He moved behind the desk and sat down. Through the open doorway that led to the reception room he could see Della coming back for the afternoon. "What do you want me to do?" he asked.

"During the debate, we've got a bunch of speeches lined up. We thought we'd let you deliver the clincher. You know—ex-POW calling for military action for freedom lovers everywhere. Really spice it up. This is your chance to shine, because everybody will listen to you. I hear you've got a tough reelection campaign coming up. Handle this speech right and it'll put you over the top."

"I'm not sure how I feel about this," Martindale said.

Keller ignored him. "Give us about fifteen minutes, and we'll try and get a vote right after. The resolution won't amount to a hill of shit, but this could be great for the party."

"Fifteen minutes," Martindale repeated and wrote it down on the desk blotter. It *was* time to think about November. The voters in his district were split pretty evenly between the parties, and his opponent was rich, giving him an unlimited campaign fund.

"Oh, and Hugh," Keller said, 'I've seen you walking with a cane before."

"I need one sometimes when the pain's bad."

"Okay. Make sure you have it with you tomorrow. It'll look good under the circumstances."

Martindale nearly laughed. At last the years of torture were turning into an asset.

Indian Ocean—Somewhere Off Sumatra
April 15—High Noon

Seaman First Class Riley Withers lay on the wing of the A-7E Corsair and worked on his tan. Stripped to the waist and wearing shorts, he braced his back against the upslanted wing, sitting in the crease where it folded up. They called him Red because of his hair and the usual look of his face when he got too much sun. Today he was being careful, putting cream on his nose and checking the time religiously.

The sky was a brilliant blue from the flight deck of the *USS Carl Vinson*, the pride of the nuclear fleet. With two reactors to power the steam turbines, she was the fastest thing afloat, capable of thirty-three knots when pushed to it, and it sure seemed to Red that they were pushing.

Something was up. They'd been towing planes onto the flight line all morning, half of *Vinson's* ninety Corsairs and helicopters already on deck, with more coming. They'd been told they were going on maneuvers in the South China Sea, but he didn't believe it, not the way they were roused and sent on their way in the middle of the night.

"I'd rather be dead than red on the head!" someone called from nearby.

He turned to see Greggson, in uniform, running in front of a grinding tow truck on the now-crowded deck to reach him. The wide flight line stretched way off in the distance, its edges jammed with wing to wing aircraft.

He slid around to face the man. "Aaron," he said, "I thought we were going to catch some rays."

"We've been put on alert," the man said, his deep tanned face creased with worry. Huge binoculars hung from his neck. "You'd better get in uniform, pronto."

Red slid off the wing, onto the deck. "What's up?"

"Word has it we're going to Vietnam."

Red laughed, shaking his head vigorously. "Real cute, asshole."

"Honest to God, Red," Greggson returned. "There's some kind of trouble down there with the Russians. Come here."

He led the man past the grayish white planes with the Navy stars on the sides, to the edge lifts. Nearby, surface-to-airs were being loaded into the Sea Sparrow launchers.

"Look," Greggson said, pointing. He took off his binoculars and handed them to Red, who held them up to his face, getting cream from his nose on them.

The deck of *Vinson* sat more than a hundred feet above the waterline, affording a panoramic view of the ocean. They skimmed it, blue-green, glinting sparkles of sunlight in the bright afternoon. There, spread out all around them, were ships. He picked out two cruisers, one a California class, and a destroyer. He swung the glasses around and saw frigates, plus refueling support, amphibious landers and mine warfare ships.

"The whole fucking Sixth Fleet's here," he said low.

"And we're joining elements of the Seventh out of Subic Bay," Greggson said. "All of Yankee Station."

Red pulled the glasses off his face and looked at Greggson. "What the hell's going on?" he asked, and the chill sea air was making goose flesh stand up on his arms.

The man shook his head. "I don't know. I don't think anybody does."

"We could throw a major party with all this hardware."

"Yeah, a worldwide party."

Red brought a hand to his mouth. he was nineteen years old and had joined the Navy to get away from his domineering mother. "You don't think . . ."

"We're sailors," Greggson laughed. "We're not supposed to think."

Above the noise on deck, another sound was making itself heard—jet aircraft. They both looked up to see a whole squadron circling the fleet, spiraling closer, the planes breaking off in different directions, but still circling.

"What are those?" Greggson said.

Red handed him the binoculars. "You're the trained spotter," he said. "You tell me."

Greggson took the glasses, held them up to his face. He

squinted into the afternoon glare, bringing the glasses down slowly a moment later. He looked at Red.

"Well?"

"They're MiGs," he said quietly, "Russian MiGs."

PROTESTS TO FOCUS ON CENTERS

LOS ANGELES, (AP)—The nation's college students should be focusing their political efforts on the collection centers designed to raise money to pay the ransom of over two thousand American servicemen still in Vietnam, according to David Eddings, founder of Students for a Strong America.

"We've got to gear our efforts first and foremost to stopping this left-wing conspiracy," Eddings said. "It's a step we can take, right now, toward putting America back on the right track. Our enemy right now is Nancy Henderson and the NAMWives group."

The Students for a Strong America (SSA) is a loose coalition of protest groups from around the nation's campuses put together by Eddings to try and deal with the current political crisis and to take firm steps as far as future governmental action goes.

"We're a protest and lobbying group," Eddings said after a rally last night. "This is just the beginning. We intend to make this country strong again."

XXX

White House Press Room

April 15—2:30 P.M.

Maurice Benstock stared directly at the camera, willing his feelings through it, trying to open that synergistic pipeline that existed between himself and the audience.

So far, things were moving according to schedule. Prescott, as he had suspected, was trying to make trouble. But it wasn't anything he couldn't handle. He had to keep forging ahead for the good of the country. What he was doing was right and just. America had been a great country once and could be again. It was all a matter of approach and finesse. It was World War III, the attritional war of terrorism—and America was going to win it.

"The pictures we're about to show you were taken at a marine outpost not forty miles north of Saigon," he said, face grim. "The year was 1968, the year of the infamous Tet offensive. This New Year pastime of slaughter and attrition was to become a regular feature until our pullout. If you think the Vietnamese are human beings just like us, watch these films and think again."

The picture switched from Benstock's face to a series of shots taken at an overrun outpost. It wasn't pretty. The men had literally been butchered—hacked to pieces. Heads lay everywhere with wide, frightened eyes. Boys no older than teenagers disemboweled to die slowly in the hot sun, their insides baking. It was war in its impolite extreme, and everywhere the camera panned too quickly, Benstock would have the frame frozen so it could be fully appreciated.

His voice continued over the visuals. "The people who did this, the people who ordered it done, are the same ones who pretend to hold out the hand of friendship today. They are the same ones who cry over the decay of their country now, and yet they were capable of this. . . ."

The scene changed to a montage of film taken after terrorist bombings in Saigon. This time, women and children were added to the stew. They lay, cut and screaming, amid broken restaurant tables and glass and mortar, the camera intimately caressing their final moments on earth.

"They're not our friends," Benstock said, "any more than the mad dog is our friend. Life means nothing to them, not those of their prisoners, not their own. No, my friends, there is nothing we can do with the Vietnamese if we give in to their demands. There is no common ground upon which to meet them. Strength is all they understand, the kind of strength that enabled them to do this. . . ."

The scene switched to the jungle. An entire company of soldiers had been hung upside down, naked, from the trees and left to die that way, most of their hearts eventually

bursting from the extra exertion of trying to pump blood back
through the system.

The scene switched back to Benstock. "We want those
boys back more than anything," he said, eyes moist. The
camera tightened on his eyes. "But we must do it through
our own strength, our own resolve. Nothing else will work.
There's not a person in the government who really believes
the prisoners will be released if we pay the money. The cold,
harsh reality is that ransom money, once paid, does nothing
to insure release. We must put that thought out of our minds,
especially those of you who have been moved by the emotional and highly subjective pleas of the so-called, NAMWives
organization, about which we have been receiving some
startling information." He looked at his watch, then smiled.
"Our time for this hour is up. We'll be back with further
developments in two hours. Until then, remember that the
transmissions you are seeing from Vietnam are designed to
play on your sympathies, and that the personal pleas of the
prisoners could very well be extracted through force. Until
then, good-bye."

He smiled at the camera until the red light went out.
Then he sat back in the chair, the hot lights on his face
cutting off, leaving his flesh tingling. He took the towel from
under the table and wiped his forehead. Sincerity was
exhausting. He remembered why he had gotten out of the
business.

Steve Holmberg, one of his assistants, moved onto the
small set, dropping a stack of mail on the desk. The network
cameramen, the only other spectators in the large room, took
off their headphones, chatting aimlessly and smoking cigarettes.

"Did the letters the way you wanted," Holmberg said,
his suit too large for his slender frame.

Benstock sat up, nodding to the forty or fifty letters and
cables that lay before him. "That should be enough. How do
these run?"

Holmberg hitched up a leg and sat partway on the desk.
"Three to one in favor," he said.

"Good. We don't want to get carried away."

"The President wants to see you as soon as you get the
chance. He's getting his hair cut."

Benstock stood immediately, picked up the stack of
carefully chosen letters.

"Wish me luck, Steve," he said.

Holmberg shook his head and slid off the desktop. "You don't need luck, Benny," he replied. "You always make your own."

Benstock moved off the stage where press conferences were usually held. There was no press here today, though, except for the cameramen. There was nothing to question and no one to question it. The government was simply issuing statements of fact in the person of Maurice Benstock. If he was occasionally stepping over the boundaries of unbiased journalism, it was because it was necessary under the current circumstances.

He walked across the pressroom to the sidedoor, then turned to watch Holmberg gathering papers together at the set's desk.

"How's that other film coming?" he called across the room.

Holmberg smiled while tapping the papers into a neat stack, his eyes on his work. "The lab people are nearly finished with it," he said. "You'll have a chance to look at it before it airs."

"Excellent," Benstock said, then gestured to the room. "See you later, everybody."

He turned and walked out then, a chorus of good-byes following him into the hallway. The barber shop, along with a tailor shop and drug store, sat on the same hallway, on what they called officially, sublevel-A, and unofficially, the mall. He moved along the hall until it teed, then took the left fork.

The shop was not far from the intersection. The door simply had Barber stenciled on it. This was where Kennedy had gotten his famous windblown look, and Reagan his "natural" color. The barbers who worked here were on call twenty-four hours a day.

Benstock knocked. A Secret Serviceman immediately opened the door a crack, flinging it wide when he made visual recognition.

Herrod sat in the center of the room in a large barber chair, while a small man in a white smock moved around him with comb and scissors. This trim was to maintain the look that the President never changed.

Herrod looked tired.

"I can tell you're worrying too much," Benstock said,

smiling, then moving to the chair to pat the man's arm. "That's what you've got advisers for."

Herrod managed a weak smile. "Sometimes I have to do my own worrying," he said. "I'm watching the whole damned world in turmoil and I still can't figure out what my part in all of it is. Do you know I spoke with Doksoi on the hot line a little while ago and he's afraid that all of our arms talks are right out the window."

"He said that?" Benstock replied.

"Of course not," Herrod said. "But it doesn't take a psychiatrist to figure out that the phrases 'suicidal overreaction,' and 'out of our control' mean big trouble for all of us."

"It's not over yet, Mr. President," Benstock said, unwilling to be pessimistic in the face of his own success. "We can still pull this out."

"I hope you're right," Herrod replied, brushing hair off the dial of his wristwatch. He pointed to its face. "Time is beginning to run out already. Three days nearly gone, with no progress in any direction. Have we gotten any word from Prescott?"

Benstock shook his head, catching a glimpse of himself in the large mirror above the rinse sink. "Not really. Just that he's working on our problem in Chicago and hopes for results soon."

"I'm sorry I sent him now," the President said. "He's always been a levelhead in tough situations."

"You really need him where he is," Benstock said.

Herrod nodded tiredly. "I just hope I'm doing the right thing. The fleet's on its way to Ho Chi Minh City and the Russians are already in place. I can't turn on the television without seeing demonstrations or hunger strikes or federal walkouts. Maybe I've handled this thing wrong from the start."

"Don't believe it," Benstock said, and dropped the stack of letters into Herrod's lap. "Your support is out there and it's solid."

Herrod bent his head to the letters, a smile gradually lighting his face. "Mostly support," he said.

"Since our broadcasts began," Benstock said, "support has run consistently at three to one."

"All right," one of the Secret Service said.

"That's the best news I've had since this thing started," Herrod smiled. "Benny, you're a godsend."

Benstock wiggled his eyebrows. "My mama told me that when I was just a baby," he said.

Herrod continued to page through the letters. "Honest to God, I had worried over our TV stance, especially about your going after the MIA wives. But this . . ." He held up the letter stack. "We're reaching the people, letting them know *our* viewpoint for a change. You've given us a solid voice, and I'm grateful."

"This is only the beginning, Mr. President." Benstock beamed. "By the time this is over, we'll have all America solidly behind us where they belong."

"What about NAMWives? I hear they're suing us."

"I'm not finished with them yet," Benstock said. "By the end of the road, they won't be a problem anymore. With your permission, I'd like to go after them even harder."

"Benny," Herrod said. "At this point, you're the only thing I have going for me. Do whatever you need to do. I leave it to your discretion. You're my media expert. That's what we pay you for."

"Yes, indeed," Benstock said, taking back his stack of carefully picked letters. He could switch into high gear now. "Yes, indeed."

NOBELIST DONATES PRIZE

DENVER, (AP)—The winner of last year's Nobel Prize for science has donated the proceeds of his award (around one hundred thousand dollars) to the NAMWives collection drive. Franklin Bonier, winner for his pioneering work in genetics, said, "Nancy Henderson is one of the great people of our age. She is an active force in a glacial world. For that she has my congratulations and my condolences."

Dr. Bonier teaches microbiology at the University of Colorado at Boulder.

XXXI

Camp Friendship

April 15—10:00 P.M.

Ferguson's face did nothing to betray his inner turmoil. Ridley watched the outdoor monitor carefully, appreciating in small measure just how plastic the boundaries of reality really are.

Ferguson sat in the yard, a contingent of American progeny sitting all around him. The children were beggars mostly, but tidied up for the occasion. Several of them stood near the big man, hugging him or touching his scarred and pitted head in naive fascination.

"We all want to go home," Ferguson said. "Vietnam has been like our home for a long time, but we want to be back among our own kind. Our government has . . . abandoned us. We've been deserted by those who should have worked the hardest for our return. Only you, the citizens of the United States, can help us. They need the money here, they really do. All they want is the same chance at life that we enjoy in the States. Is that so much to ask? We've destroyed them. The least we can do is give them a helping hand."

Tears rolled helplessly down his cheeks, and only Ridley knew that he was crying for his own loss of self-respect—the only thing that had kept him alive all this time. Ferguson risked much for them. He had agreed to appear on television to alleviate suspicion about the chain of command, but should they actually escape, he'd be in line for any retribution the government might contemplate against those who spoke out. He risked his future and his good name. He risked the ideals he held most dear. And he did it willingly, without complaint, simply because Jason Ridley had asked him to.

And only the top links in the chain knew of it.

Ridley slowly turned his head, looking around the yard. Large pole lights brightened the area in sections, deep shadows filling in between the lights. The huge fuse box for the yard lights sat outside the high fences and would have to be taken out. Here again, the AWOLs came in handy. One of them, even now, stood in the shadowed part of the yard, near the fence, looking toward the cameras. On the other side of the fence, his Vietnamese wife tended a chicken stand. They spoke casually, passing information back and forth. The pull of the wives was toward their husbands, not their country.

Within the crowd of onlookers to Ferguson's betrayal was Jenkins. He watched the filming with a hard stare, occasionally casting his unconvinced gaze toward Ridley. Whatever Ferguson's little show was doing for their captors, it hadn't fooled Jenkins. Though he was still unwilling to admit it to himself, Ridley knew that Jenkins would have to be eliminated as a problem—one way or the other.

Ferguson had his arms around several of the children. "Free us, people of America," he said. "Free us to return to our families. I've taught the children a song today. We'd like to sing it for you now." He looked to a girl of about fourteen who sat next to him.

The girl looked around, all wide dark eyes and reddish hair. Her face was as vulnerable as dandelion fluff.

"Go ahead, sweetheart," he whispered.

Then the girl began, in a clear high voice, the words she had learned phonetically that day. "Oh beautiful, for spacious skies. For amber waves of grain. . . ."

When Ridley heard the words he felt a hand closing on his own heart, his lips involuntarily joining the song. Others were doing the same.

"For purple mountains majesty, above the fruited plains. . . ."

"Just what the hell are you up to?" Jenkins said from beside Ridley.

Ridley turned to him and answered with another question. "What's gotten into you, Harry?"

"I know you've got something planned, you son of a bitch."

"America, America. God shed His grace on thee."

Ridley's lips were quivering. "Please, Harry. You're going home. We're all going home. Stop being paranoid. Jesus Christ, please leave it alone."

Jenkins hand was on his arm, squeezing hard. "I'll never leave it alone," he said. "This shit may fool the slants, but not me."

"Take your hand off, Harry."

"And crown Thy good, with brotherhood..."

"I'm gonna stop you, Jase," Jenkins said. "If I have to kill you myself, I'm gonna stop you."

They stared hard at one another, nothing but fear and hatred between them. Plastic reality.

"From sea to shining sea."

Everyone was crying when the song ended. Jenkins pulled roughly away from Ridley and strode up to the director.

"I'm next," he said.

The Frenchman was nodding. "Good, good."

Ferguson got up and wandered away from the shooting, while the children quietly filed off, worried that if they had been bad they wouldn't get the rice they had been promised.

Head low, the big man walked across the yard. Ridley wanted to go after him, to thank him, but too many eyes watched. It was as if the entire camp, the entire city, wondered what Jason Ridley had on his mind.

Jenkins walked proudly into the center of the area of TV lights, a small man in a khaki jumpsuit hurrying up to powder off the shine on his head caused by the lights.

"Do you know your speech?" the director called from behind the cameras.

He nodded, eyes set in fierce determination. Ridley hardly recognized him. In the span of three days his friend had been replaced by some sort of metaphysical changeling. Nothing made sense. Nothing seemed real.

"Action!" the director called.

"Me and my buddies have been betrayed," Jenkins began, his fists angrily bunched up in front of his face. "We've been abandoned, left for dead, by the ones who should have cared about us. It hurts me bad. It hurts all of us. How can you leave us here this way, Mr. President? I hear your name is Herrod. I remember another Herod once..."

Ridley couldn't stand it. He jammed his hands into the pockets of his corduroy jeans and walked aimlessly across the yard. All he wanted was distance, distance from Jenkins, from the prying eyes.

He hadn't asked for any of this. Why did it all have to fall on him? He'd spent twenty years having his every action controlled and now he was supposed to deal with the complexities of an international incident. Jenkins had said the

President's name was Herrod. He wondered how many there'd
been since Nixon.

Scattered groups of prisoners stood around the yard,
small groups to avoid trouble with their jailers. They talked
and smoked, occasionally laughing uneasily. Some of them
were his people, passing vital information, or at least they
hoped it was vital. Maybe they were all just kidding themselves. As he passed each group someone would invariably
whisper to the others, everyone turning to watch the senior
officer walk by, everyone wondering if he was going to try
anything. He wondered what the people in Washington were
wondering. What would President Herrod expect him to
do?

The atmosphere was charged, the air alive with rumor. If
things persisted he saw no way to avoid arrest. Perhaps that
was best. Perhaps things would proceed more smoothly if he
were out of the way.

Without realizing it, Ridley had walked toward the communications bunker, its air conditioner humming into the night's
heat, the huge satellite dish sitting atop the flat roof like a
wart.

He stopped short of the building and stared at it, the
television monitor cameras on the corners turning to lock on
him. Seconds later the door opened, Colonel Tin stood there
in full field uniform, the red stars on his collar bright against
the drab khaki, the Dai Ta Khong Quan ampulets taking up
his whole shoulder. The two men locked eyes, Ridley's
apprehensions melting under the glare of those dark, featureless
orbs. He found the inner strength that had been lying
dormant for so long.

This was the battle he had been sent to Vietnam to fight
so many years ago. He intended to win it no matter what the
cost.

...WHO'S ZOOMIN' WHO?

—Miami Herald

XXXII

Chicago, Illinois—Sheraton Hotel

April 15—Late Evening

The phone had rung for the fifteenth time in her ear before Nancy Henderson hung up her end. She was through kidding herself that Sid and the kids had simply been out and would be back. It was way past the children's bedtime. That afternoon she had called his office to find that he'd asked for a leave of absence. A call to the children's daycare didn't help either. They had never shown up that day. Why couldn't he understand that she had to do this, that until this chapter in her life was closed it would always eat at her, always try and make her feel guilty for every bit of happiness she ever experienced. It wouldn't have been so bad if her relationship with Billy had been awful; but it hadn't been. They had been separated when the idealism had been high, and first love had been at its most intense. Maybe that's what scared Sid so, that competition with a dream. Maybe that was the demon she had to slay for all their sakes—especially her own.

The statements Sid had made on television had hurt her deeply, yet she found herself incapable of anger at him. He approached life forthrightly and simply. Could she have prepared him better for this? Billy Phillips had always been a taboo subject between them by mutual, unspoken consent, both of them perhaps hoping that ignoring the fact of his existence would somehow affirm that he had never existed. But try as she might, his ghost had never left her. Now, because of it, she and the man she loved were having to negotiate their relationship over the airwaves of the world.

All around her the suite was filled with women on telephones, high-pitched chatter punctuated by ringing bells. Installers with large utility belts and gray jumpsuits continued to put in more phones. As soon as one was installed, a woman was there to answer it. A local corporation had donated an 800-number to NAMWives, and the calls were coming in from all over the country.

It was a madhouse. Everything was in high gear of necessity. In four days they not only had to have the gold, but had also to transport it halfway around the world, losing another twelve hours in the process. A time-study expert had been brought in specifically to study this problem and had promptly called it a physical impossibility. Nancy had just as promptly fired him and gotten back to work.

"Nancy," came a voice behind her.

She saw Marsha Ridley, the woman's face drawn and tired.

"You need some sleep," Nancy said.

Marsha smiled, her mouth slack. "I can take it if you can."

Nancy used both hands to brush back her long hair. "Who said I can take it?" She smiled. "What's up?"

Marsha tilted her head toward the open frontdoor. "That . . . man by the door is from the Associated Press."

Nancy looked. A short, older man with a round, fleshy face and slicked-back gray hair stood gazing around the room, his lips fixed in a permanent sneer.

Marsha rolled her eyes. "He insists on talking to you."

"Okay," Nancy said, patting Marsha's arm. "I want you to see if you can get through to the L.A. collection center. The last I heard, there was trouble with demonstrations."

"What'll I tell them?"

"To hang on," Nancy said. "We've got part of the tree calling policemen in the area who are also veterans. I think we can work up our own security force."

"Got it."

Nancy turned and walked to the reporter. She stuck out her hand. "I'm Nancy Henderson," she said.

He took the hand reluctantly. "Jess Harper," he said in a slight southern accent highlighted by alcohol. "You sure got yourself a big job for such a little lady."

She gave him a cold stare. "I'm thirty-five years old," she said. "I've earned my own living since the age of nineteen and it hasn't been easy. I've given birth twice and had one miscarriage. I've been lied to and slandered by the government, treated like shit by people who wouldn't give me the time of day, and left wondering for half my life if my husband was alive or dead. At the present moment I'm engaged in a project that we hope will save a couple of thousand lives. I won't ask you to justify *your* existence, Mr. Harper, but if you've got something to ask me, do so because I'm real busy."

He opened his mouth to say something, thought better about it, then said, "How do you expect to raise and transport so much gold in so short a time?"

She took a breath. "You see the phone lines," she said. "People call here from all over the country, and we refer them to our nearest collection center. All the major cities have them, manned by disabled vets. From there, the gold is flown to our central receiving location to prepare for overseas shipment."

"Where is your central receiving location?"

She smiled. "That's classified."

"Where have you gotten the planes for such a major operation?"

"Donated, Mr. Harper. The planes have been donated.

Our movement is touching people from all walks of life. Many have volunteered their private aircraft, along with their time, for this worthy cause."

"That's a lot of gold to be taking away from the American economy and shipping overseas."

"Being mostly in the form of jewelry, it is coming from sources that won't affect our economy whatsoever. I'm glad you asked that question."

"Are you and your present husband, ah . . ." He looked down at his pad. ". . . Sid going to get a divorce over this."

"Of course not," she said calmly, while her stomach knotted up.

Harper looked up at her. "The man has accused you of treason."

"No, he hasn't."

"Mrs. Henderson . . ."

"You will please restrict your questions to the issue of the MIAs. My relationship with my husband is none of your concern."

Harper pursed his lips flipping pages on his notepad. "How do you respond to the repeated attacks in the media by President Herrod?"

"Mr. President will have to answer to his own conscience and the American people for his vicious lies and innuendo. Although I think his attacks are a testament to the strength and vitality of our movement." She looked at her watch. She was late for a strategy meeting with Joey Nhu. "Now, if you'll excuse me, I have a previous . . ."

"One more question, please," Harper said, his voice syrupy.

Nancy looked at him, at the gleam in his eye, and knew this was the real reason he was talking to her. "Just a brief one," she said.

"This will be easy," he said. "Yes or no will do. I'm trying to confirm a rumor. Is it true that you are working directly with North Vietnamese agents in this country in regards to the raising and transporting of the gold?"

"No," she said, trying to keep the tremor out of her voice. "It's not true."

Jerry Prescott stood looking out at the lake. He held a glass of scotch in his hand, but it had gotten warm. Alcohol had always been convenient before, a lubricant to help him

slip through the rough places, but it didn't do anything now.
Facing himself was a chore he could only handle alone. Nothing
would make it easier, nothing but honesty could help at all.

He turned to put his drink down. Myrna was sitting, soft
and quiet, her stockinged legs curled up under her on the
barstool.

He immediately felt guilty when he saw her. "I'm sorry,"
he said. "I invited you up here to reestablish contact and all I
do is pull inward."

"You want to talk?" she said, ignoring his words. "Maybe
it would help."

He sat on the other stool, swiveling to face her. Back in
the bedroom he could hear Tod trying to get through to the
White House without any luck. It was a scenario they had
played out many times that day. And if he had ever doubted
Benstock's intentions, he didn't anymore. This had his finger-
prints all over it. Except for Tod and the marine at the door,
they were alone. Politicians get used to traveling in large
groups and having no privacy. The respite was welcome.

"I'm worried for Nancy Henderson," he said, putting
down the glass and sliding it away from him. "I think they're
setting her up for real trouble."

"She knows that," Myrna said. "She accepts every bit of it."

"But I don't, dammit," he replied. "Benstock's lining her
up like a duck in an arcade. He's building a case against her,
just waiting until her connections come out into the open to
lower the boom."

"Her connections?"

He reached out and took her hands, marveling at their
softness. What kind of idiot would have let this woman slip
into the background of his life? "Somewhere down the line,
if she hasn't already done it, Nancy Henderson will have to
negotiate with the other side. They'll have to make arrangements for transportation and exchange. I see no way she can
keep those things secret, especially with such little time left.
The way things are going with the hate campaign on TV, I
think she'll be arrested for treason."

Her brows narrowed in concern. "You think this is all a
waste of time then?"

"There's too much at stake, too many people involved,
for it to remain a secret," he said. "I think she's done for just
as soon as they make even a small case against her."

"I've seen enough here to know that will make a lot of people really angry."

He nodded. "That's the crazy part. I don't think Simon could recover from such a thing. He'll ultimately come away looking like some horrible monster. He's put all his faith in Benstock, who can't look beyond the momentary gratification, the false gratification that comes through the television."

"It sounds like our Mr. Benstock can't tell the difference between fantasy and reality," Myrna said.

He laughed dryly. "It's not that he can't tell, but that he doesn't think there *is* a difference." He let go of her hands and leaned an arm on the bartop. "Let me ask you a question: If you were in the position that Nancy Henderson's in, what would you do?"

Myrna didn't even hesitate. "I'd do exactly what she's doing, no matter what the government said or did."

"Why?"

She pulled her legs out from under her and stretched. "I don't think the government means more than the people," she said. "And I couldn't go on living if I knew I had let you die without doing everything *I* thought was right to save you. Prison would be nothing compared to the hell I'd go through otherwise. Now I get to ask you the same question."

He stared at her, knowing she realized the question was one that was running deeply through him, that its answer affected much more than the present situation. His entire adult life had been spent in service to a government that he had felt did the greatest amount of good for the greatest number of people. But it was all in question now.

"I don't know if I'm ready to answer that yet," he said.

"I'm afraid, Jerry," she replied, "that you'll have to...and soon."

He lowered his head. "I know."

There was a knock at the door as the marine let Charlie Johnston in. The man hurried across the length of the suite talking as he walked.

"I just got finished with her people," he said. "They've agreed to a meeting at ten." He reached the bar, looked at his watch. "Thirty minutes from now."

Jerry looked over at Myrna. "Thanks," he said. "You've helped."

She nodded. "Want me to go with you?"

He stood, tightening the knot on his tie. "Would you mind?"

"Not at all. Let me comb my hair."

They walked back to the bedroom to find Tod staring at the silent phone. He looked at them, disappointment showing on his face. "I've tried it in ten different directions and can't get through to anybody higher than an assistant to an assistant."

Prescott cuffed him good naturedly on the arm. "Guess neither one of us has the pull we used to," he said. "Don't worry about it."

The man nodded, forcing a smile. "Sorry, Mr. Secretary."

"We haven't pulled all our rabbits out of the hat, yet," Prescott replied, thinking Benstock a fool to believe he could really keep the lines of communication closed. He'd just have to go around the long way.

The TV in the bedroom played silently, Jerry watching it as he slipped into his suit coat. It was the morning of the fourth day in Ho Chi Minh City, and the daily broadcasts were in full swing. When *he* saw the same morning, how much will his life have changed? He felt like a great weight suspended from a constantly unraveling rope. And there was only one way to fall.

Joey Nhu slugged down another bourbon and pointed a wagging finger at Nancy. "This country's been nothing but shit for me," he said, a slight heaviness to his voice. He sat at the desk chair and poured himself another.

"Don't you think..." she began.

"Shut up," he said evenly. "This is my operation, Nancy. *I* do the thinking." He drank again, set it down. "Ever since I got back from Nam, it's been one job to another. Restaurants, sales... they'd keep me just long enough to get them moving good, then they'd trump up some reason to get rid of me. The last job I had was as the kitchen manager at a Holiday Inn. I was bringing in more business than they could handle, and they fired me because they said I was stealing food. Hell, *everybody* takes a little home with them."

"There's something we need to talk about," Nancy said.

Joey stood up, poking his own chest with an index finger. "I'm twenty times smarter than anyone I ever worked for. Those sons of bitches just had the power to keep me down. Well, they're all going to see."

Nancy hated this. She cringed every time she had to deal with him. If only there were another way. "Would you please talk to me for a minute. There's something very important we have to discuss."

He sat back down, face hard. "Everything's under control," he said. "Don't you worry about it."

"I don't want to fly the gold into Vietnam," she said.

"You're full of shit, too," he said.

"You're going to have to listen to me."

"Who the hell do you think you are?" he said, fixing her with his eyes. "This is already set up. You can't come waltzing in here and change my schedule."

"I can and I will." She was trembling inside but had sworn to herself when she had come in that she wouldn't let him intimidate her.

"You don't do what I say, lady, and your old man's gonna die, get it? I pick up that phone, make one call, and he's dead already."

"I'll take the chance," she said, folding her hands on her lap so he wouldn't see how they were shaking.

"We've already made the deal with Air France. There's no other way."

"You'll have to understand my position," she said. "If I simply turn the gold over to you, I have no way of assuring your end of the bargain. Once the gold is gone, it's gone. I must have more control than that."

"I'm an honorable man," he said.

"I won't debate that. It's not the issue."

"It's *exactly* the issue," he said, and brought a hand down hard on the table. She jumped, and he smiled. "I've worked very hard setting this up. I don't care what you want. I don't give a damn what you think you need. I'm in charge, not you. We do it my way, or you can pick your little middle-class ass up off that chair and walk out of here right now."

"That's it?"

He sneered. "You read it loud and clear, sweetheart."

She stood, legs weak. "Well, I guess that's it, then." She turned immediately, walking toward the door, desperation closing in on her.

"Where the hell do you think you're going?" he asked thickly.

"To make other arrangements," she said, and opened the door, walking into the hallway.

She moved slowly to the elevator, mind whirling. If Joey

Nhu had done anything, he had made her aware of just how tenuous her position really was. What to do now? Should she try and get in touch with the Vietnamese herself, and would they still insist on Nhu's plan?

She pushed the elevator button, walking in to the empty car. The door slid closed, boxing her in. When she reached out to push the down button the door slid open again. Joey Nhu stood glaring at her.

"Come back," he said.

She followed him back to his room, his movements jerky from the alcohol. She had backed him down twice and, in so doing, understood much about his character.

"Just for the sake of debate," he said when they had closed the door, "what exactly did you have in mind?"

She took a breath. "I'll fly the gold to a neutral country with a good port," she said. "Then we load a freighter and meet at a prearranged spot in the high seas. When we've heard the prisoners have been released, we turn over the ship. Otherwise, we scuttle it."

"That's stupid," he said. "We'd have to involve another country."

"Stupid or not," she said, "those are my terms."

He stared at her for a full thirty seconds before speaking. "I tell you what I'll do, Nancy," he said, the superiority back in his voice. "I'll call my people and back your plan to the fullest just to show you what a nice guy I am. With me behind it, you might just get what you want. Will that square us up?"

"Just about," she returned, and walked to the desk, picking up the half bottle of bourbon sitting there. She carried it to the bathroom.

"What are you doing?" he asked, following her in.

She moved to the sink and uncapped the bottle. "I'm doing *you* a favor," she said, and began pouring the dark liquid into the sink.

Barrows had insisted that the hallways and elevators leading to the meeting room be totally secured by the military before Prescott went in. There was too much emotion running through the hotel to insure the secretary's safety in crowds. Jerry had reluctantly agreed, but as he and Myrna walked the vacant halls, Tod and Charlie behind, he realized he felt a lot better this way, a lot more able to think rationally.

A small group had congregated down the hall, Nancy Henderson and several of her people. They looked tired, worn out from worry and lack of sleep. He found himself feeling sorry for them again, and got angry at himself for the loss of objectivity.

"Don't go any farther than you intend to go," Myrna said, squeezing his hand. "It's easier to add things later to the discussion than to try and take them back after you've said them."

"I don't even know who I'm speaking *for*," he said. "Am I here to defend Benstock, or Simon, or what?"

"It's the truth you're looking for, Jerry," she replied, then drew a sharp breath. "Though, God help me, I hate politics so much I'm not even sure what motivates my advice."

"Self-interest I can appreciate," he said, and leaned down to kiss her on the cheek.

They reached the room. The door was already open, a marine sergeant standing at parade rest just within. Everyone nodded uneasily, silently, as if words were the enemy here. And perhaps they were, Jerry Prescott thought.

Prescott shrugged, looking around. "Shall we?" he said, motioning through the door.

"I'd like to make a request," Henderson said.

"Of course," Prescott replied.

"I want to meet with you alone," she said. "Just the two of us. Everyone else stays out here."

"Do you really think..."

"That's the only way I'll do it."

He looked at Myrna, who barely nodded in return.

"I'm amenable," he said, turning immediately to Barrows. "You and Charlie stay out here."

Tod nodded, recognizing the tone of voice and responding in kind.

"Somebody order coffee," one of Henderson's entourage said.

Nancy Henderson turned to the older woman beside her. "Marsha," she said, "I don't know how long we'll be, but you're in charge. No interruptions unless it's an extreme emergency."

Jerry shared one more look with Myrna and moved into the room, the marine leaving as he did so. Nancy followed him, then closed and bolted the door behind them.

Nancy took a desk chair and pulled it across from where Jerry was sitting. She looked exhausted, but not tired, as if she were moving with some sort of determination that overcame the body. He knew the feeling well, had experienced it himself during the Cuban missile crisis in '62 when he was one of Kennedy's aides. She still wore the suit she had worn during the press conference. The silence between them became embarrassing.

He had been saving up a bit of honesty, and impulsively decided to use it to break the ice. "I'm sorry," he said, "about what they've done to you on television. I think it's terrible."

"Not terrible enough to do anything about," she said.

He felt his fists clench reactively. The words kept wanting to choke in his throat. He had spent so many years selling the program that the truth was a subject he instinctively avoided. Not this time. Not this time.

"I've been calling the White House all day," he said. "They're avoiding me. I'm unable to get through to the President."

He watched her face strain in confusion. "What do you mean?" she said, and he knew she was having just as hard a time believing his words as he had saying them.

"Why did you want to meet with me alone?" he asked.

"We've been making speeches all day," she said. "If we brought people in with us, we'd just make some more. Time is so short . . . if we can't approach some sort of honesty, there's no reason to meet."

"That's why I told you about my phone calls," he said.

She looked hard at him. "You know that I hate you," she said.

He lowered his head, then looked up at her. "We don't have the time to deal with that, either," he said. "Besides, it doesn't really matter what we think of each other, just so long as we can find a point of communication."

"Can we?" she asked. "Can we do that?"

"I pray that we can."

They looked at one another, the air between them like a wall. And he could see her future, could see how the machinery of government was going to eat her alive because she had the gall to disagree.

"I'm scared shitless," she said at last.

"You should be. This television campaign is designed for one reason alone: to arouse the public against you so they'll applaud your arrest whenever your Vietnamese connections are exposed."

She stiffened, eyes going wide. "Who said anything about Vietnamese connections?"

In that instant he could see how truly frightened she was. He also knew that she had already made her connection.

"This doesn't have to be true confessions," he said. "I'm not interested in how or through whom you transport your gold."

"Then what are you interested in?"

He stood up and took off his jacket, throwing it on the bed. "I don't know," he said. "Maybe my own self-respect."

"I don't know what the hell you're talking about, Mr. Secretary."

Jerry sat back down. "Look, I'll lay it out for you as neatly as I can." He leaned forward in his chair, using his hands as he talked. "You've gone against the government because of your ideals. But the government is bigger than you are, has more money and more manpower. If they want to, they can screw you to the wall. And from what I've seen on the TV, they want to."

She searched his face with her eyes. "Have you got any suggestions?"

He sat back and shrugged. "Sure. Give it up."

"I won't do that."

"Yeah. I know."

The silence came again, and it was even more uneasy this time. Nancy finally broke it. "Funny," she said. "You're the last person in the world I'd want to be with right now, but you're the only one who understands."

He nodded. "I'm afraid for you," he said. "I'm afraid of what's going to happen to you and afraid of what's going to happen to me afterwards. I didn't want to come to Chicago but Simon Herrod asked me to as a friend." He shook his head, tightening his lips. "This television stuff is Maurice Benstock's idea and it goes against everything I stand for."

He stopped talking and looked at her. Myrna had said that it would be easier to add to the discussion afterwards than to say the wrong thing, but he couldn't help himself. He quite simply couldn't live with the thought of anything hap-

pening to this woman. Maybe he blamed himself for the past
and wanted to expiate his sins, or maybe she simply embod-
ied the problems that had been plaguing him for years.
Whatever the reason, he found himself unable to keep from
reaching out to her.

"Benstock has had the President's switchboards tied up
all day, including the red phone. He means to have his way
on this."

"Which is, taking care of me."

"Right."

"How can this happen?" she said, voice cracking. "I
though this was supposed to be a free country."

He shook his head. "I have no answer for you."

Her face hardened. "Pretty convenient for you," she
said, voice strong again. "Poor Mr. Secretary can come in and
transfer his sins over to the nice lady, then walk away clean,
sadder but wiser."

It was her turn to stand up. She walked around to lean
against the back of her chair, staring down at him from the
superior position. "If it bothers you so much, do something
about it."

"Like what?"

"Oh, you're so clever Jerry, until it comes time to pass
out the guts." She walked up close to glare at him. "Call a
press conference. Blow the whistle on Benstock. Bring it all
out into the open. The people would believe you. If your
remorse is so genuine, do something about it."

"B-But Simon Herrod is my friend, I . . ."

"And my husband's going to die in Vietnam!" she screamed,
shaking with rage. "And it will be your fault. At least Benstock
believes in what he's doing. What do you believe in, Mr.
Secretary? What kind of explosion does it take to move *you*
to action?"

There was a commotion out in the hall, the sounds of
shouting, a scuffle outside. Henderson looked at him once,
then turned, walking toward the door.

"Nancy!" came muffled voices. "Nancy!"

She put her hands on the door. "What is it?" she
shouted.

"Turn on the TV! The TV—quickly!"

She flared back around, watching Jerry intently as she
moved to the set and turned it on.

The picture focused. It was grainy and old, but recognizable. Nancy Henderson was there, looking younger, but not much different. The woman she called Marsha was also there, and some other women he recognized from the Nixon days. They were all shaking hands with a group of smiling Vietnamese.

"That's Paris," she said, her voice low and husky.

"Nineteen seventy-three," he said, "when I took your delegation to meet with the peace negotiators. But something's wrong, I . . ."

"You used to be in these pictures," she said. "They've cropped them so you're missing."

He reached out and turned up the sound. Benstock's voice purred with authority. ". . . found these films in our CIA research facilities. This was taken by hidden camera during the Paris peace talks."

"Hidden camera!" Nancy said. "We were there with the government!"

"It clearly shows four members of the NAMWives organization in conference with North Vietnamese officials."

The scene changed to one of Benstock sitting at his desk. He had a fuzzy, blown-up photo of the scene just shown. The camera pulled in tight on the face of each woman.

"We've managed to identify all of these women," Benstock said. "Marsha Ridley, then-president of the group; Sheila Fredericks, vice-president; Nan Tompkins, secretary. She has since died mysteriously in the Middle East . . ."

"Mysteriously?" Nancy said. "She was in a plane crash on vacation."

"And Nancy Henderson, who then went by the name of Nancy Phillips."

"God, they make a married name seem like an alias," she said.

"These women met for several hours with the North Vietnamese and when they left, they carried away information."

The film came back on again, showing the smiling women leaving the gray stone structure on a busy city street. Nancy carried a briefcase.

"That held the list of dogtag numbers of confirmed dead," she said.

The picture froze with the women smiling, then focused in on the briefcase. "What were the contents of this case?"

Benstock asked. "We may never know. But isn't it interesting, so many years later, that the names of Billy Phillips, Jason Ridley, Murray Fredericks, and Vincent Tompkins all appear on the survivors' list from Camp Friendship? What incredible plan could they have hatched that day so long ago?"

The picture switched to a close-up of Benstock. "Are the events of the last few days somehow related to all this?" His eyes were staring hard at the screen, boring a hole right into the audience. "Ask yourselves this question: How could an organization as small as NAMWives hope to raise such large amounts of cash in such a short time, transport it, and negotiate for the prisoners' release without help from the North Vietnamese? I'll answer the question for you—they can't. This is Maurice Benstock. I'll be back tomorrow with more on this and other related stories."

Jerry reached out and snapped off the television. "I'm really sorry," he said.

"Just get away from me you son of a bitch," she whispered.

He stood immediately, moving toward the door. Nancy picked up the desk chair and swinging it viciously, put it right through the television screen.

Sid Henderson sat in the den at his mother's house, the shades drawn against the afternoon, the television replaying the story about Nancy's visit to Paris during the peace talks.

This made no sense to him. His wife would never do the things they had accused her of. For the first time he began to realize that she could go to jail for the type of thing they were showing. She may be screwed up, but she wasn't a criminal.

The phone had been ringing all day, his mother taking the calls, telling the media leeches on the other end that her son wasn't there. That's why the shades were drawn. He was hiding. A grown man with two children was having to hide in his mother's house.

He heard the phone ring in the other room, a knock coming on the front door at the same time.

"I'll get it," he called, moving out of the den to the front door.

He pulled it open, coming face-to-face with a television camera.

"Mr. Henderson!" A female reporter wearing too much make-up said. "You *are* here."

"Get out," he said low. "This is private property and you're trespassing."

"We just want to ask you a few questions about the reports the government has been running about your wife's activities."

"I don't know anything," he said. "Go away."

"Will you testify against her if there is a trial?"

"If you don't get off this porch right now I'm going to shove that camera down your throat, lady."

She backed off, taking the cameraman back a few paces with her. "We represent the public," she said. "This is news they have a right to know."

"Do they have a right to know lies!" he yelled. "Do they have a right to hear slander?"

The woman smiled slightly. "Then you feel that the reports we've been seeing are not the truth?"

He opened the door, stepping out onto the porch of the old white-frame house. He smiled back at her. "You want a statement?"

"You bet," she answered.

"All right. I'll oblige."

"Wait," she said. "Let us bring the camera in close."

He stood patiently while they moved in and focused.

"Okay," she said. "Shoot."

"Gladly," he said, and looked directly into the camera lens. "People of the United States of America... fuck you!"

He turned and walked back into the house, slamming the door behind him. He leaned up against it, his mind in turmoil. What was going on? What in God's name was happening?

CHURCH ATTENDANCE UP

WASHINGTON, (AP)—The nation's churches are doing a booming business since the development of the hostage situation in Vietnam and the subsequent involvement of the Soviet Union. "We're bursting at the seams," said United Methodist spokesman Rev. Larry Meens in a phone interview. "We have prayer vigils going nearly around the clock, and that's all over the country," he said. "I guess people turn to God when things get rough. Listen, I'm not complaining. Maybe it will stay like this after the crisis is over."

A random sampling of other churches showed the same pattern all over the country. In related developments, it seems that not everyone is taking his solace in church. The nation's liquor stores are also reporting sharp increases in sales.

XXXIII

Bangkok, Thailand— Don Muang Airport

April 16—3:37 A.M.

"May I see your passport, Mr. . . . ?"

"Perkins," Cassady said, pulling the pipe out of his mouth. "Richard Perkins."

He reached in his jacket pocket, and pulled out the last of his passports, handing it to the small brown man at the counter. A line of similar counters stretched out on both sides of him, others from the flight sleepily moving along, sliding their luggage up the counter to be examined in the pale yellow lighting of the humid airport.

"You have no visa," the man said to him, as he examined the photograph, then checked Cassady against it. It had better match, he was wearing the same beard he had worn for the photo and the same thick-lensed glasses he could barely see through.

"I'm a professor of comparative religions on holiday," Cassady said. "I'm here to study Songkran."

The man brightened, brown eyes shining. "You like our water festival, then?"

Cassady nodded. "I was here long ago, during the war. I enjoyed water festival very much then."

The man put his hands together and bowed slightly. "*Sawad dee, cap,*" he said. "Welcome back."

Cassady returned the gesture. "*Sawad dee, cap.*"

"I will look at your baggage now."

Cassady slipped the small overnight bag up to the customs inspector. The man opened it, going through the few essentials it contained, having no idea it was lined with money.

There was a glass partition beyond the customs counters. Beyond that, several Thai military stood, carefully watching everything. And next to them, a tall, brooding American, who could have only been station personnel.

There was a small commotion at the counter beside him. An extremely large man with kinky blond hair and a red face was arguing with the customs agent, who had turned and summoned the officials behind the glass.

"What's the 'old up?" the man asked loudly, in a booming Australian accent. He was dressed in khakis and combat boots.

The uniformed officials rushed in, followed by the American.

"He carry guns," the customs agent said, pointing to a .45 and a disassembled rifle in the man's luggage.

"Of course I bloody-well carry guns," the man said. "I'm a hunter. That's what I do."

"You have papers?" the American asked. "Permits to bring these things in here?"

"You bet I got permits," the man said, fumbling through the papers in a small, hand valise he carried. "I'm here to take the royal family on safari. I've got enough papers to choke all of you."

One of the officials reached for the .45, the man shoving him away. "There you . . ."

They grabbed him then, pinning his arms behind his back as he struggled, shouting at them the whole time.

Cassady's man closed the suitcase, rolling his eyes at the commotion. "All Thailand not like this," he said. "You have good time here."

"I know I will," Cassady said.

The man stamped his passport in several places, signing under the blue ink of the official seal. "You stay fifteen days, no longer. If you want stay longer, go to American Embassy and get visá."

"Thank you," Cassady said, bowing. He picked up his
bag and walked past the struggling Australian, into the airport proper. The American was looking at a wirephoto of
Cassady, trying to make the Australian's face fit the photo
without success.

He changed some dollars into baht, moved toward the
front entrance. The airport was quiet, nearly deserted. Some
Indians and Japanese strolled around.

It felt good being here, like breathing fresh air after a
long confinement. Between missions, he and Kim had taken
R and R in Bangkok, weaving themselves into their own
personal world where they knew no one but each other. It
had been during dinner at the Oriental's Nomandie Grill,
while they watched the small boats packing the *Chao Phya*,
that she told him she was pregnant with his child, a child she
was later to lose through miscarriage. He almost hadn't gone
back after that trip, and a million times since had wished he
hadn't.

He reached the long glass doors that led into the warm
night. Another American was coming in, his white suit dripping
wet, water festival in full swing. It was a religious celebration
of spring, where birds and fish are set free and water is
sprinkled on the hands of Buddha and the monks, the bonze.
It is also the time when people throw water on their
unsuspecting neighbors, everyone joining in the good-natured
fun.

The man who passed Cassady, however, was not enjoying
himself. He cursed under his breath as he hurried along,
clutching a briefcase to his chest.

Cassady moved into the night, walking to the first of a
line of cabs in front of the airport. The cabbie had his cap
pulled down over his face.

"*Taow rye* Embassy Row? he asked.

The man sized him up, saw he had an American, and
said, "Twenty baht. Long trip."

"Sim," Cassady said. "Not so long a trip."

"Ten baht, okay," the man said, and was still probably
making a killing. Cassady climbed into the back of the
English Ford, and they were off.

Richard McKinley hurried toward customs, embarrassed
every time someone turned to stare at him in his wet suit.

Damn those cabbies. It was if they lay in wait just for him. Water Festival lasts for a week and had only two more days to go. He had known very few dry moments for the last five days.

He spotted Franklin near the customs area, watching some Thai military handcuff a man who was twice as big as they. The man was screaming incomprehensibly.

Franklin waved him over as soon as he saw him. The tall man raised an eyebrow as McKinley walked up.

"Raining?" he asked.

McKinley handed him the briefcase without responding to the question. "Just got this telex in," he said. "They've made Cassady's cover."

Franklin opened the wet leather case and extracted the classified document. "Richard Perkins," he read, "coming in on an AJ-14 from DOD."

He reached into his pocket, pulling out a folded-up copy of the passenger manifesto. He ran his finger down the list of names until he found it. "He's on this flight!"

The customs area was full of passengers. Franklin told the Thais to release the Australian, then hurried through the glass doors. "Passenger Richard Perkins," he called. "Will passenger Richard Perkins please step forward."

"Mr. Perkins already here," one of the customs officers called. "He just left."

Franklin pushed through the crowd to reach the officer. "What did he look like?"

The man put hands up to his face. "He have big beard," he said, "and smoke pipe."

McKinley had walked into the confusion. "I passed him on the way in!"

"Get him!"

McKinley hurried back out through the airport, wondering if he'd be using the .38 that hung under his arm. He'd never fired the gun outside the range, and the thought exhilarated him.

He ran through the sparse crowds in the wide open structure, then outside. There was only a line of cabs with sleeping drivers, and the hot wind of the Bangkok night.

Cassady took off the beard and makeup as they drove toward the cluster of tree-lined streets that held the palatial embassies of many countries. Bangkok was asleep right now, waiting out the night. Only tourists out late from the night spots, and roving bands of Thai youths braved the darkness. Within an hour, though, the monks would leave the local *wats* and begin their day by begging for food before the sun came up too hot, and soon after, the local canals, the *klongs*, would fill with thousands of small skiffs—local merchants selling their wares in the floating markets.

They passed the ramshackled dwellings with rusted tin roofs on Phayathai Road, onto Rama IV, and the beginning of the rich housing. When they neared the intersection of Silom Road, Cassady tapped the driver on the shoulder. "Stop here," he said.

"This not near house," the driver responded.

"*My pen lai,*" Cassady responded.

The man shrugged, then turned to look at him, his mouth falling open at the sight of a beardless Cassady. He hit the brakes immediately, screeching to a halt in the middle of the wide boulevard.

"*Dee mark,*" Cassady said, climbing out of the back of the car. He handed the incredulous driver the ten baht they had agreed upon, then gave him an extra ten for a tip. "*Corp Coon.*"

The man stared at the money in his hand, mumbling "*Sawad dee, cap,*" as Cassady hurried off into the darkness.

Cassady stayed close to the shadows by the high embassy walls as he hurried along Silom. It had been a long time since he'd been here, but he'd find the place again just as soon as he got near the Russian Embassy.

He spotted it at the end of the block, immediately looking for the old converted palace annex that sat catty-corner across the street.

He stood on the corner, in the shadow of a stand of banyon trees, and watched a Thai police cruiser slide past. He couldn't be very far ahead of them at this point and would have to be extremely careful. The building he sought was where he thought it would be. He ran across the wide, empty street and through the open, street-side doorway.

The annex had once been a hunting lodge when Bangkok was nothing more than wild plum orchards at the turn of the century. It had been converted to apartments years ago, and the Bangkok CIA station had bought up some of it as part of their CI operations, keeping an eye on the Russian Embassy.

The building had a facade of white stone, but the sloping pagoda roof was still intact, as was the small, ornate spirit house that was set on a pole in front.

He took the marble stairs up two at a time until he reached the fourth floor. He walked a long hallway, lit only by a candle on a high stand, and stopped in front of the apartment at hall's end.

He gave two sharp knocks, then waited a few seconds before giving two more. He repeated this procedure several times until he heard a sleepy-sounding voice on the other side.

"Who is it?"

"A friend. Open up."

"Who is it?"

Cassady smiled. "Remember the Gemini bar in Saigon?"

The door flung open immediately, a man in a wheelchair on the other side. He wore a T-shirt and boxer shorts that didn't hide the fact that his legs were gone from the knees down. "Cassady, you son of a bitch!" he yelled. "Get your ass in here!"

"Hey, Tully," Cassady said, walking inside, looking back down the hall before closing the door.

The man wheeled the chair out of the way with powerful arms to allow passage. "I figured they killed you off long ago," he said.

"I thought you heard," Cassady said, bolting the door. "Only the good die young."

"You son of a bitch," Tully said, his face and paunch gone all to flesh. "You son of a bitch. How many asses did we kick in the Gemini that day?"

"Fifteen," Cassady said. "One for every day I had to spend in the stockade."

Tully threw back his head and laughed loudly. "I got less time for a murder there once."

Cassady set his suitcase on the floor and looked around the apartment. There was a large living room, mostly taken up by the tools of Tully's business. A small TV camera sat before a blacked-in window, pointing across the street at the Russian Embassy. It juiced a picture onto a monitor of the west garden of the embassy. It was Tully's job to watch that garden, recording any conversations that took place there to send along to the Russian lip-readers.

He also had decoding equipment, plus a telex, and large-spool tape decks. Electronic gear was strewn around here and there. Off the living room was a well-lit kitchen that had a bathroom and bedroom attached to it. A head was poking around the bedroom doorframe.

"Who's the company?" he asked.

Tully looked quizzical. "Nobody," he said. "A local. Come on out here, sweetheart."

"I have no clothes," a woman's voice replied.

"Just come on out and meet my friend."

A naked Thai girl walked through the kitchen and into the living room. She had raven hair spilling way down her back, her smooth skin the color of bronze.

Cassady stared hard at her, taking in the whole length of her body. She returned his gaze boldly and put her hands on her hips—a prostitute.

"This is my old friend, Cassady," Tully said.

The girl was beginning to wake up and smell the dollars. "Your friend want skivvy show?" she asked.

"No," Cassady said. He spotted a flower-printed shift on Tully's worn sofa and picked it up, throwing it to her. "Get dressed. Go home."

She frowned deeply and looked at Tully. "You say I stay all night."

"You just do like the man says," Tully replied, sitting back and stroking his chin. "I'll pay for all night."

The girl's face lit up and she slid into the dress, sitting on the couch to slip on her four-inch heels. Tully pulled some cash out of the side-pocket of his wheelchair and tossed it on the couch.

She stood, stuffing the money into the front of the dress. "You have me back sometime?"

"Yeah," he said. "Sometime."

She left without another word, Cassady locking the door behind her. "A little young for you," he said.

"I have to take the thrills where I can get them, don't I?" Tully replied. "I sure don't get a lot of satisfaction out of my work."

"Beats inactive," Cassady said.

"Yeah."

Tully had worked with Cassady in Nam until he lost his legs to an American Bouncing Betty in '73. He had worked at the Bangkok station ever since. His kind of surveillance was usually done by an elderly couple, but Tully was perfect for the work.

His arms were huge, the result of constantly working out with weights, and he could wheel his chair around like a demon in a cage.

"Let's have a drink," Tully said, slapping his hands together. "Not often I get the chance to shoot the shit with an old friend."

"I don't have a lot of time," Cassady said.

"Got time for a drink," Tully replied.

He wheeled to the kitchen table, Cassady following him in. A bottle of Leaping Deer sat on the wooden top. Tully got glasses while he took a seat. The house lizard sat atop the small, American-made refrigerator—staring.

"Been a lot of years," Cassady said.

"Since '75," Tully said, wheeling around with the glasses and setting them on the table. He had a cardful of punch-out capsules of some sort. He poured them each a glass full of whiskey, then popped one of the pills off the card and stuck it in his mouth.

"What's that?" Cassady asked.

"A little preventative medicine," Tully replied, swallowing the pill with a drink. "Tetracycline. In case my little friend has anything contagious. Wondered if I'd ever see you again."

Cassady frowned, taking a drink. "After I finished with the Seventh Day Adventist rehab hospital, they sent me back to the States and never let me come back."

"You still work for the company, though?"

"Oh yeah."

"Get around a lot?"

"Some."

"How'd you know I'd still be here?"

Cassady drank deeply. He had taken some crystal meth. before getting off the plane and his brain was moving at a hundred miles an hour. He could barely feel the liquor going down. "Found you in the files."

Tully ran a hand through thinning hair and finished his drink, immediately pouring another. "Don't think you'd breech security to make a social call."

"Well, you're right. I need something."

"And what could old Tully do for you?"

"I need some hardware and some information. I got in a sticky situation with the locals and had to unload all my ordnance."

Tully drank again, his eyes studying Cassady. "You on business?"

"Yeah."

"Why don't you just deal through the station?"

"'Cause I came to you, Tully."

Tully wheeled away from the table and disappeared into the bedroom. Cassady could hear him rummaging through drawers. "What sort of information?" he called back.

"I need transport, bad," Cassady said. "Who's still in business?"

"Where you want to go?"

"Up country. Has Nickademis still got that Huey?"

Tully wheeled back in, a blanket folded up on his lap. "I haven't heard anything different," he said, and lifted the blanket up on the table. "God, I wish I could get out in the field again. You don't know what it's like, sitting here watching myself get old, knowing I could be replaced by a fucking monkey." He stared at Cassady. "I wonder what they'd want you to do up country. Ain't nothing up there but Cambodia."

Cassady ignored him and unfolded the blanket. A 9-mm Uzi lay there, just the right size for his suitcase, a .45, and a K-bar knife, plus several boxes of ammo.

"I can pay you for these," he said.

"Fuck that. Just seeing you's pay enough. Just knowing that you're still out there kicking ass." The man poured another drink. "God, what I'd give..."

"Is Nickademis still in the same place?"

Tully shook his head. "Naw, but I got a number for you." He pulled pencil and paper out of the sidepocket and scribbled some numbers. He dropped it on top of the stack of weapons. "Why does this seem fishy to me?"

"You're getting paranoid in your old age," Cassady replied. "You know I can't tell you everything."

"Something's fishier than that, old buddy." He picked up the glass, studying the liquid within. He looked aging and bitter, a man who had nothing left and nowhere to go. "I think you're into something weird and I don't think it's business at all."

"Don't push it, Tully," Cassady said, standing. "Five

minutes from now I'll be out the door and out of your life. Just leave it at that."

"Sure," Tully said, and drained the glass. "Then I can get back to dying."

Cassady got up and retrieved his suitcase from beside the front door. He opened it on the table and began loading the weapons into it. Tully watched him, silently following his movements.

It began to feel close in there, the smell of peanut oil thick in the heavy air. He finished with the suitcase and shut it, sticking Nickademis's number in the tweed jacket pocket.

He snapped the catch on the lid and shared a look with Tully. Two men on the thin edge of eternity, both desperately trying to think of reasons not to jump to the other side.

The decoder buzzed loudly on the other side of the room, breaking the silence. Then it shuddered to life, clacking a message on the typer beside.

Tully jerked his head to the machine, then turned back. He was smiling. "Now what in the world could that be at this time of night?" he said, his voice almost singsong. He jerked his chair around in that direction.

"Let it go for a few minutes," Cassady said. "You don't need to look at it now."

Tully seemed happy, almost exuberant. "But, it's my job, old buddy. Good jobs don't come along that often for us handicapped workers. I've got to be conscientious."

He rolled quickly over to the printer and pulled a long sheet of paper out of it, reading quickly. He shook a finger at Cassady. "You've been a bad boy," he said.

Cassady moved to him, looking down at the man. "Give me an hour," he said. "That's not too much to ask of our friendship, is it? One lousy hour. I'm trying to break out of this."

Tully reached out and patted his arm. "Sure, Cassady. Sure."

Then those arms pulled hard, jerking Cassady down onto the chair, hands around his neck. He was choking, thumbs pushing into his windpipe. He tried pulling back, jerking, but just pulled the chair across the floor.

He started pounding on Tully, lashing out, but couldn't get any force behind the blows. He was bent over the chair, reality fuzzing around him.

Then, instead of trying to pull away, he dug in his toes and pushed, the wheelchair going backwards. They banged aside the coffee table, bouncing against the ragged sofa, tipping the chair.

The blow loosened Tully's grip, the man grabbing the sofa to keep from falling over. Cassady fell off, coughing, hand to his throat.

He struggled to his feet, still gasping for breath. "Damn . . . damn."

Then Tully was there, hands reaching back to the sidepocket. "You son of a bitch!" he yelled.

Cassady shook his head, saw the cut-off riot gun in the man's hands and dove backward, toward the kitchen.

The blast was deafening in the small room, chips from the floor where Cassady had been flying everywhere. Tully pumped, as Cassady leaped for the table and his suitcase.

He hit the table at the sound of the blast, falling over with it, grabbing the suitcase. Tully was still coming, pumping as he rolled.

Wham!

A cabinet beside him caved in, dishes shattering, falling in pieces. Cassady half crouched, charging for the bedroom, Tully no more than ten feet from him and still coming.

He slammed the bedroom door, snapping the latch to lock it. It smelled of sweat and sex in there and was totally dark. He fell across the bed, fumbling with the latch on the suitcase.

The shotgun fired again, a large hole blasting through the door, light from the kitchen pouring through.

Cassady got the case open, grabbing the .45, feeling for an ammo clip in the darkness.

Another blast, the handle exploding off the door, blowing the whole thing inward. Tully was there, silhouetted against the kitchen light.

Cassady felt the clip, his hands shaking wildly as he tried to shove it in the butt of the gun. He heard Tully pump just as he snapped the clip in place.

He rolled off the bed, the blast from the riot gun tearing into the mattress, down filling the air like snow. He came up firing.

He missed with the first one, Tully pumping again. The second one kicked the gun from Tully's hands, the man sagging in the darkness. The third shot brought a loud groan as Tully pitched violently to the side, the chair falling over. He fired again, just to be sure, but it probably wasn't necessary.

Cassady sat in the darkness beside Tully's bed, breathing heavily. He had to get up and move, had to keep going.

He stood on shaky legs and stuck the pistol into the waistband of his pants. His edge was gone now. It was even-up from here on out.

THURSDAY

PARIS—The French government today called for the use of "moderation" by the United States in dealing with the current crisis in Vietnam. Speaking for the government, Foreign Minister Jacques Borodin said, "Under other circumstances, the U.S. would probably aid Vietnam anyway. Why risk nuclear war over a few dollars?"

Asked if he thought that ransoming hostages was a viable way for governments to fill their coffers, Borodin said, "Now you're putting words in my mouth. This isn't the same thing...not the same thing at all."

—REUTERS

XXXIV

The White House

April 16—Midmorning

The young marine scanned the appointment schedule. "I only see his name on here, Mr. Speaker." He turned the list so Sam Fulton could look at it.

"I see that, son," he said, his soft-spoken voice a counterpoint to his bearlike size. "My secretary must have made a mistake when she set the appointment. Mr. Prescott is supposed to go in with me."

The man looked up. "I'm sorry, Secretary Prescott, but if your name's not on the list, you're not authorized for a meeting time."

Fulton looked at Prescott, Jerry trying hard not to laugh when the big man winked at him.

225

"Well, I guess that's it, then," Fulton said, scowling deeply at the marine. He took a notepad and pencil out of his blue serge sport jacket and leaned down to squint at the nameplate on the young man's breast. "I didn't bring my glasses. Is your name Pickett?"

"Yes, sir."

He carefully wrote it down. "Well," he said, putting the notebook away. "I guess that's it. There's no reason for me to go in without the secretary of state, so I guess I'll leave, too. When Simon asks why a Democratic Congress folded up like a rose in an eclipse during debate today, I'll just refer him to you, Corporal Pickett."

The men turned to walk back through the confusion of the White House entry to a slate-gray Washington spring.

"Excuse me, sirs," the marine said sheepishly.

They turned to stare at him.

"I think I just found your names."

A minute later, they were standing by the first-floor elevator, waiting for a car up.

"I appreciate it, Sam," Prescott said, rubbing a hand across his face. "When I called this morning, the whole day was booked. They weren't expecting me back, so they had no time for me."

"Ain't no big thing, Jerry," he said in his Kansas drawl. "Simon don't really need anything from me. He just wants to pep-talk me for the debates today. You look dead on your feet."

Jerry was surprised. "That good, huh?" He pulled back on his shoulders, stretching his back muscles. "Been up most of the night. Can't take that like I used to."

The elevator arrived, some Pentagon brass stepping out before they could get in. The doors closed, Fulton pushing the third-floor button. "I can't even shit like I used to, Jerry," he said. "What the hell's goin' on with them women up in Chicago?"

"They want their husbands back," Prescott said.

"They're going to get themselves in trouble if they ain't careful. I don't think Simon's into fucking with them."

"How's Congress looking at that?"

Fulton smiled, his fleshed-out farmboy face lighting up. "We're all too busy pulling knives out of our own backs to worry about some other fellers' wives," he said. "The Repubs are screaming for World War Three, and we're caught somewhere between castrating the dinks or jacking them off." He shook his head. "Ask me, I think we oughta just make it illegal to watch television like that preacher said."

Jerry laughed. "That'd cure a multitude of ills," he said.

As they made their way to the Oval Office, Prescott was amazed at the number of military personnel he saw in the halls. He assumed that some sort of mobilization would take place in conjunction with this, but somehow he had misinterpreted the scale.

After sitting up all night pondering the turn things had taken, he had decided to fly back and confront both Herrod and Benstock. It was time the President knew what his media liaison was doing with all that power. It was time to put a stop to it.

He had no luck making an appointment through his office in the State Department. Then he had simply found out who did have appointments and picked his quarry. Sam was more than willing to help him get in to see the President.

When they reached the President's door, several men were filing out, all members of the National Security Agency council, as he, himself was. No one had notified him of a meeting.

They exchanged greetings and moved into the large office. Herrod, in a gray suit, was standing with Miller Angostis and Benstock.

"Jerry, welcome back," Benstock said, shaking hands. "Pretty rough in Chicago?"

"You should know," Prescott said.

"Jerry!" Herrod called, waving him over. "You missed the meeting."

"Nobody told me about it," Prescott said, moving up to Herrod and Angostis. He shook hands with both of them, the CIA director's limp response sending a chill through him.

He had never liked Angostis. There was something unearthly about the man that sent a chill through him. He knew there was a need for men like Angostis in government, but like the ivy that was climbing the back of his house killing everything else, he preferred not to think about it.

"So you have a man in Vietnam now?" Herrod asked.

Angostis flicked a look at Prescott that said, move away.
Jerry made it a point to stay.

"We have a man in country," he said. "Exactly where, I
don't know."

"We're not in contact?"

The director shook his head. "We can't afford a radio
message being picked up. The only thing we have going for
us is surprise. I assume there's nothing we can do anyway. If
the prisoners don't escape, we're right where we are now. If
they do, the fleet will pick them up outside the three-mile
limit."

"God, I'd love to know what's going on there," Herrod
said.

Angostis fixed him with dark eyes. "So would I, Mr.
President. Is there anything else?"

Herrod shrugged. "Keep me posted on any . . . developments or whatever."

"Yes, sir."

The man turned to leave, Benstock intercepting him
before he got away. "Is there any connection between that
stuff in Baltimore and you people?" he asked.

Angostis narrowed his eyes, choosing his words carefully.
"Just what are you referring to?"

"Russian agent dead in Glen Burnie," Benstock said.
"Burned down house that the local cops are blaming on the
FBI."

"Perhaps you'd better ask the FBI," the director said.
"Domestic security is their job, not mine."

He moved around Benstock and got to the door. He
turned once, as if waiting for someone to say something, then
thought again and hurried out.

"Jerry said he wasn't notified about the NSA meeting,"
Herrod said to Benstock. "What happened?"

Benstock showed empty palms. "I plead guilty to that
one," he said. "I just assumed he'd still be in Chicago, so I
had his name struck from the list."

"My assistant could have gone," Jerry said.

"Your assistant quit day before yesterday," Benstock said.

"*Someone* could have gone," Prescott said, frustrated.
"Okay?"

"Sure, Jerry," Benstock said, in a patronizing voice.
"Take it easy."

"Take it easy," Prescott repeated. "I've been trying to get through to somebody here for two days and finally had to sneak in with Sam, like some kind of a pickpocket."

"We spoke just yesterday," Benstock said, his voice low and calm.

Jerry worked for that same coolness, but he couldn't get the anger out of his tone. "I wanted to talk to Simon, not you," he said. "You are the problem I wanted to talk about."

"Gentlemen," Herrod said, but he was fixing Prescott with angry eyes. "Can't we bring this down to a little friendlier level? We're dealing with a major crisis here. I really don't have the time for petty bickering."

"That sounds great to me," Benstock said.

"Maybe I should leave," Fulton said, looking at his watch.

"No," Herrod said, still looking at Prescott. "This is your meeting time, Sam. I really want to keep on schedule."

"I won't take but a minute," Prescott said.

Herrod took a breath, the consternation still on his face. "Okay," he said. "Let's sit down and see what the problem is, but we really don't have a great deal of time." He looked at Fulton. "That okay, Sam?"

The Speaker had already taken a seat on an overstuffed leather chair by the fireplace. "I can park it here just as easy as anywhere," he said. "Besides, this sounds interestin'."

"Well, let's all . . . park it," Herrod said, directing them to the comfortable meeting area in the corner of the office.

Jerry took a chair that was the twin of Fulton's, Benstock and the President sitting on the facing sofa. A TV was playing silently, the Vietnamese's morning offerings. A large man with a pitted and scarred head was sitting with a group of children.

"Now, what's the problem?" Herrod said.

"Have you seen the stuff he's been putting on television about the NAMWives group?" Jerry asked, nodding toward Benstock.

"Not all of it," Herrod responded. "Why?"

"It's full of lies and innuendo!"

Benstock laughed. "It may be full of innuendo, but I don't think there are any out-and-out lies."

Prescott tried to keep calm. "The one last night did

everything but come out and accuse Nancy Henderson of consorting with the enemy for the last decade."

"I'll admit we stretched the truth a bit with that one," Benstock said, "but it does nothing but mirror the intent she's exhibiting now."

"What the hell is that supposed to mean?" Prescott said.

Fulton chuckled. "It means he's reaming them before the fact, Jerry."

"In case you guys don't remember," Jerry said, "we're supposedly living in a free country. You can't accuse someone of a crime until after they've committed it."

"They will," Herrod said coldly.

Prescott narrowed his eyes and stared at a man he hardly recognized anymore. "I don't understand, Mr. President."

"I'll make it very clear, Jerry," he said. "We are faced with a crisis of major proportions, the greatest threat to this nation since the Cuban missile crisis. The Soviet Navy's off the coast of Vietnam, and we're all armed. They have issued some strong statements that make it clear they will fire upon us if we should in any way breech the security of the Vietnamese, with whom they are bound by treaty. The power base is shifting over there, and I really believe they are prepared to do just what they say they'll do to solidify the new order."

"What has this . . ." Jerry began, but Herrod stopped him with an upraised hand.

The President continued. "I've been forced to put the military on yellow alert. We're moving our nuclear subs into target position now. This is a time of extreme national emergency, and the clock is working against us. We can't have a bunch of wild-eyed women walking in and trying to get in the middle of that."

"And if you let them pay the money, the crisis is over," Prescott said.

"And have this government made a fool of?" Benstock asked.

"So what's the foolishness worth?" Prescott asked. "How many lives? We've already lost our integrity by lying about those women."

"You still don't get it, do you Jerry?" Benstock said. "This is war, media war. And if we don't fight it as well as they do, we'll lose everything just as surely as if they dropped nukes on us."

Prescott put his hands in the air. "You make it sound like the truth is something that we can pack away like our winter clothes and use whenever we feel like it."

"The *truth* is what we say it is," Benstock said, and for the first time ever, Prescott saw something akin to intensity on the man's face. "Grow up, Jerry. There's a new world out there."

Prescott looked at the President. "How about you, Simon? Is that what you think, too?"

Herrod slumped for a moment, thinking, choosing his words. Fulton listened intently. "Listen," he said finally, "my job is to hold together the Republic. I feel we must deal from a position of strength. I also feel we must meet the enemy on his own terms, his own territory. Those women are, in my estimation, a threat to the country right now, and yes, I do feel that they must be conspiring with a foreign power in violation of the Constitution. I will do whatever is necessary to stop them. If I can discredit them on television, then it not only stops the movement but kills interest in the movement's followers. As soon as I find those foreign connections, I'll arrest the ringleaders and put a complete stop to it."

"The end doesn't justify the means," Prescott said.

"Platitudes we definitely don't need," Benstock said. "We're making up new rules here."

"You're rationalizing," Prescott said. "If we can't live our ideals, what's any of it worth?" He was floundering badly. He looked to Fulton for support. "What do you think, Sam?"

Fulton frowned at him. "I think we should have given them money back in '75 like Nixon promised." Prescott just stared at him. "Sorry, Jerry. I'm out of my league with this one. I'm just a countryboy trying to make a living."

Benstock was beaming. "Looks like you're the Lone Ranger," he said.

Prescott stood and looked at Herrod. The man wouldn't meet his gaze. "I think when the lies get out, the American people are going to rise up against us and kick us all the way back to where we came from."

Herrod stood, his shoulders slumped. "We've been friends for a long time," he told Prescott. "Please don't judge me too harshly. Believe me when I tell you I'm just doing what's right for the country. If you really want to help those women, go back to Chicago and convince them to stop this nonsense at once. I won't allow it to go on."

"You offer me very little choice," Prescott said. "If this is the new world, I want no part of it. You'll have my resignation on your desk later today."

"Unacceptable," Herrod said. "This is a time of national emergency and I can't be without a secretary of state. You'll just have to stay on until the end of the week."

End of the week, Prescott thought. End of the world.

DIRECTIVE J-47B ... DOD 16 APRIL
TO: HQ NATIONAL GUARD,
MAJOR GEN. ABRAMS
RE: EMERGENCY CLAUSE 14-C

This serves as official notification as per 1600 this date, all active reserves are to be put on standby (yellow) alert. Initiate chain of command accordance with SOP sections 30a through 46. Further instructions pending.

SURVEY SHOWS COUNTRY SPLIT

NEW YORK (AP)—The latest Harris poll shows a nearly fifty-fifty split in the country over the issue of MIA hostages. "The divisions have been very clear," said Lou Harris, whose firm conducted the poll. "In young people below the age of twenty-five, the breakdown is nearly eighty/eighteen and two against paying the ransom. In people over twenty-five, it breaks down sixty-nine/twenty and eleven for payment, with the low undecided numbers due to the extreme television saturation this issue has had.

"This is one of the strongest responses we've ever had in a poll," Harris said, "the people who answered our survey being opinionated in the extreme."

Other factors polled at the same time were whether or not the U.S. should intervene militarily and whether or not this issue could lead to a larger

confrontation with the Soviet Union. On the issue of
military action, the percentage breakdowns were
nearly identical to the divisions found in the ransom
question. On the confrontation-with-Russia issue,
however, the poll showed startling results. Of those
polled, nearly 80 percent felt that this issue could
lead to nuclear war with the Soviets. "It doesn't jibe
with the other results," Harris said. "Perhaps because
of the coverage, we've arrived at some state of
national paranoia."

The polls were conducted at shopping malls
nationwide on Wednesday.

XXXV

Baltimore, Maryland

April 16—Noon

The smell was the first thing that struck Nancy Henderson
as she stepped out of the rental car on Pratt Street. They
were a block from the renovated harbor area, its pungent,
salty odor drifting on a wet breeze, mixed with the exotic
sweet smells of the McCormick Spice Company just down
the street. Gulls called overhead, bright white against the
gray backdrop of a drizzly day. Afternoon traffic hurried past,
thick downtown traffic. Beyond the traffic and the building
she could see the masts of the USS *Constellation* rising from
the old frigate's permanent berth in the harbor.

"All this talk of treason is a bunch of bullshit," Joey Nhu
said as he got out the driver's side of the Pinto and locked it.
"Its not fair. They can't do that."

Nancy took a breath, looking at the old, red-brick building.
"Comes with the territory, Joey," she said, tired of the discussion,
the same one they'd had since they left Chicago. "You can't
expect to go against the government and have them be happy
about it. They'll do what ever they need to, to stop us."

"I just want you to remember that I lose my effectiveness
if my identity becomes known." He shook his head, black hair

falling into his face. "So, if anything...happens, you leave me out of it at all costs."

She stood next to the car, waiting for him to join her on the sidewalk. "If anything happens," she replied, "your 'effectiveness' won't mean a thing to me. We stand or fall together. You're a big important man, you should be proud of your role in this."

"Hey, I'm not afraid of a little heat," he said. "I've got friends...you know? One phone call and I'll be off the hook." He moved around and joined her.

"Then stop worring about it," she said harshly. "We're committed. Let's just go with it."

"Committed," he said halfheartedly. "Yeah." He guided her toward a metal door beside a garage opening. "Let's get off the street."

Using a key, he opened the door. It was hot, a baking smell thick in the atmosphere. They moved through a dark entryway into a large, open warehouse.

A number of Vietnamese hurried about, wheeling carts full of jewelry over to the large smelters that were set in the back on a platform. Men with large gloves and black-lensed glasses grabbed handfuls of jewelry out of the carts, dropping them into the vats; while down the line, molten gold was spouted into forms making easily transportable bullion. Several trucks and passenger cars were parked within, their American drivers standing in groups, chatting and smoking cigarettes while their vehicles were being unloaded.

"I set all this up, myself," Nhu said.

"When?" Nancy asked.

The man looked at her quizzically. "About a month ago. Why?"

She shrugged. It was difficult for her to accept the predetermined nature of all this. Everything seemed to be happening so spontaneously. She wondered how long they had been watching her, at just what point they'd decided she'd be the one to help them.

"Wouldn't it be easier," she said, "to take the gold as is, instead of melting it down?"

"Easier," he replied, his mouth turned down, "but far less profitable. We're smelting to separate the gold from whatever metals it may be mixed with—tin or lead, what have you. What gets poured into the molds is pure."

That made sense to her. She looked around, her gaze settling on the stacks of bullion set on metal pallets in various sections of the building. There seemed to be a lot of it. It was then she noticed that most of the Vietnamese were carrying guns.

"I guess the obvious question," she said, "is, how much have we got so far?"

"I'll find out," he said, and moved away, his two-inch heels clicking on the cement floor of the dimly lit building.

Nancy walked to the Americans who awaited the unloading. She felt small and insignificant. She had to keep reminding herself that this was *her* operation.

Three men stood beside a milk truck with the name Cloverland Farms Dairy written on the side. They all turned to watch her as she approached.

"Hi," she said. "My name's Nancy Henderson. I'd like to thank you for what you're doing for the prisoners."

They brightened. One of the men put his hand out. "I'm John Hartly," he said. "It's good to see you out here in the trenches."

"They've really turned the heat up, haven't they?" one of the others said.

She forced a big smile. "They haven't burned us yet!" she said with enthusiasm. "How are the shipments coming?"

A swarthy man in gray coveralls and a Pontiac patch said, "Slowed down after all they've done. We may get close, but I don't think we'll get it all."

"We'll just do as good as we can," she replied. "Any trouble at the local collection centers?"

Their eyes hardened. "Some," Hartly said. "A bunch of fool kids from the colleges are demonstrating and throwing rocks, but we've handled it so far." He looked at the floor. "They're so young, they just... don't remember."

"Nobody's been hurt, have they?" she asked.

The man in the overalls answered. "Not yet. We're hoping for the best."

"Nancy!" Joey called from across the warehouse. He was waving to get her attention, hurrying across the wide floor.

"See you guys later," she said, and went to meet him.

"I think they're on to us," he said, voice shaking.

"What do you mean?"

He pointed back to the smelting area, speaking quickly.

"They told me a black van's been driving around here a lot, parking in front of the building, then driving on. I think the government's figured it out."

"Just take it easy," she said. Joey's head was turning, eyes darting back and forth. "We haven't done anything wrong. We've gathered our donations here, that's all."

"What if they figure out who I am?" he asked, voice too loud.

"I said to calm down," she said in a coarse whisper. "If they do, they do. We'll just take it as it comes."

She put her hands on his shoulders, trying to calm him. "Just hold together for one more day," she said. "We'll get this stuff on the planes tomorrow and you'll be finished."

He nodded. "One more day," he repeated automatically.

"Now. How much gold do we have right now?"

"Gold," he said absently, then put a hand to his head. "We've got over a billion, but the stuff coming in has really slowed down."

There was a beep from outside, Nancy and Joey turned to the big garage door. A Vietnamese, hand on his holster, ran with mincing steps across the warehouse, pushing a button beside the door. There was another beep, and he released the garage door. It automatically opened with a grind, a Good Humor ice-cream truck waiting in the drive.

As it drove in, Nancy and Joey stepped outside, gazing up and down the streets. A black van with long, mirrored side windows was parked across the street.

"There it is," Joey said, voice cracking. "What'll we do now?"

"We get inside to begin with," she replied. "Then we go about our business."

They moved back into the warehouse, garage door crying as it slowly descended.

"I want to get what we've already done out of here," she said. "And for God's sake, get rid of the guns."

"I'm not authorized for that," Joey replied, bravado long gone. "I'm supposed to keep it all together."

She just stared at him. "Get on the phone and make sure everything's set up for the planes out."

He went to a glassed-in office at the side of the building. She knew she had to start taking some charge of this end of it. Joey Nhu could no longer be trusted. She'd have to do it herself.

* * *

Steve McKenna caught the woman squarely in the view-finder of the videotape camera and zoomed in, getting a good headshot of her and the unidentified Vietnamese.

"ID positive," he said to David Markley. "Got a great shot of her."

"It's her all right." Markley spoke into the telephone receiver in his hand. "I think we got the place for sure."

He listened intently for a moment, McKenna shutting down the camera when the people went inside and the door came down.

"Yeah," Markley said. "We've already ordered up the tap. Do you want to send some more men over here and we'll go in?"

"What charge?" McKenna said. "Have they done anything to violate federal law?"

"Sure," Markley said into the receiver. "I get it."

He hung up the phone. "We're going to wait for awhile," he told McKenna. "We'll work their phone and see what happens."

"What if the phones don't turn up anything?"

Markley leaned to the glovebox, unlocking it with the ignition key. He pulled out a .38 long-barrel, opening the chamber to check the load. "It don't matter," he said, snapping the chamber closed again. "The gold will not be leaving that warehouse." He stuck the gun into his shoulder holster. "And that's official."

XXXVI

Somewhere Over Cambodia

April 16—Morning

The Huey's blades throbbed, the dull thud of concussed air, as Cassady stared down at the teak forests of eastern Cambodia. He was supercharged on speed and adrenaline. As soon as they had passed over the Mekong River he had begun to feel new life pulsing through him; his feelings, so long dormant, reawakening.

"That looks like a good place down there, motherfucker," the Greek said, taking the big cigar out of his mouth. He pointed to a large rice paddy, pale green against the deeper greens of the never-ending forest. "You let me set you down there pretty quick, okay?"

Cassady looked, tan faces under white coolie hats turning to stare up at them, trying to decide whether to run or stay. Judging from the amount of Cambodian-Vietnamese fighting they had passed so far, he didn't blame them. "No," he said, tapping the fuel gauge. "We still got a little gas left, Nicademis. I'm going to get my money's worth."

"Come on, gimme a break, Cassady," the dark man returned. "I always been good to you."

"And you were always paid for it," Cassady said, sitting back in the seat and shifting the Uzi off his lap. He wore a light print shirt, white pants and Ho Chi Minh sandals. His own coolie hat was in back, in the troop area, hanging from one of the still-in-place M-60 mounts, along with his duffle.

"How am I supposed to get back?" Nicademis asked.

"Find some gas."

"Inna middle a this?"

The Greek had been there longer than any of them. He had come to Vietnam as a mercenary in the early sixties, and stayed after, somehow "acquiring" the Air Force Huey. He maintained his own outpost near the Cambodian border, making a living taking big game hunters into inaccessible areas and making occasional soirees into enemy territory for the company. The chopper was still in good shape, though all nationality markings had been painted over with camouflage.

"We've seen enough trucks and fighting," Cassady replied. "There must be plenty of gas floating around."

"They fight all the time here," Nicademis said. "Chinese and Charlies, Cambodians and Thais, Charlies and Cambodians. I get crazy trying to sort it out."

"And everybody pays you."

The Greek puffed rapidly on the cigar and rubbed the thick black stubble of his beard. "Yeah. Ima good guy, just tryin' to get along, you know? I'm not crazy like you."

Cassady took the large map from under his seat and unfolded it. "We ought to be over the border by now," he said, "getting near Tay Ninh. I figure us to have enough fuel to make it there."

"No way we gonna make Tay Ninh," Nicademis said. "The fuel's not gonna last that long. I'll set you down soon, okay?"

Cassady refolded the map. "You'll get me there, my friend. One way or the other." He stared hard at the man. "Okay?"

Nicademis fixed him with brown eyes for a moment, found the hardness there, and shrugged. "Maybe we make Tay Ninh," he said, smiling wide.

They continued on, thunderheads building to the east. Cassady watched out the window, feeling it all come back. It had been many years since he had been here. He hadn't lost the feeling. The way his blood pounded, Vietnam was yesterday. He thought of Kim, her naked body twitching on top of the sheets, the overhead fan beating time like the chopper props. Everything had been larger than life, every second an eternity of living. There had been excitement everywhere. Love had walked hand in hand with Death, and they were the same thing. God, he wanted her. He hadn't had sex since leaving Nam and right now, this instant, was the first time he *had* wanted it. He was awakening from a long slumber, and he was hungry.

The engine coughed, sputtered, then caught again.

"We gotta get down!" the Greek said.

"Look," Cassady said, pointing to the distant north.

A city of twenty thousand sat nestled in the teak forest, a wide band of rice paddies surrounding it. Tay Ninh—fifty miles from Saigon. A paved road wound through its center, disappearing to the south and east in the thick forests. It was a poor city of tin huts and French colonial public buildings. The bright red Vietnamese flag with inlaid gold star flew from the government house.

"You see," Nicademis said. "Charlie military."

Cassady saw. Several units of North Vietnamese regulars were bivouacked around the city, trying to fight the same sort of conventional war against the Cambodians that America tried to fight against them. Nothing changes.

"Well, there oughta be plenty of gas, then," Cassady said. "Find some level ground and put her down."

The engine sputtered again, the Huey losing altitude. It

tried to catch, Nicademis frantically working the choke to squeeze the last bit of juice out of it.

"I think we go down here," he said.

And they did.

They came in at a forty-five degree angle, just clearing the treetops to bang hard in the center of a wild marijuana field twenty feet high. The engine gave out completely fifteen feet off the ground, dropping them rudely to bounce on the spongy ground, pungent green stalks blocking their view, sticking through the door spaces to come in the cockpit.

"You done it to me good, motherfucker," the Greek said, angrily climbing out of the chopper and trying to slam his door against the stalks that filled the space.

Cassady had moved to the back of the Huey to retrieve his gear. Coming around to Nicademis, he found the man sitting crosslegged on the ground.

Cassady put on his coolie hat, then reached into the duffle. He pulled out a stack of American money four inches thick. "Here," he said, dropping the bundle in the Greek's lap. "Buy some gas with this."

The man stared up, eyes wide. "So much."

"Means nothing to me," Cassady said, then started off, quickly disappearing into the brush while the Greek counted out the best part of fifty thousand dollars.

DEMONSTRATORS JAILED

LOS ANGELES (AP)—Two dozen student demonstrators were jailed following a rock and bottle throwing melee near the Watts collection center here today.

"They just went wild," said LAPD Lt. Tom Hagee after the arrests which have followed two days of violent demonstrations against the NAMWives gold collection drive.

Police were called in after collection center security guards were unable to hold back the crowds. The collection center was sacked and its workers, mostly disabled veterans, a great many of them hospitalized.

"This is just another example of left wing oppression," said demonstration leader David Eddings, whose coalition, Students for a Safe America (SSA), has claimed responsibility for riots all over the country. "Our voice is strong. It cannot be silenced."

There is no report yet on the number of injuries.

XXXVII

Camp Friendship

April 16—Lunchtime

It wasn't working.

When Charlie had brought in the big tent and set it up in the yard, everyone had gotten excited about the possibilities— movies, real American movies. It would be the prisoners' first real glimpse of the States since they had left two decades before. And for Ridley it had meant something more— opportunity. It was the golden opportunity to get away from Jenkins's watchful eyes for a time.

Ridley had surrounded himself with his comrades, his people taking up a block of several rows of folding-chair seating. Jenkins had been effectively frozen out. There, in the darkness, Ridley would have a few hours of the concentrated planning time he needed. In some strange way he couldn't shake the notion that Harry was trying to do him a favor, was trying to keep him honest until all went well and they were sent back home, there to laugh about the whole experience over a few beers while having an outdoor barbecue with their wives and families. The thought brought depression, and Colonel Jason Ridley had to shake it because he, now, was responsible for the lives of two thousand men.

But it wasn't working, the movie idea.

Several days before it had occurred to Ridley that Charlie was controlling the prisoners' experiences, that Tin was giving the men the America they knew and loved, so as to whet their appetite for it in a positive way, so they'd behave in order to get it for good and all. It was a fantasy world that didn't exist: Creedence Clearwater and bell-bottom pants and hippies. It was the prisoners' fantasy, and the proof was what was happening in the movie theater.

They were showing two films, two slices of America that were supposed to make the men hungry for more. And in so showing, Tin proved he knew nothing about the American mind.

The first film was called Star Wars, and they were told before the showing that this was the most successful movie ever made. What came on screen confused and angered the prisoners. They were waiting for a movie about life, about their friends and what was happening in the world. What they got was a technological fairy tale, a children's movie dressed up for adults. It was obviously a film for children, yet its complexity of hardware and technical jargon was beyond men who had spent so many years just scratching to stay alive. They wanted meat and got a new toy instead. The fact that they couldn't understand the new toy simply frustrated them. Many realized for the first time that, perhaps, there was a world out there that had passed them by.

The next film fared even worse, though it wouldn't have at one time. The Vietnamese announcer had summed it up very handily when he walked out in front of the screen holding a flashlight up to his face to be seen.

"Everyone make love in America," he had said. "Everyone make bom-bom alla time. They all have good time, and want you back to have good time, too. You watch this and see."

They had rolled the film. It was a hard-core sex movie, the kind that he had watched at smokers for years; except this one was flashier, almost like a regular movie, and in color to boot. It was all there—men with huge dicks, blonds giving blowjobs—but the boisterous reception Charlie expected didn't come, except from a few of the AWOLs who were perfectly happy where they were. For the most part the men saw past the sex to revel in the glimpses of home life and relationships. It made them think vividly of what they had left, and the juxtaposition of those thoughts and feelings against the sharp edges of hard-core sex was more than many of them could bear. There was open weeping in the hot, enclosed tent, many of the men leaving the theater as the film progressed.

As far as Ridley was concerned, he hoped they'd show several more. This was the strategy session he needed.

"So it's the harbor then?" Ferguson asked from the seat behind Ridley, his voice masked by the click-clicking of the projector.

"I don't see any other way," Ridley returned. "If we can make it to the harbor and get down the Saigon River to the sea, we've got three miles separating us from international waters. Any other way we cut it, we've got to go at least three hundred fifty miles across Cambodia to get to Thailand. I don't know if we could make that."

"Plus the fact that there's a war going on there right now," Shinsky, the one-armed man, said.

"There's something else," Larry Frank, the AWOL leader said. He shifted uneasily in his seat beside Ridley.

"What is it?" Ridley asked.

"I sent my wife down to the harbor to see what boats were there, what kind of enemy strength we'd have to worry about."

"Yeah?" Ridley said.

"Everybody's talking at the docks. The word, is that the Russian Navy *and* the Seventh Fleet are anchored just outside the three-mile limit."

"Son of a bitch," Ridley said, sliding down a little farther in the seat. On screen, a woman with huge breasts was being fucked from behind by a man wearing a three-piece suit without the pants.

This was an international incident of major proportions, Ridley realized. If what Frank said was true, they'd *have* to make the harbor. He mopped the sweat off his face with a torn up T-shirt as the responsibility just got heavier. "Do we have a map, yet?"

"We not only have a map," Frank said, pulling a folded-up piece of paper out of his sock, "but it shows the best routes to the harbor."

"Don't give it to me," Ridley said, sticking his hands in his pockets. "Give it to Ferguson. He's cooled off."

Frank slipped the note back to Ferguson. "Troop concentrations are shown on it," he said. 'We've found a roundabout route that can get us through most of the army. Our major problems will come at the harbor itself."

"We can't worry about that now," Shinsky said from Ridley's left.

"We still have the problem with support," Ferguson said.

"Let me take care of that," Ridley replied. "Don't worry about it. Can we get the lights doused?"

"Whenever you say," Frank said, "When do we go?"

"The sixth night," Ridley said, and reached in his breast pocket for his own cigarettes. He tapped one out, put it between his lips. "We'll do it in the middle of the night: Take out the guards and get their weapons, douse the lights, get the trucks, and crash out right through the fences."

"Take out the guards... how?" Slater, the other Hanoi Hilton alumni, said.

"We'll have to kill them," Ridley said.

"That could make it tough on those who stay behind," Shinsky said.

"Yeah," Ridley replied. "That's the idea." He lit his cigarette and inhaled, speaking as smoke came back out with the words. "I want to get that communications shack if we can, also."

"What the hell," Ferguson said.

There was an orgy going on in the film, masses of flesh heaving and grinding. "I think this is almost over," he said. "I'm going out first. You guys follow, but not together."

He moved past a score of knees before getting into the aisle, his head blocking the projector light for several seconds until he had passed it. He walked directly toward the out flap, wanting to turn and take one last look at the screen and not doing it because he wanted to. What he had planned would probably end his life within a day. He didn't want to know what he was missing.

As he walked into bright daylight, Ridley noted a long line stretched out in front of the tent. He turned back to look at Tin's air-conditioned bunker and saw Harry Jenkins knocking on the door and being allowed entry.

He took a deep drag on the cigarette. They'd be coming for him soon, probably that afternoon.

COALITION FORMED

CHICAGO, (AP)—Over two hundred MIA support groups across the country have joined forces with NAMWives to help in the raising of cash to pay for the release of American servicemen still in Vietnam, according to Marsha Ridley, media liaison for NAMWives.

"The response has been tremendous," Mrs. Ridley said. "Virtually all the support groups are with us on this, including MIA parents organizations, disabled vets groups, The Red Cross, self-help groups, and senior citizen action committees.

"Our membership roll is up over fifty thousand right now," Ridley said, "and believe me, they're all active right now in this fund-raising project."

XXXVIII

Washington, D.C.— House of Representatives

April 16—2:23 P.M.

The representative from California was having the time of his life, and the packed gallery which had been listening to heavy doses of party politics all day, was responding in kind.

The man was on his feet, microphone in one hand, the other on his hip looking like a standup comedian. "I'll tell you what they ought to do," he said. "They ought to put commercials in it and make it a weekly series. The ratings would go through the ceiling!"

The halls rang with laughter, the echoes bouncing back down from the rotunda like a thunderstorm. Many in the gallery applauded.

"They could put it on opposite *Dallas* and call it *Uncle Ho's Heroes*."

The laughter reached a crescendo, forcing Sam Fulton to frown and pound his gavel. "I don't want to have to clear the gallery," he said, cocking a wicked eye up at the spectators who totally surrounded them. "But I will not let the business of this body be disrupted by these outbursts."

Several women ran down the gallery stairs and unfurled a banner to hang over the edge of the loft. It read FREE THE PRISONERS NOW. There was a minor commotion as security guards hurried over to remove the women, who simply went limp and had to be carted off. When things finally settled down again, Fulton spoke.

"Mr. Swan, please try and keep your remarks germane to the issues of this debate."

"I'm sorry, Mr. Speaker," the representative said. "I was simply using humor to make a very simple point. It seems to me that the debate itself is harmful to the escalating situation in Ho Chi Minh City. What has made this situation so volatile is the publicity it's receiving. What would happen, gentlemen and ladies, if we simply ignored it? What would happen if we simply refused to play the game?"

Hugh Martindale sat listening to Swan, just as he had been listening to the others all day long. This was a game to all of them to be manipulated to advantage. What if the man was right and the reality they were dealing with was all created by the television? Did that make it any less real? And how do you tell the wives who haven't seen their husbands for so many years that they should just ignore the situation and it would go away?

He was sick to death of all this. As he looked around the floor he saw most of his colleagues either reading the paper or chatting in small groups, laughing and pointing. Several of the older House members were sleeping, heads lolled back on their chairs. Sleep had been a torment to him the last several days. In his dreams he was back at the Hanoi Hilton, watching the camp commander tear up the letter from his wife that the Red Cross had brought. The letter he had waited years to get and that he'd never read. The prison-camp days that had unfocused themselves into gentle, dim pictures over the years were now back full, their reality harsh and brutal. And just the knowing that many of his friends were still living that reality made him feel guilty and dirty.

The guilt was the worst part. He knew it wasn't rational or even logical, but he felt that his years of freedom after captivity were somehow wrong while the others still suffered. He had left too soon and done too little. He wondered if the other POWs felt the same way.

He and Janie had fought the previous night. When she

heard that Keller wanted him to make the bombing speech she had gone to pieces, accusing him of everything short of child molestation for even considering it. He had tried to explain to her that he had to think of the party and of their future. He had tried to make it sound sensible the way George Keller had made it sound sensible to him, but it didn't work. She had spent the night sleeping in the living room, the first time they had been separated for the night since his return from Hanoi.

Damn. The trouble with politics was that as soon as you got elected to office, it immediately became a job. Once it became a job, you thought in terms of keeping it. And as soon as keeping the job became the priority, all sense of right and wrong went out the window. You were simply trying to earn a living.

A pretty blond page was shoving a folded note in his face. She was only about seventeen with vibrant green eyes and a scrubbed-clean look.

"Who from?" he asked, taking the paper.

"The minority leader sends his regards," the girl said, flashing her eyes, the message clear.

"Thanks," he said, ignoring her and unfolding the note. It read: GOT YOUR SPEECH READY? YOU'RE ON TOMORROW, PROBABLY IN LATER MORNING. I'M COUNTING ON YOU TO PUT US OVER THE TOP. GEORGE.

Martindale crumpled up the note, sticking it in the pocket of his sport jacket. He slid down a little farther in his chair, trying to ease the pressure on his throbbing leg.

MOSCOW

April 16—Evening

It was chilly in the office, the cold not being helped by the bleak wind that was blowing through the telephone lines. Alexander Doksoi took a sip of bourbon to keep warm and listened to President Youskevitch making excuses.

"We've always made concessions to the military," the man was saying. "What's the big problem all of a sudden? Have we not always been a blend of the civilian authority and military strength?"

"This is different and you know it, Andrei," the first secretary replied. "There's no threat to us at work here. The Americans simply want their people back, and I can hardly say that I blame them. Our intervention means nothing but international trouble."

"And what about our mutual defense treaties with Vietnam?" Youskevitch replied.

"There's no question of defense involved," Doksoi said. He drained the glass and poured another drink. "They want their people back and nothing more. President Herrod has spoken to me at length about this. What happens if they go into Ho Chi Minh City to take them back? Where does that leave us?"

"Choice compels choice," Youskevitch replied.

"Don't be a fool, Andrei!" Doksoi said. "Dolgoruki just wants me out of the way so he can return things to the old ways. That world doesn't exist anymore. We need the trade and the friendship of America. We can't afford to feed our people as it is."

"You misunderstand, my friend," Youskevitch said, his voice syrupy. "I take no sides here. I just happen to believe that—"

"I don't want to hear it!" Doksoi said, a headache forming behind his eyes. "Andrei . . . you carry an amount of support in the politburo. Dolgoruki can't override me on this without your support. I'm asking you, begging you, to throw enough of it my way to overrule him. If not, I'm afraid we'll be fighting a nuclear war in the South China Sea at the end of this week."

"You're being overdramatic. This is merely a display of solidarity and friendship for one of our allies. Nothing will come of it."

Doksoi slammed a fist on the desktop. "And what if the Americans go in?"

"They won't."

"What if they do?"

There was a pause on the line before Youskevitch spoke again. "Then it will be a problem totally for the military," he said.

Doksoi took the phone from his ear and stared at it before letting it drop gently back on its cradle. Dolgoruki's

KGB connections went deep. He probably had something on Youskevitch to be able to pull his chain so tightly.

He sighed, giving over to the inevitable. The glass of American whiskey set glistening on the desktop. He wondered if he didn't have some capitalist blood in him somewhere.

He picked it up and drank deeply, ruminating on the end of the world. That, he decided, would make Dolgoruki very happy. Entropy, the man would call it, arrogantly reminding people of his scientific background. Total entropy.

XXXIX

Camp Friendship

April 16—Around 9 P.M.

They didn't come for Ridley until after dinner, when everyone had settled in for the night. For dinner they had had a cookout, with hamburgers and barbecued chicken cooked over coalpits dug right in the hard-packed ground of the yard. There was even beer on ice. The atmosphere seemed strangely congenial, even the guards were loosening up and laughing with the prisoners. Underlying the spirit of camaraderie, however, Ridley could sense many eyes turned to him at all times.

They had brought a crate of comic books in then, new ones, and the prisoners gleefully tore into the sweet-smelling pages, learning more about the twists and turns in modern America from them than they had from any other source in the last two decades.

Ridley went back to the barracks early, while most everyone else was still outside, singing and getting drunk in the deepening night. He lay on his bunk, smoking and planning, surprised that his mind continued to function rationally despite the strange emotions that ran through him. Or was he rational? There was no way to tell anymore, no yardstick against which to measure himself. All he had to go on was his code of conduct as a soldier in the Air Force of the

United States of America; it was the point of rationality for all
of his people—a shared reality.

Everyone had stayed away from him after word got
around that Jenkins had paid a visit to Colonel Tin. Emerging
plans were issued through someone who had contact with
Ferguson. They were being forced to depend on the AWOLs
again, the only people in camp with boating experience on
the Saigon River. Getting down that stretch of river to the sea
was going to be the major challenge if they were able to
escape the compound itself.

After a time the others began to slowly trickle in,
sweating under the overhead fans, swatting the mosquitoes
that came in with them. When Jenkins didn't respond to
curfew with the others, Ridley knew they were going to come
for him. It happened after the party had broken up completely.

He saw the guard come in, looking around, just after
lights out. He threw his cigarette to the floor and rolled over,
feigning sleep. Within a minute a hand was shaking him.

"You wake up now," the man said softly, so as not to
disturb anyone else. "You come with me."

Ridley got to his elbows. "I want to sleep," he said, but
the man simply shook his head.

He sat up slowly, with a sense of the inevitable. He was
still dressed, so sure he was of his fate. He slipped into his
shoes and stood, lighting another cigarette before he was led
outside.

A nice breeze took the sting off the hot night as he was
led across the compound toward Tin's bunker. The firepits
had been extinguished and they smoldered all around like
some nightmare-smoking landscape. The smells were of cooked
meat and charred wood.

The door to Tin's bunker was opened immediately upon
his arrival, his cigarette taken away, and he was ushered back
into its tomblike coolness directly to the office.

Tin, still in uniform, and Jenkins were in there drinking
tea. The delicate room of porcelain figurines smelled of
incense. A radio playing atonal Vietnamese music was working at a respectable level in the background.

Ridley ignored Jenkins and spoke immediately. "I protest being brought away from my bed in the middle of the
night," he said, "and request that I be allowed to return to
sleep right away."

Tin simply smiled, indicating a chair beside Jenkins. Ridley saw another one on the opposite side of the room and headed for it instead, pulling it up within reach of the desk the Colonel sat behind.

"You will have tea, Colonel Ridley?" Tin asked.

"No, thanks," Ridley said, looking at Jenkins, who was making himself right at home with tea and a rice cake. "Why have you brought me here?"

"I want to tell you some news," Tin said. "We have been getting reports from America, and it seems the money to rebuild our country is being raised by the citizens of the United States, who are converting their gold jewelry into a more usable form. Our dream is rapidly becoming a reality."

"What's that got to do with me?" Ridley asked.

Tin took a sip of his own tea, eyes bright, face intelligent. "I am a dedicated and patriotic Vietnamese citizen," he said. "What I do, I do only for my country. I think our little... production is having a very fine, nonviolent effect. Just think of it—my country is rebuilt and yours gets back its heroes—and the only cost, a piece of metal off some rich American's finger. Don't you see what a wonderful, unselfish thing this is for everyone involved? What better way for our two nations to stabilize relations again. Perhaps our cultures could once again become good friends, like the Japanese or the Germans."

Ridley stood. "This is politics," he said. "It has nothing to do with me." He indicated Jenkins. "I'll leave you and your friend to discuss it."

"Sit down, Colonel," Tin said, the smile still on his face. Ridley sat.

Tin then stood and walked to one of the rosewood tables containing his figurines. He picked one up, a brightly colored peasant girl in coolie hat balancing a long pole with buckets on the ends on her shoulder. Frowning, he used a handkerchief to wipe some dust off. "No matter how tightly we seal the building, Colonel Ridley," he said, "dust always manages to find its way in."

He brought the statue over and set it on the desk in front of Ridley. "Its takes a delicate hand to form and then paint these. It takes care and deftness, the kind of deftness I've tried to use in constructing my little plan for rebuilding my country. But the dust still gets in and spoils things." He picked up the piece and brought it down hard on the desktop, shattering it. "A beautiful thing, once ruined, retains no beauty at all."

The man went around to the other side of the desk and came back with a small trash can. He began sweeping the broken porcelain off the desk and into the receptacle. "This was my favorite piece," he said, real sadness showing in his voice, "but I break it to remind myself how easily my dream for my country can be shattered." He nodded toward Jenkins, both men treating him as a piece of the furniture. "Your friend tells me you are planning an escape."

"Then my friend is a liar," Ridley returned quickly. "Or maybe years of torture and abuse have simply unhinged his mind. You can certainly understand that, can you not?"

Jenkins was on his feet. "You got something going, Jase, and we all know it."

"You will be silent, Captain." Tin said, turning to stare at the man. Jenkins nodded and sat back down. Tin returned to sit at his desk.

"Let's be honest with each other," Ridley said. "I haven't exercised command prerogatives in over twenty years. Besides that, I've got an 'army' of cripples and mushbrains, to say nothing of the deserters. We're unarmed and locked up in the middle of a hostile city as far away from home as it's possible to be and still remain on the planet. Now you tell me what it is I'm supposed to be plotting?"

"Something crazy and stupid I would suspect," Tin said, again drinking from his tea. "Americans seem to have a genetic affectation for acts of heroic lunacy."

"We don't corner that market, Colonel," Ridley replied. "Or have you forgotten Dien Bien Phu, or perhaps the monks who immolated themselves, or the terrorists who went up with their own bombs?"

"That was a struggle we were destined to win," Tin said.

"What am I doing here?" Ridley asked.

"I quite simply don't want anyone hurt, Colonel Ridley." Tin took a breath and leaned across the desk to get closer to Ridley. "I don't want war. I don't want to kill anyone. You and your men have suffered. In my opinion, you've suffered more than enough to compensate for what you did to my people. I bear no ill will toward any of you. You could never succeed in an escape attempt. It would only bring death to your people, and probably retributions and death to mine. The Vietnamese people, again, would be the ones to suffer. Innocents, once again, thrown on the fires of war. As human beings, can't we forget everything else and work together to make this thing happen?"

"It's interesting that you put all the burden on me," Ridley said, meeting Tin's gaze fiercely. "You knew what the risks were when you began this enterprise. You're the one who started the ball rolling, not me."

"But if you'd just leave it alone," Jenkins said, "everything would be okay. Why do you have to keep getting your nose all bent out of joint. It's that damned Ferguson; he's the one putting all these notions in your head."

Ridley glared at him, not realizing the depth to which Jenkins's treason would reach.

"But Captain Ferguson spoke before our cameras yesterday," Tin said. "Are you saying that *he* is instrumental in an escape plan?"

Jenkins hesitated, looking between Ridley and Tin. "Please, Jase," he said. "Give it up."

"You haven't answered my question," said Tin.

Ridley looked at Tin. "My friend is not well," he said. "He's been following me around like a damned fool for two days, trying to catch me at something. It's embarrassing."

Tin stood and moved for the office door. "You will come with me, Colonel Ridley," he said. "I have something to show you."

Jenkins was up, moving toward the door with them. Tin frowned at the man.

"You'll stay here," he told Jenkins. "We must talk again."

Jenkins lowered his head, returning to his seat.

Tin opened the door and walked out into the cool hall, Ridley right behind.

Ridley knew he'd have to find a way to warn Ferguson and any others his former friend might implicate. He should have taken care of the man before he became dangerous.

"You will find what I have to show you very interesting," Tin said over his shoulder as they walked. "We are capable of many things here at Camp Friendship."

They moved past several guards, through a doorway leading to the control room. Two of the Frenchmen manned the control booth—a small room full of television screens and spinning wheels of videotape. Ridley could see all the tiny screens that monitored the camp cameras. There were other screens and a large control board from where they directed and edited the television stuff being filmed at the camp.

Tin spoke to the man in fluent French, both of them laughing. Then they stood, gathering together some personal articles, and moved out the door, closing it behind them. The lighting was subdued in there, most of the illumination coming from the altered reality of the television screens.

"We not only send our little tableaus over the airwaves from here," Tin said, smiling again, "But we receive also. We received a transmission this evening you may find of interest," He held up a small black case. "Videotape, Colonel. Have you ever seen it?"

Ridley shook his head.

Tin shoved the case into an opening on the control board. "In America everyone owns their own videotape machines." He snapped the lid closed on the tape. "In my country, we don't have enough to eat. Watch."

The two men sat in the darkened booth. A large television screen in the middle of all the others showed static for several seconds before juicing a picture. It was an American television program called, *Good Morning, America*, and a man was sitting in an easychair, interviewing a middle-aged woman.

"No, David," she was saying. "Those films were dummied up, changed somehow."

"That's a pretty serious charge, Mrs. Ridley," the man said. "Can you back that up?"

"Secretary of State Prescott can verify it," she replied. "He was also in that picture, though the administration had him cropped out."

Jason Ridley stared in horrified fascination at the screen. "M—Marsha?" he said. "Marsha!"

"That is your wife," Tin said.

He watched her, feeling totally disassociated from his body. She was there, older, with hard lines of strain around her eyes and mouth. The years hadn't been kind to her—was that because of him? And he realized how completely time had passed him by when he looked at her. She was years away from him, a lifetime. She appeared so self-assured and in control, not anything like the shy little homebody he had left behind. This was his wife on her own. All this she had accomplished alone, without him.

"Where is Nancy Henderson right now?" the man on the TV asked.

"She is overseeing our operation, David," she replied. "And before you ask me again, I'm not going to tell you where she is."

Both of them laughed.

Ridley looked at Tin, who was watching him intently. "Is she . . . has she . . ."

Tin shook his head. "You have a loyal wife," Tin said. "She never remarried. She awaits only you and has worked unceasingly for your release since you were shot down. Her whole life is geared around your safe return to America. She is second-in-command of the organization that is raising the money to rebuild Vietnam. We feel your wife is a great hero over here. Do you see now why it is so important to me that we work together? Please, Colonel Ridley. I don't want anything to happen to you. I don't think your wife could stand it."

Ridley's eyes held the screen, mesmerized. There were no tears in him, only a deep and profound sense of loss, and then anger that the years could rob him so. He wanted to reach through the screen, to touch her, to thank her for the devotion he hardly deserved. He thought back to the count-less times he had hurt her unintentionally, and sometimes, not so unintentionally. He was trapped in his prison; she had entered hers of her own free will—because of him. And now they were in direct opposition.

He hung his head, whatever was left of his emotions completely excavated, scooped out. It was more than he could bear, more than anyone could bear. His sorrow was anesthetizing. He felt numb, a mind operating without a body.

"You have a son of twenty-eight," Tin said. "He's a doctor in Cleveland, Ohio. Your daughter is twenty-seven. Currently divorced, she's living with her children..."

"Stop," Ridley said, raising a hand. "I don't want to know any of it now."

"When?"

"Later," he cried. "After you tell me what I must do."

Tin let out a sigh of relief. "Now, Colonel Ridley," he said. "We can get down to the business of setting you free."

XL

Silver Springs, Maryland

April 16—9:47 P.M.

Jerry Prescott looked at the travel brochure from the Bahamas and thought about his own honeymoon. He and Myrna had met in New York in 1958 while working to get Jack Kennedy the Democratic nomination. Both were young, as all Kennedy people were, and had fallen in love first with politics, then with each other. They had met Simon Herrod around the same time, the three of them fast and close friends from the start. After Kennedy got the nomination, they were all three elevated to more prestigious positions in the party organization, doing advance work in states where the senator was to speak. Jerry and Myrna had married out of desperation, hoping it would get them sent around together as they sojourned through the country. It didn't work that way.

They had married in Maryland in a civil ceremony, other campaign workers their only attendants. They'd had one night together before Jerry was sent to Minnesota and Myrna to California. That had been the beginning of the end of Myrna's love affair with politics, and, undoubtedly, set the tone of their relationship over the intervening years.

"Dad," Randy said. "Earth calling Dad."

Jerry shook his head, smiling at Randy and June on the other side of the card table. Myrna reached over and patted his hand. "Sorry," he said. "I was somewhere else."

"Somewhere pleasant, I hope," Myrna said.

He looked at her. "I was remembering our wedding," he said.

She frowned. "Oh. That."

He shrugged sadly, Myrna returning a casual smile, an it's-really-all-right smile.

"I want you all to stay as long in the Bahamas as you want to," he told them. "You only get to do this once."

"What—travel or have a honeymoon?" June asked.

Randy laughed and put his arm around her, hugging her close. They were so young, so optimistic. "You'd better not have any other honeymoons," he said.

They all sat in the den, television turned off at Jerry's request. He was disgusted with the whole business and his part in it and just needed to be away from it for awhile. When Myrna had suggested that Randy and June come by and talk about their honeymoon wedding present, it seemed like the perfect thing to get his mind off Nancy Henderson and Vietnam.

"We talked about two weeks," Jerry said. "I think we should make it three."

"Wow!" June screamed, jumping up to come around the table and hug him. "Thank you."

"I've never seen you so calm during a crisis," Randy said. "What gives?"

Jerry shook his head. "There's only so much a human being can do before he has to back off and take it easy."

The red phone rang.

They all turned to stare at it. From the spare room off the den Tod Barrows stuck his head out.

"Don't need you now," Jerry told him. The man nodded once and disappeared back in the room. He looked at the others, Myrna already standing and gathering drink glasses.

"Jerry will need to be alone for this call," she said, busily moving around to hide her frustration. No matter how they kidded themselves about freedom and privacy, they were never more than a telephone call away from responsibility.

"We need to be getting along anyway," Randy said, he and June standing. "We really appreciate . . ."

"I'll walk you out," Myrna said, moving in that direction, the phone still jangling. She turned to Jerry. "If you're not too long, I'll be upstairs."

He nodded somberly. "Sorry," he said, then turned toward the phone. What would happen if he just didn't answer it? After all, the world turned without him just fine. If he didn't pick it up, they'd have to go to some other fool and make him pick his up, that's all.

He moved automatically to sit on the couch, wondering what voice would be on the other end. He picked up the receiver. "Prescott."

"Jerry," came a familiar voice. "It's Simon."

"Mr. President," Jerry said. "I somehow didn't expect it would be you."

"Who then?"

"Don't know," Jerry said, knowing something was up. "Maybe the Russians got a wrong number."

"We've got an interesting little problem here," the President said. "I'm going to ask for your help in solving it."

"What is it?"

There was a slight hesitation on the line, just enough to make Jerry know that Herrod was searching for just the right words. "It has to do with that damned NAMWives group," he said finally. "They're raising a big stink about those films taken in Paris."

"Sure they are," Jerry said. "They got screwed."

"I'm not here to debate that point," Herrod said, his voice laced with anger. "I'm fighting a war on several fronts here and I've already made my decisions."

"Then what do you need me for?"

"Okay," Herrod said, "NAMWives is screaming for you. Somehow they know you were in those films and have been cropped out of the picture. They're saying they want you to come forward and corroborate their story. Obviously, we can't do that."

"But they're right," Jerry said.

"We make right," Herrod said, and he sounded just like Benstock. "Look. We've got those bitches coming and going. We found their warehouse this morning and we'll be moving in to confiscate their gold tomorrow morning when the paperwork is finished."

"Confiscate?"

"Yeah. Having that much gold is in possible violation of the Sherman-Clayton Antitrust Act. Owning gold is no longer against the law, but artificially manipulating the market *is*. Just the possession of that much gold shows intent to manipulate."

"I don't know if that could hold up in court," Jerry said, and stretched out on the couch.

"Who cares?" Herrod replied. "All I need to do is buy some time so they'll miss the Sunday deadline. I don't give a rat's ass what they do after that. Meanwhile, I've got people working on establishing connections with the Vietnamese, so we can slap the treason charges on the Henderson woman."

"I don't like it, Simon," Jerry said. "I'm telling you as an adviser and as your friend that the whole thing stinks. Let them pay the goddamned money. It won't be any skin off your nose."

"I'm the President, " Herrod said. "I've already made this policy decision. Your job is to keep your mouth shut and do what I tell you."

"Okay," Jerry said, angry. "I'll bite. What is it you want me to do?"

"Just stay home, Jerry," Herrod said. "Lay low. I'll tell the press that you're on a secret diplomatic mission for me to Vietnam and can't be reached for comment."

"I haven't practiced law for a few years, Simon," Jerry said, "but doesn't that make me an accessory?"

"Don't joke," Herrod said.

"Who's joking? Your boy got himself in hot water, and now you're running to me to help you cover it up. Legally, what does that make me?"

"You're being really stupid about this," Herrod replied. "We're just fighting fire with fire and we don't need a big battle in the press until after this business is all over. You just screen your calls, keep your head down, and in a couple of days this will be over and done with. Then those bitches can sink back to the muck they climbed out of. All except Nancy Henderson. We're going to make an example of her."

"I think that it's you who's being stupid," Jerry said. "Why don't you back off and let Benstock take the blame he deserves on this?"

Herrod took a harsh breath. "You want the truth?" he asked. "Okay, I'll give you two reasons. First, I know I'm right. I know I'm doing what's best for the country as a whole and not just for the self-interest of a few people. Second, Benstock was working for me when he overstepped, *if* he overstepped. The boss always has to take the ultimate flak for what his people do, and I'd sacrifice a thousand Nancy

Hendersons before I'd put myself in a position like that. Do I make myself clear, Jerry?"

"Yes, Mr. President."

"Good. Now this is what I want: Stay home, talk to no one about any of this, and don't let anybody know you're there—reporters can be really persistent. Got it?"

"Yes, sir. What about Benstock?"

"What about him? Mr. Benstock will continue to do the job we're paying him for. What else is there?"

Jerry almost said, cancellation, but thought better of it. "Nothing, I guess."

"Okay." Herrod's voice sounded relieved. "I've got to go to a meeting."

"Good-bye, Mr. President."

"Good-bye."

Herrod hung up immediately. Jerry sat staring at the receiver in perplexity, then hung up. He stood, seeing Tod at the door again. "Mr. Secretary..."

"It's nothing, Tod. I won't need you anymore tonight."

"Thank you," Tod said, and the door reclosed.

Jerry stood, stretching. He felt old, totally used up. Nothing seemed to mean anything, nothing seemed real save the rantings of whomever he was talking to at the time. He was beginning to feel very far away from things, as if he had stopped moving and the politics had kept going. He didn't fit into the scheme of things anymore. He didn't belong. Maybe he was simply being foolish as Herrod had suggested. His cynicism hadn't completely lobotomized his ideals, leaving him only partially cured.

His legs were heavy as he slowly moved across the entry and up the stairs. So, Nancy Henderson was to be the sacrificial goat. He felt bad for her. And to make matters worse, she wasn't even going to get to free her husband for her treason. It wasn't fair and it wasn't just no matter how he looked at it. And the question rapidly became, was he going to compound the problem by acting as accessory after the fact? He knew that idea came from Benstock and it made him even madder—the man was trying to alleviate his own guilt by spreading it around.

When he entered the bedroom Myrna put down her book and looked up. "How did it go?"

"I need your advice," he said. "I need it badly."

She patted the bed beside her. He walked over and sat, putting his hand on her arm. "If you were me," he said, "and knew that Nancy Henderson's gold was going to be confiscated in the morning, would you try and do anything about it?"

"Like what?" she asked.

"I don't know—warn her, I guess."

She removed her glasses and lay them on the nighttable. "There's more, isn't there?"

He nodded. "Simon wants me to go into hiding so I won't have to talk about the Paris films."

"Is that legal?"

He laughed. "Depends on how it comes out in the end. If Simon wins, it's legal, if not, we all go to jail for conspiracy." He lowered his head. "He also intends to prosecute Nancy Henderson for treason."

She reached out a hand to him. "Oh, Jerry—no. That poor woman has been through so much."

"More than anyone should have to go through."

"And you can help her."

He nodded. "At the risk of my entire career, of everything I've worked my whole life for."

"Let me ask you a question," she said. "If you don't help her, will you be able to live with yourself?"

He held her hand, bringing it to his lips. "If I don't help her," he said softly, "will you be able to live with me?"

She reached her arms out to him, hugging him close. When she pulled away, her eyes were filled with tears. "Things haven't been so great for us for a long time," she said, and laughed, wiping her eyes. "Understatement of the year, right?"

He nodded.

"But I've discovered something in the last few days," she said. "I still love you very much and, more importantly, I still respect you. I know that at this point, you'll make the right decision—there's too much good in you not to."

"You'd help her, wouldn't you?" he said.

She raised her eyebrows. "In a heartbeat, wouldn't you?" Then she began to hum, very softly in her off key voice, the theme from *Camelot*. Kennedy's song. It had also been their wedding song.

He reached for the telephone.

* * *

Joey Nhu paced at the end of the telephone cord as if he were tied to it. He gesticulated wildly with his free hand while he talked, a cigarette bobbing between his lips.

"What do you mean, he's not available?" Joey said. "I know he's there. His secretary said he'd be home tonight. It's urgent that I speak with him!"

Nancy Henderson sat on the bed and watched the Vietnamese carefully. Most of her day had been spent calming Joey down as he tried to make the final arrangements with Air France for the transportation of the gold.

"Listen, you fucking bitch!" he yelled. "You put your goddamned husband on the phone right now! And I . . ."

He pulled the phone away from his ear and stared at it. He turned to Nancy. "She hung up."

"I don't blame her," Nancy returned. "I'd hang up if you talked to me that way, too."

"Shit!" He slammed the receiver down and slumped into the room's desk chair. "Something's wrong. This morning, everything was fine, now suddenly, no one's available. What the hell is going on?"

"Would you just take it easy," she replied. "We don't have time for another scene. Perhaps we'd better try and make other arrangements."

He glared at her. "What kind of arrangements? What . . . do we just call up American Airlines and say, 'yes, we've got two hundred tons of gold we want flown to South Vietnam right away'?"

"I don't know what other arrangements," she replied calmly, "but I'm beginning to think that Air France has changed their minds. We'll need to be doing something. Perhaps one of the Moslem countries . . ."

"This is the only way," he said with finality. "If this doesn't work, we're screwed."

"Easy for you to say," she replied. "All you do is walk away and protect your precious little ass. I'm all out in the open and my husband is a prisoner. I've *got* to find another way."

He stood, lighting another cigarette on the butt of the one he was smoking. He jammed an index finger into his own chest. "You do it without me," he said. "I'm not risking myself for the likes of you."

"Oh?" she said. "What about the homeland? I thought you were a patriot."

The phone rang. Joey grabbed it before the first ring had echoed away. "Yes?" His face fell. "Yeah. She's here."

He held out the receiver, Nancy standing to take it from him. "Henderson," she said.

"Nancy, this is Marsha."

"How are we holding up?"

"Not well," the woman answered. "Most of the collection centers are shutting down. The television attacks against us are doing the job."

"We're noticing the downturn on this end," Nancy said, "but we're going to get pretty close I think."

"Nancy . . . there's something else. Jerry Prescott has just gotten in touch with me."

"Where is he? He is going to come forward?"

"He wouldn't say. All he said was that he had to talk to you right away."

"Me? Why?"

"He gave me a message," Marsha said. "I'll quote: 'Tell Nancy that if she doesn't contact me right away, it's all over.' That's it, the whole message."

"He gave you a number?"

"Yeah." She read off the number, Nancy staring at it curiously.

"Let me call him," Nancy said. "Stay near your phone. I'll get back to you."

"Okay." Marsha hung up without another word.

"What is it?" Joey said nervously. "Something else gone wrong?"

She began punching numbers into the phone. "I don't know yet," she returned.

"What if . . ."

"Shhh. It's ringing."

Myrna Prescott answered the phone after the first ring.

"This is Nancy Henderson," Nancy said. "I believe your husband . . ."

"He's right here," Myrna said. "Hold on."

Nancy looked at Joey. The man was walking around, nervously looking at his watch, then walking to peek through the window curtains to the street, fifteen stories below.

Prescott was on the phone. "Nancy, I'm so glad to have reached you."

"So, what is it, Jerry?" she said. "Coming out of hiding to try out the truth?"

"We've got to get by all that," he replied, "and we've got to do it now. You don't have much time."

"What do you mean?"

"I had a call from the President just about thirty minutes ago. He knows where you're hiding the gold and intends to confiscate it."

"How?" she asked, not really believing him. "It's my gold. He has no right."

"Just listen to me," the man said, just the barest hint of deep concern in his controlled voice. That made her listen to him. "He's putting the paperwork through now. He's using some old anti-trust legislation to say you intend to manipulate the gold market by hoarding. They'll be out there sometime during the morning."

"I don't believe it."

"That's not my problem," he said. "I felt the obligation to tell you and I've told you."

"Why?" she asked. "Why would you want to help me?"

"You may or may not believe me," he said, "but I'm on your side. I hate what they've done to you and what they intend to do to you. I couldn't stand by and let them stop you cold without a fighting chance."

She looked at Joey. His eyes were wild as he paced the room. "This is so hard for me to believe."

"Have you seen anything suspicious around your storage place?" he asked.

"No, I . . . wait. A van. A black van has been driving around the building."

"Use your head," he told her. "An operation of this magnitude would be impossible to keep under wraps for very long. And look at what the administration has done so far to keep you from freeing those men."

She couldn't ignore the weight of evidence that was piling up. "Would they . . . could they have tapped the phones there?"

"It's standard procedure," he said. "Although I can't tell if it was done in your case."

She knew then what had happened to Air France. The early calls had been tapped and the government had put pressure on the French to withdraw their support. "Why have you kept silent about the Paris films?" she asked.

"I was ordered to," he said.

"But . . ."

"Look. I'd come out now, but perhaps I can do you more good on the inside at this point, you know?"

She thought about that. "Maybe you're right. It's just so hard to change my mind about you. This could be some sort of setup."

"You've got two choices," he said. "Either believe me or not. One way or the other, the proof will come tomorrow."

"Tomorrow," she repeated, her brain spinning. She had to make the choice and she didn't even have the luxury of waiting until tomorrow to do it. She thought of him, thought of the look on his face when he saw the Paris films with her. He'd have had no reason to be there if he knew those films were going to be shown. "I believe you," she said at last.

"I'll be at this number whenever you want to reach me," he said.

"I won't thank you," she said, "for doing the right thing."

"I'd never expect you to. Good luck, Nancy Henderson. Godspeed."

"Good-bye."

Jerry hung up and turned to Myrna, a strange thought going through his head. "I hope that *our* phone isn't bugged," he said.

She patted his leg. "Don't worry, my love," she said. "I'd have bored to death any eavesdroppers a long time ago with my conversations."

He smiled at her.

"How do you feel?" she asked.

"Good," he said. "Clean . . . scared shitless. If this gets out, I could go right down the tubes with Nancy. But somehow I'm not as frightened of that as I was before I made the call."

"Do you think it's a little hot in here?" she asked.

He looked at her through narrowed eyes. "Not especially. Do you want me to open some windows?"

She shook her head, a strange little smile playing on her lips. "No," she said, sitting up straight and tugging at her nightgown. She began to wriggle out of it. "I think if I just get out of this, I'll be more comfortable."

The gown came off, drifting to land on him. She was naked, the covers pulled down to her thighs.

"That's better," she said. "You know, you look a little hot to me, too."

He was beginning to get the idea, and his body, he could feel, had already gotten the idea. He stood, stripping quickly, his penis already erect, rock-hard.

"How convenient," she said. "You've got a handle."

She reached out and took his penis in her hand, pulling it, and him, onto the bed with her. It amazed him how easily they fit into one another's arms after all this time, how comfortable—and exciting—his wife really was. She was squirming softly, running her hands up and down the length of his body. He rolled partially on top of her, his own hands coming into play as she moaned softly.

"Why?" he whispered into her neck. "Why now?"

"You asked for my opinion," she said, then cried out softly as his hand closed over her sex. "You cared about my opinion."

"What if I wouldn't have taken your advice?"

"Mr. Secretary," she said, "you talk too much. Come here."

After many years in politics, Jerry Prescott had finally learned to do what he was told.

Joey Nhu was throwing clothes into a suitcase as Nancy Henderson tried to talk him out of it.

"It's over!" he practically shouted. "I don't give a damn about you or your fucking husband. I'm not going to do time over this. It's stupid!"

"If I go down, Joey," she said, "you're the first person I'll implicate, so help me God."

"I don't believe in God," he replied.

"You can't get away from this," she said.

"You watch me," he said. "I've got some operating expenses left. I'll be out of here and in hiding before they even know what's happening. I know I'm dead here. At least on the run I'll have a chance."

"How can you stand yourself?"

He closed the suitcase, snapping it shut. "Low expectations," he said, and grabbed it off the bed.

He moved toward the door while she stood helplessly, watching. Suitcase in hand, he opened the door and was gone.

She stared at the empty space for a moment, desperately readjusting to the situation, then she walked to the door and shut it.

She moved back to the desk and picked up the phone, dialing the house operator. "Yes," she said. "I need a cab downstairs right away."

XLI

Ho Chi Minh City—Khank Hoi Docks

April 17—Just Past Midnight

Cassady stood near water's edge watching the Saigon River etch its course to the South China Sea. The smells were fishy and stale, the river broad and deep enough at this point to berth the large freighters that kissed the wide, covered wooden docks. Farther to the north was the bulk of downtown Saigon. At the end of Tu Do Street he could just make out the Gothic spires of the basilica of Our Lady of Peace Cathedral, his reference point for finding Camp Friendship.

The docks were mostly deserted, though units of the army were stationed up and down the whole river, watching for any rescue attempts by sea. He had simply walked the area out in the open, scoping it out, thinking Vietnamese. He walked with confidence. He thought Vietnamese; he acted Vietnamese. No one questioned him.

Cassady remembered the last time he had been here, April 29, 1975. The docks had been crowded that day,

mobbed. He had left the embassy compound looking for
Kim. She had promised to meet him at the gates, but no one
could have foreseen the thousands who had crowded those
gates, Vietnamese sympathizers who feared bloody retribution when the armies of the North took over the city. He had
desperately searched the mobs to no avail, then stole an army
jeep and raced across town to the docks, thinking she may
have tried to get out on one of the barges leaving from there.

Tan Son Nhut Airbase was already in flames to the
northwest, Dodge City processing decimated, making fixed
wing evacuation utterly impossible. The crowds that jammed
the docks were no longer people, but a machine of hysteria.
North Vietnamese mortar stations had sprung up just on the
other side of the river and the cries of *phao kick*—incoming—
were echoed by a thousand voices whenever another shell
whistled overhead.

There was no way he could have found her there, among
the smoking ruins of the docks and barges, among the scores
of trampled bodies that covered the wooden floors. When he
had gone back for the jeep it had already been stripped clean
by teenaged gangs called cowboys, forcing him to steal a
bicycle for the long ride back to the embassy.

He had returned to see Americans in flight. Unable to
live up to their commitment to evacuate their most valuable
Vietnamese allies, the marines left at the compound had
simply retreated, using their M-16s to keep the nationals at
bay. They had escaped up the embassy stairs, blocking doors
behind them as North Vietnamese tanks entered the city
itself. And that's where the final evacuation had taken place,
from the roof of the embassy. At the last moment Cassady had
realized that life without Kim was no life at all and had
determined to stay. For his decision he had gotten a concussion from a gun butt and three days of unconsciousness.

He watched the river, flowing always flowing, flushing
out the good and the bad, carrying it all to the great one. He
had often speculated that, perhaps, that concussion had killed
him—he had certainly felt dead since then. But now he knew
that was false, for the life had begun to flood back into him as
soon as Vietnam had been within smelling distance of
Nickademis's Huey. He'd find Kim, too. He was certain of
that. What they shared had gone way beyond human relationship; their connections were chemical, spiritual. They

understood one another in an elemental way that defied logical description—simpatico, was the word that came to mind. He *knew* she was alive and in the city. Her heartbeat would draw him, its rhythm so like his own.

There was a mass of large fishing boats docked up and down the harbor, along with several Russian-made gunboats. He'd have to watch those. His years with the SEAL team naval operations would pay off now.

He was surprised at how few troops and gunboats controlled the river. They'd actually have a chance in boats if the defenses stayed the same. It was about thirty miles downriver to the sea, but the real test would come in the first ten, where many small river islands would force the boats close to the eastern shore gun emplacements.

That wasn't his problem, though. All he'd agreed to do was get the prisoners free and on the boats. After that, they were on their own. He'd be staying behind, trying to make it to Thailand with Kim.

He turned and took in the whole of the night city and its tall, tall trees and French-colonial buildings. She was out there. He could feel her. After a decade, her presence was still like a beacon to him.

He wondered if she could feel him.

FRIDAY

MOSCOW (AP)—The Soviet Union demanded today that the United States "remove its presence" from the South China Sea. In an editorial in *Pravda*, the official Soviet newspaper, they said that the U.S. was "interfering with the Soviet Navy's training exercise and behaving in an aggressive fashion" and called for their immediate and unconditional withdrawal.

BENEFIT FETE HELD

What shines like the sun and never tarnishes? If you guessed gold, you're right, and there was plenty of the glittery stuff on display at last night's **Golddigger's Ball,** a charity benefit held at the beautiful Downtown Hilton.

Host **Don Regall** and his wife **Nancy** were resplendent in heavy gold chains to go along with the ball's theme. Don said that everyone had to wear a gaudy gold item to be donated to the MIA gold drive sponsored by the local chapter of NAMWives.

People-watchers had plenty to look at, as **Joe** and **Marie Price** waltzed in, both in gold lame with real gold studs to hold their outfits together. **Jane Fitzwell** looked beautiful in a taffeta evening gown with lace bodice, her earrings fashioned from old twenty-dollar gold pieces. Local artist **Mary Feigal** showed up in white tux, gold rings on each finger of her hand. Her husband, oral surgeon **Tom Padgem,** delighted the audience with a set of solid gold "chattering teeth."

Also in attendance...

—JoAnn Fullerton
Fresno Sun

XLII

Baltimore, Maryland

April 17—Dawn

Miller Angostis pushed the button on the limo's power window and watched it *whir* down, letting in the rank Baltimore morning. A thick, smelly fog had rolled in from the Chesapeake Bay and he could barely see the half block to the old building that was the object of so much scrutiny and debate.

"What are they waiting for?" Russ Buchner said from beside him. "They've been in place for almost an hour."

"I suspect," Angostis said as he rapped on the partition that separated front from back, "that this is a big enough publicity event that Will Cain would want to be involved in it personally."

The director sipped coffee, tasting like the thermos metal it had come from. All around them were unmarked cars, each carrying four men, parked in expectation of the raid. A large garbage truck with dumpster arms sat directly across from the building. Occasional heads could be seen poking up from nearby rooftops. And through it all, the dirty fog drifted lazily, turning the whole scene to a dreamlike haze.

This was local stuff, FBI and Treasury Department territory, but the director couldn't resist the visit, if for no other reason that it would make Will Cain, bureau director, mad as hell. He smiled and took another bitter sip.

"Did you pick up the latest from the Bangkok Station before we left?" he asked, settling back into the softness of the rear cushions.

Russ Buchner nodded, frowning. "Cassady hired a Greek mercenary to fly him into Nam by chopper," he said. "He ran it until it was out of fuel, crashing fifty miles from Ho Chi Minh City."

"So we must assume the gentleman is there now," Angostis said, grudging admiration coloring his voice.

"Yes, sir. Cowboy is also en route."

Angostis took a long drink, then tossed the rest of it out the window. "I should have gone with my original impulse and sent Cassady anyway."

"Could you have controlled him, though?" Buchner asked.

Angostis turned to stare at the man, smiling slightly. "You may make it in this business yet," he said.

"There." Buchner pointed.

A late-model Oldsmobile slid past them to angle up to the curb a little farther up the street, a government license plate shining through the fog.

"That's him," Angostis said, opening his door and stepping out. Buchner got out the other side. They walked toward the car.

A tall, gangly man with a pronounced neck climbed out of the driver's seat, carrying a small briefcase. He smiled crookedly when he saw Angostis walking up.

"A little out of your jurisdiction, aren't you, Miller?" he asked.

"Vested interest," Angostis said. "I promise I won't get in the way."

The man raised an eyebrow. "I *know* you won't get in the way," he said. "Seems like you and your boys have been quite busy playing around here lately as it is."

"I don't know what you're talking about," Angostis replied.

Cain fixed him with an unwavering gaze. "No, I guess you don't," he said, then turned to Buchner and extended a hand. "Name's Will Cain."

Buchner looked at Angostis before returning the handshake. "Russell Buchner."

"Well, Miller," Cain said, "looks like we're just a couple of days away from the big one."

"We're always a couple of days away from the big one," Angostis replied. "My people are on the job."

Cain shrugged broadly. "Think I'll keep stocking canned goods just the same," he said.

Other men were walking toward them, the garbage truck

starting up with a wheezing grind. Angostis could see the barrels of several rifles aiming down from the surrounding roofs. As his men approached, the FBI director's face solidified.

"Look," he told the small group that had gathered, "this is a touchy issue. I don't want any kind of trouble unless it's absolutely necessary. Think first. That's an order. Return fire only." His eyes drifted to rooftop level. "Chuck, do your men know that?"

A small man in a bulky suit that obviously concealed body armor nodded. "They are aware of the delicate nature of this operation," he said.

Cain nodded, his Adam's apple bobbing. "Good." He handed the man some folded-up papers. "Here's the search warrant and authority to confiscate. You may proceed when ready."

"Yes, sir."

The man took the papers and strode off toward the garbage truck with his men in tow. The truck was jockeying around, getting into position to ram the large gargage door at the front of the building.

While Angostis, Buchner, and Cain stood at a distance, the small army of thirty men cautiously approached the garage doors, weapons out and ready.

"Okay!" the small man shouted, waving the garbage truck forward.

The truck ground into gear, its pickup arms out in front like ram's horns. Then, all at once, the big door slid up, opening the passage for them to enter.

The truck stopped, the crowd of men ran into the maw of the building. Angostis, primed for the sound of gunfire, found himself disappointed when there wasn't any. He shared a look with Cain and they started forward, the small man coming out of the building seconds later. He shrugged broadly.

Cain broke into a trot, Angostis and Buchner hurrying to keep up. They reached the small man, who just said, "It's nothing..." before they passed him and found out for themselves.

They had walked into an empty building. Smelting equipment took up one end of the structure, but there was nothing to smelt. They were looking at the inside of a large vacant warehouse.

"Maybe it's hidden..." Buchner began.

Cain glared him to silence. "Two hundred tons of gold is not going to be that easy to hide," he said.

"A shame," Angostis said, the humor evident in his voice. "Looks like you made a big mistake."

Cain turned away from him. Five Oriental men were being led toward them, their hands interlocked on top their heads.

"What the hell's going on here?" Cain demanded of the men. "Where have you taken that gold?"

"Mr. Director . . ." one of the agents began.

"Shut up," Cain snapped, then turned back to the Oriental. "Where? What have you done with it?"

The agent spoke up again. "They don't speak English, sir."

Cain glared at his man, then at the bobbing, smiling faces of the Vietnamese prisoners. He sagged physically. "Take them to the local bureau," he said. "Get an interpreter over there to question them."

He turned to see Angostis grinning at him. "Think you got a leak, Will," the man said. "If you need any professional help plugging it, let me know."

"Just get the hell out of here, Miller," Cain replied, "before I throw you out."

Angostis shook his head. "No need to be ungrateful," he said. "I can't wait to see the President's face when he hears about this."

"Fuck off."

Miller, still smiling, turned and walked casually out of the warehouse, Cain spitting on the floor behind him. The small man in the body armor came trotting up, the weight he was carrying wearing him down.

"This place backs up to another warehouse," he said. "I think they must have gone through the other place and used trucks a block over."

"Yeah," Cain said. "I want you to blanket the area with men. Ask the whole neighborhood if they saw anything. I want a list of everyone who knew about this operation. Somebody tipped it off, and I want him found—and quick."

"Yes, sir."

Cain looked up to see Angostis's limo sliding past the garage door. "Chuck," he said. "Do we have a file on that son of a bitch?"

The man shook his head. "I don't know. He was after Hoover's time."

Cain took a long breath, and the anger was still there. "If we've got one, I want to see it. If we don't have one, I want one started."

US REJECTS SOVIET VIEW

WASHINGTON, (AP)—In a statement aimed directly at the Soviet Union, the Herrod administration asserted the right of freedom of the high seas. Reacting to an editorial in *Pravda*, Media Liaison Maurice Benstock today said, "The freedom of the high seas is preeminent, despite what our more closed-minded neighbors would like to think."

Asked, then, if the administration was not going to acquiesce to Soviet demands, Benstock replied, "We'll sail our ships anywhere we damn well please."

XLIII

Silver Springs, Maryland

April 17—9:05 A.M.

Jerry Prescott used the hammer to drive the last of his row of stakes into the moist ground of his garden. It was already warming up, the early sun burning off the last of the night's moisture in his wide backyard.

He straightened, feeling the tightness in his lower back, then bent again to tie the stalk of the young tomato plant to the stake. A good deal of Maryland was sandy and still filled with seashells from its prehistoric days underwater—the perfect environment for tomatoes. Growing tomatoes was a statewide obsession. The secretary had always grown more than the family could eat, but what was left was ground up and put back in the soil for next year.

He used bread-twist wire to fix the last plant to the

stake. New life had sprung up all around him, budding
mimosa trees filling out to cover the ugly gray of the wall that
totally surrounded his property. He felt new himself. Whatever the consequences of his relationship with Nancy
Henderson, he knew he had done the right thing. Fear was
there, too, fear of reprisal, but it was far outweighed by the
human commitment he had made.

Apparently his warning to the woman had been timely.
There had been no word of a warehouse raid at all, the
morning television filled only with Vietnamese broadcasts
and more of Benstock's attacks on the NAMWives, this time
accusing them of lesbianism. He at least had to give the man
credit for creativity.

He heard a noise toward the far corner of the yard.
Thinking it a squirrel, he stood and took several steps in that
direction, hoping to get a good look. Then he saw a jeans-clad
leg hoist over the wall on his side.

His immediate impulse was to run. He turned toward
the house, looking for Tod or Charlie, so ingrained was the
fear of assassination. They weren't out there. He took a
couple of steps toward the house, as the rest of the body slid
over the top of the cinderblock wall.

It was a woman. She dropped to the ground, crouching
behind the tree. He calmed himself with deep breaths.
Nancy Henderson had just snuck into his yard.

She saw him and stood, coming around the tree. He
waved her back, his head darting frantically back and forth
between her and the house. She concealed herself once
again, and he casually walked the twenty-yard distance to her
tree, kneeling beside it to pretend to pull weeds.

He glanced quickly up at her. Her face was drawn, dark
circles under her eyes. Her cheeks and sweatshirt were
streaked with dirt. "What the hell are you doing here?" he
whispered loudly.

"I had to talk to you," she said, as if that were all there
was to it.

"You know my number."

"I couldn't use the phone for this. Where are your
bodyguards?"

"Inside somewhere . . . I don't know."

"Can you trust them?" she asked.

"What are you talking about?" he said. "We've committed treasonous acts against the government of the United States—their employers. It's not a question of trust at this point."

"Good," she said. "You've already put yourself in the boat with me. We need to talk somewhere a little more private."

"Nancy," he said, "I've done all I can."

"Just hear me out." She reached a hand out to him. It was cut in several places and deeply calloused, as if she had been doing heavy manual labor. "Please," she said, laying the hand on his arm.

He turned once more to the house, then back to her. "Stay here," he said, and pointed to the backdoor on the wide expanse of brick. "That door leads to my den. They have a room just off it. When I give the all clear, work your way around the wall to the garage. There's a door on the side there. I'll come around and let you in."

She nodded, her eyes frightened, but determined. "Thanks."

"For what?" he said. "For being a fool?"

She shook her head. "You're no fool."

He stood and moved quickly across the lawn, quietly opening the den door and poking his head inside. Myrna was moving around in there, an eye on the television as she watered plants. She smiled when she saw him, words forming on her lips; but he silenced her with a hand. She cocked her head. In the room beside he could hear Tod on the phone with his station chief, a television also coming muffled from there.

He held up two fingers to Myrna, then pointed to the room. She nodded, face quizzical.

He ducked back outside and waved frantically, Nancy hurrying in response to the agitation of his movements. Then he came quietly in, moving right to Myrna and taking her elbow. He silently led her out of the den, past the front staircase and down the long hallway to the garage.

"What in the world..." she said as they reached the garage.

"Nancy Henderson is out there," he said.

Her eyes widened fearfully. "Why?"

He shrugged. "She wants to talk about something. I'll need you to help me."

"Anything."

He squeezed her quickly. "You'll get to see how a spy feels," he said, winking.

They entered the garage, filled with all the lawn and garden clutter that seems to grow in such places, plus a Cadillac and a Mercedes sports car. It smelled vaguely of chemicals and gasoline and springtime. He moved to the door to the outside and let the woman in.

"Oh, my," Myrna said when she saw how Nancy looked.

Nancy looked apologetic. "The bad penny," she said.

"Okay," Jerry said, excitement building up in him. "Myrna, I want you to watch at the den door for Tod or Charlie. Talk loudly to them if you see them, I'll try and get Nancy up the stairs to the master bedroom and meet you up there."

Myrna nodded. "Now?" she asked.

He smiled at her. "We've come this far. . . ."

She returned the smile and left the garage immediately, all of them feeling the web of conspiracy tightening just a little more.

Moments later they sat in the bathroom off the master bedroom, several locked doors between them and the men who could just as easily be their jailers.

Nancy stood at the sink trying to clean her face a bit, her hands so sore she could barely use them. "We got it all out," she was saying, "somehow. It was a madhouse. We all ran around like we were crazy. We were still getting it out when the FBI and Treasury people were surrounding the warehouse. I don't think we had a ten-minute start on them."

"But you got it all away." Jerry smiled from his seat on the edge of the tub.

Nancy turned, wiping her face with a washcloth. "Thanks to you," she said. "But now we need to take the next step."

"What step is that?" Myrna said.

Nancy looked from one to the other. "Help me get the gold to Vietnam," she said quietly.

"I thought you had made arrangements," Jerry said.

"They fell through. I talked to the Air France people this morning and they said the government has threatened to take away their American routes and confiscate all equipment in this country if they help us. They've backed off."

"The warehouse was bugged," Jerry said.

"And we're not," Myrna said, "or we'd have heard about it already."

"Where's the gold now?" Jerry asked.

Nancy put down the washcloth, Myrna getting her a towel from the linen closet. "Thanks," Nancy smiled, taking the towel. "It's in a field near the airport."

"A field!" Myrna said.

"A tobacco field," Nancy said, shrugging. "I had nowhere else to take it. "We put it in the field, then threw tarps over it so it wouldn't look like El Dorado from the air."

"I'm having a hard time picturing how much we're talking about," Jerry said.

Nancy set down the towel and held her hands up to span the size of a brick. "Over thirty thousand ten-pound bars," she said, smiling at Jerry's amazed whistle. "Plus quite a bit that hasn't even been processed yet. That's why I look the way I do. It was quite a job."

"And what can I do?" he asked.

"Find me some planes," she said. "We've made tentative arrangements with the government of Malaysia to land there. Then we'll have to try to find a boat or something to do the transfer at sea."

"I don't have access to planes . . . I mean, not without going through government channels and getting us all arrested. You'd have to move this stuff today. What about your Vietnamese contact?"

"Gone," she said. "He ran out when things got tough."

"So you have no contact with the other side right now?" She shook her head.

"Actually not a bad thing," he said.

Her eyes widened. "What do you mean?"

"I have some friends in the French government," he said. "They're in this up to their necks anyway, but would never be able to admit it publicly. If we . . . you went through a third party, it would look like negotiation instead of conspiracy. They could act as a go-between."

"Would they do that?" Nancy asked.

He smiled. "Why not? If it worked out, they'd come off looking like international heroes and peacemakers. That still doesn't solve the problem of transport, though."

"You're not thinking enough, my love," Myrna said,

leaning against the wall with folded arms. "We do know someone who has airplanes."

He shook his head, drawing a blank.

"Our future in-laws," she said.

"Oh, I couldn't . . ." he began, but Myrna stopped him.

"It wouldn't hurt to ask," she said. "You know how strongly Fran feels about this issue, and you know how David gives in to Fran."

"But this is so much larger than that."

"Larger than people?" Myrna said. "Larger than people caring about one another? We could load the planes in secret, then give a press conference saying they were flying over to give the prisoners comfortable transportation home when they are freed."

Jerry walked to her and took her by the shoulders. "Do you have any idea what you're suggesting?"

"*Lèse-majesté*," she said, her high-school French still good. "High treason."

He ran hands through his hair. "Jesus, why couldn't I have been born a Republican? I'll bet they don't worry about things like this."

"David probably won't do it," she said. "He'd stand to lose everything, too. Call him, put your cards on the table. If it goes, it goes."

"We haven't been charged with anything," Nancy said. "We're doing the right thing here. The President isn't the Pope, for God's sake. He's not infallible. We just disagree with him, that's all. I thought that's what this country is all about?" She looked at Jerry in exasperation. "We need to make people understand that. We're not criminals, we're humanitarians, and nothing's come down to suggest that another humanitarian *shouldn't* help us achieve our goal. I've given this a lot of thought. It seems to me that we're only in trouble if this *doesn't* work. It'd be tough to argue with success."

"I'm pretty sure I know where I can get you a freighter," Jerry said. "And I can use my contacts to finalize your arrangements. So, once we get the gold to Malaysia, all we have to do is sail it through the Seventh Fleet and the Russian Navy and we're home free."

"It's worth a try," Myrna said, Nancy moving to hug her.

"If we're wrong, we may all go to jail for any one of a hundred reasons," Jerry said.

"It's worth a try," Myrna repeated.

Jerry sighed deeply, knowing that his wife didn't realize the ramifications as he did. They were on the verge of giving up everything, including a country. He read something once that stuck in his mind now. "If I had to choose between betraying my country and betraying my friend," he said, "I hope I should have the guts to betray my country." He reached out, hugging both of them to him. "I'll make the call."

Sid Henderson sat at the breakfast table with his mother, pretending to read the paper, his coffee growing cold in the cup.

"I heard on the radio this morning that Nancy's a fugitive from the law now," Naomi Henderson said, pursing her small lips the way she always did when faced with unpleasantness.

Sid just touched her with his eyes. "I really don't want to talk about it right now," he said.

The phone rang in the living room, cutting like a cleaver into the conversation. "How can we not talk about it?" Naomi said. "Because of her, all our lives have been thrown into turmoil. I can't stand hearing that thing ring anymore. I spend all my time answering it, being harassed as if *I* were the criminal."

"Why don't you just unplug it?" he said. "Nancy might be a lot of things, but she's not a criminal."

"It has to be answered!" Naomi stood abruptly, clearing dishes off the table, the phone still jangling in the background. "I'm all alone here since your father died, and my lady friends call to check on me. If I don't answer..."

"All right," Sid said. "All right." He stood quickly, nearly knocking over the coffee. "I'll get it."

He walked to the living room. Timmy was sitting on the floor watching TV while Jeremy slept in his playpen. He picked up the receiver just long enough to hear the syrupy radio voice on the other end and dropped it back on the cradle.

He went into the kitchen, watching his mother stacking dishes in the sink. He carried his cold coffee over to her.

"I don't know how you can defend her after all she's done," she said without looking at him.

"What *has* she done?" he asked, exasperated. "What... exactly *has* she done."

Naomi stopped and turned to stare at him. "For starters, she's abandoned her husband and children and ruined all of our lives."

The phone rang again.

Naomi put a hand to her forehead. "Is there never any end to this? Why in God's name did you ever have to marry that woman?"

Sid laughed dryly. "Because I loved her!"

"I think it's time to give Harvey Ponts a call."

"The lawyer? What for?"

"Custody," she said. "You need to get full custody of those boys right away, so she can't hurt them anymore."

Timmy ran into the kitchen, pointing back to the ringing phone. "Mommy's call?" he asked. "Is that Mommy?"

Sid went to one knee, taking the boy in his arms. "No, son, it's not Mommy."

"Your Mother's gone far away," Naomi said, and turned on the water in the sink. "She won't be back."

"Mother!" Sid said, as Timmy began crying into his father's shoulder.

His mother had been right about one thing. Nancy's leaving had torn them all apart from the inside out.

NAMWIVES LEVELS CHARGES

CHICAGO, (AP)—In its strongest statement to date, the NAMWives organization charged the Herrod administration with purposefully doctoring film of a meeting between NAMWives leaders and North Vietnamese officials in Paris during the 1974 peace talks. In an angry news conference spokeswoman Marsha Ridley accused President Herrod of "the worst, most vicious smear tactics American politics has ever seen. You'd expect to see this from a common criminal, but not from the President of the United States."

According the Ridley, current Secretary of State

Jerry Prescott was also at the Paris meetings, which
were open, not secret, and held with the United
States's blessing. Prescott, she said, was actually in
the film being shown on American television, but
was cropped out of the current version.

Asked if she could prove her allegations, Mrs.
Ridley said, "Gladly. Bring on the secretary of state.
Ask him."

Secretary of State Prescott could not be reached
for comment. NAMWives currently has a $2.5 bil-
lion defamation-of-character suit pending against President Herrod and the United States government.

XLIV

Camp Friendship

April 17—9:47 A.M.

Colonel Tin sat in his air-conditioned office, reading the
speech Jason Ridley had written for television broadcast, a
tight smile occasionally turning the corners of his lips.

"Very good, Colonel," he said. "You are a man of consid-
erable intelligence and talent."

"I've had a great deal of time to think," Ridley returned,
trying to read Tin's face to no avail.

Tin smiled broadly and creaked back in his desk chair.
"Nice that we can joke like comrades," he said. "I do indeed
have respect for you, Colonel. I think in other circumstances
we could have been friends."

"I understand a lot of things now that I never allowed
myself to dwell on before," Ridley said, and he thought it
possible that Tin actually believed him. "We all look at life
through our own eyes. After watching Marsha on the TV last
night I realized that maybe seeing life through the eyes of
others will allow for understanding."

Tin slid the speech across the table to Ridley. "Your talk
reflects that idea," he said. "It's a moving plea for mutual

understanding that I think will cap off all of our efforts here. I salute you."

"When will I deliver it?" Ridley asked, picking up the papers and folding them to put in his pocket.

Tin stood, thoughtfully lighting one of his small cigars. He looked around the room slowly, as if reaffirming the truth of his life-style. "Tomorrow morning, I think," he said. "That way we will be broadcasting for the American prime-time audiences. Your speech, as commanding officer, will carry a great deal of weight in America. I think it will break down resistance once and for all."

Ridley stood also. "I hope so," he said. and reached out a hand to Tin.

The man looked surprised and pleased, returning Ridley's handshake with vigor. "This gives me the greatest pleasure, Colonel. Let's hope this is the first step toward global understanding."

"The first step," Ridley repeated, almost sure now that Tin was falling for it. The man was just arrogant enough to think his plans infallible. It could be his downfall. "I look forward to tomorrow."

"As do I," Tin said, leading him to the door. He opened it, patting Ridley on the back as he walked out. "This is an historic occasion, my friend."

Ridley turned to him as he walked down the hall. "I pray that all goes well."

Tin smiled. "Include me in your prayers," he said, flicking ashes into his hand to keep the floor clean. "I'm not allowed."

Ridley walked gratefully into the sunshine, wanting the heat to burn off the clamminess of Tin's bunker. Tomorrow, he thought. Tomorrow. He'd stayed alive all these years for tomorrow. His duty had kept him alive specifically for tomorrow morning.

As he walked across the yard he saw Larry Frank in the prescribed place, leaning against the outside of his barracks in the early shade. He tugged at his thick black beard, paying no attention to Ridley's advance.

Ridley walked near the man, facing away from him, and pulled the pack of cigarettes out of his breast pocket. He put one in his mouth, then cupped a hand around a match to light it.

The flame danced in the breeze, but lit the cigarette. Ridley puffed hard to get it going. "He's tumbled," he said. "Tomorrow morning."

"We'll be ready," Frank said, then moved away from the barracks, walking toward the vendor stands just inside the gate, Ridley continuing on his way.

As he walked he noticed someone keeping pace with him at a short distance. Thinking it Jenkins, he turned and looked, surprised to find he didn't recognize the man. He stopped walking, pretending to watch an impromptu songfest that had begun on the stoop leading up to a barracks, a group of men singing off-key and clapping out of time.

The man was watching him, he could feel it. Seconds later, a body was pressing up against him, a voice whispering in his ear. "Are you Lieutenant Colonel Jason Ridley?"

The man was so close, nearly climbing up his back. He made to move away, but a strong hand gripped his arm and held him still. "Yes, I'm Ridley."

"You're ranking officer here at the compound?"

"We don't follow military protocol here," Ridley said, and the grip tightened on his arm.

"I have a forty-five automatic stuck in my belt, Colonel," the voice whispered. "Do you feel it pressing against you?"

The man pulled closer and Ridley could feel the weapon. He nodded.

The man moved away slightly. "I must talk with you. Every second I stay here in the open my life is in jeopardy."

Ridley turned and looked at the man. Steel-gray eyes stared back, cold and hard—the eyes of a killer. He was lean like knotted rope. He was tensed, ready to spring. This wasn't one of the prisoners.

"Who are you?"

"I'm here to help you escape."

"Who are you?"

"Not here," he said, his eyes drifting to the others who crowded around the man on the stairs leading the songs.

"They have guards and cameras everywhere," Ridley said.

The man nodded. "We'll need a diversion." He bent and picked a handful of grass from around one of the stilts the building was resting on. He threw the grass in the air, watching the wind drift. "Follow me."

The man turned and moved off immediately, Ridley following behind in confusion. It was happening too fast. Who was this man? Where did he come from? How did he get into camp? He decided to not give anything away, to let the man make himself known, to wait . . . to hope.

The man moved to the next barracks in the line and turned to Ridley. "You're smoking a cigarette," he said. "Do you have matches?"

Ridley nodded dumbly, taking the pack out of his pocket and handing them over.

The man strode up the wooden stairs and looked in the building. Seconds later he was back down the stairs, moving off quickly. "Come on!" he ordered.

Ridley hurried after him. "What did you do?"

"I set a bed on fire. Let's get downwind."

"You did what?"

"Come on."

They moved into the matrix of barracks, going several rows in to where they were completely surrounded by the buildings. Even as they walked, shouts began to reach back to them, a plume of smoke drifting gray-white on the breeze.

"You're insane," Ridley said.

"I just don't have the time, Colonel," the man said. He navigated them between buildings, just under one of the cameras attached to the wall. There was a lot of shouting now, men and guards running from all directions toward the bright orange fire that was evident at roof level, the dry wood of the building going up like a match. The smoke was drifting through camp right toward them, shrouding them, as sirens began sounding all over.

"We'll have a little time now," the man said, casually. "The guards will move to the perimeters to cover any escape attempts. It will take awhile to sort through the confusion."

"Who are you?" Ridley asked again.

"I'm with the government."

"Which government?"

The man glanced around quickly. "Look. I was here during the war. I know where I can get my hands on enough weapons to give you a fighting chance if you want to escape."

"Why should I believe you?" Ridley asked. "Tin could have sent you in to set me up."

The man's lips tightened imperceptibly. "Ask me anything you want—but quickly."

"How did you get in?"

"I waylaid a bomity-bom vendor and bought his cart and permit in gold," the man said. "Then I put Vietnamese clothes over these clothes and came in with the others. Then I tilted my umbrella, took off the outer clothing and drifted around with the prisoners. See?" He pointed to his sandaled feet. "I'm still wearing Ho Chi Minhs. If we don't get caught here, I'll get out the same way."

The smoke was rolling thick all around them. Even if they were on camera, they'd be unrecognizable. A hand-drawn pumper tank on a two-wheeled cart passed their notice between buildings. It wouldn't be enough to put out the now-huge blaze in the distance.

"Are there anymore of you?" Ridley asked.

The man shook his head. "We could have never gotten a force in here. Have you made any plans for a break?"

Ridley stared at the man. Nothing in his experience had prepared him for this meeting. He couldn't imagine Tin setting his own buildings on fire, yet the nature of their game had gotten relatively sophisticated.

"What's the capital of Texas?" he asked finally.

"Austin," the man said, a smile just barely creasing his lips before disappearing. "You've got to decide quickly or you'll get me killed."

"How did you know who I was?"

"I drifted around, keeping my ears open. You're the topic of conversation around the whole camp."

Ridley nodded. That was true enough. In the distance he could see a French camera crew attempting to move a minicam atop another building to take pictures of the fire. "We've set a break," he said, "for late tomorrow night."

The man nodded. "Good. What's the plan?"

Ridley hesitated only slightly. "We've had some help from the outside, the wives of the AWOLs who were put in here with us. They've mapped us a route to the river and worked out plans to cut power and phone lines. We'll jump the guards and fight our way out from there, then see what happens at the river."

"Did you know the Seventh Fleet's anchored out at sea?"

"Will they cover us?"

"If they don't you're dead," the man said. "I'll take care of the gunboats at the docks and make sure you have boats waiting. They'll be marked with red flags. You have transport?"

"Their motor pool has plenty of trucks. We'll manage."

The man took the cigarette from Ridley's mouth and drew on it. The fire had gotten larger, another building catching. Elements from the local fire department could be heard approaching in the distance.

The man turned to the sound. "I may get out in the confusion," he said. "Will your escape route take you past the cathedral?"

Ridley nodded.

"Okay. Look for a truck parked right in front. The key will be under the seat. It's full of weapons. Take it."

"What about you?"

"You probably won't see me again after today. I have to keep moving." He took another drag on the cigarette and handed it back. "Do you have full support?"

"I will have by tomorrow," Ridley said grimly.

The man noted Ridley's tone and said, "We each have our jobs to do, don't we?"

Ridley looked at the ground and nodded.

All at once the man jumped to the side, running around the edge of the building. There was a struggle. Before Ridley could do anything, the man came back, dragging someone with him, hand clamped over his mouth. Jenkins. Ridley jumped him, too, and they shoved him against the building. A K-bar knife was in the man's hand.

"You stupid son of a bitch," Ridley told Jenkins.

"You know him?" the man asked. "Can we trust him?"

"He's an informer," Ridley heard himself say.

The hand came off Jenkins's mouth, going to his throat, pinning him, gasping, to the wall. "I knew . . . it," Harry choked out. "I . . . knew . . . it."

"Harry . . ." Ridley said.

The man looked at Ridley, his face understanding but firm. "I've got to . . ."

"I know," Ridley said, then looked at his friend's frightened eyes. "Let me."

He took the knife. "Oh, Harry," he said. "I'm so sorry, so . . ."

"Jase . . . please, don't . . ."

Ridley plunged the blade into his heart, ripping down. Jenkins's eyes rolled back immediately, blood pumping furiously from his chest, his body sagging to the ground.

"What do we do now?" Ridley asked.

The man was already bending to Jenkins's still-twitching body. "Not much we can do," he said. "Help me."

Ridley knelt, his arms and hands weak, shaking. Honor. Duty.

"We'll just shove him up under the barracks. Give me a hand."

They pushed the body between the building stilts and jammed him as far under as they could, the body not visible to casual observation, then stood.

"They'll find him," the man said.

Ridley nodded. "At head count if not before."

The man's expression never changed. "Rough," he said.

"Yeah," Ridley replied, and found that his emotions hadn't been as gutted as he thought. "Rough all the way around."

The fire department was clanging through the gates, a big pumper truck.

"I've got to go," the man said. "Anything else?"

Ridley shook his head. "No," he said. "We've taken care of it all."

"We'll never meet again. Good luck."

"Same to you," Ridley said. "Same to you."

The man turned and strode resolutely into the drifting smoke and, like a specter, was gone in seconds. Ridley stared after him, then down at the ground where the blood had turned the sand dark.

He kicked dirt on the place, all the while wishing to God this was some sort of crazy dream he'd wake up from, and all the while knowing it wasn't.

He turned to walk off, then came back around and bowed his head, saying a prayer for the best friend he'd ever have.

PRESCOTT ON DELICATE MISSION

WASHINGTON, (AP)—In the latest salvo in the war between NAMWives and President Herrod, the White House today termed the organization's accusations concerning films taken at the Paris peace talks "pure fantasy." Speaking for the administration, Media Liaison Maurice Benstock said, "These women are grabbing at straws. I feel kind of sorry for them."

Asked about the claim that Secretary of State Jerry Prescott actually participated in the talks and the film, Benstock said, "Let me set the record straight on that once and for all. To my knowledge, Jerry Prescott wasn't even in Paris during that time. The reason he hasn't come forward is simple, he's involved in some very delicate negotiations with the Vietnamese right now and cannot be reached. But don't worry, he'll straighten this out soon enough."

Asked if he knew why NAMWives was attacking so adamantly on this particular issue, Benstock replied, grinning, "They're women. You figure them out."

XLV

Baltimore, Maryland— Friendship Airport

April 17—2:00 P.M.

"Have you got the coordinates, Jean?" Prescott asked the French ambassador, static on the phone line plus the drone of jet engines making it almost impossible to hear.

"Yes, Jerry," returned the voice, "but I'm not exactly sure how you want this to be handled. This is as a private citizen, yes?"

"Yes and no," Jerry said. "I'm acting officially unofficial."

"You straddle fences, my friend."

"Just as long as I can. If you get in trouble, I'll say I told you I was acting in the name of the government."

The VIP lounge was filled with people, confusion bottling up everything as timing became more and more the biggest hindrance to their success.

Nancy Henderson stood near Jerry, looking out the huge picture windows of the plush lounge toward the beehive of intersecting runways. "There goes number three," she said.

"Now the business of the boats," the ambassador said in Jerry's ear. "Explain that again."

Jerry watched the World Airways jumbo jet lumber down the runway, bloated under its heavy load. It seemed to take forever to get airborne, but it finally did, turning immediately eastward as it began a slow ascent. The planes, six of them, were loaded to their limits.

"We want to be met at those coordinates in a civilian boat, nothing military or governmental," Jerry said as he watched Fran Durbins moving around the lounge, chatting in her flamboyant way with the others, mostly volunteer workers loading gold, or airline officials. She had been most instrumental in this operation, her unflinching humanism a backbone for her husband when he faltered over the idea. "We'll be in a Liberian freighter. We'll simply exchange boats, with the understanding that each will be given back to its respective owners when this is all done."

"Got it."

"We will not turn over the boat, however, until we know the prisoners have been released. We'll scuttle it before we do that. Make sure they understand."

"Don't worry," Jean Callan said. "They want this to work as much as you do. Do you have all the gold?"

"No," Jerry said. "But we'll come up with nearly eighty percent of it. That's the best we can do, take it or leave it."

"I'll also pass that along," the ambassador replied. "Although, under the circumstances, I think they'll find the terms acceptable."

"The press conference is coming on!" Fran called, turning up the sound on the lounge TV. "Quiet everybody."

"Should I contact your embassy in Malaysia when we arrive?" Jerry asked.

"Yes," came the distant voice. "We'll forward all information there."

"And everyone is aware that this must be handled with the utmost secrecy?"

The man chuckled. "We will try to, how do you say it?...plug our leaks."

"Good," Jerry said. "Jean, I don't know how to thank you. I..."

"Don't say it," Callan replied. "We have been friends for too long, played too much bridge together. My country has a self-interest in this too, you know."

"I appreciate it anyway," Jerry said, a hand covering his free ear so he could listen above the noise of the television. "Good-bye and good luck."

"You're the one who needs luck," Callan said. "*Au revoir.*"

He hung up, giving the thumbs up sign to Myrna, who stood on the other side of the room watching. She smiled in return, hurrying over to join him.

"Jean is interceding for us," he said, Nancy sighing beside him as Myrna and he embraced.

"Why won't you let me go with you?" she asked into his shoulder. "We should be together through this."

He pulled her away from him by the shoulders, staring hard at her. "You know why," he said. "If something should...happen, I'll need you to take care of things."

Nancy moved to put a hand on Myrna. "He's right," she said. "The fewer people we put in jeopardy, the better off everyone will be."

She smiled weakly. "I know."

"Besides," Jerry said with a smile, "you've got a wedding to plan."

"Maybe we can have it in the federal penitentiary!" Fran called from the floor in front of the television, the whole room laughing nervously.

David Durbins came on the TV screen, live from another part of the airport. Everyone bunched in close to hear him.

He was smiling in his easy Southern manner, his relaxed-looking face showing none of the tension that was undoubtedly tearing him apart. He read from a prepared statement, his eyes bobbing between the paper in his hand and the audience. He was standing beside one of his ticket counters, a plethora of microphones positioned on poles near his mouth.

"As president and chairman of the board of World Airways," he read, black-frame glasses sitting near the end of his nose, "it is mah decided pleasure to announce what we're

calling Operation Airlift. Beginning right now, a small fleet of
our planes is takin' off for Bangkok, Thailand. With that
country's kind permission, we will be waiting there for the
release of the hostages being held in Ho Chi Minh City, so as
to provide them with the comfortable and accommodatin' ride
home to their loved ones they are entitled to. Ah have seen
to it that six of our finest planes have been specially outfitted
for extra comfort and enjoyment, and that quality medical
care will be available on board for those who might need it.

"We do not do this for thanks or personal gain, but only
out of a deep appreciation for what those men have gone
through in all of our behalfs. Our efforts aren't much, but
they're our best, and our most preciously given. To those of
our regular customers who've been inconvenienced by the
diversion of our aircraft, I can only apologize and hope that
you understand the special nature of our circumstances.

"Best wishes to the prisoners, and to the citizens of the
United States, the greatest country in the world. Thank you."

Everyone in the lounge broke into spontaneous applause, Fran whooping and shaking her arms in the air. Jerry
moved to her immediately, reaching out a hand to help her
up off the floor.

"We couldn't have done it without you," he told her, a
large smile consuming her face.

"Listen," she said, tapping his arm, "I'm getting to be a
part of history in the making, and maybe I've made my own
little contribution to peace. It should be me thanking you. I
haven't felt this good in years." She threw her arms around
him, her large dangle earrings bouncing against his face.

"I don't know how you did it," he said. "David could
lose millions on this deal."

She moved away from him, shrugging off the remark.
"Hey, this'll be the best publicity he's ever had. We'll just
hack it off the advertising budget."

"Mr. Secretary," a voice called from across the room.

Prescott turned to see a man in World Airways overalls
waving from the doorway.

"Excuse me," he told Fran, and moved through the
crowd to reach the door.

"We're about ready," the man told him, his face slack
from exhaustion. "Number five is set to taxi and number six is
almost done loading."

"Thanks," Jerry said, patting him on the shoulder. "We'll be right down."

He turned to get Nancy's attention, but she was already watching him. He raised his arm, twirling his hand in a circle, and she felt the excitement surge within her. She started to walk toward him, then looked at the telephone and knew there was one more thing she had to do.

She held a finger in the air, Jerry looking at his watch and nodding. She moved to the phone, almost frightened to pick it up. This was it. She was taking irrevocable steps now and she had to try to reach her husband and family one more time. She hadn't spoken to Sid since leaving for Chicago a million years ago. If their life together was over, he was going to have to tell her that.

With shaking hand, she dialed her mother-in-law's number on the VIP WATS line. If she could only reach him, try one more time to tell him what was in her mind and heart. She'd given up hoping to convince him of the rightness of what she was doing. All she could hope for was his eventual forgiveness.

"Hello?"

It was Sid. She had so expected to hear his mother's voice that the words caught in her throat. Now that she had him, she didn't know what to say.

"Hello?" he said again.

"S-Sid?" she said in the small naive voice that had served her as a teenager.

He didn't answer for a long moment. "It's you," he finally said. "Didn't think I'd ever hear from you again."

"Why?" she said too loud, tears coming unexpectedly to her eyes. Several people turned to stare at her. She tried to control her voice. He sounded so cold. "You're my husband. Why shouldn't I . . ."

"You've gotten pretty famous," he said, the bitter edge still there. "I even had to enroll the kids in another preschool under a different name."

"Oh, no," she said, her wall of control powdering to dust. "I never wanted any of this to happen."

His voice broke with suppressed anger. "Never wanted it?" he said loudly. "Hell, you begged for it. You went to a great deal of trouble to find it. Don't bullshit me, Nancy."

She was too numbed to argue with him. "Are the children a-all right?" she asked.

"How can they be all right? They don't have a mother anymore."

She broke down then, all the tears she couldn't find over the last week coming at once. "Oh, Sid. I love you," she cried, voice cracking. "Please don't hate me. Please. You and the boys are my whole life."

"You're lying," he said, but his own voice was choked. His mother was badgering him to hang up. Nancy heard him cover the receiver, the muffled "shut up," coming through anyway.

"Sid," she said. "Please. I don't know if I can... live without you."

"Why didn't you think of that before?" he asked quietly.

"I did," she whispered.

Prescott was at her arm, his eyes concerned. "We've got to go," he whispered.

"Come home now," Sid said. "Renounce this thing and hop a plane back. We can be together tonight."

"I can't," she said through clenched teeth.

"Why?" he asked, his own voice cracking.

"I've got to be whole again," she said in a monotone. "I've got to bury my past."

"I've never cared about that," he said. "I just wanted you as you were."

"But I care about it! Me!" She was shaking, Prescott putting an arm around her shoulder to steady her. "I've lived in the shadows so long, Sid, I don't know what the sun looks like anymore. Don't hate me for that. Please don't hate me."

There was a long silence on his end of the line until finally, very quietly, the phone clicked off, the connection broken on his end.

She cried silently, Jerry holding her, taking the receiver out of her hand to hang it up. The room had gotten deathly quiet, everyone staring around uneasily, the TV bringing them all to attention.

"We interrupt this program for a special bulletin."

Everyone turned to the screen, Jerry walking a still-sobbing Nancy up to stand in front of it. A network newsman was looking directly at the camera.

"We've just gotten word from the State Department," he

said, "that a Vietnamese-American named Joseph Nhu has surrendered to the Baltimore police today. Mr. Nhu told government interrogators that he is in the employ of the government of the Republic of Vietnam as an insurgent, and that he, along with NAMWives leader Nancy Phillips Henderson, planned the massive campaign that is attempting to transfer several billion dollars worth of gold from America to Vietnam."

A videotape came on screen showing Joey Nhu being moved from a Baltimore police car to an unmarked government car, his hands cuffed behind his back. Famous at last, Nancy thought. Then they showed some recent file footage of her in Chicago.

"Mrs. Henderson is at-large at the moment and is currently being sought under a federal arrest warrant, charged with conspiracy to commit a treasonous act and violation of the Sherman-Clayton Antitrust Act. More as things develop."

Prescott took her by the arm, his overnight bag in his free hand. "Come on," he said. "We've got to keep moving. We can't stop now."

They walked quickly among the trainlike machines that carried baggage and meals to the planes, past the men with the earphones who guided the big machines in, finally stopping at one of the hangars.

"This will all work itself out," Prescott told her. "Just hold yourself together."

Forklifts were moving, lifting skiffs loaded with tarp-covered gold bars into the cargo bay of the 747. The man who had spoken to Prescott in the lounge directed them up the long stairs leading into the plane.

Myrna went up with them, but kissed her husband good-bye at the doorway, tears filling her own eyes. It passed for Nancy in a blur, as she tried desperately to get herself together.

The pilot came out of the cockpit, shaking hands with Prescott. "Mr. Secretary," he said.

"We really appreciate your volunteering for this," Prescott told him.

"I flew over there, too," he said. "We've got to be finished with it."

"No one's to know you've got passengers," Prescott said.

"I understand."

Then the man was looking at her. "I want you to know," he said, "that I'm proud to make your acquaintance." He took her hand, his warmth pumping life back into her. "I think you're a great American."

"No, I'm not," she sniffled, returning his handshake. "I just drew the lucky number."

He smiled at her. "Better buckle in," he said. "We'll be out of here in a minute."

"Thanks," she replied, moving with Prescott back to the seats in the first-class section.

Gold filled the passenger compartment, the floors and seats, bricks in double rows stacked atop one another. Prescott cleared a couple of seats for them and they sat, each lost in thought.

A minute later she shook her head, laughing.

"What is it?" he asked, and the plane began to taxi out of the hanger and into the sunshine.

"All this," she said, gesturing around. "Here I am sitting here with hundreds of millions of dollars worth of gold and I don't have a nickel in my pocket." She looked down at her trashed jeans and sweatshirt. "God, I don't even have a change of clothes. I must look a mess."

He looked at her, shaking his head. "You're beautiful," he said. "Just beautiful."

They moved into priority position on the flight line, then began their charge at the runway, using as much of it as they possibly could before climbing sluggishly into the air, the controllers in the tower wondering why they were having such a difficult time taking off.

The phone felt hot in Sid Henderson's hand when he hung it up. He had steeled himself against her, had hardened an internal shell made purely of reason that didn't allow for the existence of emotion; but when he had heard her voice on the phone, so small, so vulnerable—*his* Nancy—he could feel the wall crumbling. God, why did he love her so much?

"You're a fool, Sid," Naomi said, tears wetting her cheeks from his rebuff. "Just like your father."

He stared hard at her. "Dad was human," he said. "That's all."

She turned and walked into the kitchen and began putting away the groceries she had just bought. "Your father used me like a mat under his feet. He made a fool out of me with God knows how many women before I finally wised up and got rid of him. I've suffered more than you can imagine at that man's hands, so don't you come around here defending him."

He followed her into the kitchen. "How can you be so bitter after so many years?"

She flared around, eyes flashing. "Because I wasted my whole life on him, and now bitterness is all I've got left. You'll see. I tried to protect you from that woman. She never got through when *I* answered the phone. But now..."

"She's called before?" he asked.

Naomi Henderson's face paled slightly. "I didn't want to upset you," she said quietly.

He moved to her, taking her gently by the shoulders. "Oh, Mom. I've got to handle this on my own." He moved away from her. "I was here when you threw Dad out," he said. "I remember it like yesterday. He made a mistake, then told you about it. You never forgave him, even though he tried for years to get you to take him back."

"He got what he deserved," she said.

"Did he? You've always seemed so ... triumphant in your misery. You've worn it like a badge."

"Stop it!" she said.

"The wronged woman," he said. "What kind of cross is that to carry through life?" And he realized he was talking more to himself than to her. He moved to the brown shopping bag on the kitchen table. A supermarket tabloid was folded into the top. He started to pull it out. "Isn't there forgiveness in you anywhere?"

"No!" she snapped, hurrying to pull the paper out of his hands. "He betrayed me, put me through a living hell. Every woman I would see on the streets, I'd wonder, Is she the one? Is it her? You can't know the shame I lived in."

"What's in the paper?" he asked.

"Nothing," she said, and put it in a drawer.

As soon as she walked away from the drawer he moved to it, taking out the paper.

"Leave that alone!" she said.

He unfolded the front page bannering the headline: WIFE DITCHES HUBBY FOR MIA LOVER. He looked quizzically at her, only going back to the paper when he noticed how white her face had gotten. The article promised to expose the "untold story" of Nancy Phillips Henderson. And then there was a picture. He recognized it right away. It had been cut from a larger photo.

"This is one of our wedding pictures," he said. "I wonder where they got . . ."

She turned away, and he knew the truth. "You gave them this picture."

She looked at the floor. "You need to just cut the cord and get her out of your life. I'm only trying to protect you."

He expected anger, but he felt only calm. "You want me living here so you won't be lonely," he said. He dropped the scandal sheet on the table and started out of the kitchen.

"Where are you going?" she demanded.

He turned to stare at her. "Back to join the human race," he said. "I've got to face it all sometime. Today's as good a day as any. Who knows? In a couple of days, there may be no human race to join."

"... saying the city can no longer afford the costs of the aquarena. In other local news, that hunger strike by area residents protesting the hostage situation is entering its fourth day. More from David Vickers on the scene. . . ."

"Thanks, Frank. That wailing you heard me is the sound of ambulance sirens going down Vanguard Street. Local doctors have donated their time to care for the women down here, but many of them are getting sick due to the unsanitary conditions and dampness underground.

"I'm standing here with Joe Andrews, son of Marcie Andrews, the unofficial leader of this group. What's the situation, Joe?"

"Well David . . . I just flew in from Cleveland today, so I don't know much. I know there's a lot of sick women down there, suffering from exposure and lack of food. They brought my mother out awhile ago . . . at her age, I'm surprised she lasted this long."

"Is this sort of thing typical of your mother?"

"No . . . no, she's never done anything like this before to my knowledge. She was very close to my brother; Mark. He was killed by friendly fire in 1968. She came to hate the war and what it stood for. The thought of all of that coming to a head again was just more than she could bear, I guess."

"Now that she's been taken to the hospital, is that the end of the vigil?"

"No, David. Absolutely not."

"What happens now?"

"M-my mother couldn't even sit up down there. I watched a rat run across her legs. Still, she refused to leave until I made her go. I guess the least I can do for her, and for Mark, is to take her place down there."

"Any statements?"

"Yeah. Pay the money!"

"This is David Vickers, KING-TV, Seattle. Back to you Frank."

XLVI

The White House

April 17—4:17 P.M.

Simon Herrod stood looking out at the silent crowds who stood vigil on Pennsylvania Avenue, just outside the big gates. There were perhaps three thousand of them. They carried no placards, shouted no slogans. They were just waiting. For five days there had been demonstrations and riots and fighting, the youth of America polarizing behind him while the older ones, the ones with memories of loss and grief, fought him at every turn. Then everything turned silent. With word that the Seventh Fleet and the Russian Navy were squared off in the South China Sea the demonstrations tapered off. There had been no progress in negotiations. In fact, the Vietnamese had adamantly refused any attempt at negotiation. And now the deadline was less than two days away.

The entire world waited. Suddenly the rhetoric was meaningless as the specter of a confrontation between the superpowers hung like an impending thunderstorm over all. Everyone wondered one thing: What would the President of the United States do when the moment came? And no one, especially the President knew what that decision would be.

"I don't believe it," Herrod said, turning around to face Miller Angostis and Maurice Benstock. "I've been friends with Jerry Prescott for nearly thirty years. Hell, we both fought over the same woman. He's loyal and hard-working, absolutely incapable of the kind of betrayal you're accusing him of."

Angostis stood in the center of the room, hands on his hips. "The connections are inescapable, Mr. President," he said, walking to the big desk and laying a hand on the file folder that sat atop it. "Just read through this. It lays it all out."

"It's all circumstantial," Herrod said, desperately wanting to believe in Prescott. How could his oldest friend desert him at a time like this? How could a man who had served government so faithfully for so many years, suddenly betray his trust? It didn't seem possible.

"You know how he was about all the television exposure we were getting," Benstock said from the couch. "He feared it so much he hated it."

Herrod shrugged. "Jerry and I have disagreed over things for years," he said. "I've always appreciated his honesty. That hardly convicts him of anything."

"Don't blind yourself to this," Angostis said. "It could hurt you."

Herrod looked hard at the man. "Maybe you'd just better explain that," he said. "You convince me why I should think my secretary of state is a traitor."

"All right," Angostis said. "Just bear with me. Did Prescott want to go to Chicago for you?"

"Well . . . no," Herrod said, moving to the coffee service to pour himself a cup. "I think he felt . . ."

"Guilty," Benstock said. "He felt guilty because of the way he had treated those women when Nixon was president."

"Would you not agree," Angostis continued, "that he was furious when the Paris films were shown?"

Herrod set his cup and saucer on the edge of his desk. "He felt they were manipulative propaganda."

"Okay," Angostis said. He began moving around the room, talking faster as he made his points. "Just follow me for a moment. Somehow, Nancy Henderson knew about the raid on her warehouse. Someone told her. Did Prescott know?"

"Yes, but..."

"Just for the sake of argument," Angostis said. "We'll debate it later. Nancy Henderson received a call from someone Joey Nhu called, 'higher up.' She apparently spent the rest of the night moving her gold. But to where? We had already put the clamps on Air France, so, in essence, she seemed to have nowhere to turn—except for her good friend, the one who had tipped her off, Jerry Prescott."

"Now wait—" Herrod began.

"Just for the sake of argument," Angostis said.

Herrod nodded, picking up his cup to drink.

"Sometime this morning, Prescott slipped away from his Secret Service protection. He took his own car and left, unannounced. His men found the remaining cars to have flat tires."

"All of them?" Herrod asked.

"Yes, Mr. President."

Herrod set his cup back down. "Go on," he said, folding his arms across his chest.

"We began searching for Nancy Henderson," Angostis continued. "That much gold would be difficult to hide. About an hour ago we found what we think was a hiding place. A tobacco farmer complained to police that a lot of people had gone through his fields in trucks. We went there and found evidence that a major hauling operation had taken place in the field. The field is located within a few miles of Friendship Airport in Baltimore.

"All at once, out of the blue, World Airways announces it's going to send planes to Bangkok to bring the prisoners back upon their release. Where do they leave from? Friendship Airport. And it just so happens that the president of World Airways is David Durbins, father of the girl Jerry Prescott's son is getting ready to marry."

Herrod sadly looked down at the carpet. "I didn't know that," he said.

Angostis walked up to stand in front of the man. "Now the planes are long gone. There is no more trace of the gold or of Nancy Henderson or Jerry Prescott. The planes were loaded in a hangar, in secret."

Herrod moved behind his desk. "Even I'm smart enough

to see the truth when it hits me in the face," he said, and the entire turn of events was beyond his understanding. "How could he do it?"

"This business has turned everyone around," Benstock said from the couch. "Jerry just started thinking with his heart instead of his head."

"It's got to be more than that," Herrod replied. "He's a decent, honest man and one of the highest officials in the country. He couldn't have just gone off half-cocked to commit treason."

"I think," Angostis said, "that he may have felt betrayed himself. I believe he felt your propaganda efforts were... dishonest."

"We had no choice," Herrod said. "We just met them on their own battlefield."

Angostis shrugged. "Maybe he didn't have the stomach for that kind of fighting."

"And maybe," Benstock added, "he's the remnant of a world that no longer exists."

"Kind of like those men over there in the prison camp," Herrod said. "Can we get the planes back?"

"Not at this point," Angostis said, "but we've made arrangements with the Thai government to pick them up when they get off the plane, and to confiscate the gold."

Herrod nodded. "If he would have only tried to understand things from my viewpoint," he said. "He was always so damned pigheaded." He looked at Angostis. "When we arrest him, I want it done quietly. I don't want to have to stand up to this until the hostage business is over with. We'll just take him and the woman and salt them away somewhere for now."

"There is another way," Angostis said.

Herrod narrowed his gaze. "What do you mean?"

"This is going to be a real embarrassment to you, Mr. President, no matter how it works out," the man said, his voice flat, inflectionless. "But, you know, people have accidents all the time—planes fall out of the sky, cars get into wrecks—people get hurt, killed."

Herrod stood up slowly, fighting to control himself. "I'm going to pretend you never said that," he told Angostis, "and I'm absolutely positive you'll never say anything like that again."

"Yes, Mr. President," Angostis said, but he shared a long, knowing look with Benstock.

"What about the prison break?" Herrod asked.

"My man is in Ho Chi Minh City," the director replied. "If the break occurs, will the Seventh Fleet cover their retreat?"

"If the break occurs," Herrod said slowly, "we will go to red alert. Beyond that, I don't know. Good afternoon, Mr. Angostis."

"Good afternoon," the man said, and moved immediately for the door. He slipped quietly out.

Herrod rubbed his face with his hands. "God, I don't think I've slept more than an hour at a stretch since this thing started."

"It'll be over soon," Benstock said.

"Will it, Benny?" he asked.

"Nobody wants war," Benstock said. "It's all bluff. It'll come out fine."

"We're doing the right thing, aren't we?"

Benstock stood and moved to the desk, leaning across it on stiff arms. "We're doing the only thing," he said.

Herrod nodded. "Too late to change now, anyway," he said, then pointed a finger. "I want you over there."

"What?"

"I want you over there in the South China Sea on the fleet flagship. That way I'll have my right arm on top of any situation that develops, and you'll also be able to make sure the 'right' news gets sent back."

Benstock looked at his watch. "Can I make it this late?"

Herrod picked up a phone. "We'll vac you over to Andrews," he said, then put up a hand. "Get the copter revved up. I'll need it right away." He hung up the phone. "Then we'll send you over on an Air Force jet. There's plenty of time."

"I've had an overnight bag packed in my office," Benstock said. "I just need to call my wife."

"We'll take care of that," Herrod replied. "Just get down to the pad."

Benstock moved toward the door.

"And Benny," the President said, the man turning back to him. "If you see Prescott . . . ask him, why."

"Yes, sir," Benstock said, hurrying out the door.

Herrod stood, shuffled to the window and looked out again, staring back at the silent people who stared in.

The House of Representatives
April 17—4:49 P.M.

Hugh Martindale sat at his desk in the House chambers listening intently to the patriotic speech being made by the Republican representative from Nevada, Morris Allen. Allen, he knew, was a Mormon, and the Armageddon speech he was making sounded like it might have been a sermon he had heard recently at the Temple.

The chambers were full today, everyone waiting for the end of debate before voting on the Resolution issue. The almighty Resolution, the nonbinding, time-wasting procedure elected officials go through to make their constituents think they're doing something vital for the country. Pain flared in the back of Martindale's neck, a bad headache to counteract the pain in his leg that had intensified the closer he got to his speech.

His duty to the party was clear, the resolution suddenly an important link in the chain of his political future. But all he could think about was Vietnam.

"We've got to bring the righteous sword of Justice to bear on those who would do us harm," Allen said in a monotone. The man shifted uneasily from foot to foot, the microphone held closely to his mouth. "There is nothing to debate. There is nothing to negotiate. We must use our God-given might to go in and smite our enemies and bring those boys home to our bosom."

Martindale reached back and massaged the muscles on the back of his neck, trying to ease down the headache. God, wouldn't Allen ever shut up? What did he know about it? What *could* he know about it?

He could smell the human feces, his own, as he was pushed across the cell, knocking over his *binjo* pot in the corner. Pizza Face took his head then, pushing it down into the decomposing glop before raising him up and shoving the metal bar through his trussed-up arms, twisting until he felt his shoulders were being pulled to pieces.

"Who organized this religious service, Captain Martindale?" Snake Eyes, the interrogator had asked him over and over.

He had never answered, couldn't answer through the pain. And he knew, really knew...

They never wanted him to answer.

The pain flared again in Martindale's head, and he knew he couldn't stand it anymore. His body was telling him what his mind denied. "Mr. Speaker," he said, eyes closed, into his own microphone, listening to the echo, surprised at the pain in his own voice. "Mr. Speaker."

"The chair recognizes the representative from Ohio," Sam Fulton said, his eyebrows raised in a bemused expression.

Martindale stood, rotating his head, trying to ease the pain. "Will the representative from Nevada yield the floor?"

He turned to look at Allen, who was looking up at George Keller, the minority whip. Keller smiled, a cat with a mouse, and nodded broadly.

Allen cleared his throat. "I gladly yield to a great American, Representative Martindale."

"Thank you, sir."

"You have the floor," the Speaker said.

Martindale looked around as if he were trying to impress every detail of the House chambers indelibly upon his memory.

"Distinguished gentlemen and ladies," he said softly. "I want all of you to think about something." The chamber was deathly still. "A democratic republic, like any government, is a collection of people who stand to represent the hopes, dreams, ideals, and feelings of the people it serves. Government exists for the will of the people, not the other way around. A government is not a living organism, nor is it a reality beyond that given it by its citizens. No government should be stronger than its citizens—none. All is subject to change.

"Those men over there are martyrs to a government, not to a people. They are the expendable goods of barter to a system that neither wants them nor needs them. They have given the best part of their lives to hang on the cross of government—not the cross of the people. Because the people want them back alive. *I* want them back alive."

He felt moisture on his cheeks, but didn't wipe it off. "They have sacrificed everything that we hold dear, and now are being sacrificed again. What for? National pride!" He pointed to Allen. "Or even worse—election returns!"

The House erupted, the Speaker pounding his gavel for quiet.

"Will the representative yield?" Allen called angrily, other voices echoing it.

"No!" Martindale said loudly. "I'm nailing myself into the coffin, I might as well do a proper job of it. Let me tell you the truth of the situation. If we do anything besides pay that money, those men will die. There are no other alternatives. They will die so that our country can maintain its posture for the rest of the world. Well let me tell you something, no pride is worth death. A nation that feeds its lifeblood to the flames for pride is not worthy of that blood.

"Pay the ransom, America! Forget the national ego and the political pepperheads like my esteemed colleagues and let those poor men live out their days in peace. So help me God, they deserve it."

The chambers broke into angry shouts and scattered applause, but Martindale didn't hear any of it. He turned and walked out of the huge room, slightly favoring his bad leg. He knew he was finished in politics, but he didn't care. If his years in the prison camps had taught him anything, it had been the lesson of respect for life above all. That was the key, the reason they were all there.

His headache had gone away.

VIOLENCE SPREADS

LOS ANGELES (AP)—Collection centers for the NAMWives's drive to raise ransom funds to free captive American servicemen held in Vietnam have increasingly become the targets of vandalism and violence, the FBI said today.

Citing a turn to the right on the nation's college campuses, the Washington bureau listed 113 incidents of violence between student demonstrators and personnel working the collection centers.

"The kids mean well," said FBI spokesman Arthur Teem, "but they tend to get a little overzealous in the expression of their feelings." Asked if there was anything being done to halt the spread of violence in these student demonstrations, Teem replied, "Maybe on the local levels they're doing something, but there's nothing we can do. By the time we set up any kind of study or anything, this whole thing will have blown over."

In the three days of demonstrations, there has been property damage totaling $23 million and 520 people hospitalized, including 31 paraplegics beaten by protestors at the South Los Angeles collection center. Fourteen people have died.

XLVII

Ho Chi Minh City, Vietnam

April 17—2:30 P.M.

Cassady rode his bicycle down tree-lined Tu Do Street toward the cathedral. The streets were full of military, but the civilians paid them little heed, going about their daily affairs. There seemed to be little tension in the air, the atmosphere more one of relaxed festivity for the many soldiers—this despite the threat that waited at the headwaters of the Saigon River.

The sidewalk cafés were filled with uniformed Asians, occasional Russian technical personnel dotting the open-air tables in small groups. The Russians held no status among the Vietnamese. They were generally poorer than the Americans had been, generally ruder and more ill-kempt. If there was any apprehension anywhere in the city though, it was mirrored in the faces of the Russians. Perhaps they, above all, understood the immensity of the chain of events Colonel Tin had set in motion. They, better than anyone, knew the magnitude of the horror that sat barely thirty miles from them. Unless something was done quickly, Vietnam, and perhaps the rest of the world as well, had less than forty-six hours to live.

The cathedral sat at the head of the street. When Cassady reached it he turned toward the old Presidential Palace. A right would have taken him to Camp Friendship, near what was once the American Embassy.

He had spent a part of the morning looking for Kim. She had once had residence at the Hotel Catinat on Nguyen Hue Boulevard. The Pink Nightclub, the favorite hangout of the high-rollers in the old days, had been located in the hotel. But all that was changed now. Ho Chi Minh City had no money for nightclubs, or for any other diversions. Kim was long gone from the Catinat which had been turned into apartments. But it didn't matter. He'd find her.

He felt good. The city hadn't changed much save the leveling out of its wartime frenetic pace. From what he saw on the streets, the black market still seemed to be operating, which meant the criminal underground was still intact, which meant some of his old contacts would still be around.

The Presidential Palace stood in the distance, shining brightly in the hot afternoon sun, the huge flag rippling gently in the wind, its gold star glinting on the red background.

He turned down a narrow alleyway several blocks before reaching the palace, waving off the fish and vegetable vendors who walked into the street to accost him. He passed two Buddhist monks in saffron, who raised their arms to cover their faces from the haze of dust he had roused on the dirt street.

The pavement would turn into dirt road a mile or so later that eventually led to Tan Son Nhut Airbase, but Cassady wasn't going that far. Several small hootches were nestled in the jungle along the path. They had belonged to locals who had worked for the Americans at Tan Son Nhut in clerical or janitorial positions. Poor by American standards, they were wealthy compared to the other Vietnamese, living what could be considered an extravagant life-style. One of these, Kim Van Kieu—who boasted of being related to the great Vietnamese poet of the same name—had worked both sides of the street. A janitor by day, he had played the blackmarket by night, making deals he had consummated at the base for American goods and equipment. He in turn sold the G.I.'s drugs and women.

Kieu had been Cassady's best friend and contact during the war years, and it was in the American-built air-raid shelter in his backyard that an amount of firepower was cached. There were weapons buried all over Vietnam. In fact, American weapons were buried all over the world. It was a Pentagon priority.

The trail got too undergrown to take the bike, and he got off and walked it until he spotted Kieu's house in a small clearing to his right. He made his way down, leaving the bike hidden just off the path.

The house was wooden, unpainted, with a rusted tin roof. Rice paper covered the open windows, the smell of palm oil seeping out into the yard. Chickens scattered at his approach, an old dog barking once before whining and running up to him. A monkey stared in mock concentration from under the house, a long piece of rope keeping him tied to one of the supports.

Cassady ignored the dog and strode up the rickety steps to the door. The smell of joss sticks mixed with the perfume of the palm oil. He knocked.

A moment later a woman opened the door, clad loosely in white gauze, a turban of the same material wrapped around her head. It held together a small crown of straw topped by a sash. In her hand she carried a bamboo cane. When she saw Cassady, her eyes widened in horror.

"You've come back," she said in English.

"*Chao ong*, Thuy Kieu," he said, bowing slightly. "Who died?"

"You devil!" she said angrily. "Go way!"

She tried to slam the door on him, but he held an arm out stiff and stopped it. He watched her eyes, the anger turning to fright.

"*O day khong duoc yen*," she said, looking back in the house, then back at Cassady.

The man laughed. "No place is safe for me," he replied. "Where's your husband?"

She just stared at him, her lower lip trembling slightly.

"Look," he said. "All I want is the key."

She put a finger to her lips. "*Phai im lang.*"

"I must have the key."

"No key. You go way."

She tried to shut the door again, met the resistance of his arm again. This time he shoved back, the door banging open.

Cassady shoved her aside and strode in. Several children were prostrating before an altar upon which sat a picture of Kieu hung with a garland of white flowers. They all wore white, the mourning color. A teenaged boy, dressed in black leathers, leaned against the wall looking disinterested. A cigarette bobbed in his mouth. The altar was covered with food—rice, tea, and sweetcakes, offerings for the dead person's soul.

Cassady took off his coolie hat, throwing it on the floor. Moving past the children, he went into the family bedroom, Kieu's wife hurrying behind him.

"He dead," she said. "Go now."

The body lay on a narrow pallet underneath a mosquito netting. A white kerchief was placed across his face, a knife upon his stomach to ward off devils. Beside the bed sat an open coffin, a white silk shroud laying loosely across it.

Cassady looked at the woman. Her face, once beautiful, looked strained and aged, her eyes edged deep from constant tears. Whenever she looked at Cassady, her face held nothing but horror.

"What happened?" he asked.

"He sick long time," she answered, the white-clad children standing just outside the door. "After war he go to reeducation center and get sick."

Cassady grunted. "Where's the key?"

"Gone," she said. "No key. You go now."

He stared at her for another second, then turned to the body. He grasped the mosquito netting, pulling it aside. He had to check the body—just to be sure.

"No!" the woman screamed loudly, throwing herself at Cassady. One of the children, a little boy, wrapped himself around Cassady's leg, biting.

He shoved the woman aside, pulling the kerchief off the face. It was Kieu all right, but he seemed to have the face of an old man. It looked as if his death were a blessing.

The boy sank his teeth into Cassady's leg, pain shooting through it. He reached down, grabbing the boy by the hair and pulling him off. Thuy came at him again, and he grabbed her.

"Tell me where the key is," he said, shaking her violently.

Her dark eyes caught his. "You trouble," she said, crying, sinking to the floor—an old woman's trick. "Please go. I have no key."

Cassady stepped back a pace from her, taking the .45 out of his pants and leveling it at her head. "You'll tell me where the key is now," he said. "If I leave without it, I must kill you because you could turn me in. If you give me the key, you are my accomplice." He cocked the pistol. "Decide now. I will kill your family, too."

She stared up from the floor with eyes of horror, then looked to the children, the leather-clad boy watching behind the others.

"It must be now," he said softly.

She nodded, rising slowly. He followed her out of the room and past the silent children. Cassady looked at the older boy.

"You come, too, cowboy," he said.

At the word cowboy, the youth brightened, following Cassady and his mother out of the house and into the dusty yard. They all moved around the back of the house, Thuy stopping to pick up a small shovel that lay, rusted, on the ground.

The sky began to rumble to the east, the day's rain moving rapidly in. A wet breeze drifted through the surrounding jungle, setting branches and leaves flapping like rippling sails.

Thuy stopped walking, bending to dig at the base of a sack tree, its sap a deadly poison. She dug quickly, her voice singsonging a Vietnamese lament. Cassady looked at the boy. He was staring at the gun that Cassady still carried at his side.

Cassady held up the weapon. "You like guns?" he asked.

"Gun okay," the boy said, admiration in his voice.

"Maybe I'll get you some if you want, okay?"

The boy smiled wide. "Okay."

Cassady watched the woman dig. He could use the cowboy and his friends to help him find Kim.

"Aieee," the woman whined, her shovel banging into something solid. Cassady shoved her out of the way and bent to the hole. A small metal box was partially uncovered.

He worked quickly, uncovering the box. Thuy had taken the opportunity to run back to the house, but the boy stayed, watching the whole operation quizzically.

Cassady stood, the box in his hands covered with moist earth. He found the hinge and cracked it open, a large key within. He took the key, tossing the box farther into the dense jungle.

"You want guns?" he asked the boy.

"Yes," the boy said, lighting another cigarette. "Do I kill for you?"

Cassady shook his head. "I just want you to find somebody. How many in your gang?"

"Twelve," he said without hesitation. "I do my father's business."

"Your mama doesn't approve," Cassady replied.

The cowboy spit on the ground, thunder cracking loudly in the distance.

Cassady took out pencil and paper, jotting down the name. He handed the paper to the boy. "You find where this woman is for me, and I'll give a gun to everyone in your gang."

The boy looked at the paper, smiling. "Street woman?"

Cassady's jaw muscles clenched. "Yes," he said.

The boy nodded. "I find, no sweat."

Cassady grabbed the back of the boy's head, jamming the gun into his neck. "You meet me on the Khank Hoi Dock at six o'clock, or I'll come and get you."

Eyes wide, the boy nodded. Cassady released him and he ran off. With the key grasped firmly in his hand, Cassady looked back at the house, trying to remember what things were like so many years ago. A small rod poked slightly out of the center of the roof. He aligned himself perfectly with it in respect to the house, then turned toward the jungle and walked.

No trees obstructed him for about twenty feet. He remembered now: ten paces to the right of the linden tree. He made the turn, walking into thicket, counting his steps.

He practically tripped over the concrete slab. It was completely covered by undergrowth. Moving quickly, he stripped away moss and thicket, revealing the entry to the bunker. A stainless-steel keyhole protruded an inch out of the slab. The long key fit perfectly, turned a click, then slid open a panel containing a number-coded combination.

That part was easy. Cassady punched up the numbers for his birthday and heard a lock spring within the mechanism. He grabbed the side of the concrete pad and pulled. It slid out of the way revealing stairs down.

A box of self-lighting flares sat on the first step. He opened the box and took one out, popping off the top to bright white, spewing light.

The stairs led down ten feet to the storage room. Cassady took the walk and came out into an intact arsenal. In the throbbing light of the flare he could see it all: cases of M-16s and M-60s, grenades and launchers, handguns and crates of ammo. It all sat there, packed up for moving, just waiting for him.

He could have never done this without his SEAL training. He guided the motorized junk along the locks, slipping up to the next gunboat in the line and tying down. The docks were as full as they had been empty the night before, smells and colors blurring together like a carnival. It was cool, everything slick-shiny from the shower that had just fallen. The crews on the gunboats seemed relaxed, sitting on the decks with their uniform shirts hanging open and smoking cigarettes or marijuana. He'd wave and smile up at them, and they'd return the gesture, sure, perhaps, that their Russian allies would keep them all safe.

Cassady had spent the afternoon acquiring boats, using a local contact to rent ten large craft for several days, paying in gold. And now he was incapacitating gunboats one by one, in the middle of the afternoon.

He walked to the dock-side of the brightly painted wooden ship, looking at his watch. Kieu's boy should be around soon. Cassady'd have to watch for him. Exhaustion was beginning to overtake his body despite the speed. But with any luck, he'd be able to grab a little sleep tonight—with Kim.

Ten-foot lengths of chain lay side by side on the portside. He picked one up, coiling it around his arm. The chains fit perfectly around propeller blades. When a gunboat would start its engine, the chain would foul the prop, leaving it dead in the water.

He moved automatically, at home in a society where the basic skills of survival were most important. He and Kim could set themselves up like the Greek, doing the odd bit of work he was specialized in from time to time. The company was mad at him now, but if he could put himself in a position to do them some good, they'd come around.

He slipped out of his sandals, hoisting himself up on the gunwale, his feet dangling. The chain hung heavy on his shoulder, almost enough to sink him and keep him sunk. When he went down, it would be impossible to see anything below the surface. He'd have to make it over to the big gray ship and feel his way down to the prop.

Above, they were laughing on the gunboat deck as one of the sailors took pot shots at gulls with a .9-mm pistol. This was Cassady's chance. Without a second of indecision he tossed his hat onto the deck and slid quietly into the dark waters, where he began his battle to complete the job before the chains dragged him all the way down to the bottom.

NAMWIVES LEADER MISSING

CHICAGO, (AP)—As her campaign to raise gold for her husband and the other MIAs in Vietnam picks up steam, NAMWives leader Nancy Henderson appears to be among the missing. "She's taking care of business," said Marsha Ridley, spokeswoman for the group. "Beyond that I can't say."

Henderson, who's not been seen for two days, is the mastermind behind the move to raise the ransom money despite the government's objections. She has become, in the space of a few days, one of the most recognizable figures in America.

"She's with the gold," an unidentified woman from NAMWives said. "Find the gold and you'll find Nancy Henderson."

Finding the gold has proven to be as difficult a task as finding the woman. Reports have come in from all over the country saying the gold is hidden in various places, but so far, all leads have proven false. How long Nancy Henderson can remain hidden from view is a matter of speculation.

XLVIII

Camp Friendship

April 17—Late Evening

Colonel Bui Tin sat in his blue silk robe and matching pajamas and yawned into the telephone, responding in French from time to time as the ambassador spoke rapidly, outlining the changing plans in the gold exchange. Tin's personal regimen was austere, his belief in keeping his body healthy and strong an almost overwhelming obsession. Sleep was most important to him, its loss a major irritation barely justified by the importance of the call.

"Jean," he interrupted. "Jean." It took a few seconds for the ambassador to hear him and clear the line. "This man . . . Prescott. Can we trust him?"

There was dead air on the line as the messages went back and forth. The ambassador's voice came back, distant but clear. "He is an old friend and a good man. I trust him."

Tin picked the small cigar, his only vice, off the rim of the ashtray and brought it to his lips, barely inhaling. "Do they have all the money?"

"No. Jerry told me they could get about eighty percent."

"Jean—"

"Just listen to me," the man said. "They're having to sneak this around as it is. The government is trying to confiscate all of it. There can be no more gold. If you are to have a deal, this must be it, and we must keep everything a secret."

Tin exhaled a long, gray streamer, then put the cigar back in the ashtray. "All right," he said, satisfied enough. "But we will have to do a quick examination of the gold before we take control of the vessel and consummate the deal."

"Will you call a moratorium on any action while you examine the gold?"

"Yes."

There was knocking on the door.

Tin covered the receiver with his hand. "Go away," he called in Vietnamese.

The knocking came again, more insistent. Something was going on.

"About this Joey Nhu . . ." the ambassador was saying.

"Let me see what I can do on this end," Tin said. "This person has proven a great embarrassment to me. I think we will simply disavow knowledge of him."

"You have everything I have."

The knocking continued.

Tin covered the mouthpiece. "Just wait!" he called, then went back to the phone. "I will do all required on my end and will meet Mr. Secretary Prescott in..." he looked at his watch, "just under thirty-seven hours at the coordinates listed."

"Good. I'll relay that through our people in Malaysia and get back to you if there are any changes."

"It's too late for changes, Jean," Tin said. "Good-bye."

"Good-bye."

Tin hung up the phone. Everything was falling into place. With any luck, the gold would be in his possession within a day and a half with no one hurt, no real face lost to anyone except the American hierarchy that didn't seem to understand honor anyway.

They were cutting it close to the time limit, but there was nothing he could do about that. And if the workings of his plan led to confrontation, to global warfare—so be it. Those were the choices of other people and had nothing to do with him. He'd spent his life breathing the fetid air of war. Its odor no longer frightened him.

He picked up the cigar and looked at the door. "Come in," he called.

The door opened, a young corporal coming in fear-fully, his hat forever turning in his hands. "Colonel, sir..."

"Yes, yes. Surely this can wait until morning."

"The dog, sir," the young man stammered. "One of the camp dogs..."

"What are you babbling about?" Tin demanded, drawing on the cigar.

"We chased the barking dog," he said. "It was trying to get at something under the barracks. We found ... we found ..." He turned to the door and motioned to someone outside. Four men entered, carrying a body on a flat skiff.

Tin was out of his chair, moving around to them. He came up next to the body, staring into the unseeing eyes of Harry Jenkins.

He centered his mind on that face, forced himself away

from the ramifications to deal with this one step at a time. "Did you find the weapon?" he asked.

"No, sir," the corporal replied, looking at the ground.

He turned dark eyes upon the man. "Look at me," he ordered. The man's eyes rose to his. "You will roust out the entire camp. You will strip-search each one of them in the yard, then go through the buildings inch by inch. Anything you find —anything—will be brought to me and that prisoner detained."

"Yes, sir."

"And you will have Colonel Ridley brought to me immediately. Put the body on the floor and get out."

The men moved quickly, silently, leaving Tin with the burden he wasn't prepared to bear.

"You were a weak, broken excuse for life," he told Jenkins's hulk, squatting to get near the head. "You were a frightened little animal. I could see it in your eyes. I'll wager you brought all this on yourself, sneaking around, snooping into everything." He spit on the body. "And now, dead you can hurt me when you could never hurt me alive."

Outside, he could hear voices and running feet, lights coming on all over the compound. And now what? Did Ridley have something to do with this? Was this somehow connected with the morning's fire? Something was going on and he had to stop it now, before it got anymore out of hand.

He could hear them shuffling down the hall toward his door. Ridley the enigma. Ridley the inscrutable. They knocked. He moved behind his desk, sitting, trying to regain some measure of composure.

"Bring him in," he said.

The door came open, and there was Ridley, dressed only in trousers, several long scars running across his torso. A guard held onto each of his arms. He stared down at the body, his face totally unreadable.

"Leave us," Tin said.

Ridley was pushed into the room, the door closing after him. The two men, alone, stared at one another.

"What are you trying to do to me, Colonel?" Tin said, standing, unable to keep his seat.

"I don't follow you," Ridley said.

Tin walked around the desk, tightening the sash on his robe, his fists clenching. "First the fire, now this. Why did you kill him? What did he find out about you?"

"He was my best friend," Ridley said solemnly.

"Are you trying to say you didn't do this?" Tin still held his cigar. "Don't insult my intelligence. I'm going to have to ask you what you have planned and I will have the truth from you."

"Harry was my friend," Ridley replied calmly. "I remember how he used to be—before. No one remembers that but me. He had a great many enemies here, the way he used to sneak around."

Tin flared around, his face strained. "I don't believe you!" he yelled, then calmer, "I thought we had an agreement?"

"We do," Ridley said.

Tin's fists came out in front of him—all of his planning, all of his emotion—in jeopardy. "Why did you do this?" he asked.

"I feel I am being threatened here," Ridley said, "in violation . . ."

"Don't say it!" Tin screamed.

"I did nothing," Ridley replied. "There are no plans, no secrets. I've kept to myself all day, rehearsing my speech. I'm sorry if that doesn't fit into your slots, but that's the truth of the matter. I have no idea what happened to Harry."

"The truth can be gotten out of you," Tin said softly.

Ridley smiled broadly. "That's been tried before," he said. "Death holds no more mystery for me. If that's the level upon which you want to play the game, Colonel Tin, I will accommodate you gladly. That will be the only thing I would really have understood since I was brought here."

Tin narrowed his gaze. "You mean that, don't you?"

Ridley moved up to the body, bending to shut the eyes. He looked at his friend through the dispassionate eyes of war, from the place where soldiers go to survive their own emotions. "I think you've gone a little soft," Ridley told Tin. "We all play the game of life and death here. I don't know if you're really ready to face up to the extremes you've set in motion."

Tin moved back to his desk, sitting heavily. "We've had enough death," he said. "At some point life must go on."

Ridley moved to stand across the desk from him. "Then let us all go . . . now," he said. "Set us free. I'll bet you get the money anyhow."

"I haven't gone that soft, my friend," he said, staring hard at Ridley. "Whatever comes, I'll do my duty. Much of my life, the life of my country, has been spent in revolutionary struggle and sacrifice on a level your captivity has just barely allowed you to appreciate. I'll do what I must, Colonel Ridley. Depend on that."

Ridley straightened. "And what must you do about Jenkins?"

"I think I'll use your cowardly friend," Tin said, staring over at the body. "We'll see where the sentiments lie. We'll display him in the yard and tell the truth about his death— that he was killed by terrorists of his own kind. Then we'll ask for information." Tin smiled. "Yes, we'll promise protection to those who wish to step forward with information about this crime, or anything else that may ruin the chances of their release."

Ridley shrugged. "It's your party."

"And as to you," Tin said, standing and coming around the desk again, "I think we will proceed with our schedule. You will deliver your speech tomorrow as planned, although you will be closely watched. If you are, indeed, blameless in your friend's death and are telling the truth about everything else, time will bear that out."

He walked to the door, pulling it open and turning back to Ridley. "If you are lying, however, you will find out exactly how soft I've gotten. You will have to deal with, how did you say it? . . . 'the extremes you've set in motion.' Think about your future, Colonel. Think about your courageous wife. Embrace death if you wish, but ask yourself why."

Ridley nodded then, beyond words, and walked out of the air-cooled office and into the hot night. All the prisoners were lined up, naked, in the yard, Tin's men going through their clothing like grave robbers.

XLIX

Ho Chi Minh City, Vietnam

April 18—1:56 A.M.

The house almost looked respectable. Located at the end of a tree-lined street in a small, merchant-class neighbor-

hood, it could almost pass for a family dwelling—except for
the cars that came and went during the course of an
evening, sometimes staying until very late while uniformed
military drivers slept in the front seats or smoked cigarettes,
wishing they were the ones who had been invited for a
visit.

Cassady had watched three of them that night, all at
different times, neatly dovetailing one visit after another. He
had sat, perfectly still, in the back shrubs, listening to the
laughter, or the sex sounds. Once he had caught a glimpse of
her. She had run, naked, onto the wide veranda on the
second floor of the white, French colonial house, a gross fat
man, also naked, chasing her while they both laughed. He
had caught her then, or she had let him, and he had thrown
her over his shoulder and carried her back into the house. As
he watched the man run his hands all over her, he was taken
by the fact that her wild beauty, so sharp when she was
young, had grown into an elegance that made her all the
more desirable.

Cassady waited until he saw the lights in the house
go out one by one and knew she was through with her
"visitors."

He crept quietly up to the backdoor, prayer flags
flapping gently from the doorpost and the veranda support
pillars.

He bent to the old lock and inserted one of his picks. It
came open easily and he walked into the darkened house.

Kim had done well for herself. Her furniture was delicate, polished wood, richly laquered. The house was crammed
with the knickknacks the Vietnamese loved, small, spindly
things that bespoke the riches it took just to keep such
delicacy intact. Thick, Persian carpets highlighted the polished wood of the floors. If she'd been pining away for him,
she certainly hadn't let it stand in the way of her looking out
for herself.

He topped the stairs, moving toward the light. It was the
bedroom, wide open and luxurious. The bed was large, the
light blue satin sheets wadded and tangled from the evening's
gymnastics. Erotic art covered all except the mirrored
wall.

Across the room was an opening that led to a bathroom with a marble floor. The sound of splashing drew him in that direction. He tossed his hat on a chair and quietly went through the opening.

She was there, within touching distance. She sat in a tub nearly full of water, entirely immersed except for her head. She was washing her long, sleek black hair, her eyes closed from the shampoo that slid down her round face.

He watched, his mouth going dry, his whole body overcome with an ache he had kept sublimated for longer than he cared to imagine.

She slid down in the tub, her head going underwater to rinse out the soap. When she came back out, she pulled her hair back and opened her eyes to stare at him.

There was no start, no hint of fear or surprise. They stared at one another for several seconds, tentacles reaching invisibly across the room to wrap him beyond hope. He'd never leave her again. He knew that already.

She smiled slightly, a kittenish motion, and stood, her lips full and parted. She was sleek, like one of her statues, her beasts still full, the dark nipples large and jutting. Water dripped from her as she stepped out of the tub and walked to him, arms outstretched.

He felt numb and weak, then strong and confident. She fit herself to him, their bodies molding perfectly. She moved against him with a sharp intake of breath. Eyes flashing, she pulled his gun and knife out of his pants and set them on the washstand. Then she fit herself to him again, rubbing against his loins, moaning softly.

He tilted her face to his and searched her eyes. It was as if they had never parted. The look they exchanged was personal and magnetic, full of understanding and acceptance that reached a level far beyond the physical.

"You bitch," he whispered, crushing her open lips to his. She laughed around his probing tongue and pulled herself up his body to wrap legs around his torso. She pulled her face from his, eyes wicked, mouth stretched in a wide grin. He laughed back, moving his hands down under her buttocks to support her. She began bouncing against him.

He turned, carrying her that way out of the bathroom to fall on the bed, her hands going feverishly to his pants, trying to pull them off.

He rolled off her and slid down his pants as she all but pounced on his erect penis, pulling on it, kissing up and down its length.

She slithered against him like a snake, all over his body at the same time, and when he couldn't stand it anymore, he pulled her atop him.

"I haven't had a woman since the last time we were together," he said, pulling on her wet hair, using it to draw her face close to his.

"I've had every man since the last time we were together," she said, reaching a hand back to steady his penis while she mounted him.

"It's your job," he said, then groaned loudly as she sank on him and began to pump.

They ground against each other like a well-timed machine, each understanding the other's needs and responding to them. Their sex had always been perfect, since the very first time, and nothing had changed.

When they were finished, they lay back in one another's arms and watched the overhead fan. "I love you," he said.

She laughed. "You love me because I don't make you feel so nasty."

He crooked an arm under his head, his body relaxed, his mind at ease. He was home. "I'm not nasty when I'm around you."

She knelt beside him, pointing. "You're nasty all the time. We're both nasty." She ran hands across his hard, muscled chest. "I missed you, nasty man. All these years go by and I think I forget you." She shook her head, her eyes flashing. "Why do you come back?"

He pulled her down beside him, reveling in the feel of her, his hands never satisfied, never getting enough. "I came back to get you," he said.

She laughed again, her own hands busy. "You could have come back anytime," she replied, breathing heavily when she found he was erect again. "I think you're back for those men."

"What men?"

She slapped his thigh. "No lies with us, Cassady," she said, and shook her finger at him.

He pushed her onto her back, rolling on top of her. "I'll be finished with them tomorrow night. Then we'll be free."

"Free to do what?" She reached between them, slipping him back into her.

He moved slowly, losing himself in her softness and beauty. Her eyes fluttered as she rose to meet his gentle thrusts.

"Free to . . . go somewhere," he said, "to pick up our life."

"Ohhh." Her eyes opened, staring at him in amusement. "Do you have money for all this?" she asked, knowing the answer in advance.

"A little," he said. "I spent most of it getting here. Do you have any?"

Her hands found his buttocks and she grabbed, trying to hurry his pace. He always could draw it out to where she knew what it felt like to be the client. "Not much," she said. "Oh, yes . . . that's good, baby, so good. Money's scarce these days. Even the generals don't have much. Not like—ooh—good old days with American money. Do they know you're . . . not going back?"

"Honey"—he smiled—"they don't even want me here at all. "I came anyway."

She wrapped her legs around his back, holding him tightly. "They'll come after you."

"Fuck them," he said.

She brought his lips down to kiss. "Oh, no," she cooed. "Fuck me."

He moved faster, watching her face flush, her mouth come open, gasping. She hadn't changed. It was just like before, just like he knew it would be. So many dreams, so many . . .

He was alive again, a corpse brought back from the dead. And he could feel it building up in him, the coiled spring, ready to unwind. From somewhere far away, he heard her screaming as she clung desperately to him, sobbing out her love and her devotion. And then he was screaming, too, then falling, drifting lazily.

He lay on the bed, totally drained, unable to even move. "Can I stay here tonight?" he asked, seventy-two hours without sleep finally catching him.

She smoothed his hair. "Yes, my love," she said, kissing his forehead. "You sleep now. Rest well."

"One question," he said, words slurred. "Why didn't you show up at the embassy that day?"

She just looked at him, knowing he wouldn't understand the answer.

Then he was gone. She cuddled up to him, amazed at the effect he still had on her. Poor Cassady, everybody's pawn. She didn't show up at the embassy that day because she felt she deserved a better life than he could ever offer. What she hadn't counted on was the bond that tied them permanently together. They were, both of them, incomplete without the other.

But this time was different. This time the circumstances could work in their favor. Cassady was a dedicated man, but not very pragmatic, clever but thoughtless. A lot of money was tied up with those prisoners, and there was no reason why they couldn't have some of it to start their new life together.

In the morning she'd take care of it. She'd fix it so they would never have to worry about money again. She kissed him softly on the shoulder, then rolled over and fell into a deep and untroubled sleep—the best sleep she'd had in years.

SATURDAY

BENSTOCK TO VIETNAM

WASHINGTON, (AP)—In a surprise move today, President Herrod's media liaison, Maurice Benstock, was sent to join the Seventh Fleet in the South China Sea. Meeting with reporters briefly before boarding the helicopter that would take him to Andrews Airbase, Benstock said, "I'm on my way to Vietnam to bring the truth to the American people." Among other duties, the ex-newsman is to supervise the press coverage of the standoff between the Seventh Fleet and the Russian Navy, along with the negotiations with the Vietnamese. "It's a big job," he admitted, "but handled right, we'll bring this thing right into the living rooms of America so everyone can see what's going on."

Obviously hurried, Benstock spoke with reporters for only a minute before boarding and taking off. As he climbed into the cockpit he was asked if he had any last comments. "Yeah," Benstock said. "Somebody call my wife Arlene and tell her I won't be home for dinner."

L

Kota Bharu, West Malaysia

April 18—7:00 A.M.

Jerry Prescott and Nancy Henderson walked down the ramp from the 747 with Jeff Frankel, their pilot. The sky was heavily overcast, a light drizzle falling, misting everything. Beyond the simple airport stretched a tropical paradise of vibrant green jungles and white beaches the Portuguese explorers had found worth stealing centuries before.

The flight line was a madhouse as Malay regular army troops formed lines to load the gold into the backs of Russian-made trucks for transportation to the rail line a mile distant. From there it was a short trip to the docks where the Liberian-registered freighter was already loading for the last leg of the trip across the South China Sea.

"The government is waiting for us in Bangkok," Frankel said from behind them. "I think they've got the whole setup figured."

Prescott turned to him for just a second, then continued down. "Will you guys be in much trouble?"

"I don't know," Frankel returned. "We were scheduled for refueling in Germany, but were able to do it unregistered in Paris. They filed false flight plans for us, so we'll be landing in Bangkok at just about the right time. If they don't catch us here, I don't know if they can catch us."

A roar drowned out conversation as a World Airways plane taxied quickly down the too-short runway, climbing steeply when it got off the ground. Their plane was all that was left on the ground.

They reached the bottom of the ramp, Prescott turning to shake hands with Frankel. "I don't know how to thank you," he said.

"Don't even consider thanking me," the tall, lean man replied. "I wanted to do this. Hell, I volunteered." He turned to a sleepy-looking Nancy Henderson and stuck out his hand. "Mrs. Henderson, I . . ."

She ignored his hand, giving him a big hug instead. "I'll never forget you or any of the others," she said, going on tiptoes to kiss him on the cheek.

"I won't forget you, either," he said, admiration in his voice. "Good luck to you."

"And you," Nancy said.

Frankel looked over at the refueling trucks parked under his wings. "I'd better make sure they only fill those things halfway," he said, bringing his hand up to the brim of his cap. Then he looked past them. "It appears you've got to get to work anyway."

Then the man turned, striding through the ranks of soldiers to try and make contact through hand language with the refuelers.

Prescott turned to look behind him. A small Chinese man in a white suit and hat was making his way toward them from a jeep with a military driver.

"This should be our contact," he told Nancy.

"A Chinese?" she asked.

"The Chinese have always exerted a large influence in Malaysia," he replied. "Up through the 70s they ran most everything."

"How are we fixed for time?"

He shook his head. "It's going to be close at best but, with luck, I think we can pull it off."

Nancy was beginning to wake up. She had slept through most of the flight, coming around long enough during the Paris refueling to borrow some money from Jerry and buy a black dress and shoes in the duty-free shop to replace her blue jeans. "Why did we come here?" she asked.

He smiled. "Being secretary of state definitely has its advantages," he said. "Malaysia is supposedly a neutral country, but its inclination is basically Communist in order to fit in with the rest of the area. They have no ties with the United States, so they had nothing to lose by helping us out."

"Mr. Secretary Prescott." The man approached, speaking in Oxford English, a holdover from British colonialism. "I am Mr. Thulu, unofficial representative of the Independent Republic of West Malaysia." He bowed low. "Welcome to our home."

Prescott bowed. "I am honored to make your acquaintance, sir," he said. "May I present Mrs. Nancy Henderson, the head of our little delegation."

Mr. Thulu nodded, bowing again. "We have heard of your exploits," he said. "You are quite a resourceful woman."

"Thank you," Nancy said. "I must compliment you on your English."

"It is quite unworthy, I am sure," he said. "But thank you."

"Will there be any . . . official representatives," Prescott asked.

The man shook his head. "As far as we are concerned, you have never come to our beautiful country, Mr. Secretary

Prescott." He raised his hand in the air. "You are but a cloud passing before the sun. In an hour, you will be gone. Nothing but a memory."

"A fruitful memory, I trust," Prescott replied.

Thulu smiled wide, nodding vigorously. "Yes, Mr. Secretary, a prosperous memory."

"The money has been taken care of then?" Nancy asked.

"On the first plane, Missus," he said, and used a handkerchief to wipe his forehead, "we realized our dream. Will you allow me to escort you to your transportation?"

He led them to the jeep, while yelling something in a Malay dialect to the troops who worked on the rain-slicked concrete. He helped Nancy into the back of the open car, Jerry climbing in behind her. Thulu took the front seat next to the driver.

"It's only a few miles to the docks," Thulu said, turning to speak to them. "We will make the ride by car."

"Why is the gold going into the trains, then?" Nancy asked, watching fearfully as they left the airport, and the gold, behind.

Thulu laughed. "Not to fear, Missus." He smiled. "The tracks go up to the docks for easy loading, thanks to American rubber plantations from many years ago."

Prescott turned to take one last look at the loading operations, then spoke to the small man. "My pilot tells me my government is waiting in Bangkok. Have you heard anything on this end?"

"We've heard much," Thulu replied. "Your own State Department has been calling us every hour, asking for information."

"You haven't . . ." Nancy began.

Thulu smiled again, taking off his hat to mop the humid sweat and drizzle from his forehead. "We are a very resourceful country," he said. "We've learned to be friends with our friends and honor our commitments. You are our friend. The United States of America is not."

Nancy turned to Jerry. "What is all this going to do to you?"

He shook his head. "I stopped worrying about that when we talked in my bathroom back in Silver Springs. As you said then, if this works out, we won't be in much trouble. Kind of funny, though—my own people tracking me down."

She searched his face. "I was so caught up in this... I guess I never really thought about what your involvement would do to you... your life, your career...."

He took her by the hand. "I did this for me," he said, "not you."

She nodded then, accepting it at that. Now that she had lost everything that meant anything to her, the mission was all that remained. Beyond that, her life was a huge, dark hole.

Somewhere during the ride they were passed by the train carrying their gold. She knew they were probably being robbed of millions of dollars, but the numbers were so high that a few million didn't really amount to very much, something that would have been an incredible thought to her mere days before.

They crested a high hill, gravel crunching under the wheels of the jeep. The rain had stopped, the morning sun climbing in the eastern sky. There was another rumble, but it was only the last of the World Airways planes taking off for Bangkok.

"The harbor," Mr. Thulu said, pointing. But they needed no one to tell them. The sun glinted diamond-bright off the breadth of the ocean below, the water near shore clear and green, the beaches white as sugar.

It was a small port in a deep water cove, five piers jutting out from a steel jetty. It had been cleared of all vessels save one, a large dark freighter, ominous and dirty looking, even at this distance.

"Not much of a boat," Nancy said.

"The *Queen Mary* was all booked up," Jerry said. "Best I could do on short notice."

"The Spaniard has given us some trouble," Thulu said. "He is not a good sort."

"Yeah," Jerry said, resignation lacing his voice.

"Spaniard?" Nancy said. "I thought this was a Liberian ship."

"Registered Liberian," Jerry replied, stretching his back. "Liberia will register anybody, and that's who they get."

"Who are these people then?"

Jerry fixed her with steady eyes. "Pirates," he said.

"I'm serious," she returned.

"So am I. We needed mercenaries for this, freebooters. No country would risk its ship or its world position this way."

They were moving slowly downward toward the harbor. "Can we trust them?" she asked.

"No," Thulu replied.

They made the rest of the ride in silence, pulling into the confusion on the docks within ten minutes. They drove directly onto the pier beside the railroad cars, some sort of altercation going on by the loading cranes. The ship looked even worse close up, its hull rusted in rippling waves, dark-featured men hanging over the rails forty feet above, watching intently the actions below.

"They're not loading," Jerry said. "Pull up there."

"I was afraid of this," Mr. Thulu said, wiping his forehead. "There's been much said about this man by the Vietnamese refugees who inhabit our outer islands."

They came down the pier, skidding to a halt by skiffs full of gold, the ocean below and all around them. A soldier ran up to Thulu, speaking in Malay. Nancy's attention was caught by a tall, lean man, dressed in a blue bathing suit and red T-shirt. He wore tennis shoes with no socks, a long-stemmed unlit pipe clamped firmly between his teeth. Could this be the Spaniard? He looked more like a high-school science teacher on vacation.

Thulu sent the soldier away, turning in his seat to speak. "I am so sorry," he said. "The gentleman over there is Señor Garcia. He refuses to load anymore gold unless he receives more money."

"We've already made him an incredible offer," Jerry said.

Nancy was out of the jeep. "Let's go and speak with him," she said.

"No," Thulu said, his smooth face lined with worry. "This is not for a lady."

"The hell you say," she replied, and was off, striding resolutely toward the tall man, Jerry hurrying to catch up.

"He's right," Jerry said as he caught her. "Let me handle this. We'll see what we can work out."

"No," Nancy said flatly. "I appreciate it but this is my money. I'll have to do what I think is best."

The man had a large revolver strapped around his waist. He smiled slightly, his face gaunt, like a skull. A small moustache adorned his upper lip.

"You're Garcia?" Nancy asked the man.

He looked her up and down, trying to humiliate her with his eyes. "That's right, Señora," he said around the pipe, and continued to stare.

"Seen enough?" she asked, voice cold, "Or is your childish game more important to you than doing business? Perhaps we've gotten a niño, huh, instead of a man."

His dark eyes flashed, his smile fading. "I would kill a man for saying that."

"Not one offering you so much money," she said. "I'd venture your honor is for sale a lot cheaper than the price we've offered for it. Now, what seems to be the problem?"

"I will talk to the señor," Garcia said, taking the pipe out of his mouth and pointing to Jerry.

"You'll talk to me or no one," she said. "Now get on with it. We don't have much time."

He stiffened, his eyes wandering around the pier to all the troops who lined out around them. High above, Garcia's men continued to stare.

"This job is far more dangerous than we were led to believe," the man said, eyes like an animal's. "We must ask you for more money because of the danger."

"How much more?" she replied.

He held out an open hand. "Five million dollars in gold," he said casually.

"What?" Prescott said loudly.

Nancy turned and glared him to silence. "I'll give you two million," she said. "One now, the other when the gold is delivered."

The man drew a breath. "No, Señora," he said. "That is not good enough. "We will have the full amount now or we will not go and you will be without transportation."

"Is that final?" she asked.

"Yes."

She shrugged turning to Mr. Thulu, who stood a discreet distance away. "You will order your men to begin unloading," she said loudly, turning to walk away. "We have no deal with Mr. Garcia."

She walked toward the jeep, heart pounding wildly. It had worked with Joey Nhu. Perhaps Garcia's greed could be used to keep him in line, too. Behind her, Prescott stood dumbfounded, unable to move.

She climbed into the jeep, senses reeling. Perhaps she

was being idiotic, but her position had to be established now
or they would be at Garcia's mercy later. She could hear
Thulu calling to one of his men.

"Señora!" Garcia called, and she thought she would
collapse with relief. She sat perfectly still as the man ran up
to the jeep.

"Three million," he said. "Two now, one later."

"I agree to three million," she replied, fixing her eyes on
his, blowing as cold as she could, "but it's one and a half now,
the same later."

He put the unlit pipe back in his mouth and they stared
at one another. "Done," he said, smiling wide. "You are a
tough woman, Señora."

She continued to stare. "Have the charges been rigged
to scuttle the boat if necessary?"

"Yes," he said, eyes narrowing in suspicion. "We can
blow her up real good."

"I want the detonator."

"I'm taking good care of it," he said low.

"I want it," she said. "I don't trust you, and the detonator is the only weapon I have against you on the high seas.
I'm a desperate woman, Mr. Garcia. At this point I don't care
what happens to any of us. It doesn't matter to me whether I
breath air or water. If you try to do anything but deliver the
goods as agreed, I'll send us all to the bottom without a
second thought. Do we understand one another?"

The man took the pipe out of his mouth and licked dry
lips, grimacing at the salt taste there. "You are in the wrong
business, Señora," he said, and smiled. "You and I should be
partners."

WARRANT ISSUED FOR NAMWIVES LEADER

WASHINGTON, (AP)—A Federal arrest warrant has been issued today for Nancy Phillips
Henderson, renegade leader of the NAMWives organization. Federal Bureau of Investigation head
Will Cain announced at 3:00 P.M. that a warrant for
interstate flight to avoid prosecution has been issued
against the woman, missing since Wednesday.

"We presume she's still in the country," Cain

said. There's already an outstanding warrant out against Mrs. Henderson charging her with Taft-Hartley violations in regard to the gold she's been raising to free the servicemen being held prisoner in Vietnam and, Cain said, "a charge of treason may not be far behind."

The government's handling of the Henderson case has angered many people in the country who feel she's simply a concerned citizen exercising her constitutional rights. But, as President Herrod's media liaison, Maurice Benstock, said, "If she's moving the gold, she's consorting with a foreign power, and that's against the law." Benstock stopped short of saying those charges would be issued against her, however, saying, "we'll just ride this out for awhile and see what happens."

LI

Camp Friendship

April 18—7:00 A.M.

Except for Ridley the barracks was completely empty. Nearly the entire camp was gathered around the outdoor staging area where the French were busily readjusting their cameras for the bright sunshine that was already cresting the barbed wire fences they so carefully kept out of their shots. Ridley hadn't slept. He had spent the entire night getting ready for the morning.

He had written a painful letter to Marsha, explaining, trying to explain, what it was he was doing and why. Then he had laboriously copied the letter as many times as the hours would allow, giving copies to many people to deliver if they made it out. He had tried to tell her of his love, of his happiness at seeing her on Tin's television. Then he had tried to explain the code of honor that had kept him alive until this moment and how he couldn't abandon it in these final hours. Finally, he had pleaded with her to carry on, to pick up her life and forget—no, not forget, to remember well. Life was for the living, and she was still alive.

He felt strangely exhilarated—part of it the giddiness brought on by lack of sleep, but most of it being the rush of battle. He was a soldier above all, had been his entire life. Tin was a revolutionary, which was why he couldn't completely understand Ridley. Tin dealt in reasons, in motivations, in the quality of life. Ridley existed to serve—a government, a way of life—to serve without question, to give his life, not for cause, but out of his sense of duty and honor.

The yard was full, everyone waiting just for him. The streets around the compound were bustling with another day's activity, the lives of a million people moving on their own courses, pursuing their own destinies. He took it all in, tried to memorize it, to impress it upon himself as he had never done before. It all seemed so alien, so distant. Even his own people belonged to another life far removed from his own. He tucked his shirt in, ran calloused hands through his patchy gray hair.

"Good morning, Colonel," came a voice from the doorway.

He turned to see Tin, in full uniform, smiling at him. "Good morning," he replied with the same smile. "I see I'm to have an audience."

"Word of your speech must have spread somehow," Tin said. "I suppose you are a famous man in our camp."

Ridley shrugged. "There probably just wasn't a baseball game this morning."

Tin closed the distance between them, searching the taller man's face with his black eyes, squinting slightly as if to read the mind. "I trust your resolve is still strong, your commitment solid."

Ridley returned the stare. "I'd be lying if I said I didn't have my weak moments, but don't worry. I'll deliver your speech for you. This must come to an end now."

Tin held a hand out to him. "My friend, welcome to the human family," he said. "You are not doing anything wrong by serving the cause of peace."

Ridley shook the man's hand without malice. They both had their jobs to do.

"Are you ready?" Tin asked. "Everything is prepared."

Ridley nodded, happy enough to get it over with. "I'm ready."

Ridley walked out of the barracks, prisoners lining a path for him to walk all the way to the cameras fifty yards distant. They stared as he moved, vacant eyes many of them, some narrowed in concern. The broken men, the army of shadows, they closed ranks, stiffening through some long-forgotten training as their commanding officer walked by. And if Ridley had held even the trace of a doubt, it was washed away in that instant. He held himself taller, walking with his head high, his bearing proud.

Occasional hands reached out to touch him. Many of the AWOLs were crying openly, tears running unashamedly down their cheeks.

And then, one by one, men began to salute, coming to attention as he walked past—reviewing his troops. And he returned the salutes, snapping them off the way he hadn't done in twenty years, perhaps the way he had never done. He had never felt so alive as in that moment.

A wide-open circle, ringed by Vietnamese guards, held back the wall of prisoners. Within the circle was a chair flanked by two flags, an American and a Vietnamese.

"Take the chair, Colonel," Tin said. The man was still looking at the crowd quizzically, and Ridley knew he was beginning to question the worth of this entire undertaking.

Ridley sat quickly, not wanting to give Tin time to change his mind. He smiled up at the French director. "Let's get this over with before I lose my nerve," he said.

The director nodded absently, the power of the moment affecting even him. He lifted his sunglasses atop his head, then seemed to snap to the present. "Do you need a rehearsal?" he asked.

"Turn it on and let's go," Ridley said, and he saw Larry Frank, his AWOL contact, staring at him from near the director. This was it.

"All right," the director said, turning to hold an arm up to the sun. He spoke to a cameraman. "Can you get all this?"

The man nodded, Frank moving very close to him.

The director turned to look at Ridley again. "Makeup?" he called.

"No," Ridley said. "No makeup. Let's go."

Out of the corner of his eye, he saw Tin nod his head, reaching some sort of internal decision. The man took a step into the circle, but was stopped by the director's voice.

"Ready . . . action. You are on the air."

"Ladies and gentlemen of the United States of America," Ridley said in a clear steady voice. "I am Lieutenant Colonel Jason Ridley, commanding officer in charge of the prisoners of war at Camp Friendship, Vietnam. For the past several days you have been hearing the voices of your countrymen over the television sets asking you to send money over here to pay the illegal ransom demands of the pirate government of Vietnam."

"No!" Tin screamed, running into the circle.

Then everything happened at once. Ridley's men, strategically placed, grabbed the guards, knocking them down and fighting with them over their weapons, as others shoved aside the cameramen and director so the filming could go on. Tin, yelling incoherently, reached Ridley, but was grabbed back by several pairs of hands. Ridley kept talking.

"These are not the free words of free men, but the ramblings of men who have been broken by years of torture and abuse. We are prisoners of war! Mistreated and abused. You cannot pay this ransom. It will do nothing to save our lives. . . ."

Men were running everywhere, more guards charging the circle as fighting went on all around him, shouts and curses filling the dusty air. Frank manned the camera, laughing shrilly as Ridley kept talking.

"Be strong, America! Fight! You cannot give in to terrorism in any form. They are raping your emotions, using your own humanity against you."

Guards were suddenly everywhere, swinging their rifle butts at heads, knocking back Ridley's defenders. A shot rang out, Frank falling heavily forward, taking the camera to the ground with him. More shots, prisoners crumpling to the ground as their comrades watched in horror.

Ridley turned in time to see Tin, close to him, swinging a rifle at his head. He got a hand up too late, taking the full force of the stock on his cheek, hearing his own bones cracking under the thing. Barely conscious, he went down hard to bleed into the dirt, several bodies scattered close to him.

As hands grabbed him he turned to Frank. The whole back of the man's head was missing. He slipped out of consciousness for a moment and when he came to he was being dragged across the yard, the sounds of shouting still loud in his ears. Tin was down next to his face.

"Idiot!" he screamed. "What are you trying to do? You fool! You fool!"

They were taking him to Tin's bunker, kicking him to make him walk. He was half dragged through the door. Several teeth were loose and broken, blood flowing freely out of his mouth to redden the front of his shirt.

He was taken to the communications room and pushed heavily to the floor, his head banging the cold concrete, shooting pain through him.

The French technicians in the room were on their feet, backing away in horror.

"Get out!" Tin screamed at them, and they hurried out the door, someone slamming it behind them.

Tin kicked Ridley, then got down beside his ear. "You betray yourself and your people," he said. "There are four dead. Four! And for what? Your message was cut off in here. It never got on the air!"

Ridley would have smiled had he been able to. The message was never meant to leave the camp.

"Who else was in on this with you?" Tin demanded, pulling Ridley's head up by the hair. "We don't have time to play games!"

"Nobody," Ridley said through broken teeth. "It . . . just . . . happened."

Tin's face twisted in rage, and he banged Ridley's head on the floor. "What was the plan?"

"No . . . p-plan," Ridley said, and he was rolled over on his back, his own blood nearly choking him.

Tin was standing over him, staring down in contempt. "You have wanted to have it this way from the first, Colonel Ridley," he said, voice low, nearly a whisper. "Now you shall have it. We will know who else is involved with your schemes and what further plans you have made."

Ridley looked at him, blinking through the pain and the sweat pooled in his eyes, and spoke. "Ridley, Lieutenant Colonel, United States Air Force, serial number . . ."

Tin kicked him again, the pain doubling him over. The man took a rifle from one of his men and motioned for them to hold Ridley's arm steady.

"You will tell me, Colonel, or there will be nothing left of you to send back when the money arrives."

"Go to hell," Ridley said weakly, a whisper.

Tin raised the butt of the rifle, bringing it down full force on Ridley's hand, bones breaking loudly. And Ridley screamed, as loudly as he could. He would win now.

UN PASSES RESOLUTION

NEW YORK, (AP)—The United Nations General Assembly today passed a weakly worded resolution condemning the actions of Vietnam in the hostage situation, and calling for the immediate release of over two thousand prisoners held since the end of the Vietnam War in 1975.

After two days of debate, mostly over wording, the resolution calling for "the release of the prisoners and the beginning of reparation negotiation" passed by a narrow margin, with the Soviet Union and most of the Arab nations abstaining. A similar proposal was vetoed in the Security Council by the Soviet Union. The resolution is nonbinding.

LII

House of Representatives

April 18—Afternoon

Sam Fulton sat on the top dais, looking out at the half-empty chamber and trying to fight off the effects of last night's marathon drinking bout. He couldn't get Jerry Prescott out of his head, or Hugh Martindale for that matter. Both were men with convictions and the strength to carry them through.

He had spent thirty-two of his sixty-four years in the House, ten of them as Speaker. He was looked up to by his constituents, trusted by his colleagues, and feared by his political enemies. His power extended throughout the House and far beyond. The words beloved and elder statesman were bandied about when his name was mentioned, and everyone agreed that he was the type of man representative democracy was all about. Sam Fulton knew that for the horseshit that it was.

He looked at Martindale's empty seat, knowing that the next time it was filled it would be with an unfamiliar face. He had seen many of them come and go over the years—the idealistic, the truly good. They never lasted long on the Hill.

Martindale's speech had shaken many of them, enough to keep them away from the resolution vote in record numbers. Truth and clear-cut choice were not the stock-in-trade of the good politician. The system didn't work that way. Coming out for cause was something that was only done along party lines, and Fulton had been an expert at that from the very first. Drew Pearson had once called him, "the greatest damned tightrope walker in Washington," and it had been the nearest thing to the truth that had ever been said about him.

Keller sat on the dais below him, the man who would have his seat if the Republicans controlled the House. Keller's face was ashen, his look haggard. Fulton felt a bit sorry for him. The minority leader had nearly engineered a brilliant coup in his handling of the resolution. He had been smart enough to recognize a great political football when he saw one and talented enough to make it work for his party without any real chance of repercussions. And then Martindale had to come along with his truth and his pain and screw it all up.

The gallery was practically empty as the entire world held its breath. They had all seen Benstock's pictures on the television that morning—the might of the two most powerful nations in the history of the world lined up against one another on the tip of an obscure country that was of no particular interest to either one of them. It was a sobering sight, even for Sam Fulton.

When he came right down to it, he had to admit he had never taken a real stand on anything in his life. Oh, he had been there for Johnson's Great Society, when they had passed civil rights legislation and environmental bills like there was no tomorrow; but that had been the popular thing to do at that time.

That was the common denominator to all of them in Congress—keeping the job. When the idealists came along, they were quickly shuffled out like beggars at the banquet. Few of them survived. The rest of them were all seniority teamplayers, winning and losing not important, but the playing of the game by the polite rules everything. To give the impression of activity when nothing was really happening was the game they all played.

And because he knew that and couldn't bear the knowledge, he was committing suicide, inexorably, with delicious slowness, through drink.

When Jerry Prescott had looked at him with contempt in the Oval Office, he knew something would have to give. If there had been any doubt, Martindale had put it to rest yesterday. It was time for him to move on, to get out and hope that whomever succeeded him in the job wasn't the coward he was. It would make Mary happy enough. She had begged him for years to retire.

And so, he had called a press conference for after today's session and was going to bring to a close thirty-two years of "distinguished" service. Good riddance. Perhaps it was a good sign that the republic had survived all these years even though it was populated by him and his kind.

The big clock buzzed for the start of session, pages running to close the great doors at the end of each aisle. He got through the opening business in a haze, coming up finally to the end of debate on the Vietnam resolution, which was the first order of business on the docket.

"Will there be any more debate on this resolution?" he asked, anxious now to know the outcome.

"Mr. Speaker," Keller called from below him, his hand raised halfheartedly in the air.

"The Chair recognizes the representative from Tennessee," he replied.

Keller stood, leaning tiredly against his desk. "Mr. Speaker, I move that we table this resolution out of respect for the delicate political climate surrounding it, for consideration at a later date."

Seconds came from several places, many of them Democrats.

Fulton nearly laughed. Hundreds of thousands of taxpayer dollars and government manhours wasted so that the cowards could slink away and see what was going to happen, and sure enough, many would praise them for having the good taste to back the President in a time of internal crisis. No wonder Keller looked tired. He had probably been on the phone all night. And he would, undoubtedly, come out of this like a million uninflated dollars.

"Motion to table has been made and seconded," he said. "Will there be any debate on this motion?"

The room was silent. Someone in the gallery coughed loudly, the sound echoing through the chamber. He began the process of bringing the motion to a vote, knowing the outcome in advance. He looked up at the clock, desperate for the end of session and the beginning of his life.

MOSCOW
April 18—Early Evening

Alexander Doksoi stared at his reflection in the polished surface of the wide, oblong table. As first secretary he held the place of honor at the head of the secretariat, but it was a seat he felt embarrassed to fill now that his power had eroded to a joke.

Youskevitch sat at the other end of the table, shifting uneasily. Of the other nine members of the policy-making body, Doksoi had always been able to count on an easy majority to properly implement policies, but now he knew he could count on no more than four at the outside. Though Dolgoruki wasn't there physically, his spirit controlled the meeting and the secretariat. He had beaten Doksoi in the politburo and now he was going to beat him in the inner sanctum.

The men were somber. This was the closest any of them had come to armed conflict with the United States, for there was no one left from Khrushchev's administration.

"You know we cannot deny the possibility of military retaliation, Alex," Youskevitch said. "We can never close off that option in such an emergency."

"So what happens?" Doksoi said, loosening his tie. "We have brought ourselves to the brink of nuclear war with the Americans over this nonsense. If we respond to their defense of the prisoners, the world comes to an end, but we keep our pride. If we fail to respond we are shown up as weak and irresponsible. What kind of an option is that?"

Pavrovich, the former cosmonaut, stood and moved to

the tea service at the side of the room. "Comrade Doksoi," he said, pouring a cup of tea, "it seems to me that now that we are in position beside the American fleet, it is useless to argue over whether we should be there or not. In fact, it was you who gave the order to move our Navy."

"Under pressure from the politburo, Dimitri," Doksoi said. "And I fully understand that we have now achieved an untenable position. My concern at this point is how to extricate ourselves somehow short of war."

Pavrovich commented, "It is my opinion the Americans will do nothing. They are simply putting on a performance."

"Fine," Doksoi said, standing himself. "If you are right, we will sit where we are and everything will be fine. But ask yourself, if those were our men in there and the merest danger of their imminent execution arose, what would I do?"

Pavrovich sat down again, sipping delicately, then setting the cup down. "It will not come to that," he said.

"You're a fool, Comrade," Doksoi said, wandering around the table. "All of you are. The Vietnamese know nothing of global politics. They've struggled in harsh wars for hundreds of years and know nothing save the politics of confrontation. They'll do what they feel driven to do with no thought of the consequences. I have yet to be able to reach them through any of our channels. That's how serious they are about this. The Americans won't pay the money; I'm sure of that. If President Herrod thinks action is warranted, believe me, he'll take it."

Youskevitch put his pencil down and laughed. "Stop overdramatizing, Alex," he said. "You're just angry because things have gone against you on this."

Doksoi's features darkened as he made his way around the table. He bent to Youskevitch with clenched fists. "Very soon you are going to be faced with a choice," he said, voice low, strained with frustration. "When the Americans take action to save their people, you will get a call from our flagship in the South China Sea asking for orders. You—" he straightened and pointed around the table, "—all of you, will then have to face the question that you now deny—do we end the world today? And since you want to make that decision so badly, I'm going to let you make it all by yourselves."

He turned from them, walking to the door. He reached for the knob, then turned back around. "I wash my hands of this matter," he said. "The decision, when it comes, will be yours alone. I'm going to take a few days off." He opened the door. "And when you make the decision . . . there will be no heroes. You choose between disgrace and mass suicide."

He went out the door without a backward look.

The South China Sea
April 18—6:00 P.M.

Maurice Benstock holding the microphone, spoke loudly to get above the insistent beating of the props. A small monitor broadcasting his face was operating across from him. He was using his sincere voice, the one he had always saved for funerals of state. It was a durable, compassionate voice, one that carried a lot of low-key emotion.

"We're sitting in the cargo bay of a Navy UH-60A Black Hawk above the waters of the South China Sea. The sun is beginning to wane, the oppressive heat of the day leveling off to more tolerable levels. Below you can see stretched out all around us, the U.S. Seventh Fleet, plus elements of the Sixth and the Second out of Pearl Harbor."

He looked at the monitor as the cameraman scanned the ships below. It was an impressive sight, the ample hardware of the Navy stretched out in all directions as far as he could see.

"There are over two hundred ships down there, nearly half of the entire Navy. It's quite awe-inspiring actually, but not nearly the sight it once was. When MacArthur took the Seventh to the Philippines in 1945, it consisted of over seven hundred vessels."

The camera continued to scan the ships, Benny moving fluidly with it. "This is the spirit of America come to see its sons home safely. This is the spirit that built our country, that keeps it strong."

"That's the USS *Carl Vinson*," Benstock said, "the largest, most powerful ship ever to sail the oceans. Much of the command of this operation lies with the *Vinson*, though she's not the flagship of the Seventh. That honor goes to the USS *Blue Ridge*, an amphibious command ship based out of Japan.

"Across from us you can see in the distance elements of the Russian Navy. If they're here to interfere with us, they're outgunned, though we've already identified an impressive lineup of Soviet ships. There's the *Kiev*, the only Russian carrier capable of carrying fixed-wing aircraft. We've identified several large cruisers, the *Kynda*, the *Kirov*, the *Kara*. The Russians are taking this quite seriously, but if they think we're going to back down from this, they're wrong. We're here to do what's right for the country."

He watched the monitor, saw the camera moving toward the mainland.

"And there we see the coast of Vietnam, an ignoble sight to Americans for almost three decades. Vietnamese duplicity and treachery is a horror to a culture as refined as ours. They live as jungle animals, understanding and respecting nothing save strength greater than their own. We are here to show that strength, and pray that they have enough humanity within them to respond positively.... God help them if they don't. In eighteen hours the story will be told. This is Maurice Benstock with the Seventh Fleet in the South China Sea."

The cameraman faded on the Vietnamese mainland, while Benstock pulled off his headset and wiped the sweat off his face.

The copilot had opened the connecting door between the cockpit and cargo bay and was motioning Benstock forward, his face all but hidden beneath his helmet and dark visor.

Benstock crawled the distance to the doorway and stuck his head into the profusion of instruments and computer gear. "What is it?" he yelled to the man, who had the name Varley stenciled on his helmet.

Varley shoved his helmet mike aside and cupped his hands near Benny's ear. "Cap'n Addison on the *Blue Ridge* has a message for you," he said loudly. "He says to tell you recon has spotted a freighter coming this way from the southwest at full steam."

"What kind of freighter?"

"Liberian freebooter... probably a refugee ship."

"Yeah," Benstock replied. "Maybe. Take us down. I want to check into this."

Oklahoma City, Oklahoma
April 18—Around Noon

Sid sat in front of his television and watched the government "report" about his wife. It prominently featured the statement he had made about Nancy the day he had punched out the newsman. The report made no firm accusation, but by inference accused her of everything short of the John Kennedy assassination.

There had been no word of her since the last call, the government suggesting that she was with her "contacts" in Asia, plotting, he supposed, the overthrow of the United States government.

Sid had felt a part of the process, a cog in the wheel of America until this business had come up. Now he was beginning to understand the frustration his wife had lived with for years. They were lying, plain and simple; lying about his wife, a woman who had done nothing to anybody.

God, he missed her.

The house was so empty, the children so... changed, so quiet. Naomi had accused him of being just like his father, but that wasn't the case at all. It was his mother he had emulated. No middle ground, no compromise. Do what I say or pay the consequences. For the first time he was realizing just exactly how much pleasure his mother had derived from punishing Jake, his father. Equating love with pain—the same thing he had done to Nancy.

And now she was gone, arrested by now, perhaps imprisoned. She could even be dead. And he had let her go without a word, without the least sign of how much he truly loved and respected her. More had happened to both of them in the last six days than had happened in all their years up until then. And he hadn't been man enough to handle it.

"I'm sorry," he whispered, and it rang hollowly in his ears.

They replayed his statement again and he knew he had to do something, even if it was too late. He got up and went to the phone, calling one of the local TV stations. "My name is Sid Henderson," he said. "My wife is in charge of NAMWives. I'd like to speak to the news director."

He was put through right away, smiling at the thought that he had dropped his wife's name to get in. "Just listen," he said when the man came on the phone. "I want to have a news conference but don't know how to go about setting it up."

"You've got something to say?" the man asked.

"You bet I do," he said firmly. "Plenty."

"...*so they brought the brave men down*
To Ho Chi Minh City.
Put them in cages,
They locked them away.
And we shed all our tears now, for two thousand
Heroes.
We want them back home, God,
We want them to stay."

—excerpt from
The Ballad of the MIA

LIII

South China Sea

April 18—7:00 P.M.

The cabin was dirty, as was everything else aboard ship. They called her *Viper*, and it seemed appropriate enough. It smelled heavily of petroleum and human waste. Scraps of clothing and half-eaten food lay everywhere. From brief questioning of the crew, he had found that *Viper* had most often been engaged in the business of making refugee runs from Vietnam and Cambodia to the outer Malayasian islands, robbing and raping their passengers at will once at sea. It was a situation everyone involved knew about, but tolerated because they needed the transporation.

Nancy Henderson sat across from Jerry Prescott on a wooden chair, her eyes closed, the detonator held firmly on her lap. He couldn't tell if she was sleeping or not. *Viper* rolled continually, watering badly because of the gold tonnage, and Nancy rolled with her, a part of the ship. He had never known the kind of determination the woman possessed— total obsession was all he could call it.

Someone banged loudly on the cabin door, Nancy starting, clutching the detonator closer to her. The door flew open right after the knock and a large man wearing a filthy white T-shirt poked his bearded face inside.

"The captain says you get above right away," he said in English, his accent Spanish.

Jerry tucked in his shirt and grabbed his suitcoat off the back of the chair. "What is it?" he asked, as Nancy stood, tucking the detonator under her arm.

"Big trouble," the man said, and was gone.

They left the cabin, not really sure of how to get up. They were in a long, dingy hallway with stairs at the end. They took that path, moving upward, then took every possible chance at climbing they came upon. They ended up on deck and were directed up to the wheelhouse.

A helicopter was buzzing insistently around the ship. It had Navy markings all over it and was heavily armed.

Garcia stood in the small, windowed room, watching the helicopter through binoculars, his pipe clamped firmly between his teeth. Another man stood at the helm, his arms resting lightly on the wheel.

Garcia turned to them when they walked in. "I think we are caught," he said.

"What's happened?" Nancy asked.

"Listen for yourself," Garcia said, turning up the radio on the instrument panel.

The sound came through loud and grating. "YOU WILL COME ABOUT AND FOLLOW US.... REPEAT. THIS IS A WAR ZONE. YOUR VESSEL IS BEING DETAINED. YOU WILL COME ABOUT AND FOLLOW US."

"What have you done?" Jerry asked.

"Nothing yet," Garcia responded. "I've pretended on the radio that I don't speak English."

"Any suggestions?" Nancy said, watching the chopper circle the ship, then hang in front of it.

"Scuttle it," Garcia said. He let the binoculars down to hang on his neck, and calmly began to fill his pipe. "If we send her to the bottom now, the evidence goes with her. We're free as birds."

Nancy backed a step away from him. "No," she said, drawing the detonator close. "Not yet, not while there's still a chance."

Garcia eyed the detonator. "I could take it," he said.

Jerry stepped between the two. "Look," he said, "what do you have to lose? You've got several million dollars waiting for you in Malaysia and a ship. The money's not stolen. There's no law that says you can't transport it. We have a legal transaction. I promise I won't involve you in any way in our legal problems."

Garcia's hand had been edging toward the gun on his hip. As he listened, the hand hesitated, finally coming to rest on the belt, grasping it.

"THIS IS YOUR LAST WARNING, UNIDENTIFIED VESSEL. YOU WILL COME ABOUT NOW. WE WILL LEAD YOU."

They turned to the windows. The helicopter came in tight, crossing the main deck so close to the wheelhouse they could make out the pilot and copilot. Then it cut a close circle around the ship. When it came back, it opened fire across their bow, strafing the main deck. The point was made.

Garcia reached immediately for the microphone attached to the radio and put it to his mouth. "This is Captain Jorge Garcia," he said. "As per your instructions, we are coming about. You may lead us where you will."

Jerry and Nancy sat huddled in the center seat of the dinghy, the spray pounding them whenever they crested a wave and flopped on the other side. Jerry felt foolish wearing the bulky Mae West over his gray suit, now dark with water spots. Behind them, a silent navy man gunned the outboard, its whine an insistent mosquito. In front of them, facing them, another man stared blankly, his M-16 at the ready. Both wore helmets and battle dress. Both seemed no older than teenagers.

They moved through a maze of ships toward the *Blue Ridge,* a command ship used simply as an information processing center for fleet ops; its chief function was as an intelligence gatherer. All around huge ships lay at anchor, warmakers. The sight of so much destructive power made the hairs stand up on the back of Jerry's neck. Nancy, beside him, seemed to take no notice of any of it, her head erect, her eyes fixed straight ahead.

He smiled at the sailor in front of him. "I really think you could go ahead and put the rifle down, son," he said. "We're hardly dangerous."

The young man wouldn't meet his eyes. "We're not allowed to talk to prisoners, sir," he said in a monotone, and that was the sum total of conversation.

As they approached the *Blue Ridge,* Jerry reflected on the fact that at least they hadn't been thrown in irons. Perhaps that was a hopeful sign. The ship bulged on the sides just below the main deck, forming a short subdeck. This was where the lifeboats were stored. A set of stairs with a railing jutted out of the bottom of the bulge down to the waterline. They tied up, Jerry and Nancy then being taken up the stairs.

The stairs terminated on the life boat level. It was crowded there with men and wooden ships and the heavy metal cradles that lowered them into the water.

"Pretty far from the nineteeth hole," came a voice from the crowd, and Prescott looked up to see Benstock smiling at him, a cameraman right beside recording the whole event.

"Where trouble goes," Prescott said, "can Benny Benstock be far behind. Quite a little party you've set up for yourself here."

Benstock ignored him and walked right up to Nancy, who was struggling to get out of her life jacket. "And you must be the famous Mrs. Henderson," he said, helping her with the straps. "It's an honor to make your acquaintance."

Prescott moved up to them. "This is the man who made you famous on television," he said, helping her himself.

"I know," she said quietly, and her eyes stared hard at him. "You're a sick man. I feel sorry for you."

Benstock's eyes flared, but his natural good humor replaced that soon enough. "Quite a wild ride you've given us all," he said. "I'd like to commend you for your ingeniousness in getting this far." He turned to the sailor who had brought them in. "What did you find?"

"The ship is full of gold," he said, and Benstock smiled wide. "We're guarding it now."

"What's that?" Benstock asked, pointing to something in the man's hand.

The sailor gave it to him. "A detonator, I think, sir," he said, nodding to Nancy. "She had it."

Benstock examined the detonator in amusement, clucking his tongue. "Desperate means," he said, chuckling. "Really, Jerry, you've got more of a flair for the dramatic than I ever gave you credit for."

"We are American citizens on a legal mission of mercy," Nancy said in a firm voice. "I will thank you to let us return to our business. You have no right to hold us here against our will."

Benstock cocked his head. "It's a shame," he said. "You guys would make great press... if only we could show any of this. Well, maybe some other time." He turned to the sailor beside him. "Take them to the brig and lock them up."

A sailor came running onto the deck, out of breath. He went directly to Benstock, handing him a note as Jerry and Nancy were being led out.

"Wait," Benstock said, holding up a hand. They stopped walking. "It appears you have someone who wants to talk to you. The brig will wait for awhile."

They were taken through the ship ending up in a large roomful of communications equipment. There was another room, even larger, that connected through a windowed hatch. This room was full of sailors working sophisticated electronics gear. A slender man in captain's work uniform sat at a table. He was slight and graying, black-frame glasses resting slightly down on his nose.

He stood at their entrance. "Secretary Prescott," he said, moving to Jerry with hand extended. "I'm Captain Addison."

Jerry shook the hand. "Glad to meet you," he said, then felt stupid for saying it.

"And Mrs. Henderson," Addison said, shaking her hand. "You'll excuse the rush, but there's an important call." He turned to Jerry, pointing to a red phone beside a microwave receiver.

Prescott moved to the phone and picked it up, hearing the jangle of static on the other end. "Prescott," he said tiredly into the mouthpiece.

There was a delay, then a familiar voice. "Jerry?" Simon Herrod said. "So it really is you."

"Yes, Mr. President," Jerry replied, and didn't know what else to say. He was still wearing his tie. His fingers found the knot and pulled it loose.

"How could you . . . do this to me . . . to the country? I think I'm more hurt than if you had shot me."

"We all have to do what we think is right, Simon," he answered, surprised at the strength in his voice. "I'm sorry that it had to be this way."

"You're in terrible trouble, you know," Herrod said, and his voice seemed to be tightening up.

"Yes, I know," Jerry replied. "I knew all along."

"And still you—"

"It's not too late, Mr. President," Jerry said. "We've got

the money here. All we have to do is turn it over to them and this nightmare is over."

"Stop it!" Herrod yelled. "I will not have . . ." Then his voice softened, an effort at control. "You and Mrs. Henderson are under arrest on the charge of treason, Mr. Secretary. I should have you thrown in the brig, but under the circumstances I'll give you the run of the ship if you promise not to abuse the privilege."

"I promise," Jerry said, grateful, at least, for that.

"When you come back, Mr. Secretary," Herrod said, "you must face the full brunt of responsibility for what you have done. It will not be easy for you."

"My only regret, Mr. President," Jerry Prescott said, straightening, "is that my mission of mercy was not a success."

"Good-bye, Jerry," Herrod said, voice controlled.

"Good-bye, Simon," Prescott said, and hung up the phone.

WASHINGTON, (AP)—The AFL-CIO officially called for the United States government to pay the ransom demands to the Vietnamese government. Labor president, Howard Waldrop, speaking before a convention of local union leaders here today said, "We give billions in foreign aid every year to countries who hate us. We may as well do it now and get something in return."

LIV

Ho Chi Minh City, Vietnam

April 18—9:30 P.M.

Cassady sat in the back of the old fruit truck he had stolen just an hour before and watched Vo Kieu and his people load the crates of weapons into the back. Vo's mother and his brothers and sisters were nowhere to be seen, but

Cassady didn't worry about them—they'd never do anything that could possibly jeopardize a family member.

It was black night and he could pass all but the closest scrutiny in his coolie clothes. So far all had gone according to specs. He had only to pick up Kim, leave the truck parked in front of the cathedral, and make his way to Thailand.

He surprised himself by whistling, something he hadn't done since he was a kid, and found himself looking forward to things, to life. He pulled the choke, letting it rev for a minute before idling it back down.

He checked the sideview in time to see Vo moving toward him. He looked a lot like his father as a young man, with just a touch more malice around the all-seeing eyes.

"We finish up quick," Vo said.

"Great," Cassady said, bumping hard against the rusting door to open it. He stopped down, walking to the back of the truck.

A group of young men, most dressed in leathers, were throwing the last few crates into the truck back. Cassady looked around at what was left, moving to a large pine crate stenciled with the words: PROPERTY OF U.S. MARINE CORPS, 1 CASE (THIRTY COUNT) M-16 AUTOMATIC RIFLE.

He pointed to the box, speaking to Vo, who was just then coming back around the truck. "Open this one," he said.

The teenager jumped at the crate, using a long crowbar leaning against a tree. Cassady walked back to the dark interior of the truck and peered inside, using a match to get a good look. He saw a crate of ammo for the guns and slid it toward himself. He tried to lift it out, but it was too heavy and needed help from two of the boys.

They began yelling excitedly as they pulled the weapons from the crate, fondling them gently, lovingly, looking down the barrels and clicking empty chambers on one another. He was that young once—long ago.

Vo ran up to him, his eyes wide and gleaming as he held the rifle out in front of him. "Plenty good ass kick," he said.

Cassady smiled. "You can tear an arm off with one of these, son," he said. "The whole crate's yours with my thanks."

Vo bowed low. "Thank you, Cassady," he said. "We'll make plenty good ass kick for you."

Cassady moved back to climb up into the truck again.

"You just take good care of your family," he said, slamming the door to get it closed. He leaned out the window waving back to Vo. "You're the man now, remember."

The boy smiled wide, returning the wave. Cassady ground the gears and pulled out forward, through the backyard and down the pathway to the road.

Staying off the main thoroughfares, he reached Kim's street in fifteen minutes, parking the truck at the end of the block as a matter of habit. He reached under the dash to unhook his hot-wired connection, then carefully walked to the house. He stayed in the shadows. It would be worse than stupid to blow everything in the eleventh hour.

The lights were on upstairs, the backdoor unlocked. He felt his own excitement surge and he moved through the pristine sitting rooms of her house and up the stairs to the bedroom.

She was sitting cross-legged in the middle of her large bed, wrapped in a soft blue silk robe, slowly drawing a comb through the length of her long raven hair. Her face brightened when she saw him enter.

"My love," she said in her husky voice. "I was worried for you."

He walked quickly to the bed, leaning way across it to kiss her tenderly on the lips. "Hurry," he said, straightening. "Get dressed. We've got to go. Are you packed yet?"

"There's no hurry," she said. "We can go whenever we want."

"I want to leave the guns while there's still traffic on the streets," he said, walking out onto the balcony to peer into the darkness below. He thought he saw something moving in the yard, but it was just a shadow.

"Guns?" she said.

He walked back into the bedroom, preoccupied. "Yeah, yeah. I'm leaving a truckload of guns for the prisoner escape. That's my job. If we leave now, in ten minutes we'll be free. Come on. Let's get moving."

"We're free already," she said, scooting off the bed to stand near him. Her robe had fallen open, her body still firm and young beneath. "We can leave when we want . . . or stay here if we want."

He narrowed his eyes. "What do you mean?"

She moved to put her arms around him. He responded

weakly, quizzically. "Don't you see?" she said into his chest.
"Everything's perfect now. We're together. I've worked hard
for what I have here. You can share it with me."

He took her by the shoulders, pulling her away from him
and holding her at arm's length. "What—share your whore-
house?" he asked. "You're not making sense. How could I
stay here and stay alive?"

She looked up at him with wide, soft eyes. "Please don't
be angry with me," she said in a near whisper.

His voice hardened. "What did you do?"

She looked down at the floor. He was still holding her
shoulders. "I did it for us," she said. "It didn't seem right that
we would live our beautiful life running away. I thought that
if we have each other we have everything."

He shook her. "What did you do?"

She looked at him, a touch of anger flashing through her
face, then disappearing. "I have many . . . friends in the military," she said. "I talked to some of them today and explained—"

"What!"

"Explained to them our situation. They said you would
be a hero to our people for exposing the escape plans. They
will give us money and let us live here in peace." Her lips
trembled and she put her arms on his. "Oh, my love. I could
never live in the jungle. This is my life here. We could share
it together."

"You blew my cover!" he screamed. "I'm as good as meat
now."

He let her go and ran back to the balcony. Everything
still seemed quiet. He hurried back to where she stood.

"How could you do this?" he yelled. "I can't sell out. I
never intended . . . I just had to do the job in my own way.
Jesus Christ, I'm no traitor."

She shook her head. "I don't understand you. We have
each other. What else could matter? And now, with the guns,
we can come out even better—"

"No!" he said, and ran to the balcony again. His mind
was a blur, his usual clear processes all muddied up.

He ran back inside. "I've got to get out of here," he said.
"You've got to come with me."

"No," she said flatly.

"Look, if you stay here and cover for me, you're in as
much trouble as . . ."

He stopped talking and watched the determination in her eyes. The face of a survivor. She'd never cover for him. He backed away from her toward the door. Movement was his natural instinct, his greatest friend. He had to move!

He stumbled to the bedroom door, only his animal nature intact. She was already going for the telephone on the other side of the room.

"Please," he said. "Give me some time, a couple hours. You loved me, carried my child in you."

"You've made your choice, Cassady," she said coldly. "Now I must protect myself. Yes, I carried your baby . . . and I got rid of it to protect myself. I had no miscarriage. I killed it with a coat hanger." She picked up the phone, quickly dialing a number that was familiar to her. "Your guns will help me, at least."

His hand went automatically to the .45 stuffed in the waistband of his pants. He pointed it with shaking hand. "Don't," he heard himself say from far away.

She chuckled. "You couldn't shoot me," she said. "It would be like shooting yourself."

She turned her attention to the phone, chattering quickly into it in Vietnamese, quicker than he could translate. She was blowing everything.

"No!" he said loudly.

She ignored him completely and kept talking.

He never even heard the gun go off. All he comprehended was the look of intense surprise on her face as her chest exploded, knocking her back against the wall, the phone dropping to the floor. She looked at the blood running down her naked breast, then back up to him. He heard the second shot, but just barely.

He was down the stairs, then stumbling through the darkness of the sitting room, knocking over tables, scattering knickknacks. Where was the door? Where?

Albert "Cowboy" Sorrel squatted in the bushes behind the woman's house and blended with the night. He had picked up Cassady's trail the day before through his underworld contacts and had been following him ever since in order to find out where the guns were. Now he knew. All he needed now was the plan and the when. He'd get those from Cassady before he killed him.

Cowboy had noticed Cassady acting erratically, running back and forth between the upstairs balcony and the bedroom. Something strange was going on between him and the damned whore.

And then he had heard the shots.

"Shit," he said, standing and looking quickly around. He was too tall to fit in well with the locals, so he simply relied on guts and stealth to make his way around. The street still seemed quiet. He moved partway into the backyard, trying to decide whether or not to go into the house.

Then he heard someone thrashing around downstairs. The shortbarrel .38 was in Cowboy's hand, a small silencer screwed onto the muzzle.

He saw Cassady stumbling out the door as if he were half-asleep. At first he thought the man might be shot, but he didn't seem to be hurt. It had to be *now*.

Cowboy confronted Cassady in the middle of the yard. "You made it a long way, pard," he said. "Did most of my job for me."

Cassady just stared at him with faraway eyes. Then he smiled. "Hi, Cowboy," he said, and looked down at his hands as if looking for a gun. His hands were empty. He smiled again.

"What's the plan for the break?" Albert said, leveling the .38 at Cassady's chest.

Cassady spoke in a monotone. "Park the truck in front of the cathedral and get the hell out of Dodge," he said softly. "I did *all* your work for you. You gonna kill me now?"

Cowboy nodded. "Just business, pard," he said, and pulled the trigger, the gun spitting in his hand, its muffled flare lighting the dark night for just a second.

Cassady fell heavily, without a sound. Cowboy looked down at him, grateful he was small and somewhat light. He got hold of the body under the shoulders and quickly dragged it into the bushes on the side of the yard.

He hurried across the yard and made the street just as headlights came blazing from both ends. He had time to turn once toward the weapons truck, fifty yards distant, then back toward the approaching headlights to see machine gun fire flaring. It was in Cowboy's mind to try and run, but something picked him up and knocked him to the ground. He tried to stand but was too weak. His legs had no power. He thought of crawling, but it was a thought that became locked, forevermore, in the dying cavity of his brain.

ROCKERS AX NAM FEST

Dateline Hollywood—Promoters for the hastily scheduled NAM-AID concert today canceled all plans to hold the benefit fund-raiser for the ransom release of over two thousand American servicemen still held in Vietnam. Citing scheduling problems, the promoters said it was impossible for the rock and country music stars to rearrange their schedules in time to appear and raise the needed money by the weekend.

Tom Meyers, spokesman for the NAM-AID backers, publicly denied that the cancellation had anything to do with the growing conservative youth movement that has arisen against the paying of the ransom, though he privately admitted he had been "caught off guard" by the response of America's young people. "I thought we were doing a good thing," Meyers said. "Go figure."

Music industry bigwigs are said to be breathing a large sigh of relief over the canceled funder.

—*Variety*

LV

Camp Friendship

April 18—11:04 P.M.

Ridley came slowly to consciousness, forcing himself back despite the best efforts of his body to keep him insulated from the continuing pain. He lay naked, stomach down, on the cold cement floor of the bunker, a blinding pain in his head, phlegm and blood choking him.

He coughed, spitting up. His arms were trussed behind him. It had been tough; for excruciating hours they had brought him to the pain-filled brink of madness again and again, but to no avail. It hadn't even occurred to him to tell them anything. He had learned long ago that torture only works if the victim makes the real connection between his pain and the information sought. He honestly didn't believe in that connection. They inflicted the pain; he took it. It was as simple as that.

He believed his jaw was broken, his cheekbone shattered. A lot of teeth were gone or broken. Several ribs were cracked, though he didn't know how many. Something terrible was wrong with his neck, though he didn't think it was broken. His right hand was literally crushed in uncountable places. His pelvis seemed broken, making movement impossible. He had a shattered kneecap, and all of his toes had been broken one by one. His head pain came from concussions, and he couldn't get one eye to focus at all. His spirit was still intact.

He forced himself to think. No light was filtering through the tiny windows set at the top of the bunker. An electric light burned brightly overhead. It was night. How late? Had he done enough to wake up the rest of them, to remind them all of what they still were, and of what they still were dutybound to do?

Across the floor he saw a pair of jungle boots. Perhaps activity could give him answers. Just as with Tin, he now lived for answers.

"Water," he rasped, trying to spit more phlegm out. "Please. Water."

The boots came toward him, a soldier kneeling down five feet from him to look at his face. Without a word, the man jumped up and ran out of the room.

Moments later the door opened again and the soldier came back, followed by a pair of fine, black leather shoes and black silk pants. The colonel had taken off his uniform.

He saw the soldier come toward him and he prepared himself. He was grabbed and rolled over, screaming, though he didn't know he had it in him. He was on his back, barely able to see through the blur and the waves of pain that shot through his head.

Tin was looking down at him, dressed traditionally in the short, black *ao-dai* worn at ceremonial occasions. The man's face was grave.

"You have not died," Tin said with a note of surprise. "You may still yet live if you tell us what we must know."

"I . . . know . . . nothing," Ridley said weakly. "Please. Water."

Disappointment crossed Tin's face, and Ridley realized the man had grown soft during the years of peace, that the revolutionary ardor wasn't burning as hot in him as he had thought.

"I must leave you soon," Tin said, ignoring Ridley's plea. "I go to meet the boat which will pay us our due. So, you see, all has gone for naught. Your people will be freed anyway, so why not save yourself while you're still alive and get all this foolishness out in the open?"

"Water . . . please."

"I've just received another piece of news you might find interesting," Tin said. "An American CIA agent has been shot down in the streets and killed. We had intelligence reports on him and knew he was here to abet you in an escape attempt. Your little scheme has gone all to pieces, Colonel. Are you sure you don't have anything to tell me?"

Ridley just lay there. They had gotten his contact, hopefully not before the boats were procured. It would be tougher, but not impossible. The guns. Tin hadn't mentioned the guns.

Tin knelt down beside him, lowering his voice to a whisper. "You have manipulated me into this position," he said. "I must punish you or I lose face. I do not want to kill you, Jason Ridley. Please don't make me. Give me something, anything. Let me free you."

"Fuck you, slant," Ridley said, and tried to spit, but couldn't do it.

Tin closed his eyes tightly for a second, then stood. "All right," he said, almost sadly. "The choices have all been made. You will tell us what we want to know or die in the process. I go to meet with the Americans."

He walked out of the small room, its sophisticated communications gear dark and silent. The American agent had been acting alone, so that threat had passed, Tin thought. If Ridley wanted to use them as his instrument of suicide, he'd oblige the man. Perhaps the years of captivity had unhinged him totally.

Tich Quang, a *thieu ta* and second-in-command, awaited him in the hallway.

"He is awake, Major," Tin said, drawing deeply on his cigar and holding it. "You are to continue interrogation procedures until he confides in us."

"He cannot live much longer, Colonel," Quang replied. "How careful . . ."

Tin put up a hand. "If we have one less American to send back to them, so be it. We will consider him damaged fruit."

Quang smiled slightly, but there was no humor in it. "Are there any other standing orders?"

"Keep the prisoners in the barracks," Tin said, then smiled himself. "Don't lose them." He looked at his watch. "This will all be over in twelve hours."

Quang nodded. "You can depend on me. Your car is waiting outside."

They shook hands. Quang was young, but a good man. He was leaving the camp in the best of hands. "Our time has come, my friend," Tin said. "May fortune smile on us."

"You are the dragon, Colonel," Quang replied. "You make your own fortune."

The men embraced quickly, then parted. Tin moved down the hall to the doorway and outside, exiting into an unusually hot night. An old American Cadillac was parked, motor running, by the door, the driver reading a magazine by the dome light. Tin gazed once around the camp. It was absolutely quiet, lights out, the guard doubled around each barracks.

He felt strangely uneasy, but attributed it to the drama of the moment. It was going to work out, the killing of the American agent assured it. Nothing could go wrong now despite the Russian and American navies. He opened the back door of the large car and climbed inside.

Tin leaned forward and spoke to the driver. "The docks," he said, and the man immediately put the car into gear and drove off, Tin feeling like he had left something behind as they moved through the front gates, guards shutting them behind.

Ferguson stood at the barracks window watching the Cadillac drive out of the grounds. It was close now, almost time. They had listened all day to Ridley's screams, each one making them stand a little taller. The bodies had been taken away quickly that morning, but they had left their mark. It could happen to any of them. They were in the enemy camp, and to give over to the enemy was not only traitorous, but stupid.

They had to stand together. They *would* stand together.

They had worked out their networks long before Ridley was taken away. Each barracks had its own coordinator ready to talk up the escape one-on-one. It had gotten easier as the day had progressed, as the screaming peeled away the layers of bullshit they had spent so many years putting between them and the reality of soldiering.

They would fight. If need be, they would die. It was war now. The years had melted away, the harsh light of dawn was breaking.

"Count off," he whispered into the darkness.

"One," came the instant reply from the bunk closest to the door.

"Two," came the next bunk.

"Three."

"Four."

They counted off quickly, wide-awake all of them. One hundred and fifty had voiced affirmation before the counting had finished, the entire population of Charlie barracks minus Ridley and the dead scab, Jenkins. And Ridley, Ferguson vowed, would be with them before long.

SUNDAY

LEADER STILL MISSING

NEW YORK, (AP)—In the midst of all the turmoil surrounding the confrontation between the United States and the Soviet Union in the South China Sea, the big question mark is still Nancy Henderson and the gold she raised to help free the hostages. There seem to be no firm leads as to her disappearance and whereabouts.

"We've, of course, got her contact, Joey Nhu," said Will Cain, speaking for the FBI. "But he's been very cooperative. He was with Henderson in Baltimore and left when their plans to fly the gold by Air France fell through." After that, Nancy Henderson simply disappeared, along with the gold.

No one seems to know if she found an alternate route to Vietnam or if she simply absconded with the gold. Several NAMWives representatives have been detained as material witnesses, but so far they've revealed nothing. "It's a puzzler," Cain admits. "You don't just stick two hundred tons of gold in your pocket and walk away."

LVI

Ho Chi Minh City, Vietnam

April 19—2:30 A.M.

Cassady lay quietly in the bushes, bleeding what was left of his life into the manicured garden of the woman he had loved. He had been unconscious for a time, though he wasn't sure how long. His mind was a jumble, reality passing in tiny, bright segments, then flowing back into the long blackness of the moonless night.

Kim was dead; he knew that much. He didn't really blame her for what she had done—like he, she had never known anything but survival. The difference between them was that she hadn't realized survival wasn't all that big a thing. A man he'd met in prison once had told him the real story: There are worse things than dying. As he lay there bleeding, he thought something about that.

There had been people there earlier, Vietnamese military. He had heard enough to know they had gotten Sorrel. He had found then that he was capable of movement, for he was able to drag himself a little farther into the brush as they walked back and forth, not five feet from him.

Kim had been brought out, not on a stretcher, but carried, like a bride over the threshold. Someone had put a satin pillowcase over her head, her long sleek hair partially hanging out of the bottom. There had been much excited talking for a time, then one by one the soldiers had left, one staying behind to turn out all the lights and lock up. Then he, too, was gone, leaving Cassady alone to contemplate the black night and the folly of his own dreams.

But it was intolerable. He didn't want to die there in her garden. Waiting for death was something he wasn't geared for; thinking was something that only made it worse. He took a deep breath and rolled onto his stomach, trying to get to a kneeling position.

He straightened on his knees, then reached out a hand to a small banyan tree and pulled himself up. His legs were weak, numb. The entire front of his shirt was soaked with blood. Breath came in wheezes.

Walking was an adventure. He reached the corner of the yard that fronted the quiet street, grabbing hold of an arched trellis for support. He rested, trying to get his breath, and peered around the bushes to the end of the block. He tried to laugh, but it came out a bloody cough. The truck still sat there waiting for him.

Somehow, the irony came as no surprise. He had never been a free man, never. And now that he could finish his mission, he still couldn't be free. But the duty remained—so he moved.

He somehow got down that long block, stumbling, falling, once losing consciousness for a brief period. Several small dogs barked at him, but sensing his intimacy with death, they all left quickly without rousing their masters.

Climbing into the truck was the hardest part. The cab seemed as high as Everest to him as he grabbed the steering wheel and tried to hoist himself up. He did it finally, falling across the seat and resting for a few minutes before sitting up and closing the door.

The truck complained, but started. He became totally disoriented as he drove, having no idea which direction was which. But then he caught a glimpse of the cathedral's twin Gothic spires and used them as a homer to bring himself in.

And there it was, at the head of beautiful, tree lined Tu Do Street. He bumped up partway on the curb and stopped the truck, wondering what it would be like to try to go in and request sanctuary.

An M-16, loaded and on full auto, was stuffed under the seat. He slid across to the passenger side and pulled it out. He then cradled the gun and kept watch, at ease in a familiar situation. This was the way for him to spend his remaining minutes.

He tried to think back on his life, but there was really nothing to think back on. He thought all the way to when he had used his real name, the one he had been born with. Then he laughed, coughing, when he realized he couldn't remember it.

BIAS CHARGED

NEW YORK CITY, (AP)—In private communiqués received from the South China Sea, American reporters are complaining that the government is censoring and in some cases actually rewriting their news reports. In a cable received at Associated Press offices here, A.P. Asian correspondent Mark Haworth charged, "Maurice Benstock is writing history to his own specifications."

"It's propaganda. That's the only thing we can

call it," said Wes Roberts of United Broadcasting. According to reports, all news items must be channeled through Benstock, President Herrod's media liaison, where, as Roberts says, "he (Benstock) rewrites them like a John Wayne war movie."

Reports are sketchy since all outside transmissions must go through Benstock. Haworth, admittedly, bribed a seaman first class aboard the *Carl Vinson* to send his cable. "No truth is coming out of Vietnam," Haworth's cable claims. "It's simply one man's vision of a world he'd like to live in."

No one on Benstock's staff could be reached for comment.

LVII

Camp Friendship

April 19—3:00 A.M.

At precisely the same moment three small boys ran from the shadows of the western wall of the French Embassy, scurrying along the narrow, tree-lined street that separated that structure from what had once been the American Embassy and now housed the troops guarding Camp Friendship. The camp lay several hundred yards behind, on the back edge of the embassy grounds. The children all had blue eyes, and one of them was a sandy blond. In their teeth they carried razor-sharp machetes with rubber handles.

Without a word they passed their mothers, who were even then dragging the bodies of two uniformed military back off the road and into the darkness. The way to Friendship was clear.

The boys ran quickly in the hot night, bare feet slapping the cracked asphalt. Their young hearts pounded with the excitement and the chance to see their fathers free. If the Vietnamese had made a mistake at Friendship, it was in not appreciating the basic ties of blood.

They darted off the road as they neared the floodlit

camp, breaking easily along the paths they had determined during the last several days while "playing" around the camp during the daylight hours. Time and again they had mock-staged this moment and fell into it now with a practiced cadence.

Three poles supplied the power and phones to Friend-ship. The camp's ability to reach beyond itself was wholly dependent upon these poles. The boys hit the poles on the run, wrapping themselves around like monkeys and quickly inching up. Vietnamese women, desperate for their husbands' freedom, moved silently toward the main gates armed with bolt cutters.

As each boy reached the top of his pole, he waved to the others a distance away, high above the heads of the dozing guards. Then each took the grounded machete from his mouth and began hacking away at transformer cables.

There were no watches allowed in Friendship, one of Tin's means of avoiding organization, so Ferguson simply waited, estimating time as he had done for so many years in the prison camps. He stood near the door, waiting for the floodlights to go out. All the windows in all the bar-racks had been carefully and quietly loosened during the past two days in full view of the ubiquitous cameras—patience another virtue learned after long years of confine-ment. Men lay tensed in their beds by every window, ready to spring.

Ferguson stood just out of the bite of the camera, watching one of the utility poles through a crack in the door. He stood perfectly still, feeling the sweat roll down his bald head. He was dying for action. He had waited so long and didn't even care that those he was about to make war with had probably been children when the actual fighting had gone on. They were the enemy, and long years had passed since he had tasted blood.

Ridley's screams had stopped about an hour before, though they had gotten weaker as time had gone by. He was either dead or unconscious. This fact Ferguson confined to the darkest part of his brain, the part not even he dare dwell on.

He saw movement on the pole, a fleeting shadow, and knew what it had to be. "Ready," he whispered, slight

rustling accompanying his words. He tensed with anticipa
tion. He knew it would go down, was positive it woul
happen; but when it did, it was like a miracle.

Without sound or forewarning, all the lights sudden
died. He was through the door in a second, swinging with
to kick in the head of the Vietnamese who sat on the barrack
stairs. The man grunted, falling sideways off the steps a
Ferguson followed through, coming down hard on the man
windpipe with his knee. Windows pushed out all around him
his men pouncing in large numbers on the guards wh
surrounded the barracks, felling them silently.

The man under Ferguson's knee struggled, wide-eyed a
his windpipe was crushed. Someone came behind Ferguson
retrieving the man's gun, using the butt to smash in th
guard's face.

Ferguson was up, taking the rifle. Up and down the line
along row upon row of barracks, men poured out the window
and doors, filling the night with jumping, bursting excite
ment. They had been down so long that even this brie
freedom was heady and intoxicating.

He heard a muffled groan from the direction of the gat
and knew that it had been secured. All at once men wer
running around him.

"Motor pool," he said, as guns were passed to those bes
equipped to use them. He turned in the direction of the dar
bunker, turning to the group of men who had been designat
ed as his aides. "Come on."

They charged across the yard, Ferguson wishing th
damned French TV people were housed at the camp so h
could take care of them, too. They closed the distance
reaching the bunker door just as it opened. Swinging his rif
like a baseball bat, Ferguson practically took off the head c
the first soldier who came out the door.

Without slowing, he ran into the bunker. Shadowy fig
ures filled the hallway. He began firing into the crowd
turning one way then the other, hoping the bunker itse
would be enough to muffle the sound.

More of his people poured in behind him, running fo
those still on their feet. "Search for Colonel Ridley!" h
yelled, swinging out with his rifle to clear a path down th
narrow hall. Then he found the end of the hall, kicking ope
that door.

A pale light shone in the room as a major sat at a self-contained radio, trying to raise help. He shot the man through the head. Ridley lay moaning on the floor, a metal bar shoved through his arms.

"Colonel," he said, kneeling to Ridley. He angrily drew the bar from the man's arms and threw it at the body slumped over the radio. More men poured into the room. One of them had a flashlight which he shone on Ridley.

Ferguson nearly threw up. The colonel was barely recognizable. Beaten to near death, he lay pale and bloody on the concrete, broken bones twisting his limbs to obscene angles. Ferguson bent down near his face and listened to his raspy, shallow breathing.

"Get me some fucking water!" he turned and yelled. "Quick!" He turned back to the man, smoothing his matted hair. He lowered his voice reverently. "We did it, sir. We're free."

"Go," Ridley managed. "Get . . . out."

"I am, sir," Ferguson said. "Just as soon as we get you together."

"No," Ridley moaned. "C-Can't . . . move."

Someone was shoving a glass of water into Ferguson's hand. "Get that door off the hinges," he told the man, then turned and cradled Ridley's head, bringing the water to his lips. "You wouldn't leave me behind, Colonel. This time everybody goes home."

The door was brought over and laid beside the colonel. Someone had come up with a black silk robe from Tin's office and brought it in to cover Ridley. It was placed on the door.

Ferguson gave him a little more water, then set the glass aside. "We're going to lift you onto this stretcher, sir," he said. "I know it's going to hurt, but we'll be as careful as we can. Ready?"

Ridley closed his eyes, nodding slightly. Several pairs of hands lifted him, waves of pain clenching his face, driving stakes into Ferguson's heart. They got him onto the door, his face relaxing noticeably. His arms were placed in the sleeves of the robe and it was closed over him.

Ferguson stood, feeling weak. "Let's get out of here," he said. The door was picked up by two of the bigger men, Ridley carried down the hall over the bodies of his fallen torturers. Ferguson could hear the sounds of revving engines outside.

The yard was full of trucks, men quickly loading them They were all old looking—broken hollow men—but the determination on their faces would have struck fear in the hearts of any enemy. The stronger helped the weaker, bu most were able to do for themselves. They wouldn't have lasted so many years on the work crews if they couldn't AWOLs manned the trucks, their routes to the docks memo rized. There were forty large trucks, over fifty men jammed in each wherever they could find space. Men hung from every conceivable position inside and outside the covered personnel movers.

Ferguson moved into the confusion looking all around So far, they were still undetected. "Rendezvous at the cathe dral!" he called loudly to get above the engine noise, and the trucks started rolling as soon as they were filled, the fron gates already opened by the women.

He watched as space was made for Ridley on one of the trucks, then jumped up to sit next to what was left of thei CO. The truck started with a jerk, Ridley moaning loudly Ferguson held the hand that wasn't broken.

Dust clouded the yard, and as they drove through the gates, the men silently celebrated the first freedom they had known in twenty years.

Cassady sat in the cab, hoping to stay alive long enough to see the trucks pull up. It shouldn't have mattered to him but it did. And in that he found the greatest strength he had ever known, for the man who had lived his whole life on the outside actually *did* care about something; the man who saw no meaning or reality to life around him, didn't want to die in vain. Maybe he wasn't so much like Kim after all.

When he first heard the rumble he thought it may have been distant thunder. But it was too persistent, too unbro ken. It could only be one thing.

He straightened, using the M-16 as a crutch, and opened the passenger-side door, falling to the hard ground below Trucks were pulling up quickly, their headlights lighting the area all around him in long streamers.

Men, American men, were kneeling all around him, a others were breaking into the back of the truck.

"Get me up," he said weakly. "Help me up."

They lifted him, keeping him standing because he was too weak to stand on his own. A large man with a bald head was giving orders at the back of the truck. They had formed long lines and were handing crates of guns and ammo and grenades back along the lines to waiting trucks. Lights were beginning to come on nearby, the city coming alive. They were almost out of time.

They walked him back to the big man. "Cap'n," one of them said. "We found him on the ground."

The man looked at him with fiery eyes. "You did this?" he asked, motioning around him.

Cassady nodded.

The man moved to him and took him quickly in his arms. "God bless you," he said.

"Where's the man I contacted?" Cassady asked in a near whisper.

The big man looked sadly at the ground, then inclined his head toward a stretcher of some sort that held a broken man.

"I want to be with him," Cassady said.

The big man nodded quickly and spoke to the men holding Cassady up. "Put him back there," he said, pointing to the rapidly emptying ammo truck.

They hoisted him up into the truck back, then hurried quickly off to their duties. He was astounded by the precision. Everyone had a job to do and was doing it. He tried to sit, but couldn't. He slid to a reclining position and lay staring up at the light canvas roof above.

He heard noises coming up on them, shouting. Then the firing started, ripping up the night. It was glorious. He hadn't heard noise like that since Tet of '70 in Bien-hoa. There was much shouting mixed in with the firefight, the smell of gunpowder. Bullets pinged through the truck in which he lay, zipping overhead, tearing at the fabric of darkness. The stretcher was brought over and shoved in the truck back right beside him. He thought they were mistaken at first, then he recognized Ridley through the swelling and the blood.

He rolled onto his side and looked at the man who lay with his eyes closed. "You ain't doin' much good laying there," he said.

Ridley opened one eye and focused on him, a slight

smile curling his lip when he recognized the man. "Had a hard day," he rasped. "Thought I'd take the night off."

"You top brass are all a bunch of lazy fucks," Cassady replied.

They were moving, building up speed, gunfire spewing from all around them now. Cassady raised his head and looked out the truck back. It looked as if the entire city had come alive and was after them.

He shuddered somewhere deep inside and felt a warm rush of blood come up his throat. He coughed it out. It was almost over. "I want you to do something for me," Cassady told Ridley.

"Don't ask me to dance," Ridley replied.

"When you get back, I think I've got a mother some-where..." He coughed up blood again, then shook his head to clear it. "It's no big thing... I haven't seen her since I was sixteen. But I got some compensation coming for all this. Somebody ought to get it—might as well be her, you know?"

"What's her name?" Ridley asked, then again, "Her name?"

But it was too late. The man was already gone.

Ferguson took the streets as fast as he could, following the taillights of the truck ahead. A steady barrage of fire was coming at them from all around as cross streets filled with Viet Cong vehicles.

The old Presidential Palace was looming on the right as he bounced the pitted streets, knowing he was shaking Ridley, but unable to do anything about it.

As they neared the palace, the fire increased, half-dressed soldiers stumbling out of building fronts and shooting from the palace roof. The truck in front was firing wildly, thirty or forty guns kicking lead from under the canvas cover, men hanging on the side using handguns while trying to hold on.

A hastily constructed roadblock loomed before them, the lead truck hitting it, then veering, almost turning over. Ferguson was right there, knocking broken planks aside. Men lay all over the road, some up on their knees, still firing.

A machine gun raked the windshield, blasting glass all over him. The other truck scraped the side of a building, then managed to make the street again, leaving several of its men dead on the sidewalk. One of the front tires went, and he nearly lost control, the truck pulling way to the right. But he fought it back, trying to hold the road while weaving all over it.

They hit the wide-open square of the market, bouncing wildly across the brick ground near the railway station, then veering left again, finally making their intentions known. Up until then it could have gone either way. Now they were announcing the docks. Ferguson reached to downshift and noticed blood running down his arm. He had been shot and didn't know it. No matter.

Another right turn. The docks lay just across a small tributary of the Saigon River, spanned in several places by cement bridges. The riverfront was lined with huge white buildings with neo-Grecian pillars supporting their fronts. Ferguson could smell, then see, the river as the hot sea air blew into his face through the missing windshield.

The truck in front slowed down just before the bridge, several men jumping out of the back, a crate being thrown out to them. The truck went on, and he could see them down and wiring the bridge with explosives.

He bounced over the bridge, riding on the rim of his left front tire. In the sideview mirror he could see another truck crossing the bridge. He looked forward, the lead truck no longer to be seen. But it didn't matter. He had only to follow the trail of explosions to the docks.

The truck gave out, its front axle breaking just as he reached the dock area. Gunboats were firing at them from their moorings as they set up grenade launchers to fire back. Another truck pulled up beside as he jumped out of the cab.

"Help me with the colonel!" he yelled to the men jumping off the truck, their faces reflecting orange fire a hundred yards distant. "Let's go!"

He ran around the rear of the truck, Ridley still alive in back, cradling the head of the CIA man who wasn't so lucky.

"We're almost home free!" he called to Ridley as they pulled his stretcher out and started him toward the piers.

Several explosions went up behind, one after another— the bridges—bright fireballs climbing on thin stems high into the night. They were all through now, the last trucks pulling up.

There was a dash toward the river, forward positions

trying to pin down the men on the gunboats to keep them away from their deck guns and from casting off. All along the riverfront tar fires in barrels raged on the decks of many ships, signals to the prisoners started by their wives.

"Your numbers!" the AWOLs were screaming. "Your numbers!"

Team leaders began shouting numbers from one to ten, each to lead a squad with that number to a certain boat, while the point men kept the gunboats at bay. Ferguson was number four. He ran through the crowd listening to his number while keeping track of the men with Ridley.

A tall redheaded man was standing on a crate. "Number four! Number four!" he kept screaming as his people congregated near him. Then he jumped from the crate and took off running along the water's edge, his charges yelling, "Four! Four!" and running with him.

It was confusion, but the number system was working. They ran the lane between the water and the wooden, covered piers, everyone finding their right boat.

Explosions tore through the dock roof raining splinters on them as they ran. And the docks were on fire, burning brightly, lighting the scene to near day.

One of the gunboats was freed from its moorings, but was lying dead in the water, being dragged toward the opposite shore by the current. Another was doing the same.

The red-haired man jumped aboard a boat, immediately beginning to untie it. It was a large crabber with huge thick nets slung up all over it and a sail in case the engine went out. It looked sturdy, but not very fast.

As they climbed aboard, Ferguson dropped back to walk with Ridley. "You okay, Colonel?" he yelled, but Ridley was unconscious, mercifully so.

A helicopter hovered overhead. Its searchlight was raking them with .50-caliber fire. All guns turned on the chopper. Its engine coughed as it tried to veer away, but it lost altitude quickly, crashing into the water beside one of the gunboats.

Ferguson saw a profusion of Vietnamese women and children huddled on the starboard side near thick piles of nets. No one had thought to inquire about the families of the AWOLs.

Another gunboat was dead in the water, its sailors trying

to put out a fire on deck. Many of them were jumping overboard, splashing heavily into the murky Saigon while shore birds squawked and fluttered from their roosts.

The deck was filled with men, shoulder-to-shoulder. Ferguson had Ridley set down by the port rail and huddled protectively over him. He heard the engine cough, then catch, and they were in the river, moving toward the center, the burning docks drifting farther and farther away.

Gunfire became more distant, but the lull was only temporary. The entire operation had taken less than twenty minutes. Within another twenty, boats and planes and choppers would be all over them. Nine of their ten boats had made it out of harbor. If the rest of them were to survive, they'd need help from the outside.

The worst was yet to come. He bowed his head and silently thanked God for the nameless CIA man.

LVIII

The South China Sea

April 19—4:15 A.M.

Jerry Prescott's eyes were wide open, the coffee tasting metallic on his tongue, as he sat in the com ops room of the *Blue Ridge* and watched American fighting men dying on his television screen. The room was darkened, blacked out in the combat zone. All of them, including Jerry and Nancy, were dressed for battle in fatigues, helmets, and Mae Wests. Benstock sat close to the screen, face transfixed at the spectacle of the escape attempt and the Vietnamese efforts to stop it. Captain Addison sat with his hands folded on the table, his face drained of all color. He looked at his watch constantly, and Jerry figured it was his way of breaking the emotional connection with the horror on the screen. Every few minutes he would jump up and run to the communications shack next door.

The TV showed scenes taken from helicopters that buzzed the fighting on the Saigon River. They were being sent, unedited, back to America on Benstock's orders, Jerry wondering exactly what was going through the man's mind.

Russian-made helicopters with Vietnamese markings were making runs at the eight boats still left afloat, strafing the decks and firing rockets, pulling up before they got in range of return-fire from the ships. On the periphery gunboats surrounded them, firing their deck cannons, white spray spouting the entire area. It was a bizarre standoff. The Vietnamese wouldn't shoot at the American choppers for fear of direct conflict with them, even though their airspace was being violated. The Americans stayed back because they feared Russian involvement should they intervene.

The voice of the pilot of the Navy chopper could be heard over the pictures. "They're kicking hell out of them down there, Green Leader. They can't keep this up too much longer. Request permission to render aid immediately."

"Negative Delta four-niner," came the staticked reply. "Request denied. Maintain surveillance status until further notice. Over."

"I can't stand this," replied the pilot, his voice breaking its controlled monotone. "Those are our boys down there, I—"

"Continue surveillance status, Delta four-niner. That's an order!"

One of the ships went up in a huge fireball, a gunboat scoring a direct hit from a deck cannon. Burning men could clearly be seen jumping off the decks into the swift flowing river.

Jerry felt himself jump in his chair, coffee spilling all down his front. Tears came involuntarily to his eyes. Nancy, standing near the hatch, turned from the scene, while Addison sat with fists clenched tightly in front of his face. This was insane, madness honed to organization.

Another voice through the speaker. "Green Leader, Green Leader . . . there's Russians up here, Russian choppers!"

"This is Green Leader. I'm seeking confirmation of reported Russian aircraft in vicinity, repeat, seeking confirmation of suspected Russian—"

" . . . got 'im," came the excited voice. "This is four-niner. They're all over the fucking sky!"

"This is Delta three-eight. I see them too..."

"For God's sake, let us go in Green Leader! Let us—"

"Negative, negative! Are Russian aircraft involved in the fighting? Are they firing upon our boats? Over."

"I see no indication of weapons discharge, Green Leader. Negative..."

"Who is that? Identify yourself. Over."

"This is three-eight... I see no weapons discharge from Russian choppers. They must be doing the same thing—"

"They got one! They got one!"

One of the Vietnamese helicopters was sputtering badly, its cockpit filled with smoke and arcing fire. It hovered, poised in the air for a second, then dropped from the sky like a stone.

Screaming into static, the American pilots celebrated, everyone in com ops yelling despite themselves. Then all of a sudden through the static, they heard...

"This is three-eight. Repeat. This is Delta three-eight. We've been hit. We've been hit. Oil pressure down badly, losing stabilization. I can't hold her on course. Losing altitude, Green Leader."

"His engines sparking, Green Leader. I can see—"

"Clear the air. Clear the air. Delta three-eight. Can you make it back to base? Over."

"Negative, Green Leader. I'm going to have to set it down on the mainland. Over."

"Did you see where the shot came from, Delta three-eight? Over."

"No, sir. Repeat, negative confirmation."

"Delta four-niner, Green Leader. Should I follow down three-eight and attempt rescue? Over."

There was a long pause where only static came over the wire. Jerry sat tensed, back straight, watching the fighting. It seemed like an eternity before control came back over the air. The voice seemed lighter.

"That's a roger, Delta four-niner. Institute standard rescue procedures. Over."

Benstock turned to stare at Captain Addison. "Can we do that on Vietnamese soil?" he asked.

The Captain shook his head. "No, sir, we cannot. But I'm damned glad we are!"

* * *

Admiral Nabov stood on the darkened bridge of the *Kiev* and spoke over the phone, his voice patching all the way to the Kremlin. In front of him a small TV screen juiced pictures of the American escape attempt. He was impressed and moved by their bravery—his own feelings on the matter of the hostages ones he felt obliged to keep to himself. He was not a man afraid of confrontation if it, indeed, had to happen.

"Yes, Mr. President," he told Youskevitch in a controlled voice, "the Americans have landed on Vietnamese soil in an attempt to rescue one of their pilots. I respectfully request orders on how to proceed from here."

Youskevitch sounded tired and edgy, his thoughts lost somewhere. "What do *you* think, Admiral?" he asked.

Nabov smiled and shook his head. "If we want to intervene, Mr. President, we now have every right by treaty to do so. But I must say that our two navies have drawn our might up against one another, and that might includes nuclear capabilities both above and below the water. The decision on whether to use that might, Mr. President, lies not with me, but with the secretariat—and rightly so."

Youskevitch's voice lowered to bare audibility. "Yes, of course," he said. "You're right."

"All forces are on full alert," Nabov said. "We await only your bidding. Our Vietnamese allies are requesting our intervention in the most explicit terms."

"Yes, yes, Admiral," Youskevitch said wearily. "I'm thinking."

From Tin's position just out of the mouth of the Saigon River, he could see and hear the fighting. He stood on the upper deck of the sleek white yacht and watched the distant explosions, their sound reaching him seconds later. Most of the crew of seven were up there with him, watching, fearful that they'd be caught in a crossfire should the boats make it to their position. Tin wasn't worried about that—he feared they wouldn't make it.

He turned a full circle, looking futilely into the surrounding darkness, waiting for Prescott, waiting for the money, knowing that if the man didn't show up the prisoners would die and the reprisals would begin.

Damn Ridley. He had to be behind this. Why wouldn't he understand?

He stared off into the distance, in the direction he knew the Seventh Fleet to be at anchor. He couldn't see them in the darkness, but he knew they were out there, hovering like gods waiting to crush his tiny country.

He came to a decision. It was time to break radio silence. If Prescott were out there, he needed to know now, before it was too late.

Another boat was on fire, the men on board rushing around frantically trying to put it out as the battle dragged on.

"This is four-niner, Green Leader. We've picked up the crew of three-eight and are heading up again. Repeat, rescue successful. Over."

"All right!" Addison said, slamming a hand down on the table.

The shipcom whistled, Addison jumping up immediately to push the button on the small wallspeaker. "This is the captain speaking," he said.

"Sir?" came a young-sounding voice. "We are receiving transmission from an unidentified vessel just a few miles away. It keeps addressing itself to Yankee Clipper."

Prescott stood. "That's Colonel Tin," he said, "using my code name."

Addison talked into the speaker. "Anything else to the message?"

"They want confirmation of arrival," the voice returned.

"They want their money," Nancy said. "They know that if we don't get it to them soon, all the prisoners will be dead."

"A little late to worry over that now," Benstock said, turning back to the screen. "That little drama has already been played out."

Prescott walked angrily over to him. "I'm beginning to think you like this," he said.

"What if I do?" Benstock returned casually. "Our country has been drowning in apathy for years. Maybe it will take something like this to wake us all up. You can feel the excitement generating through the air on this thing."

"Those are men out on those boats," Prescott said, walking to stand between Benstock and the television. "Real men. This isn't some TV program full of actors and commercials that wraps up in an hour or two."

"What about the Russians?" Addison asked, taking off his glasses to rub his eyes. "Where do they fit into the package?"

"We'll see what they're made of," Benstock said.

"This is real!" Prescott said. "Don't you understand that?"

Benstock stared at him with hard eyes, then stood, slowly, and walked to face the man. "Reality's what I say it is. Maybe you can contemplate that from the jail cell you spend the rest of your life in, Mr. Secretary."

Nancy couldn't stand it. She opened the hatch to "C" deck and went outside. The night was black, even the wind off the sea hot and unnatural. All around her the silhouettes of huge ships sat like deadly sentinels, waiting to unleash their poisons on the world. They were like gravestones in a watery cemetery, and maybe that's exactly what they were. Beyond the death ships she could hear the thunderlike rumbling of the fighting and watched the sky flare then subside. It was all some grisly carnival where the carousels played marches and the horses snorted blood and foam.

It had fallen to pieces, all the dreams coming to an end at once. It was no longer a case of winning anything. All the odds were now set to determine just how much everyone would lose. Yesterday she had thought she could play this game of death and at least break even. Now she understood: To play at all meant to lose. She felt silly wearing the heavy metal helmet. She took it off and stuck it under her arm.

"Mrs. Henderson," came a voice behind her. She turned to someone else with his helmet off and recognized him as one of the newsmen sent with Benstock. "Can I have a word with you?"

She nodded. He was young, a tape editor if she remembered correctly. His face was dotted with large freckles and his eyes were wide, piercing.

"We've received a network feed over the satellite that you might be interested in," he said. "I've got it set up if you've got a minute to come with me."

She shrugged. "I've got nothing but time," she said, then smiled at him. "What's your name?"

"Danny Matlock," he replied, smiling. "Come with me."

She followed him along the deck, trying to keep her

mind away from the suffering going on just a few miles from them. "How do your newscasts work with Benstock in charge?" she asked.

He turned slightly as he walked. "Not very well," he said. "Satellite feeds are all controlled by Benny. If we cut a feature, he gets full right of rejection . . . and uses it. All he wants is propaganda, and if we don't give it to him, we don't send anything back."

"What sort of propaganda?" she asked.

"Patriotic stuff," he said, and they both grabbed the rail as the ship rolled slightly. "You know, wave the flag and spit at the enemy. You'd almost think he *wanted* a war. Here we are."

Matlock took her into a room too small for what it was being used for. The major networks, plus several independents, had all their gear jammed inside the twenty-foot-square cabin. Men sat before monitors, cutting and editing, most stories that would be rejected by Benstock who controlled the feed to the outside world. Equipment was piled everywhere, and wherever it wasn't, men and women stuffed themselves. They all wore the mandatory battle dress.

Matlock took her hand. "Just stick close," he said, shoving into the confusion. "My station's over here."

Hand in hand, they pushed their way through the people and the noise, coming at last to a small corner filled with gear that had a sign stuck on the monitor screen that read: PROPERTY OF CTN, KEEPA U HANS OFF!

Matlock knelt in front of the screen and searched through a knapsack, coming out with a videotape. "This is it," he said, shoving the tape into a recorder. He pushed a button. "I'll have to rewind it."

"How can you work in here?" Nancy said, putting her free hand to her ear and shaking her head.

Matlock smiled. "We're like the monkeys in the urban crowding experiments," he said with a laugh. "Actually, most of us think we've having to wear the lifejackets to keep afloat above all the bullshit in here!"

The machine finished rewinding, and Matlock pushed the play button.

The scene was what looked like a press conference, and Nancy recognized the large conference room of the Skirvin Plaza Hotel in Oklahoma City. A man was sitting in front of a large bank of microphones, people crowding all around while flashbulbs popped continuously.

"It's Sid!" she said.

The man looked up at her from his kneeling position and smiled broadly. "Listen," he said.

"Why have you waited so long to speak with the press?" came a question from the audience.

Sid looked nervous in front of the crowd. He reached for a glass of water and sipped it with a shaking hand before answering. "To be perfectly frank," he said at last, "I wasn't sure about my feelings in this matter . . ."

Other questions began coming at him from all sides. He held a hand for silence. "Let me finish my answer," he said. "Please. My wife, Nancy, and I clashed over this issue almost from the first. I accused her of many things, some of them not very nice. And when she refused to bow to my wishes, I took that as a sign that she no longer wanted to be married to me. While she was going through her ordeals in Chicago, I broke off contact with her and moved myself and the children out of spite."

"Does that mean the two of you are now separated?"

"Separated by miles, yes," he said, wiping at his eyes. "But my heart is, and has always been, right next to her, sharing every breath with her. You see, I realized, when I could finally be honest with myself, that I was jealous. Jealous of her ex-husband, jealous of her position . . . her newfound power. I wanted to control her, to make her subservient to me. What I found, ultimately, was that I was married to a woman with greatness in her. I was married to someone whose vision far exceeded my own. It was I, not she, who needed to change. I, not she, who had no idea of what was going on around me."

"And what about the charges that have been leveled against her?"

Sid took a breath, his eyes hardening. "My wife is guilty of nothing except caring for the lives of men who were abandoned to die by their own government. She's guilty of nothing but love. If that's a crime, then this country is no longer a fit place to live." He looked straight at the cameras, his nervousness totally gone. "Nancy, wherever you are, I want you to know that I love you, the kids love you, and we'll stand behind you no matter what. Please forgive me, honey. I was a blind fool."

Matlock shut down the tape and turned to Nancy. She was standing, staring blankly. "Pretty good, huh?" he asked.

She turned her eyes to him, then broke down completely, crying loudly. He stood and put an arm around her, and she clung to him, shaking, free to be weak at last.

And all the cameras stuffed into that small room pointed in her direction, recording her reality for the seven o'clock news.

The situation had worsened in com ops. Very little fire was being returned from the ships as their ammo depleted. The helicopters had gotten bolder, coming in closer and staying longer. Seven ships were still afloat, but many of them were listing badly, taking on water from battle damage. No one could hazard a guess as to the number of casualties so far. Only the relative inexperience of the Vietnamese pilots had saved them until now.

"How far are they from the mouth of the river?" Prescott asked.

"Still quite a way," Addison said. "If we don't go in soon, there's no hope at all."

Jerry looked at him. The man's face was still drawn, strained. "Will we go in?"

Addison showed him empty palms. "The firepower of the world is sitting here right now," he said. "Would you want to make that decision?"

"No," Prescott said.

"We'll go in," Benstock said quietly. "Listen."

He turned up the sound. "This is Delta four-niner... I can't take this anymore. I'm going down to run interference—"

"Negative, four-niner. Return to surveillance duty. Repeat. Return to surveillance duty...."

"No, sir... I'm going down.... If they shoot they're going to have to shoot me straight out.... Maybe they'll back off..."

"This is Delta one-seven... I'm going down, too. We've got to give them a fighting chance."

Shipcom whistled. "Cap'n. We've picked up Vietnamese transmissions. They're putting their jets in the air."

"That's it," Addison said, jumping up and running to the

com. He punched up the button. "Get the *Vinson* on the horn. See if they're scrambling." He turned to Prescott. "If it doesn't turn right now, those men are dead."

Shipcom whistled again. "Cap'n . . . we've got the White House on the line!"

"Patch it down here," he said.

"Yes, sir. And the *Vinson* responds positively. her jets are scrambling now."

"Sweet Jesus," Addison whispered.

Benstock ran to the red phone and picked it up. "Mr President," he said, excited. "All hell's breaking loose here."

Prescott moved to Addison. "Will those jets fire on the Vietnamese?"

"Not without orders," the man said, pacing.

"This is Delta four-niner. The bastards are hanging back. They don't know whether to fire on us or not!"

"What are the Russians going to do?" Prescott asked.

Addison shook his head. "It's all guts from here on in. You call the shots."

"Yes, Mr. President," Benstock said. "We've got to go in now. We can blow them back to Hanoi if we want . . . fuck the Russians, we'll have to take care of them sometime anyway!"

Prescott shared a look with Addison. Benstock was talking like a high-school kid.

"Go in now!" Benstock said. "The cameras are running. The whole world will know we're right. Order the strike. Just say the word and we'll save those boys!"

Without realizing it, Prescott was walking toward Benstock. When he reached the man, he grabbed him and pulled him off the phone, taking the receiver from him.

"Simon, dammit, this is Jerry . . . "

"Where's Benstock, Jerry? What are you doing on the phone?"

Benstock was back, grabbing for the phone, cursing loudly, his control finally gone.

"A minute of your time, Simon. That's all I ask. Please."

He had to shove Benstock away again, Addison gaping open-mouthed at the entire scene.

"A minute," Herrod said. "Just a minute."

"Have you gone to red yet?" Jerry asked.

"Yes," Herrod said, clipped.

"This is the big one, Simon," Prescott said, trying to

keep his voice calm. "This is a lot worse than Bay of Pigs, a lot worse than the missile thing."

"I know."

Benstock stood just out of arm's reach, breathing heavily, face red.

"The boatload of gold is ten minutes away from the Vietnamese. I think we can still get them on the radio and call this whole thing off. Before you say anything, listen to me. You have three choices—let the prisoners die, go in to save them, or give them the gold. If we go in to save them, I'm afraid the Russians will have to respond. They've dug themselves too far in the hole. With that, the world ends. I don't think any of us could let the prisoners die at this point. But the gold, the gold, Simon. It's just some bars of metal, for God's sake. You didn't even raise it. You can say one word. I'll take the responsibility. Do whatever you want with me afterward, but just let me take the metal over and give it to the sons of bitches, and everything goes back to square one. This is beyond pride now. The whole goddamned planet's up for grabs and you know it. You have the power to stop it. Only you have that power. Jesus Christ, stop thinking like a politician for just a minute and do the right thing."

"What *is* the right thing?" Herrod said quietly. "No human being is qualified to make this kind of decision. I'm just a Democrat with a martyr complex. I don't have any special knowledge about anything."

"Let me ask you this: Would you rather be wrong and save the world, or be right and end it?"

"You make it all so simple."

"For once it is, Simon. Your choice is no choice at all."

Herrod took a long breath. "Okay," he said. "Take your damned gold and I hope they choke on it."

"Great!" Jerry yelled. "I'm going to put the captain on the phone so you can tell him. We've got to hurry."

"Right," Herrod said. "Thanks . . . I think."

Prescott handed the phone to Addison and turned to stare at Benstock.

"I'm going to get you for this," Benstock threatened, eyes flashing. "You're going to be made to stop hurting the country. Nothing's changed, I guarantee you that."

Prescott smiled at him. "I think your face-lift's beginning to come undone, Benny," he said, and pinched the man on

the cheek. He looked around. Where was Nancy? This wa
her baby.

He walked to the hatch and pulled it open, Nanc
Henderson standing on the other side.

"There you are," Jerry said, taking her by the arm
"How'd you like to deliver a couple billion dollars' worth o
gold?"

Her face lit up. "No kidding?"

Jerry nodded. "No kidding."

Addison hung up the phone and got on shipcom. "This i
the captain. Radio that unidentified ship and tell them th
gold is on the way. Tell them to call off their dogs!"

Nancy threw her arms around Jerry's neck. "We did it!"

Jerry returned the hug. "Let's get them the mone
first," he said. "Come on, we'd better get below."

They left, Benstock trailing behind. He walked out ont
the deck and watched them disappear around a corner. H
smiled, shaking his head. They may have the gold and the
freedom, but he still had their detonator. And he knew ju
when to use it.

LIX

Aboard *Viper*

April 19—5:30 A.M.

Jerry Prescott and Nancy Henderson stood on the mai
deck of the pirate freighter and watched the Vietnames
civilians waving from the deck of the pleasure yacht ju
twenty yards from where they were dropping anchor. Th
morning sky had lightened to the east, brightening the coa
in the distance, and the incredible armada, barely a mile i
the other direction. Distant ships seemed to fill the who
ocean beyond them out to the horizon. Above, helicopters
three nations hovered to watch the exchange, recording th
event for the eyes of the world. They seemed to travel

swarms, their beating props a constant irritant. A hospital ship lay at anchor in the distance. Large and bright white, its huge red cross seemed to glow with early sunshine.

All was quiet. On the mainland Jerry could see the mouth of the Saigon River where it emptied into the sea. Somewhere on that river the prisoners still traveled. Their lives, at least for the moment, were safe, while their captors awaited the measure of their ransom. It was metal for people, one of the most expensive commodities in the world for one of the cheapest. Jerry wondered about the relative value of life and wondered if the Vietnamese thought them foolish for paying the ransom.

A man wearing a traditional silk outfit stood on the sun deck of the yacht, smoking a small cigar, one arm behind his back. It had to be Tin.

The man took the cigar out of his mouth and shouted across to them in English. "Are there any military personnel aboard your vessel?"

"No," Jerry called back. "Are there any aboard yours?"

Tin smiled. "Only me, Mr. Prescott. Only me. What about the hospital ship?"

"Only medical people."

Tin looked up into the morning sky, already light blue. He frowned at the helicopters, but didn't say anything. He looked back across at them. "I will come aboard now. We don't have much time."

Nancy shook her head, brushing windblown hair out of her face. "I don't know whether to love him or hate him," she said.

Jerry turned to her, nodding. "We probably can't do either," he said. "He speaks for history. I think we should just be grateful that it's almost over."

"I wonder if Billy made it," she said, and Jerry realized just exactly how large the woman's stake was in this.

He put an arm around her. "I'd forgotten," he said. "So much . . ."

She smiled up at him. "Don't worry about it, okay?"

Garcia was suddenly there with them, though neither of them had heard him approach. "Does the cigar man know some of this gold is mine?" he asked.

"Yes," Jerry said. "He understands the situation. Are you prepared to take him on board?"

"We've lowered a rope ladder," the man said. "Say, you must have put something past the sailor boys. I thought we were all going to jail for life."

Nancy turned and smiled at him. "I'm sure you'll find a way to accomplish that all by yourself someday," she said.

He frowned deeply, shaking his head. "Garcia retires," he said. "I'm going to buy a villa in the mountains, and thirty women and never look at the sea again." He spat on the deck. "Thirty-one women. One for every day of the month."

"What will you do in a leap year?" Jerry asked.

Garcia grinned, a finger smoothing his moustache. "Double up," he answered.

Tin's boat puttered up to the freighter, the man nimbly climbing the rope ladder to the main deck, his men behind him.

He hurried over to them with an outstretched hand, going to Nancy first. "Mrs. Henderson," he said shaking her hand. "You are a very rare person. On behalf of my government and myself, I thank you."

"I didn't do it for your government, or you," she replied, but shook hands anyway.

The man nodded curtly, then turned to Jerry. "Secretary Prescott," he said, and they shook hands. "Someday you'll have to tell me how all this was managed. But right now, we must proceed quickly. You will please show me the gold. My experts will evaluate its relative worth. As you know, we must do this before the prisoners reach the sea. I have called a cease-fire, but am left in an untenable position should you be lying about the gold."

"Don't worry," Jerry said. "It's all there and all yours . . . except, of course, Mr. Garcia's share."

Tin turned to stare at the Spaniard. "Of course," he said. "Mr. Garcia is well-known to me. He has operated in our waters for a long time. Many people think too long a time."

The Spaniard bowed low. "Garcia retires," he said with a flourish.

Tin ignored him. "May we go below?"

"Yes," Nancy said. "The sooner this is out of our hands, the better."

Garcia led them toward the hold while the world sat poised, watching. They were taken down into the dark, away from the prying eyes.

"There are three holds," Garcia said. "The gold is split equally among the three."

They entered a large room with high, wet walls. It was dimly lit and smelled of bilge water, but gold was stacked all around. Row upon row of stacked bars, impressive by their sheer volume. Two of Garcia's men were down there guarding it from the rest of his men.

Tin called back up the stairs to his men saying something in Vietnamese. The men scurried down the stairs and began running through the stacks of gold. They carried small scales and abacuses, one of them with a portable lab he carried in a black, leather bag.

As they started to work checking the cargo, Tin, Jerry, and Nancy walked through the aisles of gold that gleamed dully in the dim light.

"You probably think ill of me," Tin said. "Blood money is the dirtiest kind of all." He put up a hand to touch the gold, then made a face. "I hate this gold. I hate everything it stands for."

He stopped. "The reason we kept your people for so many years was the fact that we hated to take blood money. We wanted to get on our feet our own way. But the Russians . . . Anyway, I use this gold to buy a future for my people. We used to be the world's number one rice producer, but no more. We were defoliated and poisoned with Agent Orange. We must take our living from below the ground now, and this gold will help us in that regard.

"We walk away from the earth, from our connection with the soil. But I suppose that's twentieth century life, is it not?"

Benstock sat with Captain Addison in com ops and watched the helicopter camera-shot taken of the freighter. They were all on there now: Prescott, the Henderson woman, even the Vietnamese. All the ducks in a row.

It was all set up so beautifully. Everything had been taken care of. He could have restored American pride in the space of a few hours and started the country back on the road to greatness. Television could have finally been used as the motivational tool it was intended to be. Well, it still wasn't too late. In fact, perhaps it was better this way. Prescott's mouth would certainly get in the way from this point on if something wasn't done to stop him.

Addison sat in the chair next to Benstock, his arms folded across his chest. "I don't know what to think about all this," he said. "I'm glad and sorry at the same time."

"You're a fighting man," Benstock said. "You know inside that you'll have to fight somewhere else because of what's going on here today."

"Maybe," Addison replied. "Though I'd sure hate to have seen us get into a dirty one on account of this. Look, they're going down below deck to count the gold."

Benstock stared at the screen, his mouth going dry. This was it. They would be below with the charges, the perfect place. He had already checked on the range of the detonator and knew he was in good shape. All he had to do was flick a switch, then drop the damned gadget into the ocean. It was as simple as that.

He stood. "Well, I think I might wander back to my cabin and clean up a bit," he told the captain.

Addison looked at him quizzically. "Not going to watch the final exchange?"

He smiled. "I've got twenty cameras recording it," he said. "I'll watch the replay."

The man nodded. "I think we're just about thirty minutes away from the end of this. The Russians haven't done anything yet, so I don't suspect they will at this point. I may stick around for the end, then catch a little shut-eye."

Benstock nodded, knowing that the excitement was just beginning. He waved casually and walked out of the room and onto "C" deck, making his way toward his cabin below where he had stashed the detonator. He moved quickly, wanting to take care of this while Prescott was in the hold. He was just nearing the stairs at the end of the deck when he heard a voice calling him.

He turned quickly back around to see Addison running across the deck to him.

"The President wants to speak to you!" he called as he ran up.

Benstock shook his head. "We'll get back with him later," he said. "There's no time now to . . ."

Addison stared suspiciously at him. "He said he wants to speak to you right now." The man spoke slowly. "It was given to me in the form of an order, Mr. Benstock."

Benstock nodded, then turned to go back to com ops,

hurrying his gait to try and get it over with as quickly as possible. "Did he say what he wanted?" he asked over his shoulder.

"No," Addison replied. "He just wanted you on the phone right then."

Damn. He hurried the length of the deck, practically on a run when he got to the red phone. "Mr. President?" he said, slightly out of breath. "You sent for me?"

"Yes, I did, Benny."

Benstock narrowed his brows. Herrod's voice sounded controlled, tightly strung.

"I've been doing some thinking over the last hour," Herrod said, almost as if he were reading a statement. "It seems to me that maybe we've gone a bit too far in this media control thing."

"Too far . . . how?" Benstock said.

"A little too carried away," Herrod replied. "Perhaps we've jumped into it too fast without studying—"

"Mr. President," Benstock said. "We've looked at this every step of the way. I've spent my entire career studying it—"

"Just the same," Herrod interrupted, "I'm not ready to go on with this right now. Until further notice, I want no more press releases issued by you that speak for this government. The networks are free to cover the rest of this thing any way they see fit without clearing it through you. As of right now, the position of media liaison no longer exists within this administration. Do I make myself clear?"

"What's clear to me is that you're going to throw me to the wolves," Benstock said.

"The wolves?" Herrod asked. "I thought the media was your friend? By the way, the networks have already been informed of the changes, so you won't have to do it yourself."

"I won't go down without a fight," Benstock snarled. "I carry a lot of weight in this country and I have a lot of access to public attention. My side will be heard."

"It's a free country, Benny. We're *all* entitled to an opinion."

"Boats coming!" someone yelled down into the hold. "Boats!"

Jerry and Nancy turned to one another. "It must be the prisoners!" he said.

Nancy turned pale, charging up the stairs with Jerry right behind her. They ran out on deck. Seven boats were right up on them, all filled with men, many wounded. Women and children could also be seen moving around on the decks. Most of the boats were badly scarred and taking water. At a distance behind were the Vietnamese boats, watching, waiting to go in if necessary.

"Oh, God, Jerry," Nancy said, grabbing his arm. "It's really them! I don't know if I believe it."

"Believe it, Mrs. Henderson," Tin said from behind. "This is reality at last."

Prescott turned to him. "Are they free now?" he asked. "Is it all over?"

Tin nodded. "The gold seems to be counting satisfactorily. I have already dispatched one of my men to contact our patrol boats and send them back to harbor."

"Thank you," Jerry said. "I thank you for that."

"I'm not a unreasonable man," Tin replied, and drew on his cigar.

The hospital ship was anchored two hundred yards distant, highly visible in the brightening day. The fishing boats were being beaconed in by cheering from the starboard decks of the ship, all personnel out and yelling their happiness and excitement.

One of the boats had pulled away from the others and was heading toward them. It was listing badly on the port side, the deck nearly touching the waterline. They'd never make it to the hospital ship.

The men were close enough to see—their old, drawn faces, the blood on many of them, the deep-set, staring eyes. Nancy leaned way over the rail, cupping her hands to her mouth.

"That boat!" she said, pointing to the yacht. "Get on that boat! We'll take you the rest of the way!"

They began waving back frantically as they bumped up against the yacht, tying up to its ladder.

Tin walked up to the rail and looked out. The first man up the ladder was tied to a stretcher. He was being lifted carefully, tenderly up the incline. Tin smiled sadly as he watched Lieutenant Colonel Jason Ridley, United States Air

Force, being lifted, more dead than alive, onto the decks of freedom. When he straightened and saluted the man, neither Prescott nor Henderson knew what he was doing.

"Do you need us here anymore?" Nancy asked Tin. "Can we leave? I—I have a lot of love and messages to pass on to those men."

Tin nodded, dark eyes shining. "We will go back to port with Mr. Garcia, then give him his boat." He looked at the yacht, at the men scrambling onto its deck. "You seem to have a crew already on yours. Our business, I think, is concluded."

Prescott and Tin shook hands once more, but Nancy was already off and moving toward the rope ladder.

Benstock ran into his cabin, hurrying to the bottom drawer of the built-in desk. He fell to his knees and tore open the drawer pulling out the detonator.

He'd have to hurry now. The prison ships were closing in. If only Herrod hadn't kept him so fucking long on the phone. The President seemed confused, unsure of who his friends were. But he still had time to solidify things if he could just hurry.

He moved back to his door, opening it slowly and looking out the crack. Then he poked his head out. The runway was clear in both directions. He stepped out onto the deck, the device held firmly in both hands.

He walked to the rail and flipped the juice button on the detonator's side. A small red light began flashing.

Nancy walked through the crowds of men and women who filled the decks of the yacht. Everyone was filthy from smoke, coughing and wheezing. The smells were of sweat and blood, the odor of death permeating everything. The wives and children did what they could for the wounded. But they were all smiling, all laughing through the pain, and it made her smile, too.

She searched for Billy, but not really. She'd search properly on the hospital ship. Right now she simply walked through the legion of the dead, exalting in the triumph of life over all.

They were getting underway, moving toward the red cross. She smiled and shook hands, assuring everyone that things were all right now. She turned and looked for Jerry. He was standing astern, watching the freighter gradually recede in the background, the fishing boat already swamped and going down fast.

And the moment froze, like a rose captured in a water globe, as the freighter cried out, a huge explosion blowing out her hull in several places, raising mammoth, white-bellied bubbles that broke and spouted water fifty feet in the air.

The sea churned and complained around them, the force pushing the yacht like a typhoon. Nancy grabbed a railing for support, her eyes glued in obscene fascination to the sight of the large boat, rolling onto its side, then sliding rapidly beneath the waves stern first.

It was happening so fast, black smoke inking out the entire scene. She watched in horror as the *Viper* seemed to slip quietly in the dark waters, disappearing within minutes.

There were two more underwater explosions, two more white-fringed bubbles, and it was over. An oil slick remained, some debris, but no people.

The helicopters still hovered, but now they didn't know what to do. And the prisoners were caught in the netherworld between the Russians and the Americans, each poised for action. And all Nancy could think about was Maurice Benstock.

A.P. TELETEXT

Central Intelligence Agency sources today refused comment on published reports in the *Washington Post* that Miller Angostis, CIA Director, is under investigation on charges that he still maintains "substantial control" over Data-Link Industries, an electronics firm that did $100 million worth of business with the federal government last year. Angostis allegedly sold out his ties to the firm he founded upon entering government. The *Post* would not confirm its sources, but said the information came from "highly placed FBI contacts."

LX

Bottom Lines

Sirens blared loudly all over the *Kiev* as Admiral Nabov repared for war. As he stood on the bridge, telephone in and, he could see pilots below, charging down the flightline oward their MiGs. Men hurried around the bridge, straping on battle dress and talking orders through the shipcom • forward gunnery positions.

The fleet was on full alert, seconds away from confrontation.

"I must have the order now, Mr. President," he said udly into the phone. "The Americans have blown up the old ship within the twelve-mile limit. Our duty becomes acreasingly clear at this point."

"How soon can you move to defend the Vietnamese?" ouskevitch asked, his voice flat, dull.

"The moment," Nabov said, irritated. "We await only our orders. We can have planes in the air within a minute."

"Have the American attacked anywhere else?"

"Mr. President, we *must* have the order now!" Nabov aid quickly. "The edge of first strike—"

"*I'll* tell you what we must have, and when," Youskevitch aid. "Now answer my question."

"There has been no other activity since the sinking of the old ship. The Vietnamese are waiting for us to move for them."

"So . . . it could reasonably be assumed that, perhaps, aere will be no more action taken by the Americans?"

Nabov took the phone away from his mouth and stared at , unbelieving. They had to fight now! Everything pointed to . He was touched on the arm by the ensign working flight ontrol.

"We have condition green on the tarmac, sir," he said. Do the planes go now?"

Nabov shook his head absently. "Hold on green," he aid, and put the phone back to his ear. "Mr. President,

403

they've attacked the people we came here to defend. A there any other options besides confrontation?"

Youskevitch didn't answer. He waited, tensed, while t might of his country strained at the leash. Finally, he sa again," "Has the attack spread anywhere else?"

"No, Mr. President," Nabov said, his voice clippe barely in control.

Youskevitch drew a long breath. "Recall your helico ters," he said, "and proceed at a...leisurely speed back your respective bases. Leave a small battle group behind cover your withdrawal."

"You mean our retreat, Mr. President."

"Discretion, Admiral," Youskevitch said. "In actions...a words. Do I make myself clear?"

"Yes, Mr. President," Nabov said, pride buckling. "Pe fectly clear."

Jerry stood for a long time on the deck of the yach watching where the *Viper* had gone down. He was looking f some sign of life, but there was none. The sea had taken t ship and its inhabitants to its dark, silent bosom and end the episode with stark finality, treating a fortune in gold a the dreams of a people as just so many more rocks on sandy bottom. The whole affair had gone from reality legend in a matter of minutes.

He turned away, watching the prisoners, smiling at t millions in back pay that would go out to them. The hospit ship loomed close, stretchers lowered, white-suited perso nel waiting on the small dock that jutted out from the h near the waterline. He had waited for the Russian respon to the destruction of the ship, but it wasn't forthcoming. surprised him to see that he was surprised that World War had not yet begun.

Nancy was making her way through the crowds, shaki hands, giving encouragement. From looking at the conditi of the men on this ship, Jerry found it nearly impossible believe they could have achieved a prison break of su incredible proportions. If ever he needed a lesson as to t possibilities of the human heart, this was it. He felt proud be included in such company, proud to have finally taken stand.

Nancy looked up to see him looking at her. She smiled and made her way over to him, pointing upward.

"The Russian helicopters are leaving," she said.

"I believe we're home free," he replied. "Finally."

"The bastard blew the ship up, didn't he?" she asked.

"Of course he did," Jerry said. "But we'd have a hell of a time proving it."

They embraced spontaneously, and Jerry realized just how much strength they had taken from one another during the ordeal.

"It's really all over, isn't it?" she asked, content in his arms.

"Not really," he replied. "The hard part starts now. You'll have interviews to deal with, feature stories, a book, probably a TV movie with three spinoffs." She began to giggle, pulling away to look up at him.

"Aw," she said, "you're just joking."

He gave her the Boy Scout salute. "Honest. I've just watched the birth of an instant celebrity."

She put a hand to her hair. "I wonder who they'll get to play me in the movies?" she asked.

"Don't joke," he replied. "Reality for us is over at this point. Everything from now on is either hype, or fantasy, or opinion, or . . . revelation."

She put a finger to his chest. "You're just being a cynical old fogey," she said.

He took her hand and kissed that outstretched finger. "Sure," he said. "But with a difference." Tears come involuntarily to mist his eyes. "I was here for this. I know it happened. I know how and I know why. And I'll never look at the world the same way again."

She put her hands on his shoulders and pulled his face to hers, kissing him deeply on the lips, lingeringly.

"We'll probably never see one another again," she said.

He smiled. "I'll come get you to autograph your book for me."

"I wish you all the best, Jerry. You're a good man."

He nodded, wiping at his eyes, feeling like a foolish old man. "That's the nicest thing anybody ever said to me."

Now they both had things to do. The noises were loud toward the bow as they came up on the dock. People running everywhere, shouting orders. There was cheering and ap-

plause as their boat cozied up with the others, the redheaded
man who was guiding her bringing it in perfectly to a small
mooring.

"The Russians are leaving!" someone yelled, and everyone cheered, and Nancy thought it funny because it was like
all the old newsreel footage she remembered from V.J. Day.
Respectability at last.

She turned to Jerry, a small crowd of people between
them now climbing up onto the swaying dock. She pointed to
the hospital ship and yelled, "Are you going aboard?"

He shook his head, an exaggerated no. "Got business on
the *Blue Ridge!*" he called back.

She made it up onto the dock with the others, moving
toward the wide stairs leading to an entry hatch ten feet
above the waterline.

"Miss!" someone called, and she turned to see a white-
suited medic motioning to her.

She moved to the man. He was holding an IV bottle full
of clear liquid above a man on a stretcher who had been
beaten severely. His face was a terrible mess, but somehow
he seemed familiar.

A large, bald man with a blood-covered arm that hung
limp at his side was crowding the doctor. "I need to go with
him," the man said, "to look out for him."

"We can do that now," the medic said patiently, and
looked at Nancy. "Could you take this for me?" He held the
IV out to her.

"Sure," she said, taking it from him.

"I've been looking out for him since we left the camp,"
the man said, concern showing on his face.

"You need to take care of yourself now," the medic
returned. "Colonel Ridley is in good hands."

Ridley! She nearly screamed, her free hand going to
cover her mouth. It was Marsha's husband! No matter how
hard they had all tried to keep the memories of the missing
alive, it had somehow never seemed completely real. But
here was the proof. Marsha's husband—her best friend's
husband—was alive, if just barely. How horrible to come this
far if. . .

"What happened to him?" she asked the bald man, and
the words were choking out of her.

"Torture," the man said casually. "He was tortured. But he never broke. Never."

She looked at the doctor. "Will he . . ."

"It's too early to tell anything," the man said with a practiced, clinical air.

Someone else came to help the bald man, pulling him up the stairs.

"You take good care of him," the man called back to them.

"Do you know how many made it?" she asked the doctor, not taking her eyes off Ridley's face. His eyes fluttered open, trying to focus on her.

They started up the stairs, two men carrying the stretcher, while the medic opened the blue robe Ridley wore to poke around on his stomach. "We had someone count," he said, not looking at her, his absorption on Ridley total, "but there was so much confusion. I think somewhere between thirteen and fourteen hundred got out. Of course, there's a lot of wounded."

"My men . . . " Ridley whispered.

"Everyone's on board, Colonel," the medic said. "You just rest. You've done your duty, now let me do mine."

Ridley looked at Nancy again, trying to slot her. They made it through the hatch, into the cool, dark innards of the ship.

"Who . . . are you?" he asked her.

"I'm a friend of Marsha's," Nancy said, leaning close to him so he'd be able to hear her over the racket. "She sends her love."

They maneuvered through the hall and into one of the many emergency rooms that were already filling with the wounded. Wheeled legs were pulled down out of the stretcher and it became a bed. They pushed it into a small room off the main room.

"Is she all right?" he asked, when the attendants left. "Does she . . . need anything?"

"Just you," Nancy said.

"Some prize," he said, trying to smile, but pain flared in his eyes and he wheezed.

"Why did they do this to you?" she asked.

He turned his head away fom her, spitting up blood. Then he turned back around. She wiped his mouth on the sleeve of her unmarked uniform. "It was the only way the could break me," he said.

Her lips trembled. "Back home we had no idea . . . we— helped raise the money to pay for your release. Did we . . . d wrong?"

"We all do what we have to do," he said, coughing again "Duty . . . to ourselves . . . is all there is. You did what you ha to do. You did right."

And through the pain and the broken body, he winked a her. She laughed loudly in return, knowing why Marsha ha married this man and why she had stayed faithful to him a these years.

The doctors came and shooed her away, and she patte his arm and drifted off into the rest of the ship. She began t search then, to search for Billy. Her mind was free of notion of any kind, and she thought about her duty to herself, wit no idea of what that was going to be.

She found him, as she knew she would. He was unhur eating ice cream in the huge, echoing commissary after brief medical exam. He was sitting with several other me talking in that damned Texas twang of his after all these years

She walked up behind him silently, the others looking u at her. One by one, they picked up their food and walked of Billy never turned around. He just sat there eating.

She sat beside him at the long table. He turned his fac to her. He had aged harshly, but perhaps some of that wou disappear in time. He was recognizable, his freckles st prominent. There was a distance in his eyes that frightene her somewhat, a strange tilt to his head that at first made he want to run away. But she didn't

She had many years worth of feelings to deal with an she didn't have a lifetime to deal with them. She had given herself physically and emotionally to only two men in he entire life, and one of them was sitting beside her, a strange but more than a stranger. A rush of images came floodin back to her that she didn't know still existed within her min She was nervous and frightened.

"Vanilla's still your favorite, huh?" she said quietly.

He smiled crookedly, that lopsided grin of his. "I'm vanilla man, all right," he said, then fell silent, turning bac to his eating.

"Are you surprised to see me?" she asked.

He didn't look at her. "Things have changed now, haven't they?" he said.

She stared down at the tabletop. "Yes," she whispered. "Everything changes."

"They didn't for me."

"I know."

They fell silent. He stared at his bowl of ice cream for a minute, then his lower lip began shaking uncontrollably. He angrily swiped his arm at the bowl, sending it skittering off the table. "It's not fair!" he said loudly, then buried his face in his arms on the table. "It's not fair."

A doctor came charging toward the table. Nancy waved him off. The man stopped, then backed slowly away. She moved her arm toward Billy—slowly, hesitantly. Then she touched him, putting her arm around his shoulder.

He turned to her, then put his arms around her, sobbing into her shoulder. "All I ever wanted to do was the right thing," he said. "Why did this happen to me?"

"I don't know," she said, stroking his sparse hair.

He pulled away from her, his cheeks slicked wet. "You look so beautiful," he said. "Are . . . are you . . . married?" He almost whispered the last word.

She nodded. "His name's Sid Henderson," she said, looking him in the eye, finding something of an old familiarity there. "We've been married for six years. We've got two kids."

"Two kids," he repeated. "What flavor?"

She smiled. "Vanilla," she replied. "Two boys."

He nodded, carefully watching her eyes. "You waited a long time."

"As long as I could," she said. "Believe me, Billy, I . . . "

He held up a hand. "Don't,'" he said. "I understand. You can't know how good it feels, you waiting so long and all. Are you happy?"

She nodded. "You'd like Sid," she said. "He's a good husband . . . a good father."

"Well, he'd better be," Billy said, making a fist, "or old Uncle Billy'll come and straighten him out."

She reached out and touched his shoulder. "It hurts, doesn't it?"

His fist shook in front of his face, his eyes brimming over. He nodded, words straining out. "It hurts so bad,

Nancy," he said, "so damn bad. I feel like I've been cheate
out of my life."

"I'm so sorry," she said, feeling stupid for saying it.

He turned to her and took both her hands in his. "No,
he said. "Don't be. You did everything you could do. You'
here, ain't you? I learned livin' out there in the jungle to g
along on just a little. And, believe me, I found out when the
took everything else away that livin's something you do fo
yourself—no other reason. I lost count of the years, Nancy
Not days or weeks, but whole years. Guess maybe I learne
somethin' about facing myself, about facing . . . things. Then
went to that damned ole camp and they got me all turne
around, tellin' me how good it was gonna be, when som
where inside I knew it wasn't gonna be like that at all." H
licked dry lips, his face calm, without judgment. "But th
colonel, he set us all straight by remindin' us about how li
is. Colonel Ridley toughed it out back at the camp. I ca
tough it out, too." He let go of her hands, turning slight
away. "I think I'd like to be alone now."

She stared at him for a moment, trying to think
something, anything to say to make it all right. Finally sl
realized what Billy knew all along, that some things can nev
be all right.

She stood. "Good-bye, Billy," she said.

"Good-bye, Nancy," he said.

She turned and walked out of the room, excited me
yelling all around her, some whistling. She thought to loo
back, but couldn't do it. And as she left the commissary sl
doubted she'd ever see Billy Phillips again.

Jerry Prescott sat in his cabin aboard the *Blue Ridge* ar
sipped on the scotch Captain Addison had provided. He fe
he had earned this one and didn't feel a bit guilty abo
drinking it.

He had already had several conversations with Herro
about the incident, the pressures of the job already settlir
back on him again. He was, of course, forgiven for his hand
the affair, and all charges concerning him or Nancy Henderso
were to be immediately and categorically dismissed. He ha
discussed his suspicions about Benstock's role in the bombir
of the *Viper*, but since it would be impossible to prove su

allegations, they both preferred to leave it at "unknown causes."

Herrod had spoken with him about the handling of the whole thing in the press, and Jerry had insisted upon the absolute truth being told, letting the chips fall where they might. To his surprise, the President had wholeheartedly agreed. The air had to be cleared. If the public went against them, that was their choice to make.

There would undoubtedly be endless debate about the course the entire situation had taken. There might even be some international repercussions. But considering the alternative, their choice seemed the right one. The sinking of the gold ship was actually quite fortuitous politically, since it effectively silenced criticism about buying off terrorists. Benstock's cameras had helped. They showed the entire episode front to back, and it would help to explain why Herrod chose the path he did. Another plus was the Russian retreat in the face of it. That was a faux pas they'd be a long time recovering from.

Jerry had even gotten a patch-in call from Myrna and he had giggled like a schoolboy through the whole thing. She had managed to embarrass him over an international satellite hookup by telling him she had bought some new negligees that he could "peel her out of like a dumpy, white banana."

There was a knock on the door.

"Come in," he called, and an angry Benstock was standing on the threshold glaring at him.

"Well, Benny," he said as the man walked in and slammed the door. "What trouble are you getting yourself into now?"

"You son of a bitch." Benstock glowered. "As soon as we get back home, I'm going to take you apart."

"How's that?" Jerry asked.

Benstock smiled. "You haven't figured it out yet, even after I rubbed your nose in it. We've got over two hundred million people waiting for us back in the States, and all of them have a little window in their house that lets people like me come in and tell them what to do."

"What are you saying?" Jerry replied, sipping casually.

"I've spent my whole life in the television business," the man said, "and what I've learned is that people will think anything I want them to think if I package it right. They're geese, Mr. Self-Righteous. They wake up in the morning and follow the first asshole they see."

"And you're just the asshole for the job, huh?"

"That's it, buddy. Truth doesn't exist. It's what I say it is, because I'm so sincere they believe me. I can jump them through any hoop I choose, anytime I want. I would have done it here, but you fucked it all up at the last minute."

"Yeah," Jerry said. "And you tried to take care of me for it, too."

Benstock laughed. "You'd have a hell of a time trying to make that stick, buddy," he said. "In fact, I've got a lawyer who's as good with juries as I am with audiences, and we could sue you for everything you've got."

"Get to the point, Benny."

"Sure," he said, his calm exterior returning, his bravado intact. "When we get back, I'm going to tell my side of all this. I've still got the connections, believe me. By the time I get through with you and Herrod, you guys won't be able to get elected as dogcatchers. I've got the power, Jerry, the charisma. People will believe anything I tell them, and I've got plenty to say."

"I'll just bet you have," Jerry replied, and set his drink down. "Maybe this time, though, it won't be as easy as you think."

"Try me."

Prescott stretched slightly. "Long day already," he said, and took another sip. "You know I promised Simon I'd secure your resignation and your promise that you'd take full responsibility for the press attacks on NAMWives."

Benstock laughed again, shaking his head. "Fat chance," he said. "I'm riding this car all the way to the end of the line."

Jerry turned away from Benstock, looking toward the bathroom door. "Did you get all that, Danny?"

The door opened, young Danny Matlock walking out with a minicam on his shoulder. He gave the thumbs-up sign. "Perfect," he said, and looked at Benstock. "I even got your good side for you."

Benstock's face dropped, his mouth opening.

"I wonder how the folks are going to respond to what you said about them?" Jerry said. It'll be interesting to see how you mesmerize your way out of that, Mr. Charisma."

"Give me the tape and I'll do anything you ask," Benstock said.

Jerry stood, moving toward the door. "Oh, you'll do what we ask, all right," he said, and pulled the door open, the sea breeze feeling good on his face, "but I believe we'll hold onto this little tape for awhile. Sort of a memento, you might say."

Benstock stood, shoulders slumped, and walked silently out the door.

Jerry, smiling, slammed it behind him. "Wonder if I'll have to fumigate in here?" he said.

"What happens now?" Danny asked.

"We do what we always do," Jerry replied. "We try and hold on and figure out what the hell is going on around us. You know, for all Benny's bullshit, he's raised some questions we're going to have to answer if we're going to survive our own technologies."

"We're not all like him, you know."

"It only takes one, Danny," Jerry said, and looked at his empty glass. "I believe I'm going to fix myself another drink. Care to join me?"

"Sure," Danny said. "But make it a club soda. I'm not much on booze."

"Kids," Jerry muttered, and went to the small refrigerator to look for the Perrier. "By the way, you know that videotape we made of my conversation with Benstock? I want you to take it out and throw it in the ocean."

"But won't you need that to keep him in line?"

Jerry pulled a bottle of Perrier out of the small refrigerator. "I don't need to be a blackmailer, Danny," he said. "We'll take a page out of Benstock's book. If he believes the tape exists, then it does. We'll let him live in the reality he's made for himself." He began pouring the club soda into a coffee cup, watching all the bubbles rising quickly to the surface to pop—one by one.

"Newstalk. You're on the air."

"Everybody's been calling in, Don, excited over the saving of the hostages . . ."

"You bet!"

"I'm also real happy, but maybe it's time, just for a

minute, that we stop and realize what all this has meant and I wrote a little prayer to . . . is it all right if I read it?"

"Go ahead."

"Dear God, we live our lives in our small worlds, taking care of our own needs and the needs of our families; but there's another world out there, much larger, that has needs too. Please give us the strength and the understanding to realize we're a part of a world family and that we have a responsibility to know about the world and what makes it run. God help us to not live our lives as blind men, but to work together for common understanding and compassion. May the unity we've known in these last hours be ours for all time."

"Amen."

LOOSE ENDS

LXI

Red Square—Spasskaya Gate

April 20—Late Morning

Alexander Doksoi walked across Red Square toward Lenin's tomb and the hunched-up figure of a man who sat on one of the benches facing it. He pulled the collar of his overcoat up just a bit around his ears, the late spring chill making itself felt.

Andrei Youskevitch sat, elbows on knees, throwing crackers to the thirty or so pigeons that waddled around the benches. Doksoi walked right up to him, scattering a third of the pigeons. They quickly regrouped, treating the standing first secretary as just another obstacle on their feeding ground.

"Chi, chi, chi," Youskevitch called, tossing large crumbs into the midst of his vocal audience.

"I thought I'd find you here, Andrei," Doksoi said, putting his hands in his overcoat pocket. "You're holding up a meeting of the secretariat."

"You'd not be anxious to go to your own execution, either," Youskevitch said, sitting back, frowning. He patted the bench next to him. "Come, sit with me for a few minutes."

Doksoi sat, looking at his watch.

"Don't worry," Youskevitch said. "There's plenty of time to do what you have to do."

"It probably won't be as bad as all that," Doksoi said. "They'll probably vote a censure. You'll just need to cast a short shadow for awhile."

"They'll be ousting me, and you know it," the man replied. "Dolgoruki will see to that."

Doksoi shrugged. "The stakes are always high," he said "the price of failure always steep. You knew that when you backed Dolgoruki."

"You managed to protect yourself, all right."

Doksoi just turned and stared at him.

Youskevitch put up both hands, crackers falling out of the small white bag he carried. "All right, all right. You didn' deserve that. I messed up. I went along with him because he's so . . . I don't know, brutish about it."

Doksoi laughed. "Brutish?"

"I'm not strong like you," Youskevitch said, then looked up at Lenin's mausoleum. "I saw him speak once, when I was a small boy." He smiled. "So much fire . . . so much optimism The revolution was so young. Everything seemed so vital."

"What did Dolgoruki have on you?" Doksoi asked.

Youskevitch turned and patted him on the arm. "If yo knew, you'd think it nothing. I'm just a bureaucrat, Alex who's been around for a long time. I'm not fit to make majo decisions. I don't have your drive or vision. Probably today' vote is the best thing that could possibly happen."

"You're a good party man," Doksoi said. "I've alway known where your heart was."

"Thank you," the president returned. "That makes m feel better. We're being photographed you know."

Doksoi cast a glance toward the State Department Stor fringing the Square and the men with the cameras in th doorway. "I'll take care of it," he said. "Don't worry. I think can save your pension, too."

"You're a good friend," Youskevitch said. "I'm only sorr that Dolgoruki isn't going out with me. He's a dangerou man. Watch out for him."

Doksoi nodded, standing. "Time, Andrei, is the key," b said. "The old guard gets older. Every day their fingers tir a little more from holding on. Soon they will let go, slip, an someone younger and stronger will take their place. Thos are the ones I'm worrying about. Come on. Let's go to th meeting."

Youskevitch stood, grunting, and dumped the rest of hi crackers there by the wall where the graves of hundreds o Bolshevik heroes were lined side by side. Then he and th

irst secretary walked the distance of the Square, back to the
Kremlin.

*he Early Evening News
April 20*

The daring escape, along with its dramatic conclusion in
he South China Sea, was viewed as a major news story all
ver planet earth. The stories slanted this way and that, but
ppeared, with slight variations, along these lines:

Shots of the MIAs being honored on the flightline of the
ircraft carrier *Vinson* filled the screen. There were happy
ices, jubilant faces, Americans celebrating a victory.

"They threw a party on an aircraft carrier today," the
ewsman on the scene said. "As you can see behind me, the
ersonnel of the USS *Carl Vinson*, are doing it up big—and
o one ask where the champagne came from. Please! The
nood here is... unbelievable! They've been celebrating all
ay long, a steady outpouring of emotion like I've never
een."

The scene switched to the hospital ship, the ward filled
ith wounded. The newsman's voice told the story. "On the
ed Cross ship, the some five hundred wounded lay in
arious stages of recovery. Since the rescue, over a hundred
ave died of wounds sustained during the escape.

"A happy note on the wounded situation is that Lieuten-
at Colonel Jason Ridley, the hero of Camp Friendship, is
xpected to recover fully from the wounds inflicted upon him
nder torture."

The picture showed Ridley, in bed and heavily ban-
aged, with a telephone up to his ear, listening intently.

"Colonel Ridley is seen here listening to the voice of his
ife, Marsha. He can't speak or respond in any way because
 wires that are running through his jaw to help mend the
roken bones."

The scene switched to a small table full of microphones.
Iaurice Benstock, looking tired, was standing before the mikes.

"On the USS *Blue Ridge* today, the flagship of the
eventh Fleet, Presidential Adviser Maurice Benstock made
 surprise announcement..."

Benstock stepped up to the microphones. "Gentlemen.
I like to read a brief statement, if you please. I'll not be

answering any questions at this time, so please, just th
statement." He cleared his throat and read from a piece
paper in his hand. "Effective immediately, I am resigning m
position as domestic affairs adviser to the President. This is
personal move and has nothing to do with politics. Further,
feel that in my zeal to represent the government's positio
during the hostage situation, I may have overstepped m
bounds in the handling of the NAMWives organization. Th
responsibility lies solely with me. I publicly tender m
apologies to all involved. I've enjoyed my time in the spo
light over the years. Now, I hope to enjoy something a b
more . . . quiet. Thank you."—

A view of ocean, a few Vietnamese gunboats anchored
"Meanwhile, all efforts to investigate the wreckage of th
freighter carrying the ransom have been squelched by th
Vietnamese government. That wreck occurred within th
territorial limit of Vietnam, and they have ordered th
no one is allowed in, even their Russian allies who they a
now accusing of betrayal."

The scene switched to America—parades and celebr
tions. There were many brief scenes strung together, showin
vocal public demonstrations all over the country as the narr
tor spoke.

"The mood was festive in the United States today, wi
many businesses letting their employees celebrate on the jo
The country is practically hysterical, a wave of happiness an
patriotism sweeping the land such as hasn't been seen sin
the end of World War II.

"While in Baltimore, Maryland, an event passed wi
the barest of fanfare."

The scene switched to Baltimore city jail, where
Oriental man was being led out of the jail and released on th
sidewalk. The man looked back and forth before walking
aimlessly.

"Joey Nhu, who several days ago became famous as t
supposed spy who helped raise the money for the prison
ransom, was released from custody today. After the denial
his identity by the Vietnamese, and once the role of the Sta
Department and the French government became apparent
the hostage situation, the man who became famous overnig
was forgotten immediately. Today he was released to return
the obscurity from which he came three days ago.

"And finally, in Columbus, Ohio . . . "

The screen filled with a picture of a residential neighborhood, a tree-lined older section of redbrick, two-story homes. Hundreds of people crowded the lawns of four or five of the houses, centering on one that had yellow ribbons tied to the limbs of trees all over the well-kept yard. An airport limo pulled up to the curb, the gathered people cheering and applauding.

"Hugh Martindale came home today. The representative from Columbus who stunned his colleagues in the House two days ago with an emotional plea to ransom back the hostages, returned to his home from Washington today to, as he said it, 'mull over his political future.' Here, shown with his wife, Janie, he is being greeted by a highly emotional crowd of supporters and well-wishers who said they were there to make sure Martindale stays right where he is in Washington.

"When asked to comment about the demonstration, an obviously emotional Martindale said, 'Maybe there's something to be said for honesty after all.' "

ABOUT THE AUTHOR

MIKE MCQUAY began his writing career in 1975 while a production line worker at a tire plant. He turned to writing as an escape from the creeping dehumanization he saw in the factory.

His first novel, *Lifekeeper*, was published in 1980. Since then, he has published thirteen others, ranging from juveniles to mainstream horror.

The MIA Ransom is his newest novel with Bantam. Others include *Escape from New York*, *Jitterbug*, and *Pure Blood*.

McQuay is thirty-six years old, and lives in Oklahoma City with his wife and three children. He is an artist in Residence at Central State University in Edmond, Oklahoma.

Relive the American Experience in Vietnam

BANTAM VIETNAM WAR BOOKS

RICHES AND HONOR
by Tom Hyman
(26141-X $4.50)

THERE'S NOT A DULL MOMENT IN THIS RACY
NOVEL DISTILLED FROM RECENT HEADLINES.
                                    —People Magazine

RICHES AND HONOR IS A RARE BIRD, A THRILLER
WITH A HEART.   —Washington Post

METICULOUSLY CRAFTED ... WITH HIDDEN
AGENDAS AND WHEELS WITHIN WHEELS ... AB-
SOLUTELY SUPER.   Library Journal

From the moment the German officer kills the Jewish
survivor at Dachau and takes his place to be rescued by the
Allies, this novel moves into high gear. Flash forward to
1982 when Grunwald (the ex Nazi) is a wealthy industrialist
being considered as the U.S. ambassador to Israel. He
saves his drug dealing son who decides to lead an expedition
into the jungles of Vietnam to find his missing brother,
now rumored to be alive.

Grunwald finds his brother who is not a prisoner but the
leader of a rebel insurgent group secretly funded by a
right-wing U.S. agency. In the meantime the industrialist
father has been kidnapped by the one witness to his decep-
tion, a communist who threatens him with exposure. All of
these plot elements are juggled brilliantly and the reader
will be on the edge of his/her seat until the very last page!

Look for RICHES AND HONOR wherever Bantam Books
are sold or use the coupon below for ordering:

Special Offer
Buy a Bantam Book
for only 50¢.

Now you can have an up-to-date listing of Bantam's hundreds of titles plus take advantage of our unique and exciting bonus book offer. A special offer which gives you the opportunity to purchase a Bantam book for only 50¢. Here's how!

By ordering any five books at the regular price per order, you can also choose any other single book listed (up to a $4.95 value) for just 50¢. Some restrictions do apply, but for further details why not send for Bantam's listing of titles today!

Just send us your name and address and we will send you a catalog!